THE
REPLACEMENT
CRUSH

THE
REPLACEMENT
CRUSH

LISA BROWN ROBERTS

Entangled Publishing, LLC
2614 South Timberline Road
Suite 109
Fort Collins, CO 80525

Entangled Teen is an imprint of Entangled Publishing, LLC.
Visit our website at www.entangledpublishing.com.

Edited by Liz Pelletier
Cover design by Louisa Maggio
Interior design by Toni Kerr

ISBN: 9781633755048
Ebook ISBN: 9781633755055

Manufactured in the United States of America
First Edition September 2016

10 9 8 7 6 5 4 3 2 1

In loving memory of my grandmothers, both of whom loved romance novels and snuck me the good stuff when my mom wasn't looking.

"You look quite well for a man that's been 'utterly destroyed,' Mr. Spock." —Captain Kirk

CHAPTER ONE

"What's with the outfit, Viv? Did a librarian and a hooker have a fight in your closet?"

"Love you, too, Jaz." I glared at my best friend. I knew my outfit said *hot date* way more than *first day of junior year*, but I didn't want my mom to notice.

My mom glanced at my tight jeans and cropped tank top. And the boring gray hoodie I'd wrapped around my waist in case I chickened out. She raised a questioning eyebrow. Wrapped in her faded plaid flannel robe, her dark curls as messy as mine, Mom looked more like my big sister than a mother. She didn't look mad so much as confused since my outfits were usually unremarkable, just like me.

"Have some sugar." I waved a donut in Jaz's face, hoping to distract Mom from my clothes.

"Thanks," Jaz said. "My mom never buys donuts."

"Tradition," Mom said. "Part of the first day of school ritual." She pointed to the poster board propped against a cupboard. "Speaking of traditions…"

I didn't have to look at the fluorescent orange cardboard to know what it said: "Vivian Galdi. First Day of Junior

Year," decorated with flowers and smiley faces. Mom wouldn't let me leave until she'd photographed me holding the poster like one of those street corner dancers waving gigantic signs pointing toward the nearest sub sandwich shop.

"You gonna do this in college, too?"

"Yep." Mom stood up, tucking her wayward curls into a loose bun. "I'll make you pose in front of a frat house with your poster."

I tugged at my shirt imagining Jake's eyes skimming over my outfit. Jake, who'd suddenly noticed me this summer after years of barely acknowledging my existence. Jake, who'd lured me to a marathon of secret, after-curfew beach kissing sessions.

Jake, who I'd been keeping a secret from my mom. My body flushed just thinking about his body wrapped around mine like a second skin.

Mom frowned. "You okay, Vivvy? You look as if you have a fever."

Jaz snorted and I shot her a death glare. She was sworn to secrecy about Jake. I hoped he'd ask me out for real now that school was back in session, and then I could tell my mom about us dating.

Since my parents had divorced when I was eight, Mom and I were tight. She knew as much about my boring life as most of my friends did. Keeping Jake a secret had weighed on me these past few weeks, but there was something about him that made me hesitate to tell anyone about our secret hookups, except Jaz of course. Seeing the concern in Mom's warm brown eyes as she studied me sent a fresh wave of guilt snaking through me.

"Let's go." Mom reached for the poster and grinned wickedly. "You, too, Jasmine. Some day you girls will thank me for documenting your passage from girlhood to womanhood."

"That's pathetic, Mom," I pretend-grumbled, following her down the worn deck steps. I actually thought the poster ritual was sweet, but this was a tradition, too: me grumbling, Mom insisting.

"Assume the position." Mom pointed to the rose trellis.

I stood under the sweet smelling arch and held up the poster to block my face. "How's this?"

"Very funny, Vivvy."

I lowered the poster, thinking of all the moments like this captured in the collage frame in our kitchen. The photos showed my metamorphosis from a chubby little girl with big brown eyes and a mess of dark curls to a curvy girl with the same big eyes and curls I still struggled to control. Along the way, I'd suffered through braces and a few bad haircuts. Most days I still felt like that pale, chubby kid hiding in the shadow of Jaz's oversized personality.

"Smile, sweetie."

I stuck out my tongue. The shutter clicked as I laughed and she kept snapping. Jaz joined me and the poses got even sillier while Mom snapped away, laughing.

Mom liked to think of herself as an amateur photographer, but her real jobs were writing a semi-famous series of mystery novels and running her bookstore, Murder by the Sea.

Mom and I were obsessed with books.

Her obsessions included writing complicated psychological mysteries that gave me nightmares and running the only bookstore within a fifty mile radius of our town. My obsessions focused on reading—romances, mostly— and blogging about them. Hardly a day passed without us engaging in passionate and funny debates about what we were reading or had tossed aside in frustration.

"We should go." Jaz brushed crumbs off her vintage Aerosmith concert T-shirt. Jaz loved those old shirts, even though they were usually covered in fur from the stray cats she rescued.

I felt another twinge of guilt as I returned Mom's extra long good-bye hug, wondering if she'd guessed my outfit might have something to do with a guy. I knew she was relieved I hadn't had any serious romances. Yet. "Guys shouldn't become an obsession," she'd lectured more than once. "Think of them as sprinkles on the donuts of life. Fun, but not necessary."

Easy for Mom to say. She had a long-term sprinkle situation going with Paul, the owner of the surfboard shop. Since Paul adored my mom and loved her weird author quirks, I approved. When Mom was so wrapped up in writing that she forgot about their date nights, he just laughed and whisked her away to fancy dinners, still dressed in her uniform of yoga pants and a faded sweatshirt. One time she left the house in her slippers and he didn't tell her because he thought it was cute. On top of all that, he was good-looking in a pony-tailed, leathery old surfer kind of way, and his son Toff and I had been friends forever.

While I packed a few donuts for the homeless guys I knew we'd see on our way to school, Jaz tried to hug our cat Hiddles goodbye, but he hissed and bared his claws. Jaz had forced the rescue cat on us, naming him after Tom Hiddleston, but our cat had none of the actor's charm.

I gave Mom another quick good-bye hug, and then we headed for the raised, paved path that paralleled the water, Jaz on her gazillion-speed mountain bike, me on my old beach cruiser. It was the slowest way to school but the most scenic, and you never knew who you might see jogging along the beach. Occasionally, movie stars escaped L.A. to head up the coast and hide out in Shady Cove. The unwritten town code was to ignore the celebs, which was easy for me but harder for Jaz.

Jaz claimed that celebrity stalking was her one weakness since as an artist she had to stay aware of pop culture. But we both knew the truth was she lusted after hot actors.

"I don't really look like a hooker, do I?" I asked as we navigated around speed walkers and joggers. I was going for sexy cute, not slutty.

Jaz laughed. "Nah...you're just showing some skin. Usually your outfits are kind of boring. No offense."

"None taken." Unlike Jaz, I didn't have a trademark style; I mostly wore leggings and sweaters or T-shirts. The aura of bookishness clung to me like a musty cape, probably because I spent half my life in my mom's bookstore.

We stopped at the overlook so Jaz could scan the beach for hot celebrities. I dug extra donuts out of my backpack and wandered over to the homeless guys hanging out on the bench.

"Thanks, darlin'," said Reg, one of the regulars. Reg was a sweet guy; he'd fought in the first Gulf War and had a daughter somewhere up in Oregon. He and his friends were as much a fixture of our town as the seagulls circling over the water.

Every once in awhile, new residents to Shady Cove floated the idea of chasing them off with anti-loitering laws, but sympathetic long-time residents like my mom quashed those movements pretty fast.

After Reg and I agreed that donuts without icing and sprinkles were a sad excuse for a pastry, I rejoined Jaz. "Any luck?"

She shook her head, then flashed me a grin. "So how's my outfit? First-day worthy?"

"Your eye shadow matches your shoes and your nails. I don't know how you do it."

She giggled. "I looked everywhere for nail polish in this shade of gold. Finally I gave up and used my acrylic paint."

I laughed, noticing that she had accidentally dipped a tuft of hair in the stuff. "Remember when we wanted to trade hair when we were little?" I asked.

Jaz laughed. "My mom accused me of 'rejecting my Korean heritage' when she caught us with the hot rollers, just because I wanted curly hair."

I was envious of Jasmine's perfectly straight, shiny black hair. "I wish I could reject whatever heritage gave me Slinky hair." When we did the required elementary school family history potluck, I brought Italian and Swedish cookies. Mom said that was close enough.

"I think you should rock what you got," Jaz said. "I love your curls. They're so bouncy and cute. They're my favorite thing to draw."

"After hot actors," I said, and she stuck out her tongue, making me laugh.

We resumed our ride along the meandering path, Jaz still scanning the beach for celebs, while I watched the Tai Chi practitioners moving in fluid synchrony.

As we intersected with the main road that fronted our school, we braked to let traffic pass. Once upon a time, the buildings that held our school had been a Spanish mission housing priests. The adobe walls and red-tile roofs drew a lot of picture-taking tourists, especially because the place was supposedly haunted. Every Halloween someone freaked out and claimed he'd seen something creepy, but Mom suspected the rumors were spread by our town's tourist office to drum up more visitors, which she was all for.

Jaz leaned over to untangle the hair sticking out of my bike helmet. "Don't worry about how you look today. Your outfit's great and your hair's awesome. I bet Jake loved running his fingers through it."

Since we'd grown up together, Jaz knew all about my insecurities. I'd survived the childhood nickname Chunky

Monkey, but part of me still cringed when I remembered crying to my Mom that I wished I were prettier. "But, Vivvy," she'd said, looking crestfallen, "you look just like me."

"Come on," Jaz said, jarring me back to the present. "He's probably waiting for you."

My heart rate skyrocketed as I searched the crowd for a glimpse of Jake. I hoped he'd put his arm around me, casually letting everyone know we were together. A kiss would be even better.

After we locked up our bikes, I tugged at my shirt which was barely in compliance with the dress code. I wondered if I'd be able to get in and out of class without my teachers staring at my stomach. This was definitely a new style for me. Maybe my outfit hadn't been such a good idea.

"There he is." Jaz tilted her head toward a crowd of surfers. We didn't hang out much with the hard-core surfers, but we knew them, mostly because of Toff. In a town this small, we'd all grown up together. It was only when we started high school that the groups splintered off as we mingled with students from neighboring beach towns who commuted to The Shady Cove Academy of Self-Actualization and Success. SCASAS. Of course, everyone called it Suck Asses.

Our school was funded by wealthy old hippies and retired movie people. The wealthy donors gave out a lot of scholarships, which was cool since it meant we were pretty diverse for a private school. And in spite of the name, the school didn't suck.

My tiny boost of sugar and caffeine-induced confidence plummeted as I watched Jake laugh with a suntanned girl tossing long blond dreads over her shoulder. She oozed sexy in an easy, beach girl way that made me feel extra pale and chubby.

All those years of love-your-body yoga classes I did with

Mom at the Herb Cottage were supposed to brainwash me, but some days I still battled my internal voice whispering "Chunky Monkey" like a lyric stuck on repeat. I reassured myself that Jake seemed to like my curves just fine, based on our time at the beach.

Jaz squeezed my shoulder. "Go say hi. His tongue will be down your throat in seconds."

A blush warmed my cheeks as a guy walking by glanced at me, probably wondering whose tongue Jaz was referring to. Embarrassed, I shot him a mind-your-own-biz glare. He cocked an eyebrow, then his eyes narrowed briefly behind black-framed hipster glasses before he moved on.

Was he new? He must not be from Shady Cove; I'd have seen him around town by now.

"Go on. Rock that hooker librarian thang like you mean it." Jaz hip-bumped me.

Why was I so nervous? Just because we hadn't texted or met up this past week didn't mean things had changed between Jake and me. Every time I'd met him at the bonfire, his eyes had lit up as he pulled me down onto his blanket for mind-blowing kissing sessions.

He'd wandered into our bookstore a few weeks ago looking like an alien scouting a new planet. "Hey, Viv," he'd said, those midnight blue eyes boring into mine. "Can you help me out?"

Of course I'd helped him. I'd collected a stack of previously loved (we didn't call them used) paperbacks for his grandma who was at his house recuperating from surgery. I'd even added one of my mom's books, autographed in her secret pen name.

"You're awesome, Viv," Jake had said. As I'd nervously counted out his change, I'd glanced up, startled to catch him giving me the full-body scope. Then I'd almost fainted at the next words out of his sexy mouth: "What are you doing tonight?"

That night, and every night after for nine days straight, we'd burned as hot as the bonfire. Well, maybe not quite that hot because I wasn't ready to go nearly as far as Jake wanted to. But he'd said it was okay that last night together when I'd pushed on his chest and told him to stop, though his "Whatever, Viv" hadn't exactly been supportive.

The morning chimes sounded and suddenly Jaz and I were swept up in the laughing, noisy crowd swirling toward the main doors.

"Chicken," Jaz teased. "You just lost your shot at some morning tongue action."

"Shut up." I glared at her, accidentally bumping into a tall, solid body as we navigated the crowd. I glanced up to see the same guy I'd noticed earlier, who'd now overheard two embarrassing tongue-related discussions in approximately three minutes.

His lips quirked, then he disappeared into the crowd.

Jaz grabbed my arm. "Who was that guy?"

"I don't know. He must be new." I frowned at her. "He's not your type, though. Glasses."

She rolled her eyes. "I didn't think you were that shallow, Viv. Haven't you heard of nerd-hot?"

That stung. If anyone knew about nerd-hot, it was me, the pasty bookstore girl and romance book blogger. "I know all about nerd-hot," I whispered, sliding into a desk next to Jaz in homeroom, tugging down my skirt. "And that guy wasn't it."

Jaz waggled her eyebrows at me. "Are you blind? Think Clark Kent. Super sexy hiding behind glasses and geeky clothes." She leaned in close. "Like Henry Cavill. Be still my heart."

I loved geek-turned-superhero as much as the next girl, but Jaz was making a big leap. "Celebrity deprivation is affecting your vision."

"Settle down everyone." Ms. Kilgore's glare landed on us, so we stopped whispering. She tossed out names, marking attendance on her iPad. I zoned out, doodling Superman capes in my notebook until Ms. Kilgore threw a verbal flamethrower that caught my attention.

"Jake Fontaine," Ms. Kilgore said as she glanced up over her reading glasses. My head snapped around.

"Present-ay," Jake drawled from the back row, smirking.

I drank in the sight of him, all messy dark hair and sculpted perfection. I willed him to look at me, which he finally did. I smiled, feeling my whole body blush as I imagined his lips on mine.

But instead of returning my smile, he stared through me like he didn't even know me.

"Sometimes a feeling is all we humans have to go on."
—Captain Kirk

CHAPTER TWO

After homeroom, Jaz and I split off until lunchtime. She was on the arts track while my schedule was loaded with honors courses. "Don't stress," Jaz said before she bolted for the arts studio. "I'm sure you'll be sitting in his lap at lunch."

The rest of the morning passed in a blur. Instead of taking copious notes as I usually did in my morning classes, I replayed Jake's cold stare over and over in my mind.

When I emerged into the sunny courtyard, my stomach twisted as I caught sight of Jake eating lunch at the surfer table. Somehow I'd pictured a different scenario these past few weeks, imagining him inviting me to join his posse or maybe bringing a few of his friends to join Jaz and me at our table.

Clearly too many saccharine Disney movies had corrupted my sense of reality. Paul's son Toff sat at the surfer table, too. He caught my eye and grinned. I forced a smile but kept walking, joining Jaz and a few of her grungy arts pals.

The artists tolerated me even though I couldn't draw a stick figure, mainly because they thought my mom was cool and they liked to hang out in our store. Listening to them argue about where to scrounge the best driftwood and scrap metal for sculptures was a distraction from Jake flirting with the blond dreadhead from this morning.

Since I'd lost my appetite, I pushed my sandwich away. A guy I knew only as Picasso, whose outfit teetered between uber-goth and beachy grunge, snatched it up. "Thanks," he grunted.

Jaz stopped eating her yogurt to glare at me. "Don't do this."

"Don't do what?"

"Don't turn into a pathetic, starving rejection zombie."

I sighed in frustration. "Don't hold back, Jaz. It's not like I need your support right now."

She leaned across the table. "Of course I support you. It's him I'm mad at. I just don't think you should give him the satisfaction of getting all mopey. He's got one shot at making me not hate him," she said. "If he doesn't come over here in the next five minutes—"

"If who doesn't come over? What's up?" Amy turned away from the driftwood argument and focused on us, twirling a long red curl around her finger. Amy floated through school like a dreamy lovechild of Ghandi and Oprah, steering clear of gossip and drama.

She hung out at my mom's store, too, reading, knitting, and sketching, and she helped me run the Lonely Hearts romance book club. But she didn't know about my secret hook-ups with Jake. I'd been waiting for some sort of public acknowledgment from him before telling her.

Jaz cut her a knowing look. "Jake the Snake."

Amy glanced between us, sizing everything up instantly. "Oh no," she whispered. "You hooked up with him?"

Jaz nodded, her handmade feather earrings bouncing for emphasis.

"Not totally. I mean," I dropped my voice to a whisper, "it was just um, kissing and uh..." I shrugged, embarrassed.

Amy sighed, reaching for her bag of yarn and needles. She always said knitting was her stress relief. "That sucks. I mean, he's a totally hot hookup, but not exactly into commitment."

"Right?" Jaz narrowed her eyes.

I shot her an annoyed look. "Weren't you the one telling me to chase him down this morning?"

Jaz sighed, dropping her indignant posturing. "I'm sorry, Viv. I was hoping…considering how much time you two spent together…I thought this time might be different for him."

Jake's deep laugh caught our attention and we all turned, just in time to see him pull the blonde dreadhead into his arms and feed her a grape.

With his tongue.

Amy made a sympathetic cooing sound and handed me a bag of chips. "You should eat. He's not worth losing your appetite over."

Horrified, I felt tears prick the corners of my eyes. I was the star of my own breakup drama, only the other half of the breakup didn't even notice.

I wanted to ask how I could possibly eat when the guy I thought I'd loved for years had steamrolled my heart, lit it on fire, then scattered its ashes to the sea. But instead I stuffed Amy's chips in my mouth, not even tasting them.

Jaz stayed after school to talk to one of her art teachers, so I left without her. I'd just strapped on my helmet when Jake the Snake sauntered over to me, splintering off from his surfer pack to acknowledge my existence.

"Hey, Viv." He stopped next to my bike, his eyes roaming everywhere but my face.

I glanced over his shoulder and saw the dreadhead

watching us curiously. *Don't worry,* I wanted to say, *he's obviously moved on.*

I hated confronting people, but maybe now was a good time to give it a try. "Do I know you?" I was shocked at the tiny bit of snark that made it past the gatekeeper of my thoughts, even as my heart raced and my hands shook.

"Hey." He raised his eyes to mine, scowling. "That's harsh."

I looked away from his beautiful, traitorous eyes and wound my bike lock around the handlebars, fantasizing that I was winding it around his neck instead. "Whatever, Jake."

He didn't say anything. Was this a lame attempt to apologize? Did he think if he stood there looking guilty I'd send him away with a few confession prayers and complete absolution? I pretended Jaz was there, poking me in the back to make sure I stood up for myself.

"M-my definition of harsh," I said, frustrated with how squeaky my voice sounded, "is ignoring the person you've been hooking up with." I glanced at him and saw his eyes widen in surprise. He definitely hadn't expected this. I pictured Jaz high-fiving me. "Also, engaging in obnoxious PDA with s-someone else…" I felt tears threaten but refused to let them fall. "In front of me was…" I sucked in a deep breath. "Not okay. At all."

Jaz would be so proud.

His faded camo Vans kicked at the ground, then he stared up at the sky and sighed, clearly frustrated. "Look," he said, "hanging out with you was…just something I did because I was bored and it was summer. I figured you knew it didn't actually *mean* anything. And summer's over now, so…" He shrugged and pinned me with a cold stare.

My body flushed with anger and mortification. I was a summer fling? We were an ancient 1950s movie where perky couples played on the beach, captured forever in freeze-frame, but discontinued once the lights came back on?

He glanced at his surfer posse, and I suddenly knew why he'd done this. Because I was still Chunky Monkey—nerdy bookstore Viv—and he wasn't about to be seen with me in the light of day.

My whole body trembled. *Must not cry.* I took a breath, then the words tumbled out, almost like Jaz was telling me what to say. "So I'm not cool enough for you to hang out with in public, right? It was okay to use me at night over the summer when no one was around but now…" I gestured toward his friends. Toff watched us, frowning.

Jake's jaw tightened. "I didn't use you."

I swallowed my tears. I could not give him the satisfaction of knowing how much he'd hurt me. "Then what do you call it, Jake? I'm not some library book you can borrow for two weeks, then return and forget about."

He smirked at me. "You're weird, Viv. But you were… available. And like I said, I was bored." He narrowed those icy blue eyes I used to dream about. "Besides," he said, "we didn't really do much. Nothing for you to get all territorial about like you freaking *own* me."

Territorial? I squeezed my eyes shut, picturing all the ways I could kill him. Sometimes I was more like my murder-plotting mom than I realized. I opened my eyes and met his hard stare, forcing a sickly sweet smile. "This has been… enlightening, Jake. For both of us."

He took a step back, half-turning toward his posse. "Whatever, Viv. I just wanted to, you know…"

I crossed my arms, waiting, but he didn't finish his thought, so I had to do it for him. "You wanted to let me know—officially—that we're done. So I wouldn't embarrass you by talking to you or making actual eye contact." I hoped he didn't hear the quiver in my voice. I needed to bolt before he saw me cry.

He rolled his eyes and shrugged. "Like I said, we hardly even did anything." His words cut like a knife as he drove home the message: I really had been a throwaway distraction. The worst part was that I knew he was right. If it had been anyone but me or anyone but him, I would've seen it coming a mile away.

But stupid me had believed all that kissing meant something. Since I'd crushed on Jake since kindergarten, I'd wanted so badly to believe he cared about me. My emotions had betrayed me, overpowering any logic, and because of it, I'd gotten burned.

Jake the Snake had just proven how he'd earned his nickname. It wasn't only because he was a snake who stole waves from other surfers. He stole hearts, too, and crushed the life out of them.

Swallowing over the lump in my throat, I took off on my bike, pedaling as fast as I could. No one chased after me or called my name. Tears blurred my vision as I rode. I took the fast way home, riding up Main Street instead of the meandering beach path, anxious to hide out in my bedroom until I could get myself under control.

I dreaded telling Jaz because I knew she'd say "I told you so." She'd warned me when I'd called her after our first bonfire hookup. "I know you think you love him, Viv, but you don't even know him. Just because he's cute—"

"Hot," I'd interrupted. "Gorgeous. Amazing."

"Do you hear yourself? You, who's always ranting about how sick you are of guys only liking girls for their looks? You're doing the same thing with him. You know his reputation."

I'd ignored her like I'd ignored the mental warning bells the few times I'd asked Jake to meet me for lunch and he'd bailed on me. I hadn't wanted to consider the possibility that he was using me or didn't want to be seen with me in public because how could such an externally gorgeous person not be just as amazing on the inside? I knew the world didn't work that way, but I wanted it to.

Right now, I felt as if the universe was punishing me for my own hypocrisy and stupidity. And I felt like I deserved it.

Mom's bookstore had a prime location, smack in the middle of Shady Cove's quaint Main Street dotted with funky stores and one-of-a-kind restaurants operating out of pastel-colored buildings that resembled life-sized dollhouses. Benches made from repurposed surfboards dotted the street, flanked by faded whiskey barrels overflowing with cascading rainbows of flowers.

We lived behind the bookstore in a house that looked a lot like our store, only smaller. Our faded blue home, surrounded by an overgrown garden of wildflowers and untended vegetables, beckoned me like a comfortable old blanket.

I started up the deck stairs to the kitchen door, but I froze when I remembered Mom wanted me at the store after school today to meet the computer genius she'd hired to automate our system.

The last thing I wanted to do was meet with some McNerd and explain our index card system to him. I pictured a skinny old guy with thick glasses and a stained *Star Wars* T-shirt rolling his eyes at the old school way Mom and I kept records.

Hiddles the angry feline met me at the top of the deck. He rolled on his back, squinting his eyes in the sun, which was quickly disappearing behind the usual afternoon fog rolling in off the water. When I leaned down to rub his stomach he batted a paw at my hand, claws out.

"I'd like to claw somebody, too, Hiddles. But I'm a pacifist." In the kitchen, I grabbed a bottle of pomegranate juice, then hurried upstairs to take off my stupid hooker librarian outfit.

I hated that I'd spent so much time primping this morning for such a jerk. I shimmied out of my tight jeans and tugged on leggings, then unearthed a faded Cal sweatshirt. I felt safe in these clothes, hiding my body from anyone else who thought they could use me and discard me like an empty candy wrapper. My eyes pricked with tears again, and I sank to the floor, hugging my knees to my chest.

I would not, could not, let this devastate me. *You're stronger than that, Viv. You're a smart, funny, enlightened feminist. Who happens to love romance novels. Who should know better than to let her hormones have any say in decisions about secret beach hook-ups.* Even if the kissing was amazing.

Hormones shouldn't even get a seat on the brain council, but mine had staged a coup this summer, taking over all rational thought and sending me straight into Jake's muscled, traitorous arms. Everyone said that guys were the ones controlled by their hormones, but girls weren't immune to their scary power. I'd just learned that the hard way.

My cell pinged, jarring me out of my self-pity trip.

"Need you at the shop. Bring cookies pls."

I leaned against my bed and closed my eyes. I'd have to postpone my breakup detox for later, when I could call Jaz. *If* I called her.

In the kitchen, I grabbed a package of Paul Newman's do-gooder fake Oreos, pausing to glance in the mirrored key holder. My eyes had the telltale *just cried her eyes out* red glow. The waterproof mascara I'd put on this morning was a perfect example of false advertising. My curly hair was a tangled mess from the bike ride home. Lovely.

Not like it mattered. I knew the regular customers and didn't care what the coder might think of me. The only potential issue was Mom, who'd zero in on my post-crying appearance and demand to know what happened. But, of course, I couldn't tell her because she didn't know about Jake.

Hey Viv, clue numero uno that maybe the whole Jake thing was a bad idea: hiding it from Mom. Thank you, non-hormone-influenced brain. I grabbed a paper towel, dampened it under the kitchen faucet, and scrubbed off the mascara stains. Not much of an improvement, but it would have to do.

I entered the store through the back door, buying a few extra minutes before facing Mom. Her laughter rang out from the front of the shop, answered by a deeper laugh. Oh, no. Was the McNerd flirting with her? Gross. I took a deep breath and navigated the stacks of books in our screened-in back porch store room, passed through the tiny store kitchen, and emerged into the main store.

Years ago, Mom had remodeled, tearing down the inside walls to create an open, high-ceilinged space full of bookshelves and a few cozy reading nooks tucked into the corners. Framed photos of Mom's favorite mystery authors dotted the walls, along with framed READ posters from the ALA. Though I didn't stalk them the way Jaz did, who didn't love pictures of sexy actors holding books? Nathan Fillion's poster had a place of honor by the mystery section because Mom loved *Castle* and I loved *Firefly*.

A u-shaped counter hid our battered desk piled high with index card boxes and paperwork. We used an old cash register that required me to make change in my head, and one of those ancient credit card slider gadgets that still used carbon paper. Tourists thought we were intentionally quaint, but the truth was Mom didn't have time to bring the store into the twenty-first century. Much as she loved the store, she loved writing her books even more, so when push came to shove, automating got shoved right out the door. Until today, apparently.

I approached Mom and the McNerd, who sat at the desk behind the counter, laughing together. Great. How was I going to fake enthusiasm when my heart was broken?

Mom glanced up. "Vivvy! There you are. I wondered what—" She paused, and I knew her Mom-scanner was assessing my bedraggled, post-breakup appearance. "What happened?" Her voice sharpened with worry. I glanced away from her, only to look right at the McNerd, who'd raised his head when Mom greeted me.

Shockingly, he wasn't an old, skinny guy in a stained *Star Wars* shirt. He was, in fact, a young, buffed guy in a clean *Star Trek* shirt. *Big difference.* His short dark hair stuck up randomly, and I wondered if it was an actual style or if it was nerd hair, like he couldn't be bothered with combing it. Nerd-hot expert Jaz might know.

I absorbed the full impact of his broad shoulders, his sexy mouth curving in a tentative smile, his steady green-eyed gaze behind the glasses, and tanned and chiseled features. This guy was definitely packing a lot of cute underneath deceptively dorky wrapping.

He adjusted his glasses on his nose, his gaze moving from Mom to me and back to Mom. Hmm…glasses. A frisson of recognition ran through me.

Oh no. The guy from school who'd heard not one but two embarrassing Jake-related tongue discussions. Was today the day all my bad karma got rolled into a giant ball and dropped on my head?

"What is it, Viv?" Mom asked, reading my face like an FBI investigator.

"Nothing," I mumbled. "But I have a lot of homework so I can't stay long." I could only put off my meltdown for so long.

Mom frowned. "But I need you to show Dallas our system." She shot him an embarrassed smile. "Such as it is."

He shrugged. "I can come back another day if today doesn't work."

His voice was much deeper and sexier than the nerd voices on TV.

"But I know your schedule's busy," Mom protested, shooting me a death glare.

"Yeah, but I'm flexible." He glanced at me and his lips quirked. And I knew—absolutely *knew*—he was remembering the overheard conversations about morning tongue action. Blood rushed to my cheeks.

Mom sighed and rustled papers on the desk. "Well, I don't know, Dallas. I hate to inconven—"

"It's fine," I interrupted. I would not be shamed into making the precious McNerd rework his busy schedule. Somehow I'd have to postpone my meltdown until later. I held up the box of cookies.

"Are these for you?" I looked into Dallas's shockingly green eyes assessing me from behind the black frames. His eyes locked with mine a few seconds longer than necessary, then he focused on the box.

"I won't say no to cookies." He grinned and held out his hand. I transferred the package to him, careful to avoid extraneous skin contact.

Mom jumped up from her chair. "I need to get back to my research." She glanced at us. "Do you know how many drugstore items can be used to poison someone? You'd be surprised."

Dallas paused mid-chew, eyes widening.

"She's an author," I explained, shooting my mom an exasperated smile. I never knew when she'd say weird writer stuff that shocked people. "A mystery writer. Killing imaginary people is her first love; the bookstore's a close second."

Mom smirked. "So many ways to die, so little time to write about them."

Dallas laughed, choking on his cookie.

"When do you need to leave, Dallas?" Mom asked.

"Four thirty."

I glanced at the cat clock on the wall. Three forty-five. Great. Forty-five minutes to spend with a stranger who already knew more about me than I wanted him to.

Mom nodded. "Well, you'll be working mostly with Vivvy—oh, excuse my horrible manners! Dallas, this is my daughter Vivvy—"

"Vivian," I corrected.

Mom ignored me because she was going to call me Vivvy forever. "And Vivvy, this is Dallas Lang. You two can work out a schedule together." Mom beamed at us. "This is so exciting. I've wanted to computerize the inventory for years."

Dallas and I avoided looking at each other while Mom gathered up a stack of papers and her Sherlock teacup, then left us, gauze skirt swishing in her wake, fuzzy slippers peeking out from under the hem. I bit back a smile, wondering how many customers had noticed.

I broke the avoidance awkwardness first, leaning over the counter to take a cookie from the package. Dallas thrust the box toward me.

"So you're new in Shady Cove?" I asked casually.

He ran a hand through his hair, and I realized that must be why it stuck up in places. It didn't look weird, though. On him it looked sort of sexy—wait, what the heck was I doing? I'd been dumped half an hour ago and I was already noticing some other guy? *Is it really a dumping if you were never together?* asked my traitorous brain.

"Not exactly," he said, settling his gaze on mine. "My family moved here last April."

I frowned. "I don't remember seeing you at school."

"Because I wasn't. Since it was late in the year, I did online classes to finish my junior year."

"So you're a senior," I said. *Duh, Vivian.*

"Yeah."

"And, let me guess…you're from Texas?"

Laughter sparked his eyes. "The name's more of a red herring. We're from Wisconsin."

"Don't try to suck up to me by throwing around mystery jargon." I narrowed my eyes and tried to look unimpressed, even though I was.

His laughter reached his mouth this time. "I wouldn't dare."

I walked behind the counter to sit in the chair Mom had vacated. The close proximity to this mysterious, potentially nerd-hot boy was unsettling. I needed to focus on the job at hand.

"So you saw Mom's desperate plea for help on Craigslist? Or was it the help wanted board in the coffee shop?"

Dallas pulled a notebook out of his backpack and glanced at me. "Coffee shop. This sounded a lot better than washing seashells."

I was still too miserable to laugh at his dumb joke, but I tried to keep the conversation going. "It must be weird to go to a new school for your senior year." I busied myself with a stack of Mom's invoices and saw him shrug from the corner of my eye.

"Wouldn't have been my first choice, but moving to the beach from the frozen tundra didn't exactly su—stink."

Was he worried about swearing in front of me? That was odd. And sort of cute. I turned slightly in my chair. "Still." I shrugged, then forced a tiny smile. "Moving here gives you an opportunity to fulfill your mission." I gestured vaguely to his shirt and stared at his neck rather than those hypnotic eyes. "Exploring strange new worlds and civilizations and all that jazz."

He chuckled softly and goose bumps rose on my arms when he spoke. "Original, *Next Generation* or *Voyager*? Not *Deep* Sleep *Nine*, I hope."

I faced him full on. This was tricky. He was clearly a Trekkie with strong opinions. I wasn't Comic Con crazy, but I did like Star Trek, especially the movies with Chris Pine. And the Next Generation series with Patrick Stewart, who also graced a READ poster on our wall.

"I like TNG," I said, "with the occasional original series sprinkled in for variety. I did a DS9 marathon last summer. Don't need to repeat it."

Dallas and I stared at each other in silence and I wondered what he was thinking. My Trekkie creds ran more shallow than deep. I suspected he was more interested in the science and space exploration aspects of the Final Frontier, unlike me, who was mostly drawn in by the relationship drama.

"Spock or Kirk?" he asked, a glint of humor in his steady green gaze.

My pulse rate sped up, even though his question wasn't flirtatious. "I have to choose?"

He shrugged. "Most people lean one way or the other."

His quiet intensity made me anxious. *Was he staring at my smeared mascara? Did he really overhear the tongue chats?*

"Isn't that kind of like asking me to choose either peanut butter or jelly?"

He laughed, making me smile for the first time since Jake had ignored me this morning.

"So..." I cleared my throat, grabbed a random box of index cards, and popped it open. I could not let my hormones suck me into another vortex of cute boy craziness. "This is the official method of tracking sales and trade-ins at Murder by the Sea." I glanced at him, surprised by the sudden worry that he might make fun of our ancient system.

He opened another index box and pulled out a card, frowning. "What do the columns mean?"

I scooted my chair closer to him, trying to ignore his distractingly sexy scent. Was that soap? Or just eau de nerd? I cleared my throat nervously. "Well, the date is obvious. Date of transaction. Number is how many books we bought from the customer. Cash is how much we paid for the books. Trade is how much we gave in store credit. And the letters are for genre. R for romance, M for mystery, etc." I glanced at him and he nodded, scribbling in a notebook. "Customers can choose store credit or cash. We give a higher dollar amount in trade credits than cash."

He stopped scribbling and turned to face me, making my breath catch. Who knew that Wisconsin grew such cute boys? I'd never thought about it; but if someone had asked me, I'd have guessed they were all beefy and red-faced, wearing foam cheesehead hats and screaming about the Packers. Somehow I couldn't picture Dallas in a cheesehead hat.

"Why do you give more in credit than cash?"

I knew why but the words took a detour on the way from my brain to my mouth. I'd felt this way around Jake at first, but the truth was we hardly talked at all on the beach. Somehow Dallas already knew things about me that Jake didn't, as in my secret Star Trek obsession. How had that happened?

"We, uh, want to encourage customers to shop in the store. Read more books."

He ran a hand through his hair again, creating random hair spikes that looked cuter every time he did it. "So, you want to keep the money in the store? Increase your profits?"

I looked away from the spiky hair and the green eyes, focusing on my index card. "Honestly, my mom doesn't care much about profit. She does okay as an author. The bookstore is more of a…personal mission."

"Yeah? Maybe I should read her books."

I glanced at him and smiled. "First you have to figure out her pen name."

His eyebrows shot up. "She doesn't publish as Rose Galdi?"

Feeling smug, I shook my head. "Nope."

"As a consultant to Murder by the Sea, it's important that I know," he said in a serious, deep voice, a glint of laughter in his eyes.

"You'll have to ask her," I said airily, trying to hide the impact his voice and laughter had on me. "I've signed a secrecy oath."

He crossed his arms over his broad chest, the chest I'd somehow overlooked when he'd bumped into me in the hallway this morning. "I'm sure I can Google it in five seconds."

"Go for it." I bit my lips, repressing a smile.

He leaned back in the chair. "I will. But before I do, let's make it interesting. If I figure it out by tomorrow, I get to borrow one of her books to read. No charge." He glanced toward the rows of shelves. "I'm sure you stock them here."

My lips twitched. He was about to embark on one of the favorite past times of Shady Cove residents: figuring out my mom's authorial identity. Very few people had done it and those who had were sworn to secrecy. Mom ensured their secrecy by inviting them to private book talk nights with wine and cheese and free autographed copies of her latest releases.

"Mom's books are always on the shelves. Some hardback, some paperback. Some new, some previously loved."

He licked his lips in a way that made me wonder what it would be like to kiss them. I spun around in my chair and grabbed another index box. I was heading to the Herb Cottage as soon as I closed the store tonight. There had to be a cure for my condition.

Dallas resumed scribbling in his notebook. "Tell me more about your record-keeping."

I tucked a strand of hair behind my ear and glanced at the clock behind us. "But you need to leave in ten minutes."

He nodded, still scribbling. "I know."

I glanced at his wrists; he wasn't wearing a watch. "How do you know? Do you have a timer inside your brain or something?"

He shot me a sideways smirk. "That's one way to put it."

"Seriously?" I spun back and forth in my chair. In my experience, lots of boys were clueless about time. Paul and Toff were always late when they joined us for dinner. Then again, so was my Mom, so she couldn't get mad.

"We should figure out a schedule for the rest of the week." He pulled his cell out of his pocket, fingers flying over the screen. "Can't do it tomorrow, but I could meet you here after school on Wednesday from three thirty until five thirty."

I grabbed a Post-it and wrote down the day and time.

"Don't you, um, need to check your calendar?" He sounded anxious.

I raised my eyes to his. "I'll remember." I gestured to his phone. "Mr. Organized."

He shrugged, looking embarrassed. "I'm, uh...sort of... particular...about some things."

"Like being on time."

He shut his notebook and capped his pen. "Exactly. Which is why I need to go. I have a cello lesson at five thirty."

I stared at him as he stood up and hoisted his backpack over his shoulders. His very broad shoulders that matched the broad chest.

"You play the cello." I stated this fact with the awe it deserved. I was hooked on YouTube videos of the uber hot Croatian cello duo who performed their own versions of popular songs.

He grinned down at me. "Yeah."

"And you're a computer whiz."

He tugged at his hair, a slight blush creeping up his neck. "I guess so."

I narrowed my eyes, trying to hide any sparks of interest that might betray me. "You sure you're from Wisconsin?"

His eyebrows arched. "Stereotype much?"

It was my turn to blush. I lowered my eyes. "Sorry." He was right; I sounded like a snob.

"It's okay, Vivian. I expected all the girls here to be beachy airheads. I'm still adjusting to the reality of Shady Cove."

My eyes narrowed as Dallas leaned down to retrieve a helmet from underneath the desk. Was that a compliment or a dig?

He stood up, and I glanced at the helmet dangling from his hand. It was white with a Union Jack flag painted on both sides, and it was definitely not a bicycle helmet.

"Do you ride a motorcycle?" My voice was a whisper. Did he leap tall buildings in a single bound, too? Maybe Jaz was right about the Superman thing.

He shook his head, one side of his mouth quirking up. "No, just a Vespa. Part of the parental bribery package to convince me to move in the middle of my junior year." He adjusted his backpack over his shoulders. "Don't forget our little wager about your mom's pen name."

I blinked, clearing my mind of the image of Dallas playing the cello, arm muscles rippling, droplets of sweat beading on his forehead.

"Wait. What if you don't figure it out? Because you won't. What do I win?"

"Hmm." Dallas rubbed his jaw. His very strong jaw. God, I was as pathetic as some of the girls in the novels I read. "Well...wagers should be roughly equal. If I can't figure it out, you can borrow my Star Trek bible. Original series episode guide, behind-the-scenes trivia, all that stuff." He tugged his helmet onto his head, the Union Jack flag's red and blue colors flashing in the sun beaming down from the skylight. "Unless you already have it."

It took me a few seconds to recover my voice. "No. I mean, I don't have it. Yeah, sure. Deal."

"Cool. It's a bet. See you back here on Wednesday." He lifted his chin in acknowledgment, then turned to leave.

I would *not* let myself look at his butt as he left the store. Things were already out of control in the Vivian hormonal department. I heard the slight rumble of the Vespa and peered over the counter as he drove off.

Nerd-hot was most definitely a *thing*.

"Too much of anything, even love, isn't necessarily a good thing."
—Captain Kirk

CHAPTER THREE

Murder by the Sea didn't have many customers after Dallas left, so I finished my homework, focusing my energy there instead of reliving Jake dumping me, or imagining Dallas bent over a cello.

I called Mom as soon as I'd locked up the store. "I have to run a quick errand before dinner."

She sighed into the phone. "But it's first-day-of-school dinner. Beach fries and hot dogs."

"We'll go as soon as I get back. I have to run to the Herb Cottage. You need anything?"

"Are you all right, Vivvy? Does this have anything to do with what a wreck you were after school today?"

"We'll talk when I get back, okay?" I locked the door behind me, walking quickly down Main Street.

Shady Cove had been a major hippie/surfer town in the sixties and seventies and was still populated by a lot of those same people and their offspring– including me. Nothing I could ask would shock or repel Natasha, proprietor of the Herb Cottage, but I still felt anxious.

Natasha was in the back of the store talking to a

customer in the age 50+ area, full of menopausal remedies and herbal Viagra. I headed to the all-natural cosmetic section and checked out cruelty-free lip gloss, putting in my ear buds so I didn't have to listen to the guy describe whatever embarrassing old person disorder he had.

My cell vibrated with a message from Jaz. *"We must talk. Amy saw u & snake after school."*

"I'll call after dinner. Busy right now."

Natasha and a balding older guy emerged from the back of the shop and I removed my ear buds.

"Vivvy, I'll be right with you." While she rang up the guy's purchase I wondered if there was a natural remedy for baldness. That made me think of Captain Jean Luc Picard from *Star Trek, The Next Generation*, which made me think of Dallas, the main reason I was here.

I tossed the lip gloss tube back into the fishbowl. Not like kissing was in my immediate future, anyway.

Natasha looked like every other middle-aged hippie chick in Shady Cove with long, straight hair and wearing an embroidered blouse, probably from Nepal or some other place she'd visited with her meditation posse, which sometimes included my mom.

"What do you need, Viv? Did your mom send you for black cohosh?"

What the heck was that? "No," I said. "I'm here for me."

Her smile faded, replaced by her "wise herbal mage" expression. "Ah. So what are your symptoms?"

"Well…it's…I guess kind of related to, um, puberty. Hormones. That stuff."

She nodded knowingly. "Cramps? I have just the thing."

I shook my head. "Not cramps."

She tilted her head. "Is it moodiness? That's very common, even for girls who don't get cramps. That time of the month can be such a chal—"

"It's not just once a month," I interrupted. Even though I was mortified, the sooner I spit it out, the sooner she could give me a cure. I took a deep breath. "It's more of a…chronic condition."

Her eyebrows shot up. "Oh dear. Have you talked with your mom?"

"No." I bit my lip. "I can't." I didn't want the anti-boy-crazy lecture from Mom. "Isn't this kind of like doctor/patient confidentiality when I talk to you?" Natasha was in my Lonely Hearts book club, and I trusted her even though we didn't always agree on books.

She tugged at her beaded necklace. "That depends. What exactly do you mean by 'chronic condition'?"

I stared at my flip-flops. "Okay. This is embarrassing, but it's …lately I've been sort of obsessed, and I don't want to be. I mean, I'm in advanced classes. Newspaper staff. I'm not an idiot." I looked up.

Natasha tilted her head. "No one said you were." Concern wrinkled her brow. "At least I hope no one did."

"No, they didn't," I replied, reassuring her. "But I'm *acting* like an idiot lately. And I want it to stop."

She leaned against one of the bottle-filled shelves. "Vivian, sweetie, you need to be specific if you want my help." Her patient smile was strained, and I realized how vague and idiotic I sounded.

"Sorry," I said. "I'm psyching myself up." I took a deep breath. "Okay, so the thing is…it's a boy." I paused, picturing Jake. Then I pictured Dallas grinning down at me in his helmet. "Not just one boy. I'm, um, turning into one of the lobotomized girls. The ones whose lives revolve around guys. And I hate it! So I figure it must be the hormones, right? And maybe you have something to fix it?"

Natasha's frown deepened. She was probably grateful I hadn't confessed any creepy homicidal inclinations, though considering my mom's profession that wouldn't be surprising.

"Well," she finally said. "I have good news and bad news. The good news is this is all perfectly normal. And this chronic obsession won't last forever. Your hormones will calm down. Eventually."

"Give me the bad news."

She twisted a lock of gray hair around her finger, her smile hesitant. "I don't have a cure for you, Vivian. You're going to have to ride it out. Have you tried meditating? Or chakra balancing?"

I groaned. Nothing on the Shady Cove alternative lifestyle menu was going to cure my disorder.

The front door opened and a young mom entered, towing a wailing toddler behind her. Grateful for the distraction, I moved toward the door. "Thanks, Natasha, but I need to get home for dinner."

"Come back any time, sweetheart. You might want to drink chamomile tea to calm your nerves. Maybe try some chaste berry or evening primrose oil."

"Yeah, okay." Her words barely registered as I made my escape.

If Natasha didn't have a cure, no one did. Maybe she was right; I'd have to ride out this crazy rollercoaster of crushes and getting dumped and feeling used. Maybe it would get easier as I got older. Mom seemed happy with Paul, but I hoped I didn't have to wait that long to connect with a decent guy.

As I walked home, I thought about what Jake had said about him being bored and me being available. Did I give off some horrible desperate girl vibe? Or was he that much of a jerk? Maybe never having a boyfriend made me especially vulnerable to the first guy who showed interest.

Even worse, maybe Jake could tell how infatuated I was with him and totally took advantage. I cut across the overgrown grass behind Murder by the Sea. If I were the heroine in a book I was reading, I'd tell myself to get a grip, to count myself lucky to be rid of such a jerk.

"Sprinkles on the donuts of life," I muttered as I entered the kitchen.

Mom glanced up from her teapot. "What's that, honey?"

"Oh, just reminding myself of your Mom wisdom."

"You'll say anything for cheese fries, won't you?"

I grinned. "Yep. Let's go."

Mom grabbed her sweatshirt for the short walk to the restaurant and we said goodbye to our cat, who ignored us as usual.

Most of the other kids who'd dragged their parents to the Doghouse hot dog shack were much younger than me, but I wasn't ashamed of my need for comfort food.

Mom ate a veggie dog while I ate a corn dog dipped in processed cheese. We sat outside bundled in sweatshirts since the evening fog was chilly.

"All right, Vivvy," Mom said. "You've found every possible way to stall and avoid me. Now please tell me why you came home from school crying."

I dipped a few fries into the cheese sauce and took a big bite. Mom narrowed her eyes, then pulled the basket away from me.

"Nice try," she said. "Swallow that bite, then tell me or no more fries."

I knew I was acting like a three-year-old, but how could I tell Mom about Jake without confessing to sneaking out to meet him? I wanted to confide in her, but I didn't want to lose her trust.

"I don't want to go into details."

Mom frowned. "I need to know if you're in danger, Vivvy. Being bullied. That kind of thing."

"It's not that." I decided to tell her the general story without specifics. "Okay, so there's this guy. And I thought he...liked me. A lot, I mean. But turns out he doesn't."

Mom's expression softened as she reached across the table to pat my hand. "That stinks, sweetie." Her frown returned. "But I don't recall you going out with anyone over the summer."

Uh oh. Time for a partial truth. "He's, um, just someone I've had a crush on. For a long time." I cringed inwardly as I thought of all the "*J + V*" doodles scrawled in notebooks, starting in the sixth grade.

"I could kill him," Mom said cheerfully. "I need to experiment with a couple of different poisons to see how the body reacts."

"Mom," I whispered, glancing around to make sure no one overheard. "Not funny."

She grinned. "I'm speaking metaphorically. But I do need to write a murder scene a few different ways, so I could use him as the victim. On the page, of course, nothing more." She grabbed a fry. "If you'll tell me his name."

"Nice try, but I'm not telling you. Besides, it doesn't matter. It's over."

We sat in silence for a few minutes, doing serious damage to the basket of carb heaven, then Mom spoke again.

"So Dallas is a nice boy, don't you think? He's smart and funny. He told me his family moved to Shady Cove because his mother threatened to leave his dad if she had to spend another winter in the Midwest." Mom chuckled. "Not exactly a motive for murder, but it might have potential."

The last person I wanted to discuss with Mom was Dallas. "He's all right," I mumbled. Mom cocked an eyebrow. She opened her mouth to disagree, but instead bit into a fry.

We Galdi girls loved us some cheese fries.

Mom drank from her water glass, then cleared her throat. "About what you said earlier, about this boy who hurt you. Are you sure you can turn off a crush? I remember when I was your age. It wasn't easy for me to turn my feelings on and off."

So Mom had been a victim of hormones, too? Was no one safe from their evil power? "I don't know, Mom. I wish I was a Vulcan, you know? Free of emotions." I'd been thinking about Dallas's Spock vs. Kirk question.

Mom's lips twitched and she spoke in a deep voice. "Fascinating, this human obsession with other humans."

"Pathetic Spock impression, Mom, but you get props for effort."

After polishing off our food, we walked home talking about unimportant stuff, which I appreciated. I knew Mom's intent was to distract me from thoughts of Jake, and it sort of worked, at least for a few blocks.

lay in bed avoiding Jaz's texts, watching an episode of the *Star Trek* original series on my laptop before I fell asleep. As I listened to Spock deflect Kirk's manic freak-outs with his Vulcan proverbs, I wondered how Spock would handle my situation.

What would Spock do if he couldn't control his obsessions? I shifted my pillows to get more comfortable. He'd deal with it logically. I closed my eyes, imagining a conversation with him.

"I think you've confused lust and love, Vivian. Humans often do. What you felt for Jake wasn't love. Search inside your human heart for the truth."

Of course he was right. I'd read enough romance books that I should know the difference. But some hot guy just had to lure me to the beach, apparently, and I forgot everything I knew about what real love should feel like.

"Perhaps you should stop looking for true love, Vivian. Satisfy this hormonal urge with a harmless crush."

Give up on love, Spock? Really?

"I recommend carefully selecting the object of your crush, rather than falling victim to your irrational hormonal condition." His pointy ears twitched. *"Perhaps the problem is not in the crush per se, but rather in your lack of control over it."*

I shivered under my comforter. Maybe Spock was right. If I couldn't control this hormonal imperative to fall in lust and/or love with somebody, maybe I should focus my attention on someone harmless. Someone boring, to trick both my hormones and my heart.

"Also," Spock continued, *"it would be wise to avoid young men who are only interested in...physical connection. Perhaps you should be more selective in the future."*

He had a point. If only I could flick a Vulcan switch to turn off my feelings and my hormones.

What I needed was a Jake replacement.

A replacement crush.

"How do Vulcans choose their mates? Haven't you wondered?"
—Spock

CHAPTER FOUR

TUESDAY, AUGUST 26

An angry Hiddles hissed as Jaz and I clattered down the steps the next morning. She paused to pet him but he intensified the hiss, adding a swat for emphasis.

"He seems upset," Jaz said as we mounted our bicycles for our daily ride to school. "You sure he's getting enough affection?"

"Please. The last thing that cat wants is affection."

Mom stepped onto the deck in her yoga pants and oversized sweatshirt that featured Hello Kitty smiling evilly and holding a knife. "Bye girls! Have a marvelous, murder-free day."

Jaz giggled. "Your mom is so awesome."

"Otherwise known as weird," I said affectionately. "Bye, Mom," I called over my shoulder. "Bye psycho cat!"

"So why didn't you call me last night?" Jaz asked. "I texted you."

Because I didn't want to hear I told you so.

I had to tell her, though. "Amy was right about Jake talking to me after school."

"Spill. Now."

My body tensed, remembering how I'd felt when he'd sauntered over to me like nothing mattered. "Basically he officially dumped me. Told me that we weren't really *a thing*, as he put it."

Jaz jammed on her brakes. "What an asshole." I circled my bike around to stop next to her. A silver-haired race-walking couple shot Jaz a glare as they sped past us.

"I know. And before you can say it, let me acknowledge that you warned me. You were right."

Jaz's face crumpled. "Oh, Viv, I wasn't going to say that. Yeah, I warned you, but that doesn't make what he did okay. Knowing someone's an ass doesn't excuse their ass-like behavior."

I gave her a tiny smile. "True."

"So what do we do about this? Key his car?"

I laughed out loud, which felt good. "His dad would buy him a new one."

Jaz nodded. "Well, revenge is bad karma anyway. I recommend ignoring him."

"Everyone always says that, but it's not so easy. Especially since he's in two of my classes and the same lunch period."

Jaz nodded, but focused on her mission as she moved toward the overlook spot to scan the beach.

"Anyway," I said, "I have an idea about how to—"

"Oh my God! Vivian, look!" Jaz pointed to a solitary figure running in the surf, a tall guy with a trim but toned body, streaky blond hair, and sunglasses. "That's Fisk Vilhelm."

I snorted. That definitely was not the *America Sings* winner who'd shot to stardom practically overnight. "No, it's not. It's probably the mechanic from Ted's Beater Repair. Or maybe the delivery guy from Wok to You. Honestly, Jaz. That could be anyone."

She turned to glare at me. "But it's not just anyone.

I know it's Fisk. Need I remind you that I'm an expert celebrity stalker?"

"No reminder necessary." I shaded my eyes and followed the guy's progress up the beach. He was definitely ripped, but that didn't mean he was a famous rock star.

"Remind me to add him to my log," Jaz said, returning to her bike.

"Like you'd forget." Jaz had started her celebrity log in the eighth grade, recording date, time, and location of sightings, along with critical details. Today's would probably include descriptions of Fisk's body and lots of exclamation points. I still didn't think it was him, but whatever made Jaz happy.

"So back to Jake," I said. We were almost to school and I wanted to tell her my plan in private. "I need to stop obsessing over him, but apparently my hormones need to obsess over someone."

Jaz glanced at me, then focused back on the road as we coasted down the hill. "You're powerless over the hormones?"

"Yes, and so are you. Don't deny it. It's a biological phenomenon. Remember what we learned in health class? The drive to procreate is dominating our lives right now. Don't tell me you don't feel this way about Lance." Lance was Jaz's genius artist boyfriend who was in his first year at RISD, so their relationship had recently transitioned from IRL to virtual. So far, I'd managed to stop her whenever she tried to tell me about their sexting and Skype exploits.

Jaz glanced at me, grinning wickedly. "You have someone in mind for this procreation activity? I could give you some pointers."

"No! That's like the opposite of what I want." Well, not exactly. I'd been tempted by Jake, but I was grateful I hadn't crossed that line with him. I didn't want my first time to be with somebody who could walk away from me as if I didn't matter.

I bounced on my feet, straddling my bike as we waited for the light to change at the crosswalk. "So anyway, last night I came up with a plan. To forget about Jake, I need to focus on someone else. A replacement crush." I paused. "Someone my body doesn't want to, uh, procreate with."

"Who do you have in mind?"

A shiver of anxiety made me glad I'd worn a hoodie today. "That's where you come in, bestie extraordinaire. I need to make a list of potential targets."

We wheeled our bikes to the nearly full racks. Not many students drove cars to school. Our town was bike-friendly, and the racks were crammed full of mountain bikes, street bikes, beach cruisers, and even a few old-style BMX bikes.

"We'll discuss at lunch," Jaz said, sounding efficient. "I might have an extra notebook in my locker."

A whiny, buzzing sound caught my attention and I turned to see Dallas arriving on his Vespa.

"Whoa. Who's got the cool ride?" Jaz asked.

"It's, um, a new guy. From Wisconsin. His name is Dallas."

She spun to look at me, fluffing out her helmet hair. "You've been holding out on me, Vivvy."

I hated when she used my childhood nickname. Usually she remembered to call me Viv or Vivian, but once in awhile she slipped.

Tugging off my helmet, I tightened my ponytail. I'd pulled the crazy curls out of my face today since I hadn't been in the mood to spend time on my hair or my clothes. My soft hoodie and worn jeans were a safe, Jake-free cocoon.

"I just met him yesterday." We watched Dallas as he dismounted the Vespa.

"Cool helmet," Jaz whispered.

"I know," I whispered back. "Why are we whispering? He can't hear us way over there."

Dallas pulled off his helmet and tugged at his spiky hair. He pushed his glasses up on his nose, then adjusted his backpack.

"Wait a sec," Jaz said. "Didn't we see him yesterday? When you asked me what nerd-hot was?" She turned to stare at me. "Tell me how you met him."

I kept my pace purposefully slow so we wouldn't accidentally catch up to Dallas. The last thing I needed was him overhearing any more conversations. "He's working for my Mom at the store. She's on a mission to bring us into the twentieth century."

"But it's the twenty-first century."

I smirked, picturing our index cards. "Yeah, well, since we're about to computerize our process, I'd say we're barely attempting twentieth century technology. You know the only reason my mom has an author website is because her publisher made one for her, right?"

"Sounds like your mom," Jaz agreed.

"So anyway," I continued, "Dallas is some sort of coding genius, so Mom hired him to help us convert the index cards into actual data."

We'd reached Jaz's locker and I waited as she pawed through the mess. "Ta-da!" She handed me a notebook with a glittery purple cover. "For the replacement crush mission."

I took the notebook, smiling. "Thanks. I'll put it to good use."

"I'm sure you will." We moved on to my locker.

"So his name's Dallas? Cute." Jaz paused. "He's definitely nerd-hot, Vivian. Put him on your list. RC target number one."

Panic surged through me. The last thing I wanted was to replace one hormone-fueled crush with another. I remembered how jittery I'd felt around Dallas yesterday. I imagined Spock warning me with his raised eyebrow face.

"No way," I said vehemently. "Absolutely no McNerds."

"Why not? You don't like the adorkable type?"

I slammed my locker shut and whirled around just in time to see Jake and the dreadhead stuck in a lip-lock. Jaz followed my horrified gaze.

"Come on." She tugged my arm. "Focus on your list. Adorkable Dallas."

"No," I whispered. "Not Dallas. I'm not opposed to cute nerds...just not him."

Jaz knocked against my shoulder as we headed to homeroom. "Give me another name, then."

"I need to think about it," I said, picturing Spock's stern gaze. "I need to handle this logically."

We slid into our chairs and Jaz gave me her patented you're-insane-but-still-my-best-friend look. "Logically? Who falls in love logically?"

"Shh." I glanced around nervously, making sure no one overheard her. "We'll discuss this at lunch. Privately."

Jake wandered in and parked himself with the rest of the surfers. Jaz shot him a murderous glare, which he didn't see since he was yawning, probably replacing the oxygen he'd depleted from all the kissing.

Ms. Kilgore took attendance and yammered about the importance of being a participatory student, joining clubs, sports teams, and all that jazz. "Surf team final tryouts are this week," she read from her iPad.

"Time to rip it!" Toff piped up. A few of his surfer bro-dudes fist-bumped him, including Jake. Toff was the star of the competitive surf team. He and Jake were probably the best two on the men's team. Even if they'd gone to one of the huge public schools, they'd still be the stars.

Toff and I had been friends since kindergarten for reasons I didn't fully understand. We were so different, but we made each other laugh, and things were always easy with him. He caught my eye and winked. I rolled my eyes at him and he pursed his lips, sending me an air kiss. His buddies catcalled and one of them said something I didn't catch.

"Gentlemen! Please restrain your antics until you've left my classroom."

God, I loved Ms. Kilgore. Our other teachers acted as if they were in a contest to be the most chill, tolerant hippie teachers on the planet. Not Ms. Kilgore.

The antics finally ceased in the surfer corner and Ms. Kilgore's voice boomed as the Buddhist chimes rang, signaling the end of homeroom. No noisy, clanging bells in our school.

"Go fill up those brains with something besides internet gossip and caffeine-fueled delusions, children." She snapped her iPad cover shut. We filed out of the room under her suspicious sentry glare. I wanted to high-five her but didn't dare.

"Put Toff on the RC list," Jaz said, falling into step next to me.

I spun to look at her. "What? No way."

She huffed in frustration. "God, Viv. Isn't anyone good enough for you? Don't tell me he wouldn't be an improvement over Jake. At least he's funny."

"I'm not opposed to funny guys. I'd prefer that, actually. But I told you, I'm taking a logical approach to this. The next time I sneak out of the house to spend the night on the beach with some guy, he'd better be worth it."

But Jaz had stopped listening. Her gaze had shifted to my left where someone had stopped next to us just in time to hear the end of my rant.

"Hi, Vivian." The voice made my stomach dance, which was not good. Not good at all.

Oh my God. Did he have a psychic radar that made him show up to overhear every embarrassing, incriminating thing I said?

"Hi, Dallas," I said, refusing to look at him.

"Hi," Jaz said, grinning. "I'm Jasmine Cho. You can call me Jaz."

"I'm Dallas," he said. "Obviously."

Jaz shot me an oh-my-God-he's-totally-nerd-hot look. I really hoped he couldn't read girl-face.

"Sorry to interrupt," he said. "But I need your cell number. I might need to change my work schedule."

I turned toward Dallas. Since boy-face was much harder to decipher than girl-face, his expression was impossible to read. I wondered how much of my rant he'd overheard.

The chimes sounded again. "I've gotta run," I said.

Dallas shoved a pen and notebook under my face. "Write fast." I glanced up and saw his lips quirk. I scribbled my number on the paper, my fingers brushing his and shooting electrical charges up my arm.

"Ciao, Vivian. Nice to meet you, Jasmine." He shot us a crooked grin and disappeared into the crowd.

Jaz opened her mouth but I poked her in the chest. "Do not squeal. Do not speak. Save it 'til lunch."

"But—"

I poked her harder. "Save it. We're already late for class."

"Fine," she said. "But I'm only pausing the squeal, not deleting it." She flounced away, as much as anyone in a vintage Ramones T-shirt and skinny jeans could flounce.

At lunch, everyone sat at the same outside tables as last year. Jake and the dreadhead were practically in each other's laps at the surfer table. Stomach twisting, I turned away, focusing on my sushi.

"Where's the notebook?" Jaz asked, unwrapping her

peanut butter and honey sandwich.

I glanced anxiously at the other Serious Artists sitting at the table. The last thing I wanted was anyone overhearing us.

Jaz glanced at them and shrugged. "Don't worry; they're too busy listening to themselves."

"Fine. But let's discuss this rationally before I commit anything to paper." I speared a piece of sushi with my chopsticks.

"You've already ruled out two excellent RC targets." Jaz took a swig from her water bottle. "I need to know your criteria if you want my help."

Amy slid onto the bench next to me, fishing an apple and crackers out of her reusable lunch bag. "Hi." She smiled at us, her amber eyes warm and bright. She'd rolled her gorgeous red hair into Princess Leia buns on the sides of her head. "Criteria for what?"

I sighed deeply and poked at my tiny container of soy sauce and wasabi. Even though I knew I could trust Amy, letting someone else know about the replacement crush mission made me nervous.

"Viv's trying to knock Jake out of her brain by replacing him with a new guy. We're making a list of potential replacement crushes."

So much for keeping it between Jaz and me. I stuffed another piece of sushi in my mouth.

Amy's eyes widened and she tilted her head, hair jewelry dangling. "Why do you need to replace him? Just go crush-free for a while."

I swallowed, my eyes stinging from the extra wasabi I'd used in my dipping sauce. "Okay, so that would be the smart choice, right? But apparently my hormones are completely out of control and must be pacified. They need someone to focus on."

Jaz and Amy shared a look that questioned my sanity.

"I don't think you can control who you fall for, Vivian,"

Amy said. She took a bite of apple, crunching noisily.

"Right?" Jaz nodded. "She won't listen to me, though."

Snapping my lid onto my bento box, I took deep, calming breaths. Why was it so hard for my friends to believe this would work? "It was Spock's idea. Metaphorically his idea, I mean." I shrugged. "It's logical, so I know it'll work."

Amy and Jaz didn't even try to hide their matching expressions of disbelief.

I retrieved the purple notebook from my backpack. "Look, either you're with me or you're not. I don't care either way. But I'm doing this."

"You know I'm in," Jaz said. "I can't let you come up with this list without my input or it'll be a train wreck."

Amy nibbled on a cracker. "I hate to see you so unhappy, Viv. I'll help however I can. But I can't think of one book club novel we've read where the couple fell in love this way."

I wasn't surprised that Amy brought up our romance book club. Even Mom had been surprised by how many people read romance novels. "People you'd never expect," Mom always said, her eyes narrowing at the customers who traipsed into the store's kitchen once a month to discuss the intricacies of shape-shifter romance, among other things.

Mom and I had a running bet to see whose meeting brought in more attendees every month: her Body Count mystery book club or my Lonely Hearts club. Sometimes she won, sometimes I did. We had several crossover members who knew they'd better show up for both meetings or else.

"I don't want to fall in love," I said to Amy. "Think of this as a matchmaker story, only instead of trying to find me a perfect match to fall in love with, we're looking for…sort of a friend-zone match. Someone safe. Someone who won't break my heart."

"If you're looking for someone safe, that won't fool your hormones." Jaz's eyes danced with mischief. "Hormones

demand action. You can't fool them with a cheap imitation."
She pointed at my bento box. "Like the fake crab meat rolls
vs. the real thing."

Amy nodded. "She's right, Viv." She stacked her crackers
into a small tower. "And, um, what if there are unforeseen
complications?"

I frowned. "Like what?"

The cracker tower's height increased, swaying slightly.
"Well, let's say you find a replacement, and you fool your
hormones or whatever. But the guy like totally falls for you.
Doesn't that make you kind of a...a user?"

The cracker tower collapsed, and Amy and Jaz busied
themselves rebuilding it, darting me anxious looks.

I squirmed uncomfortably. "Okay, so I see your point."
I sighed. The last thing I wanted to do was use someone
like Jake had used me. Maybe Spock meant I could make
myself fall for my logical choice. Sort of like those historical
arranged marriage novels in which the couple were forced
together, then eventually fell in love for real. Why couldn't I
do that, too?

"I guess what I'm doing is making a list of guys I could
maybe some day fall for."

Jaz smirked. "So you'll take them for a test run, or a test
hookup?"

I blushed. "Don't be gross, Jaz. I mean, I'll hang out with
them. See if there are sparks—but not too many. A sparkler,
not a bottle rocket."

"I still think it's risky," Amy said, popping a cracker into
her mouth. "This could totally blow up in your face."

She must have read my expression because she reached
over to pat my hand. "Hey, Viv, I don't mean to harsh your
idea. I know how much you liked Jake and how he broke
your heart—"

"Asshat," Jaz interjected.

"—but you know me: I'm a firm believer in true love. And I don't think you can force it. It just…happens."

In a flash, I was transported to fourth grade when Amy and I bonded over a book series about cloud fairies. We'd read together at lunch every day, leaning against the school building, legs stretched out in the sun, while everyone else played kickball and tag.

"I'm not looking to fall in love, Ames. I just want a simple, fun relationship. Nothing more." I glanced at Jake and added, "And nothing less." Amy raised an eyebrow at me.

"I don't think you can control that, Viv…it sort of just happens."

I propped my chin on my hands, feeling defeated. "You guys are right. It's a stupid idea. I should give up on the entire male gender."

Amy sat up straight. "Now *that* is stupid."

"Look at me," Jaz said. "Remember my rabid all-guys-are-a-holes phase when I swore off dating, patriarchal proms, and all that? Then I met Lance. I had absolutely no control over falling in love. Or my hormones, if that's how you want to look at it." She slurped from her drink. "I almost lost my feminista card."

"Feminists need love, too," I said. "I consider myself one."

"But you'd be automatically disqualified from the feminista club, based on the silly books you read," Jaz argued.

Not this again. Jaz never listened when I tried to explain how women ruled an entire genre of books as both readers and writers, and how awesome that was. I opened my mouth to argue, but Amy was faster.

"No!" Amy surprised us both with her vehemence. "I totally disagree. Girls can be strong and independent and still want to fall in love, but with the right person who appreciates all those qualities." She glared at Jaz, pointing a knitting needle. "When's the last time you read a romance anyway? It's a huge genre filled with strong heroines, and the variety of—"

"Forget it, Amy," I interrupted. "Jaz might gorge herself on TMZ but you know she's never coming to our book club." Amy was super chill, but when she talked about books she got really wound up, which was why I loved having her at book club.

"I have another reason for my mission," I said, changing the subject to defuse the tension. It was a ridiculous reason, and I'd barely acknowledged it to myself, let alone said it out loud.

Amy's eyebrows shot up and Jaz leaned forward expectantly.

"It's stupid." I took a breath. "Totally stupid, but when Jake and I were…you know…I hoped he'd be my date to the Surfer Ball."

Jaz and Amy shared a knowing glance. The Surfer Ball had replaced a traditional Homecoming at our school years ago. The surf teams planned the whole event, and it was always amazing. And ridiculous. The guys on the team wore board shorts with tuxedo jackets, and some of the surfer girls showed up in mermaid outfits. The music was usually a local alternative band. Last year all the snacks had been vegan. And gross. Still, it was the highlight of our social year.

Somehow the dance had morphed into a Sadie Hawkins thing, too, where the girls asked guys instead of the other way around. Or girls asked girls. Some people showed up in groups instead of couples, but the weeks before the dance the school was electric with the nervous energy of girls selecting their escorts.

And this year I thought I'd finally have a date. Not just any date, but one of the surfing gods himself. I'd even started planning my outfit during our intense bonfire kissing week.

So much for that.

Jaz took my notebook. Sharpie in hand, she bent over the cover while Amy and I watched. Whatever Jaz touched with her pens or brushes always took my breath away.

"You don't need a date to go to the dance, you know," Amy said. "I'm planning on going dateless and I know I'll still have fun. Come with me."

I nodded. It was always an option. But before I graduated high school, I'd like just one cliché to come true. The corsage. The cheesy couple photo. The perfect slow dance. Well, maybe not the perfect slow dance since now I was aiming for a zing-free date. But still.

My phone vibrated in my pocket. *"Ok if I work 5:00 – 6:30 tomorrow? Need 2 do smthg @ 3:30. Sorry."* I stared at the text. No matter what Jaz said, Dallas could not go on the replacement list. He rattled me too much already, and I'd only known him for a day and a half.

"Sure," I typed. *"C U then."*

"Should I let your mom know?"

"I'll tell her." I hesitated. *"Where r u? Cells r strictly forbidden in class ;)"* As soon as I hit send, I regretted it. Why had I added the wink? Was I flirting? What was *wrong* with me?

I glanced up and caught Jaz's smirk.

"Put him on the list. You know you want to."

Amy looked back and forth between us. "Put who on the list? What am I missing?"

Jaz resumed drawing with a different colored pen. "Dallas. New guy. Totally hot McNerd."

Amy lit up like a Christmas tree. "Really? I love nerds. Tell me about him." She pointed to my phone. "He's texting you already?"

"Or is he sexting?" Jaz leered at me and I threw a cracker at her.

My phone buzzed and I lunged for it as Jaz pretended to grab it, laughing.

"He's going on the list," Jaz stage-whispered to Amy. "I don't care what she says."

Ignoring them, I read Dallas's text. *"I'm stealthy. Like a ninja texter. ;)"* I laughed out loud.

"Oh my God, Viv." Jaz flipped open the notebook and started writing. "He's going on the freaking list."

"Wait!" I exclaimed. "You don't even know the list format. Plus I want to see your cover."

Jaz huffed an exaggerated sigh as she slid the notebook across the table. I snatched it up in case it said something mortifying like, "How to Fix Vivian's Pathetic Love Life." But it didn't. It was gorgeous, full of swirling colors and lots of beautiful, expression-filled eyes.

I didn't know how she captured so much emotion in a pair of eyes, but she made me feel as if I was looking at real people. In the bottom right corner, I noticed a pair of black-rimmed glasses behind which danced some familiar-looking green eyes. I glared at her, but she winked at me and took a long drink from her water bottle.

"It's gorgeous," I said, because it was, in spite of the not so subtle message she was trying to send with one particular pair of eyes. At least she hadn't drawn a naked person inside the irises like on *The Great Gatsby* cover.

"Let me see," Amy said. I gave her the notebook. "Ooh," she murmured. "You're so gifted, Jaz."

Jaz blushed. "Come off it, guys. It's just a quick drawing."

"Quick for you, maybe." I looked at my phone. "Class starts in seven minutes. If you really want to help me, I'll tell you some of my criteria."

Jaz shot me a wary look. "Okay, fire away."

"Okay, so number one and probably most important: he must not go above a five on the zing meter."

"A five?" Amy squeaked. "That's hardly anything."

"I know; that's the whole point." The three of us had invented the zing meter our freshman year. It went from zero to ten, with ten reserved for famous dream guys, like Tom Hiddleston for Jaz. Jake had been a nine for years, for me anyway. Amy and Jaz hadn't agreed, obviously seeing him more clearly than I did.

"Is this your stupid Spock logic?" Jaz asked.

I narrowed my eyes. "Do not mock the Spock. If I'd ignored Jake's zing, I'd be much better off."

"Hmm," Amy said. "But even though he's an ass, for a couple of weeks the kissing and, uh, whatever, was awesome, right?"

Jaz cocked an eyebrow. "What happened to crush-free Amy? Strong, feminist heroine Amy?"

Amy sighed and leaned her chin in her hand. "Amy hasn't kissed anyone for way too long."

We both laughed and Jaz squeezed Amy's shoulder. "At least you have standards and wouldn't waste your time on a low-zinger, unlike our friend here."

Amy gave me a sympathetic smile. "All right. Let's ignore the zing meter for now. What else, besides that?"

"He has to be smart. And funny."

Jaz nodded. "Smart plus funny automatically makes him at least a six-zinger."

"No," Amy disagreed. "The zing is all about the butterflies in your stomach, the sweaty hands. Not being able to breathe when he looks at you." She sighed, looking wistful.

I flipped open the notebook and wrote "RC Mission" on the top of the first page, then drew three columns, labeling them: Name, Pros, Cons.

Jaz shook her head in disgust. "This is how my parents decide where we go on vacation every year. And why we always end up going somewhere boring."

"Let me see." Amy read my column labels. "Oh." She chewed on a fingernail and smiled weakly. "It's, um, organized?"

Fortunately the chimes rang, sparing us all from further bickering. "Whatever," I muttered, grabbing the notebook.

Spock was never swayed by emotional arguments and I wouldn't be, either.

"One of the advantages of being a captain is being able to ask for advice without necessarily having to take it." —*Captain Kirk*

CHAPTER FIVE

News traveled fast in our school. By the end of the day, everyone knew about the cute McNerd who drove a Vespa. Judging by the random snippets of conversation I overheard, a lot of girls had a thing for nerd-hot boys.

Somehow Dallas and I ended up in the bike/Vespa parking area at the same time after school. "Hey." He nodded at me, helmet dangling from his hand. He wore a red Wisconsin Badgers T-shirt and jeans that made me want to stare at his butt.

"Oh. Hi." I pretended to look surprised, as if I hadn't been hyper-aware of him in my peripheral vision.

"Sorry I had to change the schedule. I need to run an errand, but I'll see you at five o'clock?"

"Sure. I'll be there." I tried to sound casual, reminding myself I needed to treat him like a fellow crew member on the *Enterprise*. "You ready to pay up? Cuz I know you lost the bet."

He grinned. "About your mom's pen name? Let's wait until five o'clock to settle this."

I returned his smile and zipped up my hoodie. "Hope

you brought the *Star Trek* bible."

He laughed and tugged on his helmet. "See you later, Vivian."

He revved the zoomy Italian engine and was gone, a gaggle of nerd-worshippers giggling in his wake.

"So about that list," Jaz said, suddenly appearing next to me. "We need to get serious or else you'll end up dating McNerdy, and God knows you don't want *that* to happen."

My cheeks burned. "I already have some names. And McNerdy is not one of them."

Jaz narrowed her eyes. "Excellent. I'll just swing by the store and give your list my seal of approval. Or not."

We glared at each other, then I yelled, "Race you!" and took off at full speed.

Half an hour later, we'd gorged on snacks and had taken over store duty from Mom, who'd disappeared to her home office. We sat at the desk, notebook open between us. I'd refused to change my pro/con list format, so Jaz insisted on adding a zing rating column, but that was as much as I was willing to give.

"So let's hear the names," she demanded, polishing off the last of the cookies.

Fortunately the only customer was Mrs. Sloane, a regular from the senior center. She sat in an overstuffed chair, reading jacket blurbs of western romances.

"Okay." I brushed crumbs off my shirt. "RC target number one: Iggy."

"What?" Jaz's shriek made Mrs. Sloane glance up. "Sorry," Jaz whispered. She turned her shocked gaze to me. "You do realize he's gay, right?"

"Rumor is he's actually bi, which opens the door for me."

Jaz's mouth dropped open. "No way."

I nodded. "Way. Don't you remember when he hooked up with Tara freshman year? She said he was the best kisser of her life." Which was saying something, since Tara had lots of experience.

"Viv. Get serious."

I ignored her. "Plus he's awesome. Named for Iggy Pop, British accent, Japanese cheekbones, and wicked funny. Plus we're already friends. He's made-for-TV perfect."

"As your GBF, sure. But as a replacement crush? No way."

I crossed my arms over my chest. "Look, he meets the smart and funny criteria. British accent gets at least one bonus zing point. But not too much zing."

"But he's *gay*, Vivian! As in, so not interested in luring you to the beach after dark."

Dallas chose that moment to appear at the counter.

"Hi." He tugged at his hair, not making eye contact with either of us. How much had he overheard?

Jaz squeezed my thigh so hard my eyes watered. I glared at her, but she gave me a syrupy smile, then turned the syrup on Dallas.

"Hi, Dallas. We were just discussing Vivian's—"

"Homework," I said, instantly interrupting. "We're doing homework." I glared at Jaz. "I. Will. Kill. You," I mouthed.

Dallas took a sudden interest in stowing his backpack and helmet in a corner.

Jaz giggled and stood up. "I know you two have work to do. I'll leave you alone."

Dallas approached the counter, looking adorably nervous. "Um, I can wait, if you're busy."

"No, no," Jaz said, swishing around from behind the counter. "Besides, I need to Skype Lance." She waggled her eyebrows meaningfully, making me blush.

Dallas nodded, looking slightly confused.

"I'll call you later," Jaz said, giving me a beauty queen wave.

"Oh, hey," Dallas said, recovering his composure. "Did you guys know Fisk Vilhelm is in town?"

Jaz squealed and jumped up and down. "I knew it!" She pointed at me. "I told you, Vivian. Why do you doubt my celeb-spotting skills after all these years?"

Dallas smiled at Jaz like the cheap entertainment she was. "So you saw him, too? He's pretty cool."

Jaz froze. "Wait. You met him? Talked to him? Details. Now."

Dallas glanced at me, then Jaz. "Well, uh, it was no big deal. I...sort of ran into him, and uh, he was cool." He shrugged, pushing his glasses up his nose.

"Ran into him where?" Jaz took a step toward Dallas, who stepped back, glancing at me over his shoulder like he needed rescuing.

"Uh, he was... I was..." His voice trailed away, then he cleared his throat. "I think it might be confidential, actually."

"Confidential!" Jaz squeaked. "Dallas, I know you're new here." She took a calming breath. "But it sounds like you've heard the unwritten rule that we don't hassle celebs when they're in town."

"Right." Dallas nodded. "I didn't hassle him."

Jaz narrowed her eyes. "But there's not a rule that says you can't say where you saw him."

Dallas rubbed his hand over his chin. "Good to know. But I'm still pretty sure I need to keep it a secret."

Jaz stared at me, astonished. "Vivian, tell him," she pleaded. "Tell your McNerd that I am not going to stalk Fisk."

"McWhat?" Dallas shot me a dark look, then turned back to Jaz. "Did you just call me a...McNerd?"

Jaz at least had the decency to blush. "Uh, yeah, I did. Sorry. But it's, um, not a mean nickname. It's a cute one."

She flashed him her most charming smile. "Viv's the one who came up with it. You should be flattered. She doesn't give nicknames to just anyone."

I needed to find out exactly which poisons Mom was researching so I could borrow some to kill my best friend.

No one breathed or moved or said a word for what felt like forever. From the corner, Mrs. Sloane chuckled softly to herself.

Finally, I swallowed and raised my eyes to Dallas. His mouth was a tight, straight line, and I couldn't tell if it was anger or amusement flashing in his eyes. Oh, who was I kidding? Of course he was mad, and I couldn't blame him.

"Sorry," I whispered, mortified, my face on fire. I prayed for Scottie to beam me up, but my butt stayed glued to the chair.

"I've gotta go." Jaz backed away from us. "See ya, guys." She turned and fled, pausing at the door to send me frantic I'm-so-sorry-please-don't-kill-me girl face messages. The door slammed behind her, leaving me alone with the McNerd and Mrs. Sloane, whose knowing smile indicated she was enjoying the drama playing out in front of her.

Dallas sighed as he settled himself in his chair. I couldn't look at him.

"I've been called worse," he finally said. "At least yours is clever. Sort of."

"Dallas, I…I didn't mean…"

He put up a hand, and I flinched as if he'd slapped me. "Forget it. Let's get to work."

He wouldn't look at me, which made me feel terrible. I'd thought McNerd was a cute nickname, not hurtful like Chunky Monkey, but obviously he didn't like it. He was new, trying to fit in, and he was nice…and adorkable…and now I'd hurt his feelings.

"Is this yours?" He slid the purple RC notebook toward me and I grabbed it, praying he hadn't noticed the sketch of his eyes.

He opened his laptop and his fingers flew over the keyboard. One of us had to speak, but clearly neither one of us wanted to.

"So," I finally mumbled, "what are we doing today?" I grabbed a Reese's peanut butter cup from the candy jar.

He sat quietly for a few moments, then turned toward me, his face a mask of calculated indifference with none of the humor or cute dorkiness from earlier today. I swallowed nervously. Maybe he wasn't McNerdy so much as McScary.

"I'd planned to ask about the categories of books you sell." He glanced around the store, carefully avoiding eye contact with me. "Obviously mysteries. But what else?" His gaze finally returned to me, its intensity unnerving.

I forced a smile, but he didn't return it. How could I possibly fix this?

"Well, um, we also have a romance section. That's sort of my specialty." God, had I admitted that out loud? My face burned as I rushed on. "And there's a kids' book section. Not very big but we try to keep stuff to occupy the kids while their parents browse." I took a breath. "Oh! We have a geek section, too! Sci-fi, fantasy. You might like…"

My words trailed away. Was there idiot juice instead of water in my water bottle today?

He resumed typing, but I saw his jaw clench. "Do you categorize within genres? On the shelves?"

I gulped. "Uh…"

He turned to me, impatient. "Cozy mysteries. Romantic suspense. Like that."

"Oh." I swallowed, still rattled by his cool distance. "You know about sub-genres?"

An irritated expression flitted across his face. "I did some research."

Research. I remembered the bet; maybe that could lighten the mood. I yanked out my hair elastic, fiddling with the wild curls I'd unleashed. Dallas glanced at my hair, then focused back on his screen.

"So," I said, twisting the elastic, "did your research reveal anything important, like my mom's pen name?"

He stopped typing, his fingers hovering over the keyboard. "Maybe."

"You get two guesses." Even if I gave him twenty, he'd never figure it out.

He straightened, then turned toward me, pushing his glasses up his nose. God, his eyes were so...so...

"Macy Gardner," he said.

I blinked, reminding myself to focus on his words instead of his eyes. "No. Good guess, though." Lots of people thought Mom was Macy Gardner since her cozy mysteries were set in a beach town similar to ours.

His eyebrows shot up. "Really? She's not Macy?"

I shook my head. "What's your second guess?"

He tugged his hair and glanced up. "I was sure that was it," he mumbled more to the ceiling than me.

Mrs. Sloane chose that moment to totter up to the counter. I used to wonder why she didn't buy at least ten books at once, since I knew she'd be back in two days for a new book. Then Mom explained to me that getting out of the senior center and visiting our store was probably the highlight of her week.

Smiling, I stood up to help her. "I'm sure you still have credit, but let me record this." I grabbed an index card box, recorded the transaction, and handed her the book, slipping a Murder by the Sea bookmark between the pages.

Mrs. Sloane propped the book on the counter, cover facing toward us, while she buttoned her sweater. Dallas glanced at the book then quickly looked away. *Her Wild Rider* featured a buffed, shirtless cowboy wearing low-slung jeans, head tilted down, his chiseled face partially hidden by his cowboy hat. I wasn't a huge western fan, but I followed the reviews on the blogger sites to make sure we stocked the good ones. Mrs. Sloane wasn't the only Shady Cove resident who had a thing for hot cowboys.

Even though I knew he was embarrassed, I was secretly relieved to see Dallas's cool facade rattled. Maybe now he'd be easier to work with. "Are you coming to book club on Saturday?" I asked Mrs. Sloane.

She nodded and touched her perfectly coiffed helmet of silver hair. "Wouldn't miss it, sweetie. But I wasn't thrilled with this one. I expected the dragon sex to be hotter."

Dallas choke-coughed, reaching for his water bottle.

I put up a hand. "Save it for Saturday, Mrs. Sloane. I don't want to know anyone's opinion in advance."

She dropped her book into her tote bag. "All right." She sighed. "I guess I prefer human relations to supernatural ones."

Dallas's cough increased and he slugged down more water.

Mrs. Sloane shot me a wink. "He's cute," she mouthed.

I checked to make sure he wasn't watching us, then nodded.

"See you on Saturday." I waved good-bye as Mrs. Sloane left the store.

"I bet you didn't know about those sub-genres," I said, turning to Dallas. "Cowboys and dragons."

"I know about the vampire thing," he said, not meeting my eyes.

Who on planet Earth didn't know about the vampire thing?

He cleared his throat. "I, uh, didn't realize about the dragons."

"Shape-shifters," I clarified. "They can change form from human to dragon. And other supernatural creatures. We're talking sub-sub-genres."

He finally made eye contact, unable to hide his curiosity.

"Really?"

"Yep."

I knew he had to be wondering about the physical details, especially after Mrs. Sloane's comment, but I assumed he'd rather die than ask me. I sure didn't want to tell him about this particular dragon lord's special, um, equipment. Fortunately, what happened in book club stayed in book club.

"So what's your second guess?"

It was his turn to blink in confusion.

"My mom's secret identity."

His expression cleared. "Oh, right." He frowned. "I thought I had it."

"I know. Most people around here think Mom is Macy, no matter how much she denies it." I shrugged. "But she's not."

He nodded, tugging at his hair again. "Okay…well…"

The tinkling bell sounded, and we both turned to the door. My stomach clenched as Jake and the dreadhead sauntered in, hands shoved in each other's back pockets. What was he doing here? And why did he bring his barnacle?

Jake tossed his dark hair out of his eyes in a move that used to make me melt.

"Hey, Viv," Jake said, like it was no big deal he'd crushed my heart only 48 hours earlier.

My knuckles whitened as I gripped the counter. I sensed Dallas watching me, but I refused to look at him, not wanting him to see how badly Jake rattled me.

"Hey, Jake." I spoke through gritted teeth. I didn't acknowledge the dreadhead even though I knew that was shallow and mean. I was still in the first stages of break-up grief; I was allowed to be bitter.

"My gram ran out of books again." He held up a plastic bag full of paperbacks. "She needs a refill."

Like the bookstore was a Big Gulp machine? The idiot

had no appreciation for the written word whatsoever. And I'd wasted how many kisses on him?

I sighed extra long and loud. "How much longer is she staying with you?"

Jake shrugged. "Dunno. Maybe another couple of weeks?"

I took the bag. She'd finished over a dozen books. "She reads fast," I said, more to myself than him.

"Yeah," Jake said. "She said she wants more like those, uh, what was it again?" He looked at the dreadhead for help.

Dreadhead smiled at me. She was pretty. Uber pretty, in fact. No wonder Jake dumped me. Dallas stared at her, too. Of course he'd be sucked in by the blonde beach girl spell. They probably didn't have girls like that in Wisconsin.

"She liked the Macy Gardner ones. The beach mysteries," the Jake barnacle said, tilting her pretty little dreadhead. "Is Macy your mom? That's so cool."

I bit back a sigh of frustration as Dallas chuckled softly.

"No," I snapped. "My mom writes under another name. And before you ask what it is, I can't tell you. Secrecy oath."

Dreadhead's eyes widened, then she laughed. "Whatevs." She glanced at Jake and shrugged. Jake rolled his eyes. It was definitely a *Viv's-so-weird-sorry-I-had-to-bring-you-here* eye roll.

"We have lots of Macy Gardner's books." I headed toward the cozy mystery section, determined to channel my inner Spock.

Dallas stood up and extended his hand. "I'm Dallas."

Jake shook his hand. "Jake." He tilted his head. "This is Claire."

Returning to the counter, I shoved the new books into Jake's bag. Jake asked Dallas about his Vespa and said it was sick. Claire said it was adorbs. I rolled my eyes, but no one was looking at me.

"Here." I handed the bag to Jake, who looked confused.

"Don't I need to pay you?"

I shook my head. "She had enough store credit from the ones you brought back."

"Cool." Jake looped his arm around Claire's waist and she snuggled into him. I wanted to projectile vomit all over the happy couple, but unfortunately I didn't have that superpower.

Dallas turned to me after they left. "Don't you need to record that transaction?"

"What?" I could barely focus, distracted by images of Jake and Claire kissing seared into my brain.

He gestured to the index card box. "The store credits."

"Oh." I felt a blush creeping up my neck. "I don't have a card set up for Jake's grandma."

Dallas frowned. "Why not?

Uh, because when he first came in here I was so totally flustered it was the last thing I thought of? And the second time I wanted to kill him?

"She's just visiting. I didn't think she'd become a repeat customer."

"That's...maybe not the best business practice," Dallas said softly, but he stared at his computer instead of me.

"Who are you, Bill Gates?" I snapped, then instantly regretted it because of the whole McNerd thing. I dropped into my chair and sighed. "Sorry, Dallas. I didn't mean...it's just...hard to explain."

Dallas spun his chair. "I think I got the message." He glared at me, arms crossed over his chest, those intense green eyes making my stomach flutter.

"No, I don't think you did." I swallowed, but pressed on. "Most of the time I'm actually a decent person who doesn't make fun of people, even accidentally with stupid nicknames. I'm sorry about that. But..." My voice trailed away.

What was I doing? I couldn't tell him about Jake and me. I didn't even know Dallas. For all I knew, he'd be part of Jake's snake pack by the end of the week, laughing over stupid Viv who thought kissing actually meant something. Yeah, maybe I was an idiot for hooking up with Jake, but I was also an idiot trying to blink back tears.

"Excuse me, be right back." I jumped out of my chair and scurried away. I pushed through the kitchen door and locked myself in the tiny bathroom where I splashed my burning face with cold water. At least the cold water froze the tears in their tracks.

I stared in the mirror, taking deep breaths, trying to re-center myself. *"Compose yourself, Vivian. Vulcans do not have meltdowns."* Spock's voice was stern, and slightly disgusted. Who could blame him? Spock was right; I needed to get a grip, but the tears weren't listening, staging a rebound attack. I grabbed a book off the vanity shelf and started reading randomly, distracting myself with words, my shelter in every storm.

After a chapter of a hilarious Susan Elizabeth Phillips book, I felt somewhat calmer. I straightened my ponytail, washed and dried my face, and put on some lip gloss.

When I re-entered the shop Dallas was gone. Picasso and a couple of the other art kids had arrived, settling in to sketch and argue with each other.

Picasso caught my eye as I glanced around the store. "Vespa Guy said he'd be right back." I was relieved, having been embarrassed by the length of my time-out.

"Thanks." I shrugged like I didn't care, but a tiny wave of relief snuck through me.

I sorted through the pile of books Jake had returned. As I stood up to return them to the shelves, Dallas's voice stopped me.

"Renee Larson."

"What?" I spun around. He towered over me, holding two smoothie cups from The Jumping Bean.

"My second guess." He handed me a smoothie. "Renee Larson. Author of the vampire hunter mysteries."

I laughed. "Not even. Mom's picky about vampire books. She definitely isn't a fan of Renee's." I sipped from the smoothie straw. "Chocolate and peanut butter! Thank you. How'd you know it's my favorite?"

He shrugged, his eyes darting toward the jar of Reeses' candy. "Lucky guess. You looked like you could use it after Jake left." He settled himself into his chair, then pinned me with those sparkly eyes.

Wow. Nerd hot *and* thoughtful. Dallas's lips were moving, but the *Star Trek* red alert warning blaring at maximum volume in my mind drowned him out.

"Sorry, what?"

He cocked an eyebrow. "I asked why your mom isn't a fan of the Larson books." He sucked on his straw while I tried not to stare at his lips.

I sat down, looking away so I didn't have to watch his mouth on the straw. "It's hard to explain. Mom's sort of a vampire purist."

"A what?"

"You really want to hear about this?"

He nodded. "Sounds like I need to, for business reasons." His lips quirked ever so slightly, and I hoped that meant he'd forgiven me for the Bill Gates comment. And the McNerd nickname.

I took a breath. "Okay, so basically there are readers who love the whole new-age, sparkly vampire thing. But some readers are anti-sparkle. Purists. They're all about the horror and the blood and the super scary stuff. The original vampire legends, Dracula, Nosferatu, all that stuff. Some of them blame *Twilight* for ruining vampires forever."

"Wow!" Dallas exhaled when I finished. "I had no idea it was so complex." He paused, then gave me a sly smile that made my stomach flip over. "How about you? Are you a purist? Sparkly or scary?"

As I tried to feign indifference to Dallas's smile and sparkly eyes, I was tempted to answer Team Sparkle. Where was my inner Spock when I needed him?

"I'm not as opinionated as my mom. I read all kinds of books. As long as the romance is awesome, I'm happy."

Dallas turned back to his laptop. He nodded but said nothing as his fingers flew over the keys. Was he blushing?

We spent the rest of his shift touring the store. He took notes, muttering about databases. When I showed him the romance section, he focused intently on scribbling in his notebook. I couldn't resist taking two books off the shelves to explain how the same author might write under different pen names.

"Why, um, do I need to know this?" he asked, color creeping up his neck as he glanced between the two covers. One cover had a swirly font title with a simple line drawing of a flower. The other cover, however, almost made me blush. A bare-chested, impossibly ripped guy bent over a gorgeous naked woman barely covered by a red silk sheet.

"Sometimes customers want to read every book by an author, but they might not know the author writes under more than one name. Maybe you can figure out a way we can indicate that in the database? So we can let readers know."

"Cross-listing," he said, scribbling more notes as I reshelved the books. I wondered what he thought of me reading books with covers of half-naked people. I didn't read *all* the romances, especially the super steamy ones that sometimes made me cringe, but I read a ton of review blogs so I knew which ones to stock.

I thought of the snippets of conversations Dallas had overheard about morning tongue action and Jaz saying Iggy was the last guy who'd want to drag me to the beach after dark. It was my turn to blush, wondering if Dallas had misinterpreted things.

Before Jake, my love life had been mostly non-existent. The romance in my life existed between the covers, all right. The covers of books.

I returned to the desk and busied myself sorting through Mom's pile of mail.

"I need to get going," Dallas said. "I have to babysit my sister." His arm accidentally brushed against my back as he moved behind me, making me freeze.

"Your internal timer go off again?" I joked, willing us both to stop thinking about that book cover with the red silk sheets because I knew we were.

He stopped loading his backpack. "It never lets me down."

"So you're part robot?"

He rolled his eyes. "Not all McNerds have artificial parts." He finally gave me a real smile, the first one all day. "Only a few of us get chosen for implants. I got the timer."

I laughed nervously, tucking a wayward curl behind my ear. His steady gaze didn't waver. Had he forgiven me for the nickname? I hoped so. "How old is your sister?"

"Seven."

I smiled hesitantly. "That's great. I always wanted a big brother when I was little."

"You're an only? Lucky you."

I shrugged. "It's okay, I guess." After my parents had divorced, I'd wanted a sibling, but eventually I'd found companionship in my books.

He watched me thoughtfully, then pulled his phone from his pocket. "So are you working Saturday? I'm busy in the morning, but I could come by that afternoon."

I hesitated. Saturdays were always busy plus this Saturday was Lonely Hearts book club. But maybe it would be good for him to see us in action on a busier day. "I'm doing my book club from one o'clock until two thirty. But you can come by after that."

"See you then." He paused. "I'll probably see you around school, too."

"Right." I nodded, toying with Jaz's fraying friendship bracelet. She and I needed to have a serious chat after the way she'd totally embarrassed me today.

As soon as he left, I retrieved the purple RC notebook. Homework could wait. I needed to put the Spock brain to work before the hormones took over and wrecked my life once again.

CHAPTER SIX

HUNKALICIOUSHEROES.COM
Romance Reviews for Ravenous Readers

SCORCHED BY FIRE by Declan Reever
Reviewed by Sweet Feet
Rating: Crocs*

This is a solid entry in the shape-shifter genre, though it didn't break the mold (and melt my e-reader) like Thea Harrison's *Elder Races* series. Still, it kept my interest, especially once Kevin the beta dragon showed up. I know, right? A dragon named Kevin? He's super cute, trying to get used to his dragon-ness and struggling to keep the fire-breathing in check every time he encounters the girl he's crushing on. He's terrified he'll burn her clothes off or set her hair on fire. (Teaser: one of those things actually happens the first time they kiss).

The main dragon, Ranz, is your usual scary alpha shape-shifter dude, covered with tattoos and swinging a bad attitude around like a club. He's saved from his badass ways by the love of a good woman, of course. And some super-hot bedroom scenes that are technically for older readers (don't say I didn't warn you).

I'm on Team Kevin for this one. Even though he's not the main character, he has enough scenes to make it worth your time. I hope he gets his own book. Are you listening, Ms. Reever?

*Rating Scale:
- ◆ Granny Shoes - safe for Grandmas
- ◆ Birks - lots of emotion and navel-gazing
- ◆ Wing Tips - bossy but irresistible heroes
- ◆ Crocs - Funny heroes, imperfect heroines
- ◆ Vans – testy heroes full of smarcasm
- ◆ Go-go boots - my highest rating: perfection

"It was logical to cultivate multiple options."
—Spock

CHAPTER SEVEN

"How're things going with Dallas?" Mom asked. We sat at the kitchen table, Mom sipping tea and me eating cereal. Hiddles nibbled from his bowl, pausing occasionally to hiss at us.

I swallowed quickly, trying not to choke. "What do you mean?"

Mom's brow wrinkled. "At the store? Showing him the card system?"

"Oh." I let out a relieved sigh. "It's going okay, I guess."

Mom refilled her cup from the teapot. "Just okay? He seemed quite capable when I interviewed him. I'm planning to check in with him on Saturday; he emailed me to let me know his schedule."

Of course he did. Mr. Always-on-Time probably worried I'd forget to tell her. "He's definitely smart," I said. "He asks a lot of questions about how we do stuff." I shrugged. No way could I tell Mom how much he rattled my composure. "He talked about databases yesterday. He definitely seems to have a plan."

Mom looked relieved. "Good. We also need to do an inventory after hours. I'm hoping the two of you can work a couple of late nights together to get it done."

I stopped mid-chew. "What?"

"Inventory, Vivvy. I can't even remember the last time I did it. We need to record every single book in the store and categorize all the books by genre. We should do it all in one shot, but that won't work with my writing schedule and you at school."

"Um, maybe you and I can do the inventory. Or I could ask Jaz and Amy to help." Mom gave me a questioning look. "Dallas is busy. He, um, always seems to have places to go. Cello lessons. Babysitting his sister. Stuff."

Mom raised an eyebrow. "I'm glad you're getting to know him, however, it's critical that he participate in the inventory, Vivvy. He's the one creating the database, after all."

I fiddled with my spoon. "Isn't there software you can buy that already does what you need? Did you have to hire someone to design it for you?"

Mom looked surprised. "Well, yes, there is. But I'd rather give that money to someone local. You know how I feel about supporting local businesses."

I snorted. "Dallas isn't exactly a business."

Mom's eyes narrowed. "You know what I mean, Vivvy." She sipped her tea. "Besides, I won't be surprised to see him running his own business some day."

Hiddles meowed from the floor. Grateful for the distraction, I made a few kissing noises to entice him onto my lap, but he ignored me and stalked away, swishing his tail indignantly.

"Okay, whatever," I said, not meeting Mom's eyes. I didn't want her deciphering my feelings about working late nights with Dallas in the store. Just the two of us. In the dark. Well, it wouldn't technically be dark…but metaphorically….

"Vivian, if Dallas is making you uncomfortable in some way—"

"What? No!" I yelped. I didn't want her assuming anything bad about the guy. "No, it's not that," I said, forcing myself to sound calm. "He's nice. Funny. You don't need to plot his death with poison or anything like that."

Mom frowned, studying me with her hyper-observant writer face, looking for secret motivations and underlying agendas. I tried my best to look totally uninterested in Dallas as anything other than a coworker.

"All right." Mom brushed her curls behind her ear. "It's not that I don't trust you, sweetie. I do, completely."

My face burned, remembering how many times I'd snuck out to meet Jake. "You don't need to worry about anything happening between Dallas and me."

Mom nodded. "He seems like a great guy. Probably much nicer than whoever made you cry." She narrowed her eyes at me. "I try not to be overprotective but I hate to see—"

"Um, Mom? Why are we having this conversation? It's not relevant."

Her eyebrows shot up. "Not relevant? Sweetie, you're seventeen. Trust me, it's relevant."

I jumped up from the table and put my cereal bowl in the sink. "I've gotta go, Mom. Jaz is determined to spot Fisk Vilhelm on the beach this morning."

"Oh, I heard about that. He's staying at The Lodge." Somehow Mom always knew who was at The Lodge.

"Really?" That was two confirmed reports: both Dallas and Mom. Jaz would be thrilled.

Jaz and I dismounted our bikes. She'd brought her opera glasses for spying today. She wore an old Led Zeppelin shirt with a mini skirt and wedge sandals. I had no idea how she rode her bike in those shoes, but somehow she managed.

"So do you forgive me?" Jaz asked. "For outing the McNerd nickname to Dallas?"

"I wanted to kill you, Jaz."

"I know, I know. I totally suck. I just start talking sometimes and I can't stop." She looked at me with pleading eyes. "Was it awful after I left? Did he freeze you with Kryptonite?"

"You're crazy, you know that? Besides, Kryptonite doesn't freeze. It weakens, and it weakens Superman, not the other way around."

She grinned. "Whatever. You have to admit he's totally rocking that Clark Kent/Superman vibe. Did you see those biceps?"

"No comment."

"Forgive me?" she begged.

"Yes, I forgive you but promise you won't talk about my RC mission in front of anyone else, okay?"

She crossed a finger over her heart. "I swear. On the hot body of Dallas the McNerd."

I snorted; I never could stay mad at her. "Look!" I exclaimed, pointing. Way in the distance, a guy ran along the surf's edge. It could've been anyone, but I loved messing with her.

Jaz leaned over the parapet, opera glasses glued to her face. "Oh my God! I think it's Fisk."

I laughed. "No way." I squinted in the sunlight and tried to focus on the guy. I supposed it could be him.

"We're going to be late." I grabbed my bike from its resting placing against the wall. "Let's blaze, stalker." We raced each other to the bottom of the hill, laughing.

"I'm listing that as an official sighting," Jaz declared as we hurried across the school courtyard.

"No way. It doesn't count. I refuse to sign."

Jaz liked to have witnesses sign her notebook to confirm the sightings, but I only signed when I was sure she wasn't deliriously hallucinating.

"Come on, Viv," she whispered as we slunk into homeroom. "You know it was him."

Ms. Kilgore paused her roll call as we slid into our desks. "How nice of you girls to join us. Don't mind us; we'll wait while you finish your conversation."

Laughter rolled across the room like an ocean wave. Jaz and I shared an embarrassed look. Much as I loved Ms. Kilgore's scariness, I didn't like being on the receiving end.

Ms. Kilgore resumed her droning roll call. I shot another sideways glance at Jaz and caught Toff grinning at me. He reminded me of a deranged human puppy. If he had a tail, it would always be wind-milling, knocking over everything.

Toff caught up to me in the hall after we left homeroom. "You coming to the surf comp on Saturday? It's just a qualifier, but it'll be cool."

His wavy blond hair was still damp from morning surf practice. I swore he smelled like seaweed. The guy was part dolphin, which was why I'd nicknamed him Flipper when we were kids.

"No, I've gotta work."

He gave me a fake devastated look. "Man, Viv, I'd think my almost-sister would be more supportive." He winked at me, his sky blue eyes lit with laughter.

"Right." I laughed with him. "Maybe another time."

"Guess I'll see you for dinner on Saturday then."

I stopped outside my classroom door and stared up at him. "You will?" I noticed a few girls shooting me envious looks. I didn't blame them. The shredder gods had graced Toff with the full package of athleticism and hotness, spiked with goofy humor.

He leaned against the wall, smiling down at me. "Yeah, my

dad and I are coming for dinner. Your mom didn't tell you?"

I shook my head. "She's in the middle of first-draft frenzy, so sometimes she forgets stuff."

Toff's grin deepened. "Researching cross-bows?"

"No, that was the last book. It's poison now."

"Cool."

When our parents started dating, I worried it would be awkward, but Toff took it in stride. He always found something to tease me about, but he'd never tried to move us out of the friend zone. He dated girls on the surf team; he definitely had a type and I wasn't it.

The chimes sounded from the speaker mounted right above us in the hallway, making me jump.

"Later, Wordworm," Toff said, pushing off the wall.

"Ciao, Flipper."

He tossed me a lazy smile over his shoulder then sauntered down the hallway.

"Do you want to put him on the list?" Amy whispered. She'd followed me into Lit class after Toff disappeared.

"Toff," Amy mouthed as she pantomimed writing on a piece of paper.

Jaz had suggested the same thing and I'd shot her down. I considered my criteria: smart, funny, no higher than a five on the zing meter. I knew Toff was smart, but he was one of those guys who hid their intelligence under layers of jokes. He was a surfing savant, obviously, spending most of his waking hours in the water or at his dad's surf shop. He was definitely funny. But more like class clown funny, not banter funny.

God, I was a dork. How many girls ruled out a guy because he didn't excel at witty banter?

Then there was the zing meter. Objectively, Toff was probably a solid eight on the 1-10 scale. But I wasn't entirely objective about Toff because of our parents dating. And the whole friends since kindergarten factor, which dropped him down to maybe a five.

Also, he hadn't outgrown armpit farting noises, so maybe he was more like a four. I doodled a surfboard in my notebook and drew a big X through it.

Amy's finger poked me in the shoulder and I looked up.

Ms. Sanchez's lips compressed into a thin line. "Daydreaming already, Vivian? And it's only the first week of school."

I heard scattered giggles behind me. "Sorry." I gave her an apologetic, sincere-but-distracted student smile. Her mouth relaxed slightly and she resumed her lecture.

She'd put up a slide on the Promethean board: Symbolism, a Study in Three Parts. Ugh. Why couldn't we read for fun? I knew how to analyze books for symbolism and metaphors and all that junk, but it got old. Sometimes I fantasized about taking over Lit class and turning it into a book club meeting.

"Give me your hand," Jaz demanded.

"Why should I?" I glared at Jaz suspiciously.

Jaz, Amy, and I had spent most of the lunch break hashing over my RC list, which now had three targets. But we'd argued over target number four: Toff. Jaz insisted I put him on the list while Amy sat quietly nibbling her crackers.

"Just give it to me." Jaz gestured impatiently to my hand. She gripped my wrist tightly, then stuck a marker in her mouth. She removed the cap with her teeth, then began drawing on my hand.

"Hey!" I tried to jerk my hand free, but she had me in a vise grip.

Amy leaned over to watch Jaz draw. "Perfect," she said, smiling.

"What? What's perfect?" I tried to see what Jaz was

drawing, but Amy used her hands to block my view.

I sighed and gave up, letting my hand relax in Jaz's grip. "Resistance is futile," I said.

Jaz and Amy stared at me.

"Never mind," I shrugged. "*Star Trek* quote."

Jaz smirked and my hand twitched under the felt tip tickling my skin. "There's gotta be a *Star Trek* geek we can add to your list."

Of course there was, but I wasn't going to start another argument by mentioning Dallas.

Jaz released my hand, looking like a smug Cheshire cat. "Ta da!"

We all stared at the back of my hand, which now sported a perfect caricature of me as Spock, complete with pointy ears. I closed my eyes. *Great.*

"That's awesome." Amy beamed at me. "Maybe you can use it as a geek magnet. To attract new guys for the list."

I glared at her. "We have enough names on the list. One of them is bound to work out."

Jaz snorted. "Only if you stick McNerdy on there."

Amy spoke up before I could. "No more arguing. Viv is set on this list, so we need to support her."

Jaz turned to her, annoyed. "No, we don't. Personally, I'm still completely opposed to this idea."

Amy shrugged. "I don't like it, either, but what if it works?"

"It won't," Jaz said. "But I don't get to say I told you so until it blows up in her face." She narrowed her eyes. "I was right about Jake. Why won't you trust me on this?"

I opened my mouth to argue, but my vocal cords seized as Dallas approached our table.

"Hey." Dallas nodded at everyone.

Jaz's foot kicked me under the table. Why did he look more like a super hero every day? Even his ridiculous *Dr.*

Who shirt couldn't hide his very un-geeky body.

"Hi, Dallas." Jaz gestured to Amy. "This is Amy."

"Hi," Amy said. "You're the Vespa guy, right?"

Dallas smiled, embarrassed. "Yeah. I think I should change my name since that seems to be what everyone's calling me." He shot me a meaningful glance. "Well, not *everyone*."

My lungs stopped working while Amy and Jaz giggled like idiots.

"Sorry about that," Jaz said. "You know we're just kidding, right?"

"Whatever," he said, shrugging. "I answer to a lot of weird names." He lowered his backpack from his shoulder and unzipped it. "Here." He handed me a book. "I'm paying up on our bet."

I reached for the thick Star Trek bible, secretly thrilled he'd remembered. "Awesome," I whispered. I couldn't wait to sit in my bedroom, away from prying eyes, to read it.

"Remember, it's just a loan, so I—" Dallas's voice broke off as his eyes widened. His lips quirked as he stared at my Spock hand. "Let's see it." Dallas tilted his head toward me. "Are you testing out a tattoo idea?"

Jaz laughed. "Viv's way too scared of needles for a real tattoo."

I shot her a glare and reluctantly rested my hand on the table. Dallas leaned over to check it out while Amy and Jaz sent me a barrage of crazy girl-face messages I tried to ignore.

"Did you draw this?" Dallas asked, raising his eyes to mine. He was clearly impressed.

"No." I nodded at Jaz, trying to maintain Spock-like calm. "She's the artist, not me."

Dallas grinned at Jaz. "You really captured her inner Vulcan."

Everyone laughed except me. Dallas grabbed his backpack. "Maybe I'll hire you to design my next tattoo," he said to Jaz, smiling cryptically.

Next tattoo? So he already had one? Where? And what was it?

"Dallas, wait," Jaz said. "You have to tell me where you saw Fisk Vilhelm."

He shifted nervously. "I can't."

Jaz gaped at him. "Come on, Dallas. I won't tell anyone."

Dallas shot me a questioning look. Was he wondering if it was okay to tell her?

"Viv, please tell Dallas I am *not* a super stalker or a crazy paparazzi," Jaz begged.

"Paparazza," I corrected, then took a drink from my water bottle, stalling. I couldn't see any way to answer this truthfully without upsetting Jaz, but I could tell Dallas didn't want to tell her about Fisk.

"I'm sure you'll see him again," I said, shrugging. "Running on the beach or whatever."

Jaz glared at me, then at Dallas. "Whatever, okay? I don't know why you two are keeping this a secret, but whatev—"

"Me?" I interrupted. "I don't know where Dallas saw him, either."

Jaz crossed her arms over her chest, shooting death glares at Dallas and me.

"I've gotta go," Dallas mumbled, backing away from us. "See you later, Vivian."

As he turned away, Amy leaned over the table, her red curls falling over her shoulders. "Oh, Viv, he's darling. You have to put him on your RC list."

"Ha!" Jaz transferred her death glare from Dallas's retreating figure to me. "Who does he think he is, acting all—"

"Jaz." I put up a hand to stop her rant. "I don't know why he won't tell you, but he must have a good reason.

And I swear I don't know. He hasn't told me." Dallas and I definitely didn't share any secrets. That would require a scary level of intimacy.

Her stalker fire snuffed out as quickly as it ignited. "I just want to see Fisk up close. You know I won't throw myself at him."

Amy and I shared a look. It had been a long time since Jaz had accosted a celebrity. She'd been in middle school when boy band star Zeck had blown through town and Jaz had cornered him in the coffee shop, begging him to autograph her thigh.

"What?" Jaz stared back and forth between us. "You guys are *not* going to bring up Zeck again, are you?"

Amy tried unsuccessfully to stifle a giggle.

"Anyway..." I slapped the RC notebook. Maybe I could change the subject and focus Jaz's energy elsewhere. "I'm starting with number one on the list. Iggy."

"You're an idiot," Jaz said. "The person who should be your number one just stood here flirting with you and you didn't even notice."

"What?" Dallas flirting? No way. He'd only been making good on his bet.

"So what's the plan for Iggy?" Amy asked.

"We're on the newspaper together."

"And?" Jaz prompted.

And I had no idea. The truth was I sucked at flirting. So far, I'd never been the one to make the first move. But Iggy was nice, and funny, so I hoped somehow things would just... happen.

Something needed to happen to refocus my hormones, and fast, because right now they were way too focused on Vespa Guy. And his mysterious tattoo.

"Vulcans never bluff."
—Spock

CHAPTER EIGHT

THURSDAY, AUGUST 28

I sat next to Iggy in Mr. Yang's classroom, aka the newspaper "office." Iggy glanced at me and grinned. He always looked like a magazine model, almost too perfect to be real, plus his unconfirmed bisexuality was intriguing.

"Hi." I didn't do the hair toss since I looked stupid when I did it, my curls bouncing like Slinkys growing out of my head.

"Hi, Viv," he said. "How was summer?" His lilting accent made the most boring questions sound interesting. His dad was from London and his mom was from Japan. They were both involved in the music business. That was as much as I knew, that and they were loaded with cash.

"Okay. Yours?"

He shrugged. "My parents dragged me all over Japan. Apparently I'm cousin to half the population."

I laughed, relaxing a little. "I'd love to visit Japan some day."

He nodded. "It's cool, but I missed my friends. Did I miss any summer drama?"

My face warmed as I thought of Jake. I shook my head. "I mostly worked in the bookstore, so I missed out on a lot of the drama, too." I paused, racking my brain for gossip.

"Char and Rick broke up. Big scene. She lipsticked his car when she found out he was cheating on her."

Iggy's eyes brightened with interest. "So I heard." He leaned closer and spoke in a whisper. "You heard he was having his bit on the side with a guy, right?"

It was a good thing I loved British chick lit or I might've misunderstood half of what Iggy said.

"No way!" Then I worried he'd think I was homophobic. "I mean, good for him for figuring it out, but he should've waited until after breaking up with Char, you know?"

Iggy leaned back in his chair, studying me. "It's not that simple, Viv. I'm sure it was complicated, finally being true to himself, not wanting to hurt his girlfriend." He smirked. "But she's always been bat-shit crazy. Even if he *was* straight, he should've run away screaming from all that drama."

I laughed, hoping his joke meant he hadn't been offended by my awkwardness.

Mr. Yang entered the room, voice booming. "Welcome back, seasoned journalists and seekers of truth. I hope everyone is ready for another banner year of *Clarion* news-making."

Iggy rolled his eyes. Mr. Yang was also in charge of the drama club, so everything he said sounded like a grand pronouncement. Sometimes it was funny, but it also got old.

Mr. Yang wrote in bold strokes on the white board with a dry erase marker listing the topics we needed to cover: school news, sports, extracurricular clubs and activities, volunteer stuff, blah blah blah.

Seniors got first choice, then juniors. I got to write the book review column, thanks to my insider knowledge and access to review copies. Iggy reviewed movies and other events around town, so we often edited each other's columns. His quirky writing style always made me laugh, which was a lot of the reason he'd earned the top spot on my RC list.

"Who wants to interview the new transfer students? We

have a grand total of—" Mr. Yang paused to glance at a piece of paper. "Two. A sophomore from Seattle. And a new senior, from Minnesota, I think."

"Wisconsin," I piped up, instantly regretting it as everyone turned to stare at me.

"Ah, sounds like you know him already, Vivian. Perfect. Add his interview to your to-do list." He glanced at Iggy. "You take the sophomore interview, Iggy."

"What?" I balked. "I mean…uh, shouldn't the seniors get first dibs on the interviews?"

The three seniors on the newspaper staff glanced at each other, shrugging. Trish, our editor-in-chief, spoke up. "He's all yours, Viv. We've got plenty of other material to cover." She darted a look at Nathan, the senior who covered sports. "Besides, those interviews are predictable. *Johnny is from Wisconsin and loves dogs, homework, and apple pie.*"

Everyone but me laughed. I knew I was blushing. Iggy leaned over and whispered, "Want me to do it, Viv? I'm always up for meeting new guys." He waggled his eyebrows suggestively.

Great.

"That's okay," I mumbled, digging in my backpack for my RC notebook. I flipped it open and drew a line through Iggy's name. "I have to work with Dallas anyway. Might as well kill two birds with one stone."

Iggy shrugged. "Okay, whatever." He tilted his head. "That's such a violent phrase. Who would want to kill one bird, let alone two?"

"I don't know, Ig." I doodled on the back of my notebook, not wanting to mess up Jaz's drawings on the front. I slanted him a curious glance. Maybe I could ask him to make positively sure before I moved on to target number two. "So…can I ask you a personal question?"

He angled his body toward me, grinning. "Sure. You know I love to talk about myself."

I took a deep breath, carefully planning my question so I didn't offend him or make myself look like an idiot. "Are you…" I paused. "Do you…only like guys? Or have you ever, you know, liked girls?"

He raised his eyebrows and fingered the small silver ring at the edge of his right eyebrow.

"Is that new?" I looked pointedly at the piercing, which made me think of tattoos, which made me think of Dallas and his perfectly toned body that, somewhere, housed a secret tattoo.

"Focus, Vivian." Spock's scolding was like cold water on my Dallas tattoo fantasy.

"This? Yeah. Got it in Tokyo. My mom flipped. Dad thinks it's brilliant." He narrowed his eyes, watching me closely. "I'll answer your question because I like you and I trust you. But first I want to know why you asked."

I swallowed nervously. It was a fair question since I'd asked him something incredibly personal. "Can I trust you to keep a secret?"

He nodded vigorously, leaning closer. "I hoard them like those crazy people on TV."

I fiddled with the spine of my notebook. "Okay. So, here's the deal. I'm trying to…to um, get over a bad breakup, and I, um, have a list. Of replacements."

Iggy leaned even closer. I could smell his peppermint gum as he shot me rapid-fire questions. "So you did have summer drama! What happened? Wait, what do you mean you have a list? Like a hit list of guys you fancy?"

The senior trio glanced at us and Trish frowned in disapproval.

"We're talking book plots. Movie arcs. *Clarion* business," Iggy said loudly. "Pay no attention to the lowly juniors in the corner." Nathan rolled his eyes and resumed typing on his laptop, smirking.

Iggy refocused on me. "Spill, girl. What wanker was idiotic enough to dump you?"

"Thanks for trying to make me feel better."

He frowned. "I'm not. It's factual information. You're the bee's knees, Viv. Smart, funny....cute, in sort of a nerdy way. I can't figure out why more guys don't follow you around like dogs in heat."

Wow. I'd heard of backhanded compliments, but I wasn't sure what the heck this was.

Iggy ran a hand through his hair. "That came out all wrong. I'm trying to say you're awesome and the straight guys here are tossers."

"Yeah, well." I shrugged, regretting ever starting this insane conversation.

"Who was he?"

"It doesn't matter. What matters is my new approach. I'm going to be logical about the next guy I get involved with."

Iggy fiddled with his eyebrow ring. "Logical? About love? That's bonkers, Viv."

I huffed a frustrated sigh. Why did everyone find this concept so alien? "Everyone thinks I'm crazy but I know I'm not."

Iggy ran a hand across his beautiful, kissable face. I would *not* be that cliché who fell in love with her gay friend.

"So," I plunged ahead, "the reason I asked about your orientation is...um, I put you on the top of my list. As a potential replacement."

Iggy blushed. "You did? That's so sweet, Viv." He reached over to squeeze my hand. "And if I had even one bi bone in my body, I'd be all over you. But I don't." He shrugged. "Sorry. I don't know where that rumor got started."

"Ninth grade. Tara told everyone what an amazing kisser you are."

Iggy cringed. "Oh God. That's why?" He shook his head.

"I was trying to figure out if I was absolutely positively one hundred percent gay, you know? Everyone said she was the hottest girl in our class, so…" He shrugged.

"Wow." I leaned in. "So no sparks? At all?"

He shook his head. "Zilch." His lips quirked up. "I'm so flattered I'm on your list. And number one? Wow." He shifted in his chair. "So who's number two?"

I hunched my shoulders over my notebook. "Henry Harper," I whispered.

"Henry?" He shook his head "No, no, no. We need to fix this list, and fast." His eyes darted around the room, pausing to stare at Nathan. He inclined his head. "What about him? Smokin' body. Smart. Sportsy, if you're into that."

It was my turn to blush as we both studied Nathan with his warm brown skin and dreads almost as long as Claire's. "Yeah," I whispered, "except he hardly knows I exist." I took a breath. "You might think I'm, uh, dateable or whatever, Iggy, but you're one of the few."

"I'm not going to get into one of those girlie arguments where you pretend you're hideous and deformed and I tell you how fabulous you are." He narrowed his eyes at me. "This isn't some movie cliché where I'm the sassy GBF who gives you a slutty makeover. Besides, you don't need one. That cute book nerd thing works for you."

"Gee, thanks, I guess."

"It's true." He shrugged. "Anyway, back to your list. Why not put Nathan on it?"

I couldn't believe I was about to confess my criteria and let one more person know about my mission. But Iggy might be able to help me in a way Amy and Jaz couldn't. I opened my notebook and slid it across the table, pointing toward the criteria list.

Iggy frowned as he read. "What's a zing meter?"

I squirmed. "You know."

Understanding lit his eyes. "How big is the range? One to five?"

"One to ten, but ten is reserved for famous unattainables. So technically it's one to nine."

Iggy chewed his bottom lip. "Why don't you want someone higher than a five? Don't you want...you know?" He waggled his eyebrows suggestively.

I shook my head. "I had plenty of zing with the guy who dumped me. I'm not going through that again. It totally clouded my judgment."

Iggy snorted. "That's rubbish, Viv."

I pointed a finger at him. "I mean it. I don't want to... lose my head again, and make a bad decision."

He narrowed his eyes, examining me. "Okay. If you want my advice, here it is." He grabbed my pencil and started scribbling. I groaned when I read his edits.

1. ~~Iggy~~ – *Sorry, sweetie; would if I could*
2. ~~Henry~~ *Nathan*
3. Drew – *Really?*
4. Toff – *has potential*
5. If you get this far, call me for more names.

"You know what? Let's just forget it," I said.

Iggy frowned. "I thought you wanted my expert opinion."

Mr. Yang looked up again. "I hope you two are accomplishing actual newspaper business."

"Oh, we are," Iggy said. "Unbelievably so."

I jabbed him with my pencil and he yelped.

Nathan shot us a fake scowl, then winked.

Iggy gasped. "I knew it," he whispered. "He watches us a lot. I noticed it last year, didn't you? Put him on your list."

Heat flooded my body. Nathan noticed me? Somehow I'd missed that. I grabbed my pencil and started to erase Nathan's name, but Iggy's hand reached out to stop me. "What?" I whispered in frustration.

"Where is Nathan on the zing meter?"

"Um." I bit my lip.

"Mm hm, that's what I thought."

I recaptured my pencil and erased Nathan's name. "Which is why he's not staying on the list." Way too much zing.

Iggy shook his head in disgust. "If you're not willing to listen to reason, I'm out."

"But that's the point," I sputtered. "I'm trying to only listen to reason. Nothing else."

"Nathan," Iggy called out. "Could you come here for a minute? We need your opinion on something."

"Oh my God," I whispered. "You're insane, Iggy."

Nathan glanced up, eyeing us warily.

I jumped up, grabbing my backpack. "I need to go," I said to Mr. Yang. "My mom just texted me. There's, um, an emergency at the store."

Iggy snorted. "Right. A bookstore emergency."

Mr. Yang lumbered toward us, hands on his hips. "All right, you two. Maybe you need to work separately in the future. Your chattering distracts the serious journalists."

"I'm sorry," I said. "It won't happen again." I shot Iggy the evil eye.

Mr. Yang gave me a crisp salute. "Good. Don't forget the new guy interview. And a book review. Hit or Miss, your choice."

My newspaper column was called Hit or Miss. I didn't review many misses because my goal was to get people to fall in love with books, but once in a while I published a miss so people knew I was serious about my reviews. I had to keep it PG-13, reviewing books suitable for freshmen, saving the sexier books for my blog.

I tugged on my hoodie, not looking at Iggy or Nathan.

"Your secret's safe with me," Iggy whispered.

"It better be." I turned and hurried out of the room, mortified.

Iggy jumped up and followed me. As soon as we got in the hallway, he put a hand on my shoulder. "Vivian, I'm sorry if I embarrassed you. I didn't mean to. Honestly, I'm so flattered you put me on the list, I want to help. You deserve a good guy. A great guy. Maybe I can help you find one." He paused. "Toff's your best bet. He's always flapping his gums at you."

I frowned. "Toff's a friend. *Just* a friend, but Jaz made me put him on the list. Our parents have been dating so long he's basically my brother." I sighed. "I don't know, Ig. I'm starting to think this idea is stupid, after all. Maybe I should—"

"It's not a bad idea. I support you trying to get over the breakup. Just don't jump from the frying pan into the fire."

"And you made fun of two birds with one stone?" I bit back a smile. I couldn't stay mad at him.

"I know, right?" He leaned in and gave me a hug. A platonic, non-zingy hug.

"I'm going to help. I'll peruse my giant mental database of straight guys who I think are good enough for you."

"Please don't." I glanced into the classroom and met Nathan's curious gaze. Had he heard Iggy? I shook my head. "Your help terrifies me."

He laughed and I backed away, crossing my eyes at him.

I rode home quickly and hid out in my bedroom, grateful to be surrounded by fictional boyfriends instead of real ones.

"It's logic, Spock. I thought you'd like that."
—Captain Kirk

CHAPTER NINE

SATURDAY, AUGUST 30

By Saturday morning, I'd finalized my list of mission targets, ignoring Jaz's objections and Amy's pleas for true love.

I sat at our kitchen table, dipping lemon biscotti in a steaming mug of coffee and reviewed my list.

1. Iggy (bust)

2. Henry: member of the Chess Club and Honor Society. Not quite as geeky as he sounded on paper, he had potential. And he barely pinged my zing meter.

3. Drew: Drama Club and talent show dictator. Smart but annoying. Minimal zing.

4. Toff: I'd decided to leave him on there, for now. He was a friend, and I knew I could trust him. Hopefully I wouldn't make it to number four because it might be awkward to ask him out, sort of like resorting to my cousin for a date. Besides, Toff probably already had a date to the Surfer Ball.

I wasn't sure how I'd attack the list, but today my focus was book club. I reviewed my discussion points for *Melt with You*, a dragon shape-shifter romance.

1. **How hot was Ranz, the hero?** OMG he practically

burned my e-reader screen. I didn't think anyone would disagree; but if they did, I had a list of hotness points I'd love to expand on.

2. **Should the heroine have forgiven him when he kind of cheated on her while they were split up?** He didn't 100 percent cheat. It was one make-out session with this girl he met at a club. He'd been drinking to drown his sorrows over the heroine dumping him, and alcohol affected him differently because of his dragon DNA. Plus, he felt tons of remorse.

I knew we'd have a raucous debate about the forgiveness issue. Mrs. Sloane would be in the never forgive camp; she always was, usually recommending literary castration for the cheaters.

Hiddles glared at me, meowing by his food bowl. "Good morning to you, too, buttercup," I grumbled. He hissed until I'd filled the bowl, then he buried his face in the food.

Mom was already in the store. She loved Saturdays since she could chat with customers and catch up on town gossip. I sucked down more coffee, pausing occasionally to dip my second biscotti in the strong brew. *I am not a Chunky Monkey.* I squeezed my eyes, pushing away the memory of Jake's sneer.

My phone vibrated on the table and a text lit up the screen.

"Still on for 2:30 today?"

Dallas.

Biscotti crumbs lodged in my throat as I reached for my cell. *"C u then."*

The sooner we got the inventory finished, and the sooner he finished coding the software, the better. Then he could go off and play his cello or whatever and I could focus on boring guys who didn't ping my zing meter.

...

The morning passed quickly. The Lodge was hosting a group of astrologists on a retreat. The Lodge was owned by former Hollywood celebrities, people who'd made tons of cash and decided to bail on Hollywood and L.A. It was rustic but not gross, and their biggest claim to fame was keeping out the paparazzi. Sometimes celebs in the middle of bad breakups hid out in the private cabins, but sometimes non-famous groups stayed in the main lodge, like today.

Laughter and chatter from The Lodge guests filled the store. Most of them bought armloads of books. One lady in particular, who claimed to be both psychic and an astrologer, tried her best to suss out Mom's pen name. She failed, but Mom gave her a free book for trying so hard. As I rang up her other purchases, she stared at me intently.

"Oh, honey," she whispered. "Don't do it."

I glanced up. "Don't do what?"

"You're about to make a big mistake." Her eyes grew big as saucers. "*Very* big."

Goose bumps rose all over me. I dropped her change on the counter. "Sorry." I fumbled for the coins. "I don't know what you're talking about."

She smiled sadly. "Yes, you do." She sighed, then put a card on the counter. "This is for you. To remind you to follow your heart."

I stared at the Tarot card, a riot of colors and imagery. A naked man and woman danced, legs entwined, surrounded by a border of hearts and "The Lovers" printed in a swirling font. The back of my neck prickled as I stared at the card.

Spock's voice interrupted my scattered thoughts: "*It's just a card, Vivian. It has no meaning, other than what you assign to it. Remain logical.*"

I slid the card toward the psychic. "Thanks, but you should keep it."

She shook her head. "No. Keep it; you're going to need

it." She hurried away, and I shoved the card into my pocket.

An hour later, the Lonely Hearts Club squeezed around the tiny table in the bookstore's kitchen, munching on cookies and M&M's. As predicted, we had a fiery debate about whether or not the heroine should've forgiven Ranz. Mrs. Sloane got so wound up I worried she might have a heart attack.

Amy set aside her ever-present knitting project and gave a long, prepared speech about the importance of second chances in relationships, which a few people applauded. I clapped to support Amy's speech, not because I'd ever give Jake a second chance. Natasha argued that Ranz probably had a vitamin deficiency and that was why he cheated. I wished it were that simple; but even though I trusted Natasha's herbal knowledge, I doubted a dose of vitamins would change Jake's behavior.

"What do you think, Vivian?" Mrs. Sloane demanded. "Would you forgive him?"

I leaned against the counter, thinking of Jake, of my vows to stay logical about love.

"I don't know," I said, opening a new package of cookies for the group. "I mean, he was genuinely remorseful, right? Plus… God, you guys. He was so unbelievably hot I thought my Kindle might explode. Who could resist that kind of chemistry?" I grinned and gyrated around the kitchen singing "Bow-chicka-wow-wow." I only busted out the dance moves for books that totally steamed up my e-reader.

Everyone laughed and cheered me on, then suddenly froze, their eyes focusing directly behind me. The whoosh from the door was like a cold shower on my goofy dancing. I squeezed my eyes closed. It was a guy; it had to be, based on everyone's body language.

And I could think of only one guy who'd wander into the employees-only area, just in time to see me do my fake porn star dance. I sent a desperate girl-face message to Amy. Her wide-eyed reply told me all I needed to know.

"Hi, Dallas," I muttered, refusing to turn around. Why was he even here? I'd told him to come *after* book club.

"Hi." His voice was close to my ear. Too close. I stepped away from him, still not looking at him.

"Are you a romance fan, young man?" Mrs. Sloane demanded, glaring at him with the full force of her anti-cheater rage.

I finally turned to face him. I expected him to look embarrassed, possibly even mortified. God knew I was. But instead he looked amused as well as ridiculously nerd-hot in his Spiderman T-shirt and board shorts. No way did cello-playing give a person those muscles. Or maybe it did, at least the arms. But what about the rest of—

"Vivian? Aren't you going to introduce us?" Natasha raised her eyebrows, looking just like my mom when I forgot my manners.

Wishing I could disappear, I gestured vaguely toward the table. "Dallas, this is the Lonely Hearts Book Club. Lonely Hearts, this is Dallas. He's helping us enter the twentieth century."

"Twenty-first," he corrected.

I narrowed my eyes at him. "My mom's not ready for Google glass."

He laughed, shooting me a grin that made my skin tingle.

"Can I help you find something?" I filled my voice with exaggerated annoyance because I didn't want him coming back here again during book club. It was a sacred girls-only space where people were supposed to feel safe if they spontaneously burst into song and dance.

Dallas's grin faded and he cleared his throat. "Your mom needs paper towels. Some little kid dropped his sippy cup and it exploded." He shrugged and gave everyone but me a tight smile. "Sorry to interrupt."

I yanked a wad of paper towels from the roller. "Here."

"Thanks." He hustled out of the kitchen, closing the door behind him with more force than necessary.

Everyone turned to stare at me. "What?" I sounded defensive, even to myself.

Amy fiddled with her flowered hair band. "Um, Viv, you were kind of rude to him." A circle of heads bobbed in agreement.

I sank into my chair. "Okay, I know I wasn't as nice as I normally am. But...he's just..." I didn't dare tell them why he rattled me. "It was a private meeting and he interrupted us."

Amy rolled her eyes. "You're just embarrassed because he caught you doing your skanky dance. Poor guy. It was a cleaning emergency."

"What a sweet boy," Mrs. Sloane piped up. "But now he thinks we're a den of sex-crazed vipers." She winked at me. "And pole dancers."

Natasha's eyebrows shot up again. "Now, now, Marion. Some might say 'vipers' is a chauvinistic caricature that demeans women."

Megan, our resident grad student, piped up. "True, but sometimes we get power reclaiming words used to shame us." She turned to me, eyes bright with excitement. "You know, Vivian, if you want to express your sexuality by becoming a pole dancer, that's your right."

"I don't want to be a pole dancer! I was kidding around."

Amy dissolved into giggles.

"Anyway, meeting time is up," I said brusquely, hoping to move Dallas and pole-dancing off the agenda. "I need to get back to work. What are we reading for next month?" I turned to Amy, since it was her turn to pick.

Amy's eyes shone with excitement. "I found this old book at the library, and I love it! It's sort of old-fashioned, but it's awesome. It's called *The Darkest Castle* and—"

"Oh my," Natasha interrupted. "I remember that one." She glanced at Megan. "I'm not sure what you'll think of it. You might not like the stereotypes, since the hero's one of those broody, domineering types and the heroine might be considered spineless."

Megan grinned. "Why do you think I love this book club? I need a break from storming the gates of patriarchy. Besides, you all have taught me that modern romance is full of awesome heroes who support strong women." She paused to drink her herbal tea, one of Natasha's custom brews. "None of my classmates get that because they judge without reading."

She lifted her tea cup in a toast. "So in the name of grad school research, I say bring on the broody dude! After all, I need to explore how romance books have transformed over the years." Her grin deepened as Amy clinked her teacup, returning her toast.

Mrs. Sloane sighed happily. "Sometimes a dark, brooding hero who knows how to kiss a woman senseless is exactly what the doctor ordered."

Amy and I shared a secret smile. I opened my mouth to add my support to Amy's book selection when a light knock sounded on the door. I stifled a groan. What did he want now?

"Come in," Mrs. Sloane called. "We're decent."

Everyone but me laughed as Dallas pushed through the door, looking flustered this time. Poor guy was probably terrified he'd find me stripping on the table. "Sorry to interrupt again. We need some, uh,"—he pantomimed using a squirt bottle—"cleaning stuff." He glanced at me, his eyes narrowing. "Is it under the sink? I can get it."

Was he angry with me? I squirmed, embarrassed, while Amy retrieved the cleaning liquid. Dallas gave her a grateful smile that lingered maybe a second too long and a bolt of jealousy shot through me.

So much for Vulcan cool.

I pushed away the distracting image of Dallas smiling at Amy and forced myself to resume my role of meeting leader. "I'll see if we have any copies on the shelves and check the library."

"You can buy the ebook cheap," Amy said.

"Great, sounds like we're settled then."

Everyone said their good-byes and left the kitchen, except Amy.

"Do you want to read *The Darkest Castle*? Or was that a friend perk?" she asked anxiously.

"Are you kidding? Of course I want to read it, even though I'm sure it violates every rule of the modern, mutually respectful relationship."

"Maybe." Amy shrugged. "Still, I wonder what it's like to be rescued from a bad guy, to have some gorgeous guy sweep in and save the day," Amy said. "Oops—spoiler alert."

"Well, duh." I grinned. "It's a gothic. She's got to be rescued at some point."

Amy sighed happily. "Yeah…that's my favorite part. He even busts down a door."

I put up a hand. "No more spoilers."

Amy retrieved the empty glasses from the table. "So I bet we scared Dallas from ever coming into the kitchen again." She giggled. "He's so cute."

Did Amy like Dallas? And so what if she did? It wasn't like I had any claim on him, not after the big deal I'd made about not putting him on my RC list.

McNerdy was fair game for anyone.

"Yeah," I said. "I feel bad for snapping at him." I dropped the leftover cookies into a plastic bag one by one, determined to prolong my absence from the store. I wondered how long I could stall before Mom came to drag me out by my hair to work with Dallas.

Amy squirted dish soap into the glasses and started

washing them. "Well, I kind of see why you snapped." She hip-bumped me. "You were embarrassed, right? His timing was the worst."

We laughed together as I reached for a dishtowel.

"He really is adorable," Amy said, shooting me a sideways glance. "And sweet."

I took a breath before speaking. "It's okay, Amy. If you like him. I don't mind." *Liar, liar pants on fire.*

Amy turned to face me, her hands still in the soapy sink water. "But I don't. Like him, I mean." She blew a loose hair off her cheek. "Okay, I like him, but not like that. Not that he isn't totally lust-worthy. It's just...I'm sort of interested in someone else."

Relief flooded through me. "Yeah? I thought maybe—"

She pointed a soapy finger at my chest, grinning. "You were worried I was going to move in on your territory. Don't worry. He's all yours."

My face flamed. "But he's not my territory. At all." I grimaced, drying a glass so hard it squeaked under the towel.

Amy handed me a dripping glass and smirked. "Denial isn't pretty on you."

Dallas spent the rest of the afternoon huddled over the store computer, transferring data from the index cards into the software program he'd somehow whipped up in a week. And probably trying to purge the awful images of me dancing from his memory.

Mom busied herself with customers while I worked in a secluded corner of the store, sorting through books we'd recently acquired from an estate sale. Once in awhile Mom shot a concerned glance at Dallas, then me. I knew she'd picked up on the tension between us. I tried to relax, worried that she would jump to embarrassing conclusions. I should apologize to him, but I wanted to do it when no one else was around, which was impossible on a busy Saturday.

Six o'clock finally arrived and Mom locked the door, flipping the OPEN sign to CLOSED. She turned to us, wiping her hands on her jeans. "Whew. What a day."

Dallas glanced up, then leaned back in his chair, stretching his arms above his head. I stared at him, watching his muscles practically ripple.

"Is it always this busy on Saturdays?" he asked, twisting and turning in the chair, his shirt straining at the seams. I swallowed and tried, unsuccessfully, to look elsewhere.

Mom busied herself picking up the stray books customers had left scattered on tables. "Sometimes. Depends on what else is going on in town."

Dallas stood up and started stretching his legs behind the desk. Oh dear God. I turned away before he could catch me watching him.

Mom's laughter floated across the store. "You sore from sitting all afternoon, Dallas? Believe me, I can relate; it's the writer's curse. One of them, anyway."

He stood up and hugged a knee to his chest, balancing on one leg. "Yeah, I guess. I mean, even at school we have a break between seated torture sessions."

Mom and I both laughed, but he kept his eyes on Mom, not me. He switched legs, hugging his other knee to his chest and balancing on the opposite leg.

"What are you, the karate kid?" I asked irritably.

He finally looked at me, his posture ramrod straight as he remained balanced on one leg. He was far enough away that I couldn't read his eyes, but he definitely wasn't smiling.

"Maybe," he said, releasing his knee and raising his arms high over his head. He rose up on his toes and flexed his other foot, just like the dorky guy in the old eighties *Karate Kid* movie.

Mom chuckled, and I felt her watching me, silently willing me to be civil to Dallas.

"Hey, Mom. Remember Paul's coming for dinner, right? And Toff. Don't you need to get ready?"

Her face froze in shock. "Oh my gosh. I completely forgot. What can I feed them?" She shot me a panicked look. I should've reminded her earlier, but I'd forgotten, too, distracted by the book club.

Dallas dropped his pose and leaned against the wall.

"Just fire up the grill." I felt guilty as I watched Mom frantically dig through her sweater pocket like it was Hermione's bottomless purse, full of groceries that would magically appear and save the day. "I can bike to the store and grab some grillables."

Mom bit her lip. "Okay, I guess that works. I've got salad makings, and wine," she muttered more to herself than me.

"I should go," Dallas said, pushing off the wall. "You have things to do and I—"

Mom stopped muttering to examine Dallas. "I have a better idea. Why don't you join us? It's the least I can do after making you slave all afternoon at the computer." She gave him her most persuasive smile.

He darted a wary glance at me. "Um, I'm not sure…"

Mom shot me a warning look. What did she think I'd do, anyway, un-invite him? My racing heart and sweaty palms wanted the same thing she did even though my Vulcan brain was not pleased.

"Do you need to eat with your family?" Mom asked. "Or maybe you have a date. I understand if you have other plans."

Dallas's neck reddened slightly. "I, um, don't have other plans, but I don't want to horn in on yours."

"Pfft." Mom waved her hand dismissively. "It's not horning in at all. This gives you a chance to get to know some other locals." Mom pinned me with her eyes. "Right, Vivvy?"

"Vivian," I muttered under my breath. Why was it so hard for her to stop using my little kid name? "Right," I said in a louder voice, returning her gaze. "I should run to the store." I turned to Dallas, willing my hormones to stop their party-girl chattering. "Are you a vegetarian? Vegan?"

His eyes blinked rapidly behind his glasses. "What? No, definitely not."

I smirked. "I didn't think so. Do they even have those in Wisconsin?"

"One," he said, "but we keep her locked in a cage as a traveling exhibit."

I laughed, relieved to glimpse a smile from him before he turned away to text someone. His mom…I hoped.

As I waited in line at the market, I wondered what had possessed Mom to invite Dallas to dinner. Manners, probably. Normally I'd support the gesture, but things with Dallas were definitely not normal.

What if Toff and Dallas hated each other? What if I accidentally insulted Dallas again in front of everyone? And what should I wear? And most importantly, why did I care what I wore?

As I rode home, Spock's disapproving visage rose up to lecture me.

"Vivian Galdi, it appears you've lost sight of your mission. You're about to join two young men for dinner, one of whom sends your zing meter into an unacceptably high range." Spock lowered his imaginary eyebrows in disapproval. *"I'm concerned about your apparent lack of control, Vivian. When humans make rash decisions, the*

consequences can be...disturbing."

"But it's my mom's fault!" I exclaimed. A passing jogger shot me a baffled glance. I was losing it, talking out loud to imaginary spaceship science officers.

Pedaling home, I did yoga breathing. This was not a big deal. It was just a barbecue with some guys from school. Right?

When I walked in the house, Mom looked up from the salad bowl where she was tearing lettuce. "You weren't wearing your helmet."

Dallas, standing next to my mom, paused his carrot chopping. He glanced at my mom, then me.

"Sorry," I said. "I forgot."

Mom shook her head, clicking her tongue. "Vivian, I don't know why it's so hard for you to remember a basic safety rule."

Embarrassed, I turned away, but not before I caught Dallas's sympathetic shrug and crooked smile like he was telling me his mom was overprotective, too.

As I was about to escape to change clothes, Hiddles arched his back and hissed. Paul and Toff climbed the deck stairs, laughing together. They paused before opening the sliding glass door that opened into our kitchen. Toff's grin deepened when he saw me, and he struck a bicep-curling pose. I rolled my eyes but couldn't help returning his smile.

I braced myself for Paul's bear hug, which was surprisingly strong. Or maybe not so surprising since he was in awesome shape for an old guy, probably because of all the surfing and surfboard shaping he did at his shop. As he trapped me in a hug, I inhaled the scent of ocean and herbal tea while the kitchen filled with the cacophony of introductions and laughter.

"Vespa dude!" Toff exclaimed, shaking Dallas's hand. "I saw that sweet ride at school. I'm Toff, by the way."

"Vespa?" Paul's face lit up as he joined the guys at the

counter where they talked excitedly about engines and horsepower.

Dallas didn't even notice when Mom pulled the cutting board and veggies out of his reach and resumed the carrot chopping. His animated Vespa talk made me smile, but then I reminded myself of my Spock lecture, and focused on gathering plates and silverware.

The sun dipped low over the water and I shivered against the dropping temperature. Mom and Paul sat in deck chairs, sipping wine. Toff, Dallas, and I brought the dirty plates into the kitchen.

"So you should meet me early one morning," Toff said to Dallas. "I'll show you some basics, make sure you don't do any kook stuff."

"Kook stuff?" Dallas asked, arching an eyebrow.

"Rookie mistakes," Toff clarified. "Stuff that'll piss off the line-up."

"Line-up?" Dallas raised his other eyebrow.

"The regulars waiting to take off," I clarified. "Some of the locals are sort of hardcore. They act like they own the waves."

"Totally not aloha," Toff said. "Which is why you should learn from my dad and me, so we can take you to the right places. You can't live here and not surf."

I shut off the water and stopped rinsing plates. "Yeah he can. I don't surf."

Toff shot me a grin, then rolled his eyes at Dallas. "Viv's afraid of sharks."

Dallas's eyes widened. "There are sharks? For real?"

Toff shrugged. "Hardly ever. No one's been attacked for a few years. So anyway, let me know when you want to learn, dude." Toff laughed suggestively. "Plus all the hottest chicks surf."

Dallas, whose face had paled at the mention of sharks, glanced at me, color quickly returning to his face.

Toff tilted his chin at me, eyes dancing with mischief. "Okay, maybe not all the hottest chicks surf. But most of them do."

I threw a towel at Toff. "You're a pig, Toff."

He caught the towel and threw it back. "You're breaking my heart, Viv."

I snorted. "Yeah, right."

"Viv's picky," Toff said to Dallas. "I think it's those stupid books she reads." He glanced at Dallas. "You said you're working in the bookstore, right?"

Dallas nodded, relaxing against the counter. His lips curved slightly. "Helping them join the twentieth century."

Toff looked confused. "You mean the twenty-first, dude."

"Never mind," I said, narrowing my eyes at Dallas, whose eyes danced with laughter behind his glasses.

"Computers," Dallas said. "I'm setting up a system to track inventory and sales."

"Oh, wow," Toff said. "So you're a brainiac, too, huh?" He shot me a glance I couldn't decipher. "So wait," he said to Dallas. "Does that mean you have to touch all those books with the couples practically humping on the covers?"

Before I could open my mouth to argue, Toff was at my side. He pulled me into his arms and dipped me low. "How's this for a cover pose? Take me, baby, take me now. Let me show you my love snake." He leered at me while I shoved at his chest, laughing and Dallas watched us, smirking.

"Knock it off, Toff." I pushed my hands against his chest. Heat rushed to my cheeks as he tilted me upright again, then spun us into a dance pose and glanced over his shoulder at Dallas. "First they danced, then they—"

"Shut up!" I yelled, laughing but still embarrassed.

Dallas's eyes flickered behind his glasses. His smirk was starting to irritate me, or something. It was definitely doing something that made me feel like I had a fever.

Toff finally released me and I stepped away, trying not to reward him with laughter. He was such a pain in the butt, like the brother I'd never had who lived to embarrass me.

"So you guys want to head down to the beach? Bonfire, beer, all that good stuff." Toff glanced out the window to the deck where Paul and Mom sat talking. "Should be starting to kick off."

Dallas and I looked at each other. My heart rate sped up, and I bit the inside of my lip. I should not, would not go anywhere with him. Especially not the beach. After dark. To a bonfire. That would only lead to heartbreak, as I knew from experience.

"Come on," Toff said, playfully punching Dallas on the shoulder. "You can meet some other people." He shot me a look. "Some other girls besides Wordworm here." Toff chuckled. "You can come, too, Viv. No sharks tonight."

I narrowed my eyes. "Only the human ones."

Dallas's deep laughter made my stomach flip-flop.

"No thanks," I said, trying to act as if the last thing I wanted to do was spend time with them. "You guys go without me. Go check out the *hot* girls." I shot Toff a look and he put up his hands.

"Hey, I didn't say you weren't hot. I just said that surfer chicks are the hottest." His eyes danced with laughter. "But if there was like, a hot bookworm contest, you'd totally win. Or at least place."

"Go." I pointed to the door. "Both of you. Now."

Toff laughed and pushed himself off the counter. "Put away the claws, Viv. I'm just messing with you. You know you're my dream girl." He shot Dallas a conspiratorial grin.

"Nightmare, I mean. Totally the girl in my scariest dreams."

Dallas laughed, which, unfortunately, had the same result as feeding a trained monkey. Toff jumped around the kitchen pretending to be terrified of me, hiding behind Dallas, and begging to be saved from his worst nightmare.

"Out, Flipper. Now." My face was on fire, and I needed them to be gone. I also needed to kill Toff, but that would have to wait.

Dallas hesitated at the door. "You want any help finishing the cleanup? I can—"

"Go," I said, tilting my head toward the door. "Go do guy stuff and talk about engines and hot surfer girls or whatever."

I snuck a peek at his face and wished I hadn't.

Because instead of looking as if he wanted to stay, he looked relieved that I'd told him to go.

CHAPTER TEN

HUNKALICIOUSHEROES.COM
Romance Reviews for Ravenous Readers

SHOOTING STARS by Wendy McCuthbert
Rating: *Go-go boots (with rhinestones)
Reviewed by: Sweet Feet

Author Wendy McCuthbert does it again with her latest
crossover sci-fi romance, *Shooting Stars*. She turns the
genre on its head, giving us a shy, anxious hero and a
kick-ass, smart-ass heroine who saves him over and over
again. And it works. When Alexa's not fighting off the
uber gross aliens chasing her renegade ship, she's wooing
Micah by playing the latvel (kind of like a cello, which
earned bonus points from me).

Even if you think you're not into beta heroes, give this one a
try. Yeah, Micah starts out a total SNAG (sensitive new age
guy) but by the end of the book, he's kicking some ass and
keeping up with Alexa. Plus his kisses will make you sweat.

Just put on your prom shoes and read it. Trust me.

*Rating Scale:
◆   Birks - lots of emotion and navel-gazing
◆   Wing Tips - bossy but irresistible heroes
◆   Crocs - Funny heroes, imperfect heroines (yay reality!)
◆   Vans – testy heroes full of smarcasm.
◆   Go-go boots - my highest rating: perfection.

"See? We are getting to know each other."
—*Captain Kirk*

CHAPTER ELEVEN

Sunday dawned foggy and chilly, which fit my mood. I'd stayed up late posting my blog review, started book one in a new paranormal series, then dreamt about the villain who in my dream looked a lot like Jake but also morphed into Spock.

Mom invited me to join her and Paul for brunch, but I declined. Three hours, four biscotti, and an entire pot of coffee later, my homework was finished and my hormones were comatose. Maybe pre-calc was the simple cure to my crush problem.

After showering and getting dressed, I checked my phone. My screen filled up with text notifications. Jaz had texted me not long after Toff and Dallas left, asking why I wasn't at the party. Then about an hour after that, she'd texted me that McNerdy seemed to be attracting interest from several girls. At which point I'd put my phone in do-not-disturb mode.

Most of the texts were updates on who was hooking up, photos of people posing and hamming it up, and a few blurry photos of Dallas sitting with a girl who was unrecognizable in the dark. Jaz had sent those with slurred notes like "Yur winnow is clsng," which I assumed meant, "Your window is closing."

"Whatever," I muttered, willing myself to mean it. Dallas could do whatever he wanted.

Toff had Snapchatted me a goofy selfie that made me laugh. That was his superpower, making people laugh so hard they'd forget how much he'd pissed them off.

Sunday was Mom's day to run away. She sometimes spent the day with Paul or disappeared to write. She paid me double to run the store on Sundays, so I didn't have any complaints.

Before I opened the store, I popped into the Jumping Bean for a mocha and a slice of their amazing lemon pound cake. As I was paying for my purchase, I heard a mocking voice behind me.

"Better watch all those calories, Chunky Monkey."

I whirled around and came face-to-face with Jake.

"W-what are you..." I sputtered and took a step away from him. I knew I shouldn't let some jerk tell me what I could eat, but I'd heard the clerk titter at his rude remark.

He leaned against the counter and surveyed me up and down, his lips curled in a sneer. "There was a reason we only hooked up in the dark."

I almost dropped my drink, then briefly considered tossing it in his face. Instead, I turned away and rushed out of the store, my entire body burning with anger and embarrassment.

After I unlocked the bookstore and turned on the lights, I settled at the desk, willing my body to stop shaking.

What was his damage? Why had he turned on me like this? Was it because I'd confronted him about using me? I unwrapped my slice of cake and stared at it. What if he was right? I'd always been self-conscious about my weight, even though Jaz and my mom told me there was nothing wrong with my shape.

Still... I sipped from my mocha and powered on the computer, noticing how my thighs filled up the seat of the chair.

"Am I fat?" I texted Jaz.

"WTH??? Why r u asking stupid questions and waking me up?"

I should've known I'd unleash her wrath. But her righteous anger made me feel better.

"Never mind."

"I'm awake now. Tell me what happened."

I sighed, staring longingly at my pound cake.

"Jake happened. Called me Chunky Monkey in the Bean because I bought cake."

"??!! I will kick his ass!"

I smiled at my screen.

"Forget it."

She texted a row of angry face emoticons. *"Eat your cake."*

Intellectually I knew I shouldn't give any credence to what he said. I could spout off all the feminist arguments against his shallow assessment of me. But that old nickname still hurt.

I glared at my cake. This was ridiculous. I couldn't give Jake's insult any power over me. I was healthy. I rode my bike everywhere and did yoga with Mom. So I had curves, so what? And I freaking loved lemon pound cake.

After opening my RC notebook, I started to unwrap the cake, but the bells on the door tinkled, announcing a customer.

A family strolled in—a mom and dad, a little girl bouncing up and down and babbling, and...Dallas? I slammed my RC notebook closed and stood up.

"Um, hi," I said. Everyone turned toward me, except

Dallas, who hung back from his family, looking as if he wanted the floor to swallow him up.

"Well, hello." His mom rushed forward, all smiles. She wore a Wisconsin Badgers baseball cap over her short, dark ponytail. Dallas's dad followed, smiling in a way that reminded me of Dallas. He wore a red University of Wisconsin sweatshirt with a goofy frowning badger. The little girl, also wearing a red Badgers shirt, made a beeline for the kids' section thanks to Dallas, who'd pointed her there.

"Wow, you really love your Badgers." The words popped out before I could stop them, and I immediately regretted them. Fortunately his parents laughed, but Dallas rolled his eyes. I couldn't tell if he was embarrassed for them or annoyed with me. He shoved his glasses up his nose and turned to follow his little sister.

"A lot of our wardrobe is Badger related," Dallas's mom said. "My husband taught there for years." She stuck out her hand. "I'm Jamie Lang, Dallas's mom. And that's Becca." She gestured toward her daughter, who'd plunked herself on the floor with a book.

I leaned over the counter to shake Mrs. Lang's hand. I liked that she was friendly without being condescending.

"I'm Robert, Dallas's dad." Mr. Lang shook my hand, gripping it tightly. "We thought we'd stop by and see where Dallas is earning his gas money."

I heard Dallas sigh from the kids' section. I darted a quick glance in his direction, but his back was to me.

"Yeah, well, this is it." I gestured like a game show host. "Shady Cove's marvelous book emporium."

Mrs. Lang's big-eyed gaze swept around the store. "I'm a read-a-holic, so this is great."

Mr. Lang nodded. "We're strong supporters of local business, so you can count on us shopping here. We've been meaning to stop in, but we spent most of our summer in

Wisconsin, so Dallas could have more time with his friends before moving here."

Dallas's heavy sigh drifted toward us again, and I bit back a smirk. I was pretty sure he'd beam his parents out of the store if he could.

"Is your mom around?" Mrs. Lang asked. Dallas's shoulders, which looked exceptionally broad today under his tight workout shirt, visibly tensed.

"No, she's not. Sorry."

Dallas's parents exchanged disappointed glances. "Well, another time then," Mr. Lang said. He turned toward the kids' section. "Come on, guys. We need to go."

Becca protested loudly as Dallas approached us, hands in his pockets. "I'll catch up to you in a few," he said to his parents, not looking at me. "I need to work out this week's schedule with Vivian."

"Fine," his mom said. "We'll check out some other stores. I'm sure you'll spot us."

Dallas shot a glance at their Badger logos. "Yeah. Hard to miss." His sister tugged at his hand and his gaze softened. "What's up, Becca?" She held up a chapter book. "Okay, I'll get it for you."

Dallas's parents gave him a gooey we're-so-proud-of-our-thoughtful-son smiles. Becca graced me with a gap-toothed grin and waved goodbye.

After his family left, Dallas took a deep breath and finally looked me in the eyes. Which sucked, because my inner Spock was off duty and I couldn't figure out where to focus my gaze. Dallas filled up my vision like Superman filled the big screen.

"So," I said, swallowing to coat my dry mouth, "how was the party last night?"

His body, already taut, seemed to tense even more. "Okay."

"Just okay?" I wanted to tell him my insider info told me

he'd definitely had more than an okay time. But then he'd think I was spying on him, or worse, that I cared.

He shrugged. "I met some cool people." He stepped up to the counter and his clean, minty scent made me clutch my pencil so hard I thought it would break in half.

"So this week," he said, pulling his phone from his pocket. "I'm free on Tuesday and Friday after school."

"Okay." I nodded, absently twirling hair around my finger. His eyes shot to my hair, then back to his phone. I tried to ignore how good he smelled. And looked. And sounded. *Damn it, Spock, wake the hell up!*

"So my mom asked about doing an inventory." I gestured toward the shelves. "Of everything. She wondered if you could stay after closing one night to help me. Maybe a couple of nights."

His green eyes darkened behind his glasses. "I guess that makes sense."

The bells sounded again and we both turned to see Jaz. "Hey!" She practically ran to the counter, screeching to a stop next to Dallas. She tilted her chin at him. "You're up early after such a late night."

He frowned at her, rubbing a hand over the back of his neck. "I wasn't out that late."

She waggled her eyebrows suggestively. "Uh-huh." She switched her manic attention to me, pointing an accusing finger. "You totally should've come. I can't believe you stayed home."

"I had stuff to do."

Jaz snorted. "Yeah, cuz reading books on a Saturday night is totally normal when there's an awesome party."

"It wasn't that awesome," Dallas muttered.

Jaz whirled toward him. "You seemed to be enjoying yourself." I thought of the blurry photo she'd texted me of Dallas sitting on a blanket with an unrecognizable girl.

As if he'd read my mind, his neck reddened slightly but he

didn't say anything.

Jaz spun toward me. "Did you eat your cake?" She stuck her hands on her hips, glaring.

I glanced at Dallas, embarrassed. "Um, not y—"

"Damn it, Viv, you're not fat!" Jaz turned her crazy energy on Dallas. "*You* don't think Viv's fat, do you?"

I snuck a mortified glance at Dallas, whose neck was getting redder by the second.

"I…um…no…d-definitely not…" He stared at the floor, hands jammed in his pockets, more discombobulated than I'd ever seen him.

Maybe Mom would let me padlock the door to keep Jaz out. Permanently.

"Of course you don't," Jaz said, "because you're not a moron like some people." Jaz huffed a satisfied sigh, smiling as if she'd solved global warming. "Anyway, I have news!" She was practically chirping. What was her damage? "Dallas, I'm glad you're here for this. I've confirmed that Fisk is staying at The Lodge. Totally top secret." She glanced at me. "I wonder if he's in rehab? Do they detox people up there?"

Dallas raised his head and cleared his throat. "I, uh, don't think it's rehab." He glanced anxiously between us, then tugged at his hair. I wondered if I'd ever get to find out if his hair was soft or crunchy with product.

Jaz narrowed her eyes. "For a new guy in town, you seem to know a lot about our visiting celebrity, Dallas."

He darted a glance at me. Did he want me to intervene?

"Not really," he said. "I've heard the same rumors you have."

"But you don't think he's in rehab," Jaz insisted. "Why not?"

He looked at me again, clearly sending an S.O.S.

"He's super religious, right?" I jumped in, trying desperately to remember what I knew of Fisk. I didn't follow the gossip news like Jaz, but I wasn't immune to clicking the occasional Buzzfeed link. "Christian rock—that's where he got his start, right? So definitely not in rehab."

Dallas nodded vigorously. "Vivian's right. The guy doesn't touch anything that would alter his mind."

We both turned to gape at him.

Dallas took a step backward. "I mean, that's what he always says, right? If you ever read any interviews with him. He does that one song about keeping yourself pure."

Jaz snorted. "I thought that song was about sex. Besides, it's the people who live a sheltered life who go totally crazy once they're released into the wild."

Dallas squeezed his eyes shut, looking as if he wanted to be anywhere but here. I couldn't blame him. I almost felt sorry for him, but I was more intrigued by his in-depth knowledge of Fisk.

"Maybe I'll sneak up to The Lodge," Jaz said. "See if I can spot him."

Dallas's eyes flew open. "Um, don't they have tight security up there? Dogs and stuff?"

Jaz tilted her head. "Dallas Lang. Have you been snooping around, spying on celebrities? You don't seem like the type."

He took a deep breath and shot me an anxious look. "No. I just heard about it. Toff told me he used to sneak onto the grounds til they got the dogs."

I rolled my eyes. "Sounds like Toff. He's not scared of anything."

Jaz nodded. "He was probably hoping to run into Jennifer Lawrence."

Dallas's phone pinged with a text, and he looked grateful for the interruption. Jaz caught my eye and waggled her eyebrows questioningly. I shrugged. He didn't strike me as a stalker like Jaz, but he was from Wisconsin. Maybe he was star struck.

"My parents are waiting for me," Dallas said, backing toward the door. "I've gotta go."

"See you later, star stalker," Jaz cooed, and he grimaced.

"Bye, Dallas." I smiled and his grimace disappeared, chased away by a grin that made my breath catch.

Jaz sighed, turning toward me. "He's ridiculously cute, for a nerd. Do you think we could talk him into dressing as Superman for Halloween? I want to see those legs in tights."

I shook my head. "No way. He's one of those guys who wears a T-shirt that says 'This is my costume.'"

"You sure? You don't think he's got a *Star Trek* uniform stashed in his closet?"

I froze, thinking of the *Star Trek* mini-dress I'd ordered online. What if Dallas *did* have a *Star Trek* uniform? And we wore them to the same party?

"Too bad he's not on your list," Jaz said, watching me with a smirk. "Such a shame...."

"Don't you need to be somewhere?" I glared at her.

"Yep. Heading to The Lodge right now."

"Jaz, don't. I can't bail you out of jail; I'm working all day."

"Ha. Don't you worry about me. I'm uncatchable."

Later that afternoon, my phone pinged with a text from Dallas. *"Sorry about bolting earlier. We never figured out the inventory schedule."*

"I don't blame you. Jaz can be scary." I debated, then finally sent the dorkiest text ever: *"James T. Kirk = tsk I'm a jerk."*

A row of question marks flew across my screen.

"Anagram," I replied. I held my breath, waiting. I'd just exposed the unbelievable depths of my nerdiness.

The ping of his reply made my heart stutter. *"Ok PCs = Spock"*

I giggled like the dork I was when I read his anagram reply, then sent another text.

"Inventory after closing Tue & Fri?"

He probably had a date on Friday or was going to a party

with all the new friends he was meeting. No way would he want to hang out with—

Ping. *"Sure. Both days."*

"Okay," I said out loud, trying to calm myself. *"Perfect,"* I typed.

And for now, everything was.

"This is your thirty-fifth attempt to elicit an emotional response from me." —Spock

CHAPTER TWELVE

When I handed Dallas my list of hero categories for our database, I wasn't sure who was more embarrassed, him or me. I'd asked him to add a new database field for hero types because I had a genius idea about creatively shelving the books.

He texted me during my first period class: "*Rakes of the 19th century. Category name: Tools.*"

That made me giggle, earning a disapproving glare from my teacher.

The next text arrived about ten minutes later. "*Military dudes w/tats. Category: Guns with big guns.*" I rolled my eyes, deciding not to reply.

Fifteen minutes later he sent another text. "*Billionaires who want babies? WTH? Category: no clue.*"

That one made me snort with laughter, earning another teacher glare.

I waited until lunch to text him back. "*I thought you didn't swear. Where r u finding this stuff?*"

"*WTH not swearing. Finding stuff is easy. Blog-stalking.*"

"Uh oh."

"What's up?" Jaz asked around a bite of potato chip.

I sighed. "Dallas is cyber-stalking."

She raised her eyebrows. "Seriously? He doesn't seem like the creepy type." She paused. "Though he did know a lot about Fisk."

"Not creepy stalking. Blog stalking."

Jaz gave me a knowing smile. "Uh-huh. Wonder why?" She nudged Amy, who watched me with her own speculative smile.

"He's become obsessed with sub-genres. He's amazed at the variety, especially for romance books."

Jaz and Amy shared a look. "I don't think it's the books he's obsessed with," Jaz said.

"Don't go there," I warned. "What if he finds my review site?" It would be worse than when he saw the bow-chick-a-wow-wow dance.

Amy sipped her tea. "He'll never figure it out. There are tons of review blogs and you don't use your real name."

Nodding, I took a bite of my sandwich. I hoped she was right. I suspected he'd tease me mercilessly if he ever found it.

"Don't worry," Amy said. "We won't tell him, right, Jaz?"

Jaz smirked. "Right. Entertaining as that would be, I'll maintain the girl code of honor."

"Look, he's smart, but not that smart," Amy said. "You use an avatar, not your photo. No name. No city. Nothing to give it away."

I forced a smile. "You're probably right." But the truth was, if anyone could figure it out, it was Dallas.

My phone buzzed on the table. "*Ghosts?? How does* that *work? Category: Caspers.*" I giggled, then shoved my phone in my bag. I could *not* do this with him.

Jaz shook her head in disgust. "It's like a bad movie, watching you pretend you don't like him."

It wasn't easy to ignore his texts the rest of the day,

but I did. I'd see him later at the store anyway, which my hormones weren't about to let me forget.

"Oh my God. We're so sorry, Vivian." Amy raced up to the bookstore counter, her face pinched with worry.

"Dude, please don't kill us," Jaz said, glancing over her shoulder as if she was being followed. "It was a total accident. We didn't know he was standing there." She locked eyes with Amy. "What is he, like a ninja assassin or what? I totally thought it was just us waiting for our mochas."

"I know, right? Then all of a sudden, wham! He was right there." Amy nodded vigorously. She thrust a to-go cup toward me. "Mint chocolate mocha. Peace offering."

I took the cup warily. "Peace offering for what? You guys are acting crazy."

They shared a look that made the hair on the back of my neck stand up.

"It's Dallas," Jaz said. "He knows about your RC mission."

"What!" I screeched so loudly all the customers turned to stare at us. "What do you mean?" I whispered, after everyone had gone back to book browsing.

"We were waiting for our drinks at the Bean," Amy said. "Making small talk."

I frowned at her. "Small talk about me? You call discussing my secret and personal information small talk?"

Amy could never lie under oath; her face gave away everything. "Okay, so not small talk. But we were sort of... discussing..."

"Arguing," Jaz interrupted. "About how crazy you are. About how all guys on your list are terrible matches for you."

"Except Toff," Amy said. "I was saying he's probably the

best one on the list…" Her voice faded away, and she took a long swig of her drink, her cheeks turning slightly pink.

"And I was joking about Iggy being an excellent GBF, but that he'd never be the guy you want to sneak to the beach with after dark."

Waves of anxiety roiled through me. I didn't like where this was going.

"You mean…wait…are you telling me…"

They nodded like twin bobble heads. "Dallas heard everything. He was standing behind us the whole time."

"No." I refused to believe it. Just because he'd stood behind them didn't mean he'd overheard them. Though Jaz *was* a loud talker. "No, no, no. This can't be happening. How could you let this happen? Are you *positive* he was listening?"

Amy's eyes widened. "Of course he was."

Holy. Crapoli.

Jaz straightened her shoulders. "We asked him about the Vulcan thing since you two seem to live in some parallel Trekkie universe. So we asked if he thought a person could be logical about who they fell in love with."

I fell into my chair, all feeling leaving my body. This was a nightmare. Dallas was due here any minute and now he knew about the RC mission? If I sunk deep enough into this chair, would it swallow me?

"He said it was highly unlikely," Amy said. "He said something about even Spock giving in to his human side sometimes."

"Weird," Jaz said. "But he looks cute when he talks about *Star Trek*. Sort of how you and Amy get when you talk about books."

I groaned. "What else did you tell him?"

"Everything?" Amy whispered, but I knew it wasn't a question.

"Everything?" My voice was barely audible. "Even about Jake?"

"No," Jaz said. "But when we said it was your replacement mission he said, 'Oh, replacement for Jake,' like he already knew." Jaz frowned. "Did you tell him about Jake?"

I shook my head. "He's just…observant." I remembered how he'd brought me the smoothie after Jake and Claire had left the store, when I'd run to the bathroom so he wouldn't see me cry.

I was embarrassed. And in that moment, I was pissed. "Do you guys even remember what the girl code says? Or the BFF code? You just violated every major rule! How could you do this to me, Jaz?" I saw the hurt flash in her eyes, and I knew that I wasn't being entirely fair. We'd been friends long enough that I should be used to this type of thing, but I just couldn't believe she'd been so careless.

The door swung open and Dallas walked in, carrying two cups. He stilled when he saw the three of us.

"Just go," I whispered. Then, to defuse the tension, I added, "I will kill you both later. In your sleep. I'll ask my mom for the best poison so I don't get caught."

"Don't take it out on him," Jaz whispered back. "Remember he's like Clark Kent. He'll get all flustered if you're mad at him."

Before I could respond, she grabbed Amy's arm and they bolted, sneaking through the kitchen to avoid Dallas.

Oh. My. God. They were traitors. Horrible, despicable traitors who I'd never speak to again.

Dallas didn't say anything as he stashed his stuff under the desk. He set a smoothie cup next to me and settled in his chair.

"Thanks," I muttered. I slid him a five dollar bill. I wasn't taking any more smoothie gifts from him. No way.

He ignored the money and started typing.

I wondered how I'd possibly endure the rest of the

afternoon working with him. Plus, he was staying late so we could start inventory, just the two of us.

Maybe I could fake a seizure and he'd call an ambulance. It might be less embarrassing.

"Just gonna put this in the fridge for later," I said, scooting back my chair and grabbing the smoothie. Once in the safety of the store kitchen, I tried to think of a plan, but nothing came. All I felt was overwhelming mortification. If I were starring in my own romance novel, I'd come up with a flippant one-liner that would make me seem confident and not at all concerned with what he thought.

But this was real life, and the only word that came was, "Help!"

"What's this sub-genre? Werewolf dudes?" Dallas waved a book in front of his face. We were the only ones in the store since he'd made good on his promise to stick around after closing for inventory. We'd barely spoken all afternoon but now that the customers were gone, Dallas had decided to talk.

Maybe I should joke with him. If I pretended he didn't know about my list, maybe he'd pretend, too.

Taking a deep breath, I glanced at the book and rolled my eyes. "Can you even read?" I teased, trying to force a laugh into my voice. "Obviously it's angels. List it under Lucifers and Gabriels."

He held my gaze for the first time today, making my pulse flutter. Then he flipped the book around to stare at the cover. "But he has a werewolf tattoo. And pointy ears."

I put my hands on my hips and faked major annoyance. "His tattoo is the sign of his angelic tribe. Try reading the blurbs. And his ears are totally normal."

"Why didn't we start with the mysteries? Or the sci-fi?" he asked, giving me an innocent look full of mocking laughter.

Okay, I could do this. "Because I own this category." I paused. "*Dude*."

He slanted me a crooked smile that made me reach for my water bottle.

"Fine." His shoulders lifted in a shrug. "But it's going to take me forever to figure out which weird sub-genres all of these fit into. Maybe you could sort them by sub-genre and I'll enter the data."

"That's actually a genius idea," I said.

"Well, I am a professional, after all."

I snorted, and he laughed softly.

"*Focus, Vivian, focus.*" Spock's warning voice stilled the butterflies in my stomach. Thank God I had a homework date with Henry tomorrow. Well, not a date exactly. I'd asked him for pre-calc help, even though I didn't need it.

"After I finish this stack, I'll start sorting into sub-genres," I told Dallas. "Then you can do the data entry."

He nodded, fingers flying over the keyboard. "What other hero categories do we need?" he asked, not looking up. "Do you have one for the GBF? Like your number one replacement crush target?"

All my breath whooshed out of me. So much for pretending he didn't know about my list. *Just go with it,* a voice said in my head. Not Spock's voice. Should I actually trust myself instead of Spock?

"Iggy doesn't get his own category in our database," I said, willing my blush to fade. "Besides that's not a real category since there's no chance for an HEA."

He turned toward me and tugged his hair. "A what?"

"HEA. Happily Ever After. Or HFN. Happy for Now."

He gaped at me. "You're kidding."

I cocked an eyebrow, trying to look stern. "Romance is serious business. No ones wants to be let down by a jerk hero."

He leaned back in his chair and crossed his arms over his magnificent chest, watching me with a smirk. "So I've heard."

Heat flooded my face as I turned back to my screen. "Anyway. No, we don't need a GBF category."

"So what sub-sub-sub-genre does your next RC target fit into? Since Iggy can't deliver in the happily ever after category."

My fingers froze over the keyboard. Now that he knew about my list, he wasn't going to drop it. Slowly, I spun my chair to face him. "My situation is different. I'm not looking for an HEA, or even an HFN."

He tilted his head, looking confused. "You're not looking for someone who can make you happy? What *are* you looking for?"

I forced a shrug. "Smart and funny."

"But smart and funny won't make you happy." He sounded baffled.

"It will make the replacement…tolerable."

He rubbed the back of his neck. "You're not making sense."

Should I tell him the other criteria? Was I freaking insane? On the other hand, maybe if he thought I was crazy he'd stop bugging me about my list.

"Okay, so the most important criteria is…" I took a breath and stared at my lap. "He can't have…I can't feel…" God, I was blowing this. I snuck a glance. He hadn't moved, sitting like a statue with his stupid cello-muscled arms crossed over his stupid Superman chest, his eyes fixed on me.

"No, um, zing. No chemistry. None at all." The words spilled out in a rush.

He looked at me as if I'd grown a second head. I guess *his* hormones wouldn't even consider looking for someone without zing. He shifted in his chair, leaning back slightly, his fingers clenched over his Superman biceps. I turned away and typed gibberish. I'd fix it later, but right now I had to look anywhere but at him.

"You really are trying to be a Vulcan." He sounded surprised. "I thought that was a joke."

I shook my head, still typing gibberish. "No joke."

His chair squeaked as he spun back to his own computer. "Even Spock gave in a few times. He was half human, you know. Remember that science chick? Have you seen that episode?"

"Yes," I said, "but that wasn't by choice. It was those weird spores that made him...um, hormonal." Maybe that was my problem. Alien spores activating my lust genes.

"Whatever." Dallas shook his head in disgust. "At least he didn't deny his feelings."

I twisted my hands in my lap. "But Spock left her when Kirk beamed him back to the ship. Spock crushed her heart. He never should've lost control. He hurt her, Dallas." I wouldn't let that happen to me.

Dallas cocked an eyebrow at me. "What about the Pon farr? The seven-year...um...mating ritual? Talk about losing control."

Uh oh. Dallas knew way more about the original series than I did. My skin tingled just thinking about mating rituals while sitting so close to Dallas.

"I don't know that one, but I'm done talking about it. This is my plan, and you weren't even supposed to know about it."

I jumped up and escaped to the shelves, piling books into stacks by hero category, lingering briefly over the small stack of geeky hero books. It wasn't how books were usually shelved but I had a feeling customers might like it. I shoved the small stack of nerd-hero books in the bottom of a box, then stacked a bunch of SWAT-team alpha hero books on top.

I brought the box to the desk and plopped it next to my computer. I'd do the data entry for these; I didn't want Dallas seeing the nerd ones.

An annoyed meow startled me from the vicinity of Dallas's lap. I turned, shocked to see Hiddles curled onto Dallas's denim-clad thighs.

"What the—? Where'd you find *him*?"

Dallas shot me a wry smile while rubbing Hiddles's ears. "He found me."

"But...but he hates people," I sputtered.

He shrugged, still petting the cat, whose eyes were contented slits.

"Wait." I leaned closer. "Is that purring?" Dallas and I locked eyes. I was definitely invading his personal space. I could smell his sexy eau de nerd scent, and if I wanted to, I'd just have to lean a little closer to taste his lips... I straightened so quickly I knocked into the box, sending books spilling onto the floor. Hiddles bolted off Dallas's lap, sending me an angry hiss before disappearing into the darkened store.

Alien hormone spores had struck again.

Dallas knelt on the floor, carefully stacking the books back into the box. "Not sure what order these were in." He paused, eyeing a cover. Oh no. The guy on the cover was grinning, holding a calculator. Even worse, he wore glasses. He was hot, though. Most definitely nerd-hot, as indicated by the title, *Unexpected Calculations*.

Dallas raised his eyes to mine. "Are there more books... like this?" I heard the suppressed laughter in his voice.

"Like what?" I feigned ignorance.

His lips curved into a sexy smile. "More books with... um...geeky heroes."

I dropped my eyes. No point lying because he'd just

Google it. "Yes. It's a sub-genre. Nerd-hot." I knew my face must be the color of the fire extinguisher stashed under the desk.

He picked up another book with a cover of a super hot guy wearing a lab coat. He chuckled softly and stacked it on top of the accountant. "I have the perfect category name."

"What?"

"McNerds."

My knees wobbled slightly, and I sank into my chair. "Didn't my mom say she'd buy us dinner?"

"Yep." He stopped stacking books and grinned at me. "That's another category for you. Sexy delivery guys."

I grabbed a rubber band and shot it at him. "Shut up."

He shot it back, laughing. "Why not? It could work. Maybe those UPS uniforms tear off when the guys shape shift into werewolves."

What was it I'd said about not wanting witty banter? I cleared my throat. "No. A delivery guy wouldn't work. Not enough drama to sustain an entire book. Unless he was delivering drugs or something, in which case he'd hardly be a hero."

Dallas returned to his chair, stretching his long legs out in front of him. "You take this book stuff seriously, don't you?" He removed his glasses and cleaned them on the hem of his T-shirt, giving me not only a glimpse of his six-pack but also his face without glasses. My throat went dry, and I reached for my cell. I pulled up my favorites list and called Wok to You.

I hoped they *did* have a hot delivery guy because my hormones were like drunken monkeys in the cockpit of my heart, and they needed somewhere to crash-land.

"Fascinating is a word I use for the unexpected. In this case I would think 'interesting' would suffice."
—*Spock*

CHAPTER THIRTEEN

FRIDAY, SEPTEMBER 5

"This looks great, Dallas," Mom said, hovering over the desk. He'd just given her a short demo of the software. She'd brought us dinner and eaten with us, which had both relieved and annoyed me. I'd been avoiding Dallas since the mortification of Tuesday's inventory night, but now I kind of wanted him to myself.

"Thanks." He grinned. I could tell he was pleased by her reaction.

"You two work well together." Mom straightened, shooting me a meaningful look. Mom did girl-face almost as well as Jaz.

Dallas glanced at me, then turned back to his computer. Was he blushing?

"I love your hero categories, Vivvy," Mom said. "Genius. After the inventory is finished, we'll set up a special display using them. I think customers might be confused if we shelved all the titles that way, but a display with featured titles would be great." Mom beamed at me.

"Sure," I agreed. A display shelf might be even more fun than shelving all the romances by hero category. I could do some serious decorating with featured titles. Maybe find some used nerd glasses. A cowboy hat. Some fun woo-woo paraphernalia for the paranormals.

"Time for you two to get busy; I'm heading to my office." Mom reached for a stack of papers on her desk. She paused. "Vivvy, I forgot to tell you. Take tomorrow off. You've worked a lot this week with the inventory and your regular shifts. Go to the surf competition." Mom grinned. "Cheer on Toff for me."

"You sure, Mom?" I felt Dallas's gaze on me.

She nodded. "Absolutely." She glanced at Dallas. "You should go, too, Dallas. The surf comps are fun."

"I might," he said. "I have plans first thing in the morning but could check it out after that."

"I'll probably go early," I said. "I'm meeting someone tomorrow afternoon."

Mom raised an eyebrow. "Anyone I know?"

"Just a friend from school." I shot a quick glance at Dallas, whose smirk told me he knew my plans were mission-related.

As soon as Mom left, Dallas emerged from behind the desk. "So who's the unlucky guy?"

"Very funny." I headed down an aisle and grabbed a stack of romance novels written by authors whose last name started with S. We'd be moving on to mysteries soon, which was a relief. "Actually there are two target, um, auditions, this weekend." My face burned. Why was I telling him this? "You don't know them."

"I might." He followed me down the aisle, then leaned against the bookshelf, watching me. His nerd uniform today was a Keep Khan and Klingon T-shirt and board shorts.

I sighed. "Tomorrow is Andrew. Everyone calls him Drew."

Dallas studied me, his face impossible to read. "Drama guy. I know him." Dallas stretched his arms above his head, grasping the top of the bookshelf, which was an unfair tactical maneuver since it made his muscles pop.

"You've only been in school like two weeks. How do you know Drama Drew already?" I glared at him, annoyed with how flustered I felt.

"Like I told you, it's a small school." He shrugged. "Too bad you're going to break his heart. Or the other guy's. Or both."

"What?" I spun to face him. "I'm not going to do anything to hurt him. Them. Whatever."

"We'll see about that. You know about collateral damage, right? Happens in every mission."

I frowned. Unlike Jake, I'd never hurt someone on purpose. I just wanted to see if there was a spark with Drew or Henry. Not a roaring bonfire but maybe enough of a glow that my hormones would be happy, but not too happy.

"I won't cause any collateral damage," I insisted. "People hang out all the time. It doesn't have to mean anything. The guys don't even know they're on my list."

He raised an eyebrow. "So that makes it okay?"

Flustered and embarrassed, I dropped the books in the box at my feet and put my hands on my hips. "God, Dallas. Haven't you ever just…just like, hung out with someone to see if maybe there was, you know, a spark or something? Without announcing to them that's what you were doing?"

His green eyes darkened behind his glasses, and a muscle twitched in his tight jaw. "Yeah."

"So why are you judging me for doing the same thing?" It felt as if the temperature in the store shot up to one hundred degrees. I wasn't a fight-picker, but something about him tumbled up all my emotions, making my words spew out uncontrollably.

"I'm not judging you. I'm just—" He stopped, then sighed and closed his eyes. "Never mind. I'm going back to work." He spun around and headed back to the desk. "Remember, I need to leave by closing tonight."

"I remember," I snapped to his retreating back. We'd had to postpone inventory because his parents needed him to babysit tonight. "It's just as well because my other target, Henry, is coming by to help me with homework after closing."

He turned around. "You call that a date?"

"I told you, I'm just hanging out with these guys first. No dates yet." I took a breath, then rushed on. "It's...it's because of the Surfer Ball." Why was I telling him this? Why did I feel I had to justify my mission to him? "It's the tradition for girls to ask guys to the dance. Or other girls, if that's their thing."

He stared at me for a long moment, his jaw tight and eyes narrowed. "So this...mission...it's just for a stupid dance?"

I shrugged, embarrassed. No way would I tell him I'd never been invited to a school dance or worked up the nerve to invite someone else. Or that I felt like I needed to do this to get over Jake.

I turned away to refocus on shelving books, feeling his heated gaze on me. It felt as if he was sending me an intense psychic message, but I was too rattled to consider what it might be.

After finishing my re-shelving, I resumed sitting next to Dallas, but we were back to the silent treatment. Suddenly the door burst open, and I glanced up to see Iggy making a beeline for me. Great. My ideal GBF who, according to Dallas and everyone else, couldn't deliver in the HFN or HEA department. Ig's lopsided grin encompassed Dallas and me as he approached the counter.

"Hi, Ig," I said, defeat slumping my shoulders. Once

again, Dallas was privy to way more of my private life than he should be.

Next to me, Dallas shifted in his chair. I glanced at him, not at all surprised to see his grin barely suppressing smug speculation.

"I'm Iggy," Ig said, reaching over the counter to shake Dallas's hand.

Dallas stood up and returned the handshake. "I'm Dallas. Viv has told me *all* about you."

Since I couldn't kick Dallas under the desk, I shot him a sugary smile. "I sure have." I gave Ig a real smile. "I told him what good friends we are." I narrowed my eyes at Dallas. "Ig's a great writer. *And* a great friend. Loyal. Funny. Smart."

"Two out of two criteria. Plus a loyalty bonus." Dallas smirked. "Not bad."

"What are you guys talking about?" Ig asked, confusion creasing his forehead. He fiddled with his eyebrow ring.

"Never mind," I muttered, side-eyeing Dallas who remained standing, arms folded over his chest, still sporting a smug grin.

Ig shrugged. "Okay, whatever. Anyway, Viv, I wanted to talk to you about an idea for the *Clarion*. Yang asked if you might be interested in doing a few human interest stories, interviewing some of the local homeless guys."

Dallas's grin faded. "That sounds dangerous."

Annoyed, I shot him a glare. "Stereotype much? The guys are harmless."

"Whoa," Ig said, observing Dallas's startled reaction. "Simmer down, Viv. Dallas is new. He doesn't know those guys like you do."

A needle of guilt poked at my stomach; Ig was right. I shouldn't have snapped at Dallas.

"Sorry," I said, swallowing nervously. "It's just… sometimes people make unfair assumptions about the homeless people."

Ig nodded vigorously. "Which is why you're the perfect person to write the articles."

I rubbed my forehead, wishing he had texted me instead of putting me on the spot in front of Dallas. "Why did Mr. Yang suggest me?"

"He saw you hanging out on the beach one day, having donuts with a couple of the guys."

Dallas met my gaze, a question in his eyes. "I like to bring them a snack once in awhile. Something besides what they get at the shelter."

Dallas rubbed a hand over his chin and the emotion in his eyes shifted, but to what I couldn't tell.

"Anyway," Ig said. "I told Yang you'd be perfect. Plus the talent show this year is a fundraiser for the shelter, so it's perfect. Yang said he might even be able to get the local paper to reprint some of your interviews."

"Really?" My enthusiasm ratcheted up considerably. I'd love to see my byline in a real newspaper.

Ig bounced on his toes enthusiastically. "So will you do it?"

I felt Dallas's gaze on me and wondered why I felt so awkward having this convo in front of him. I took a breath and stood up so I was at least sort of even with the guys.

"Absolutely," I said. I'd start with Reg, my favorite.

"Awesome!" Ig and I high-fived each other over the counter while Dallas frowned.

"You sure it's safe?" Dallas asked.

I rolled my eyes. "Of course it is." It was sort of sweet that he was concerned, but also frustrating.

"I'd offer to go with you, but Yang piled more stuff on my plate, too," Ig said.

Dallas rubbed the back of his neck. "I could go with you."

We both stared at him, then Ig shot me a speculative smirk.

"That's not neces—" I began.

"Great idea!" Ig interrupted.

Too bad Iggy was gay; he and Jaz would be perfect together.

As dinner time rolled around, the grungy artists who'd been arguing in the corner got up to leave. Picasso nodded at me as he pushed through the door. "Later, Viv."

Dallas glanced up curiously as he reached for his backpack. "Is he on your list?"

Startled, I shook my head.

"Why not?"

"Not my type."

Dallas rolled his eyes. "But I thought you weren't interested in guys who *are* your type. In which case, maybe he's perfect."

Flustered, I grabbed a stack of papers, pretending to look for something. "You were supposed to remind me to interview you. I need to turn in the article on Monday."

Dallas was quiet for a minute, then he pulled his phone from his pocket. "I didn't want to do the interview while I was working since I was on the clock. But I can meet you early tomorrow."

On the clock? How dorky. And cute. "How early?"

He shot me an amused look. "Need some extra beauty sleep?"

"No, I just um…" I took a breath. Why couldn't I form a coherent sentence when he teased me? And what did that beauty sleep crack mean, anyway? "What time can you meet?"

"Eight o'clock? I need to be somewhere by nine thirty."

I nodded. "Thanks." After I interviewed him, I could head to the surf comp.

"Sure." His fingers flew across his phone, then he resumed packing up his stuff.

The door swung open and Henry walked in, all gangly and gawky, looking like Robin to Dallas's Batman. Henry looked surprised to see Dallas. "Um, hi. Am I too early?"

Before I could reply, Dallas said, "Nope. But you might want to find out what number you are. I hear there's quite a list."

Henry looked confused. "What?" He shoved at his glasses, which somehow wasn't cute on him the way it was on Dallas.

I glared at Dallas, who shook his head, grinning. "I gotta go." He shouldered his backpack and headed for the door, pausing to shake Henry's hand. "I'm Dallas by the way. Otherwise known as Vespa Guy."

Henry's face lit up. "Oh yeah! Cool. What kind of mileage does that thing get? I'm doing a cost/benefit analysis of different vehicles, to convince my parents I need some type of motorized transportation. We'll be discussing it at our family meeting. I've designed a flowchart explaining the familial benefits of an additional vehicle."

Dallas glanced over his shoulder at me, raising his eyebrows. "Was there any sort of recon done for this mission? Or are the targets totally random?"

I pointed at the door. "Aren't you going to be late for babysitting? Or maybe hacking into NASA?"

He grinned at me, then gave Henry a salute. "Your country and your classmates thank you for your service to this mission. Soldier on."

"Huh?" Henry glanced between us, completely baffled.

I wanted to scream, but instead I just stabbed my finger toward the door again. "Bye, Dallas."

"See you in the morning, Spock." He saluted as he pushed

through the door, chuckling to himself. My hormones left with him, leaving no zing at all as I turned my attention to Henry.

"So." Henry dumped his backpack on the nearest table. "I was surprised you asked for my assistance, Vivian. You seem to do well in pre-calc."

Still rattled by Dallas, it took me a few seconds to absorb Henry's words. "Oh…yeah. Right. I just wanted some clarification. For the test."

Henry lined up his books and pencils in neat rows. Dallas did that, too. "I only have about thirty minutes to work with you."

"You do?" I was surprised. Maybe Henry wasn't feeling any zing, either.

He pulled out a chair and sat down. "On Fridays, we have pizza at seven thirty on the dot at my house. I've arranged for an eight o'clock mealtime tonight, allowing for travel time. Bicycle time, not Vespa time." He glanced at me, frowning. "And since my entire family is impacted by this, I'd appreciate it if we could get started."

Instead of Spock's face looming in my mind, I saw Dallas's laughing eyes and heard his sexy voice asking if my list was totally random. Sighing heavily, I walked toward Henry as if I was walking to the gallows.

At least my hormones would be able to get some sleep.

It was almost 10:00 p.m. when my phone pinged with a text. I lay stretched out in my bed, reading Dallas's *Star Trek* episode guide. I reached for the phone without looking, expecting Jaz.

"I'm guessing failed mission. Unless I totally misread things."

Dallas. My butterflies roared to life, fully rested from

their time with Henry.

"No idea what you're talking about." I flopped back against my pillows, trying to focus on my book, but that was a joke since it was Dallas's book. It was like having a part of him right here in bed with me. I flung off my blankets, suddenly feeling way too hot.

"Deflection. Good strategy but ineffective with me."

I rolled my eyes. *"I'm going to bed now. Ciao."*

There was a delay while he typed his response.

"What r u wearing?"

I gasped, flustered. I started typing an indignant reply, then his next text filled my screen.

"Kevlar? Fatigues?"

Curse him for taking something flirty and twisting it to make me laugh. I was tempted to type a very inappropriate reply, something I knew would make him blush.

But then I saw Spock's frowning face on my phone screen and heard his voice telling me to sign off.

"But I don't want to sign off," I whispered.

Spock's glare deepened. *"You must. You're losing control of your mission."*

I closed my eyes, thinking of the disastrous half hour I'd spent with Henry, faking confusion about pre-calc so he wouldn't be upset about delaying his family's pizza night. At least he left thinking he'd been useful. I thought about my plans to meet Drama Drew for coffee tomorrow. Maybe Amy was right and I should go crush-free for awhile.

But I was committed to my mission, and committed to not falling down the rabbit hole of uncontrollable emotions again. Not even with a guy who brought me smoothies and made me laugh and drove me crazy.

"Goodnight, Dallas," I whispered to my phone, but I set it aside without typing the words.

"Are you suggesting we fight to prevent a fight?"
—*Captain Kirk*

CHAPTER FOURTEEN

SATURDAY, SEPTEMBER 6

arrived at The Jumping Bean at 8:00 a.m. on the dot. Of course Dallas was already there, sitting at a corner table drinking a chai latte. I ordered chamomile tea, hoping to calm my nerves while I interviewed him.

I had a hard time getting my brain to focus on anything other than The Dallas Show. He wasn't showing off, being stupid, or acting goofy like Toff. He simply sat there in his jeans and tight, long-sleeved thermal shirt typing on his cell, pausing occasionally to give me a questioning smile, while I frantically flipped through the pages of my journalism notebook.

Where the heck were the interview questions? I'd written them out in advance to avoid exactly this situation.

Dallas cleared his throat. I glanced at him, unnerved by how calm he seemed while I was a bundle of jangled nerves.

"Everything okay?" he asked.

I bit my lip and shook my head, flipping through my notebook so fast I tore a page. "I can't find the questions I was going to ask you."

Dallas shifted in his chair, watching me as my panic

increased. He extended his arm, then rested his hand on top of mine, stilling my frantic page-flipping. Currents of electricity shot up my arm and down my spine while I stared at his hand, at the long fingers that were made for the cello, and probably other amaz—

"How about we just have a conversation?"

I raised my eyes from his hand to his face. He cocked an eyebrow, waiting for my answer, but all I could think of was how warm his hand felt on mine. My gaze darted to his hand, and he quickly removed it, cupping his chai instead.

"A conversation," I parroted like an idiot bird.

"Yeah." I heard the smile in his voice even though I stared at the table instead of him.

I willed myself to talk to him just like I would any of my friends. "Okay. First impressions," I sputtered, vaguely recalling one of the questions I'd written. "Of California. Shady Cove." I waved my hand nervously. "All of it."

He kept his eyes on me and ran a hand over his chin. I hated when he did that because of how it drew attention to his extremely kissable lips. He shifted in his chair, stretching his legs out to the side. "So, first impressions." He paused. "Overall, I'd say things here are…different than I expected."

I clutched my pen. "Different how?"

He glanced at his phone, which had just pinged with a text. He frowned slightly, then refocused on me. "Well, it looks exactly like I expected, since I Googled the heck out of Shady Cove before we moved here."

I waited, doodling circles on my paper.

"But not everything is matching up to appearances. Or my expectations."

My hand stilled. "How so?"

He laughed softly. "It's colder than I thought it would be. That fog su-stinks."

"You can say suck, Dallas. I won't be offended."

His neck reddened and he shrugged. "Bad habit I'm trying to break."

That was weird. I wanted to probe but decided to give him a break. "So yeah, the fog. It's not always like the sunny beaches you see in the movies."

"The weather's definitely better than Wisconsin, though."

I nodded and wrote, "Likes the weather."

He leaned over to see what I'd written and laughed. "This is going to be the most boring interview ever."

"So give me a good quote. Tell me something no one knows about you, Vespa Guy. Tell me a secret."

His eyes darkened behind his glasses. "Maybe later, Spock."

I swallowed, reaching for my tea. What was I doing, flirting with the one person I shouldn't be?

"Okay...then tell me about, um..." My voice faltered as his gaze stayed on mine, not blinking. "Tell me...about the cello thing." I made a lame attempt at pantomiming running a bow across strings.

"The cello thing?" He smirked, mimicking my cello pantomime.

I rolled my eyes. "How long have you played? Are you in the school band? Are you going on tour like those guys from Croatia?"

"Ah." A knowing smile played at his lips. "You're one of *those* girls."

Warmth coursed through me, and I knew I was blushing. "What girls?" I asked.

"Cello-guy groupies." He chuckled. "Those Croatians are like catnip to girls like you."

I squirmed. "I'm hardly a groupie. But I like watching those guys."

"Obviously." Laughter danced in his eyes.

"They're very talented!" I knew my protest sounded ridiculous.

He reached for a sugar packet, then twirled it on the table. "Uh-huh. And I'm sure you'd be just as appreciative of their talent if those guys were less, ah, photogenic."

I raised my eyebrows. "Photogenic? Is that McNerd code for hot?"

He spun the sugar packet. "You tell me."

Still blushing, I reached for my pen. "I think we've gone off topic. You didn't answer my question. How long have you been playing?"

"Ten years."

"Wow. You must be good."

He shrugged. "I'm all right."

Which meant he was more than all right. I ignored his false modesty and scribbled *cello expert* in my notebook. I thought of the hot Croatian cellists bent over their cellos, smoking hot in their leather jackets, their bodies extensions of their instruments, their—

"…and I'm not playing in the band."

Blinking to clear away my fantasy images, I raised my eyes. "Um, what?"

"No orchestra at the school." Dallas shrugged again. "Not enough interest, I guess, for a small school. And there's not really a permanent spot for me in the jazz band. They said once in a while I can play with them, but…" His voice trailed away.

"Huh." I doodled in my notebook. "That's weird."

"It's not a *Glee* episode, Vivian. It's not like I show up and everyone creates an entire performance based around me."

Whoa. "You don't have to be so condescending, Dallas."

For once, he looked flustered instead of me. "That's not what I—"

"Whatever." I put up a hand to silence him. I needed to get this interview over with. Fast. "Next question. What about sports? You trying out for any teams?"

His eyes narrowed. "Not surfing."

"You mean it's not like a TV show, where the new guy shows up and becomes a master surfer in a few weeks and wins all the trophies?"

We glared at each other like warring soldiers until he removed his glasses and cleaned the lenses with a napkin. I stopped breathing while I watched him, captivated by his long, dark lashes usually hidden behind the lenses.

"I don't need any more trophies." He glanced up at me.

"Why don't you wear contacts?" I blurted, regretting it instantly.

His lips twitched, but he left his glasses on the table. "I do, sometimes."

"When?" Oh my God. Hormones had taken complete control of my body, including my voice. I glanced at my arms, half-expecting to see marionette strings.

"Is that one of the official interview questions?" He was laughing at me. Maybe not on the outside but definitely on the inside; I saw it in his eyes and the tilt of his mouth. He put his glasses back on and I dropped my gaze, mortified.

"Anyway..." I cleared my throat and forced myself to resume eye contact. "Sports?"

He shook his head. "Not at school."

I frowned. "You said something about trophies, though. What are they, cello trophies?"

"No. They're for other stuff." He tugged at his hair and glanced out the window.

Now I was curious, abnormally so.

"Vespa-riding trophies? Coding medals?"

He turned back to me. "No and no."

Geez, somebody was touchy. Why'd he mention the trophies if he didn't want to talk about them? Maybe they were little kid trophies, the ones everyone on the team gets so no one feels bad. *No sports*, I wrote in my notebook.

He sighed as he read what I wrote.

"That's not exactly true," he said, sounding frustrated. "Do you have to know everything about me for this interview?"

I flinched, then closed my notebook. "If you don't want to do this, I can leave—"

"Vivian, wait." He leaned across the table, covering my hand with his again. "Don't storm off. Please." He looked genuinely distressed.

"I wasn't going to storm off," I muttered. "I'm not a drama queen."

He pulled his hand away, and his worried expression morphed into one of amusement. "Of course you aren't. There's no room on Vulcan for drama queens."

I bit back a smile.

"I'm sorry," he said. "I'm just not used to talking about myself. It feels weird."

"I'm not trying to embarrass you." I hesitated. "No one reads the paper, anyway, so you don't have to worry."

He laughed. "That's a relief."

"Soo…" I hesitated, then plunged ahead. "Sports: yes, no, or prefer not to answer?"

He dropped his gaze and fiddled with his sugar packet. "Not sports how you probably think about it. Next question."

I didn't think of myself as a gonzo journalist driven to uncover dirt, but my curiosity was piqued; however, he obviously didn't want to talk about whatever mysterious activity he did well enough to earn trophies.

"Okay," I said. "Moving on. Favorite subject in school?"

He glanced up, lips quirking. "Seriously?"

I blushed. "I know it's stupid. Just answer."

"Lunch."

I rolled my eyes. "What are you, ten years old?"

He grinned. "Sometimes."

I sighed and shook my head. "I didn't think you'd make this so difficult."

He raised a shoulder. "I told you I don't like talking about myself." He flashed me a grin that showed his dimple, making me wonder what it would be like to kiss it.

"We could talk about something else," I said, even though I had nothing in mind.

"Great idea. Let's talk about you." He pushed his long sleeves up, revealing sinewy forearms that made me bite the inside of my lip.

"Me?" I managed to whisper.

"Sure. My turn to interview you. How long have you lived in Shady Cove?" He reached for my notebook and pen and started writing on a fresh piece of paper.

"Uhh..forever. My whole life."

He looked at me over his glasses. "That explains a lot." He scribbled "forever" on the page.

"What do you mean?"

He shrugged. "Everyone knows you, and you know everyone. Makes sense." He shot me another grin. "Sports: Yes, no, or prefer not to answer."

"Bike riding. Yoga."

He gave me an assessing look but said nothing.

I squirmed, hoping he didn't think I was a Chunky Monkey. "Occasional surfing. Very occasional."

He smiled faintly. "Because of the sharks?"

"Partly that." I pictured Jake in his wet suit. "Just not my thing."

He set down the pen and leaned back in his chair. "Book club. How long have you been doing that?"

I relaxed. I could talk about that all day long. "A couple of years." I hesitated, then plunged ahead. "I have a review blog, too."

"Yeah?" He looked impressed. "What's the website?"

Ugh. Why had I mentioned it?

"Vivian? The website?" He held the pen, waiting.

I shook my head. "It's not your type of website."

He smirked. "Reviews about dragon anatomy? Cowboy action? Ropes and boots?"

My face flamed and I glared at him. "You won't tell me about your secret trophies. I don't have to tell you about this."

He narrowed his eyes. "You realize I can Google it, right?"

My stomach felt like it dropped to the floor. "Try it," I said, forcing bravado into my voice. "You couldn't figure out my mom's pen name."

His eyes flashed. "I think I'll have better luck with you."

My pulse sped up. "Why?"

"Insider information." He took a sip from his cup and grimaced.

"Cold?"

He nodded.

"Want me to heat it up for you?" His body tensed as his eyes locked on mine. Oh God. The loaded words hung there between us, so I grabbed his mug and jumped up from the table. I hurried away to shove his mug into the microwave in the corner of the store. Grateful that my back was to him, I took long, deep breaths.

When I returned to the table, he acted as if nothing zingy had happened between us. Maybe it hadn't. Maybe I'd imagined the heat I saw in his eyes.

Dallas took a sip of his chai and nodded at me. "Thanks."

"Sure."

"Do you have any more questions for me?" He leaned back in his chair. I'd never met anyone who watched me so intently but not in a creepy way.

"Packer fan?"

He rolled his eyes. "Duh."

"Does your family like it here?"

He nodded. "My mom and sister love the ocean. Dad likes teaching at UC."

"What does he teach?"

"He's in the Engineering school."

I smirked. "Figures."

Dallas smiled faintly but didn't say anything.

I cleared my throat. So far I had nothing other than basic facts. Mr. Yang wouldn't be happy. He always wanted a human interest angle. I thought of a question I wanted to ask but shouldn't. Maybe I could dance around it. "So do you miss Wisconsin?"

He blinked a few times. Now that I knew about his long eyelashes, I realized I could see them behind the glasses, if I dared myself to watch him the way he watched me.

"Sure. I had…have lots of friends there. It would be like if you moved away from here."

I nodded. "That must suck," I said, more to myself than him.

"Some days less than others," he said, his voice low.

We stared at each other without speaking, then he rested an arm on the table and drummed his fingers. "I might go back there for college, though. I applied to the University of Wisconsin."

"Good choice, since you already have the wardrobe."

His eyes narrowed, but I focused on his mouth, which was smiling. "I grew up thinking I'd go there since that's where my dad taught." He shrugged. "But now my parents are making me apply to California colleges, too. Cal Poly, USC, Berkeley. I'm drowning in college apps right now since the deadlines are coming up."

"We have the best public colleges in the country," I mimicked my mom.

He rolled his eyes. "Californians think everything here is better than everywhere else."

"Isn't it?" I widened my eyes in mock innocence, and Dallas laughed.

"Some things are. Definitely." He studied me intently, then shifted his gaze out the window.

Heat rushed through me, but I calmed myself enough to write, "Misses Wisconsin. Might go there for college."

"So, um, do you stay in touch with your friends?" I still wasn't brave enough to ask what I wanted to know.

He shifted his gaze from the window back to me. "Sure." He shrugged. "I talk to a few of my closer friends."

I raised an eyebrow. "Actual phone calls? Don't Wisconsonians have texting yet?"

His brow furrowed "Wisconsinites."

"What?"

"That's what we call ourselves. Not Wisconsonians."

"Oh." I scribbled Wisconsinites in my notebook and underlined it.

"And yes we have texting, but sometimes I like to actually talk to people."

He had a girlfriend. Guys wouldn't care if he called, but a girlfriend...

"Do you miss her? Your girlfriend?" I blurted out the words before I could lose my nerve.

His eyebrows shot up and his Adam's apple bobbed up and down. It looked as if I'd finally rattled his composure instead of the other way around. It was my turn to lean back in my chair and wait for an answer. He pushed his glasses up his nose and sighed. "So you're Lois Lane in disguise, huh?"

Did that mean I was right? He had a girlfriend back in the land of Badgers and cheeseheads? My heart felt like a ball of lead, sinking to my toes. "Just doing my job. Besides, I've been friends with Toff since kindergarten, and I've never seen him pick up the phone to call anyone but his dad."

He pulled at his hair. "Long-distance relationships are

hard." He shrugged. "But even if I was still there, we wouldn't have lasted." He took a sip of his chai, eyes fixed on me. "Just wasn't meant to be."

My heart ricocheted in my chest. Why was he telling me this? He wouldn't tell me about his secret trophies, but he'd just told me about his girlfriend? *Ex-girlfriend*, I corrected myself.

"Maybe I'll try your strategy." His eyes roved across my face.

"What strategy?" My voice sounded raspy.

"Your replacement mission. Make a list of what type of girl I want." He paused. "But I'm interested in something longer term. Not just a date for a dance. Want to help me make my list?"

I stared at him as if he'd just asked me to plan a kidnapping.

He smirked, then reached for my notebook again and tore off the sheet of paper he'd written on. "So how does this work?" He inclined his head toward my bag. "You have your replacement notebook with you?"

I gaped at him. Who had told him about my notebook? "Um, this isn't, uh, why we're here, Dallas. I'm supposed to be interviewing you, not helping you find a…a…"

"Replacement girlfriend." Laughter danced in his eyes as he watched me squirm. "Why not? Don't you want to help out the new guy?"

I huffed a sigh of frustration. "You're mocking me."

"No, I'm not. Think about it logically, Spock. You know everyone. You can help me narrow the field."

I sucked down cold tea, trying to compose myself. Help Dallas narrow the field? Introduce him to potential girlfriends? Everything in me protested, and I knew why.

Because I wanted to be the replacement.

But I couldn't. That was the whole point of my own

mission: not to fall for someone who could make me lose control. Because even if that someone seemed like an amazing person...well...letting myself get carried away again was just too scary.

"We can help each other," he said. "Since I'm new here, I can give you an outsider's opinion on your...what do you call them?"

"Targets," I whispered.

His dimple flashed, deepening as he chuckled. "Targets. Right. So yeah, I'll give you the outsider's opinion on your targets. And you give me the inside scoop on my targets." He paused. "Logically, this should work, Spock."

"But...but..." I sputtered like a cartoon character. "I don't know you well enough. To help."

"You're getting to know me. Working together in the store. Asking probing interview questions." He flashed another grin. "And I'll tell you some of my...criteria. That's what you call it, right?"

I nodded. My hormones pounded on every nerve in my body, dying to escape and capture Dallas as their personal love slave.

He started scribbling on the paper. "Number one," he said. "Easy on the eyeballs." He shot me a quick look, then refocused on his list.

"Wow," I said, my voice returning. "That's deep, Dallas. Good to know you care about the important stuff."

He flashed that stupid dimple again. "Just being honest, Vivian. Are you telling me it's not on your list? Wanting a guy you think is, uh..." He cleared his throat nervously.

"Hot," I said. "And no, it's not on my list. In fact, it's off my list. On purpose."

A frown creased his forehead. "What Vulcan stupidity is that?"

I glared at him. "Let's just say I've made that mistake

before. Caring too much about chemistry or whatever." I waved my hands nervously. "Being stupid enough to fall for some guy just because of how…" I was telling him too much. "Never mind."

"No wonder Jaz thinks your list is a bad idea." He sounded as if he'd just figured out the answer to a puzzle.

"Well, Jaz didn't get used by a jackass, so she should keep her opinions to herself," I snapped, then instantly wished I could shove the words back inside me where they belonged. I dropped my gaze to the table. How had a newspaper interview turned into true confessions?

"Would you like some more tea?" His voice was gentle now, not teasing. I nodded, refusing to look at him.

He took my cup and left the table. I practiced my yoga breathing while he refilled my mug with hot water and retrieved a tea bag. He returned and sat across from me, propping an ankle on his thigh.

"So," he said. "Now that you know I'm shallow, let's continue. Number two: she has to be smart."

I raised my eyes to meet his, but he was looking out the window. "Obviously," I said, and he snapped his head around.

"Why obviously?"

"Because even though you're shallow, pretty without smart would bore you. Eventually."

His lips twitched. "Obviously."

I took a breath. Maybe I *should* help him find a girlfriend. If he started dating someone else, I could refocus on my mission instead of him. "So, one: pretty. Two: smart. What's number three?"

"I'm not done with two. Not just smart but a certain kind of smart."

I frowned. "Like what?"

"Not just book smart. Also people smart."

"What do you mean?"

"You ever meet someone who's like a genius, but is also a total ass—uh, jerk?" He looked embarrassed.

"You can swear around me, Dallas. I'm not a delicate flower."

He still looked flustered. "Anyway, you know what I mean? The type of person who uses her intelligence like a weapon to make other people feel stupid?"

I nodded. "Sure. Sounds like you have some history there."

His eyes narrowed. "Stop digging, Lois Lane. Number three: she has to be her own person. Not someone who pretends to like the same stuff I do just to make me happy. Someone with her own interests, her own opinions." He grinned. "Someone who likes a good debate once in a while."

I took a sip of tea. It just might kill me to help him find his dream girl and watch them ride off into the sunset on his Vespa. "Okay. Pretty, smart, likes to argue." I tried to sound disinterested. "That's it?"

"Hmm…it's a start."

"Just a start?"

"Well…it's all you need for now." He tilted his head toward my bag. "Get out your list."

"What? No freaking way, Dallas." A few people turned when I raised my voice.

He grinned. "Feisty, huh?" He nodded toward the piece of paper. "Add feisty as number four."

"B-but I…I'm not…" I'd never been this flustered by a guy, not even by Jake.

He leaned over to write "Four: feisty." He raised his eyes to mine. "I didn't say *you* were one of my targets, Vivian. I just said I liked feisty. Relax."

Relax? How could I possibly relax?

"If you won't show me your notebook, at least tell me all of your criteria." He started playing with the sugar packet again.

"You already know," I snapped, bothered that he'd said I wasn't on his list. "Jaz and Amy told you everything, that day you eavesdropped."

"Confession: I *wasn't* eavesdropping; in fact, I was trying to ignore them. But Jaz is loud." His eyes practically twinkled. "Maybe they wanted me to overhear them. Ever consider that?"

I gaped at him, then leaned over the table toward him, vibrating with frustration and something else I chose to ignore. "You think you're hilarious, don't you?"

He grinned. "Most of the time. But not always. Like right now, I'm pretty sure you don't think I'm funny." His eyes kept doing that sparkling thing. "You look ready to pounce."

I started to say that I'd love to attack him but stopped just in time. "Anyway," I said. "I think the interview is over."

"Agreed. But the list discussion isn't. Tell me more of your criteria, or I'll file an official harassment complaint with the owner of Murder by the Sea, with Jaz and Amy as my witnesses."

Air whooshed out of me as if he'd punched me. "You don't give up, do you?

"Nope. It's one of my best qualities."

We stared at each other, neither of us blinking. So now we'd moved from bickering to a staring contest? It was fifth grade all over again; however, the longer I stared into his hypnotic green eyes, the harder breathing became. And thinking. I gave up, my eyelids fluttering like birds released from a cage. He blinked, too, and dropped his gaze, clearing his throat.

"My criteria," I whispered, trying to regain my composure. "One: smart. Two: funny."

He braced an elbow on the table and leaned his chin in his hand, watching me.

I took a breath. "Three: minimal chemistry."

"Yeah," he said. "I remember that one."

I ignored him and grabbed my own sugar packet to fiddle with. "He has to be um...a gentleman." I wondered if he understood the meaning underlying my words. No way was I going to say that I didn't want to date someone who'd just use me, then drop me for the next hookup that came along.

He sat up straight. "Gentleman. Opens car doors, buys dinner, all that stuff."

"He doesn't have to buy dinner all the time. We can take turns. That's not the only definition of a gentleman. I just mean that he's got to be a good person. I'm not looking for another asshole."

He tapped the side of his head. "Got it. Regular showers. Tolerates chick music." He gave me a fake look of horror. "Oh no. You like dancing, don't you?" He shot me a suggestive grin. "I know you do."

I blushed, remembering the kitchen dance he'd witnessed.

He shook his head in mock defeat. "I might not be able to help you with this mission, after all. The guys are already bitch—sorry—complaining about the Surfer Ball and the dancing."

I couldn't help smiling at how he kept stopping himself from swearing. "Are all Wisconsinites so worried about offending delicate girl ears?"

He ducked his head. "No." He shrugged. "My mom's been a freak about it ever since Becca repeated some stuff she overheard me say when I was sp—." He suddenly clamped his lips shut, looking embarrassed and frustrated.

"When you were what?" I prompted.

He shook his head, refusing to finish his sentence, so I just shrugged and spun my sugar packet. "I think it's sweet. Most guys can't finish a sentence without an f-bomb."

He cleared his throat and pushed his shirtsleeves up farther, revealing even more muscles. I really needed to check Tumblr to see if this was an actual cellist thing or if it was just him.

"So," he said. "You want a smart, funny gentleman that you have absolutely no desire to sneak to the beach with after curfew." He laughed softly. "You want a GBF."

My heart couldn't take much more of this.

He propped both elbows on the table, steepling his fingers. "What about bonus criteria?"

"Like what?" I stared at the dark hair on his forearms, and his long fingers, and—

"—but you tell me."

I blinked, embarrassed to have zoned out like an arm junkie. "I didn't catch that. What did you say?"

His lips twitched. "I said I thought we should be open to bonus criteria. Stuff that's not on our lists that might end up being important, once we notice it in someone else."

"I'm not sure about that."

He shrugged. "Well, I'm going to add it to my list." He picked up his sheet of paper and folded it carefully into fourths, then tucked it into his backpack. "I've gotta split. You sure you have enough for an interview? We spent half our time arguing." He shot me another dimpled grin.

I nodded, ignoring the fact that *likes to argue* was one of his criteria.

He stood up, swung his backpack over his shoulder, and dangled his helmet from his hand. "I can work Monday after school and stay late that night to work on the inventory; I know we need to get it done. Saturday, too. Unless you, uh, have plans."

"Nope." I shook my head. "No plans."

"When are you doing the homeless interviews?" he asked.

I side-eyed him. I didn't need, or want, a bodyguard. "I'll let you know," I said evasively.

He looked a lot like Spock as he raised one eyebrow, clearly signaling he didn't believe I'd let him tag along.

"What about your next RC target?" he asked. "No

Saturday night date?"

"I told you, no dates. We're just hanging out to see if...you know...there's any point to an actual date."

He raised his eyebrows, staring pointedly at our empty coffee mugs. "Excellent military strategy, Galdi. Covertly assess the target's strengths and weaknesses." The smile he gave me made my heart do somersaults.

"It's not a battlefield, *Lang*."

Something flickered in his eyes. "Yes it is, Vivian. And I play to win."

He turned away, his long strides getting him to the exit before I could take another breath.

"You may find that having is not so pleasing a thing as wanting. This is not logical, but it is often true."
—Spock

CHAPTER FIFTEEN

Saturday, September 6

It was a perfect day for a surf comp. Jaz, Amy, and I stood huddled on the beach in the remnants of morning fog, which had almost burned off by the time I got there. I'd missed the first heat, but it had been worth it to interview Dallas.

Toff blew me a kiss and waved. Jaz narrowed her eyes. "He's still number four on your list, right?"

"Yeah. Though I don't know why I'm keeping him on there."

"If you'd just make Dallas number one, it wouldn't be an issue," Jaz said.

"Yeah, well, apparently Dallas is on his own RC mission. And I'm not on his list."

Amy and Jaz stared at me open-mouthed.

"What! What crazy talk is this?" Jaz demanded.

I filled them in briefly on the morning's interview with Dallas. When I finished, Jaz had a huge grin on her face.

"What's so funny?"

"He's totally playing you. Of course you're on his list. I can't wait to ask him about it."

I grasped her by the shoulders and stared deep into her

eyes. "Don't. You. Dare. Seriously, Jaz, you've done enough damage telling him about my list."

Her grin didn't even waver. "Pish posh. He needed to know about it so he could make the next move. Which he's doing, obviously. I bet he plays chess."

I frowned at Amy. "Do you know what she's talking about?"

Amy shrugged. "Not this time. But I agree that Dallas likes you."

"Well, Toff sure as hell shouldn't be on her list, right, Amy?" Jaz demanded.

Amy stared at her feet, shuffling her Chucks in the damp sand and shrugged. She looked like someone from a steam punk fairy tale, her long red curls swirling in the breeze, dressed in a leather jacket and hippie dress. I envied her style since I wore boring jeans and a Cal sweatshirt.

"Let's watch the surfing, okay? I don't want to talk about this anymore." I made a show of focusing on the surfers and, amazingly, Jaz dropped the subject.

Even though Jaz drove me crazy, she'd always had my back. Yeah, she was loud and opinionated, but she was also loyal and had a huge heart. I knew her frustration with me was because she cared about me and didn't want to see me get hurt again.

The longboarders paddled out first, waiting patiently for the waves to roll in. Toff reached the line-up first, and I watched him gracefully pop up on his board when he spotted a wave. His timing was perfect, catching the top of the wave just as it crested. His feet danced on the board, and he spun his board once, twice, three times, riding the wave like an extension of the water. His teammates yelled, cheering him on, their voices swallowed in the roaring of the waves. We moved closer, our voices joining in the cheers.

Toff rode his board all the way in to the sand, laughing

and fist-pumping the air. His teammates surrounded him, pounding his back and high-fiving him. Coach hugged him, and his dad Paul gave him a thumbs-up.

"Surfing is so sexy." Amy sighed.

I turned to her and she blushed. "Yeah," I agreed. I glanced toward the team and saw Jake grab his board, heading out for the next heat. Maybe not always sexy.

Toff caught my eye and grinned. I crouched, imitating his bicep-flexing pose and he returned the pose, laughing. We unfolded my ratty blanket and settled ourselves on the sand to watch the rest of the comp. When it was time for the girls' first heat, Toff joined us, flopping down on the blanket next to me.

"Hey, beautiful ladies. Room for me?"

Jaz rolled her eyes. "You're supposed to ask *before* you sit down."

He laughed, stretching out his long legs. He'd unzipped his wet suit and shrugged out of the top half, leaving his arms and chest totally exposed. I noticed Amy sneaking glances at him, her face flushed. He was ripped, no doubt about it.

"So was I awesome today or what?" Toff joked, chewing on a straw as he watched Jake ride his wave back to the shore.

Jaz snorted. "And humble, too."

"Right." Toff winked at her.

"You were fantastic," Amy said.

"Thanks, Ames." He reached out to fist-bump her. She returned the gesture, still blushing. As I watched them, it hit me that maybe Toff was the guy Amy was crushing on. When I'd asked her who it was, she'd blown me off, saying it was nothing serious. But watching her nervous energy around Toff made me wonder.

We watched the girls paddle out, waiting for their set to roll in.

"Waves are rocking today," Toff said. "I love days like this."

I focused on Claire, watching the sun glint off her dreadlocks. The fog had rolled farther out to the ocean, and I basked in the increasing warmth. It was a nearly perfect day. The only thing better would be if Jake had a shark encounter.

"Kill it, Claire!" Toff yelled, making me jump. He chuckled. "Why so nervous, Viv? Is my manly essence totally overwhelming you girls?"

I turned to him, fake scowling. "You're unbelievable."

"In so many ways." He shoulder-bumped me and Amy looked away from us, blushing. Yeah, I definitely needed to ask her. If she did like him, he was totally going off my list. No way would I date someone my friend liked.

Claire hopped on her board, reminding me of a lithe cat. Just like Toff, she timed her ride perfectly, cresting her wave higher than anyone else and executing perfect snaps. Jake hooted, fist-pumping the air. I marveled at her skill. However I felt about her and Jake, I was blown away by her courage and ease on the waves.

"She's amazing," I said.

"Yeah, she's the best on the girls' team, hands-down." Toff leaned back on his elbows and dug his toes into the sand.

I stared down at him, narrowing my eyes. "Maybe she's the best overall from both teams."

"Wrong." Toff grinned up at me. "I think we all know who's the best on the guys' team."

Jaz threw a candy wrapper at him, and it bounced off his face.

"Dude! You're just in time to save me from being assaulted." Toff looked past me, grinning up at someone. We all turned to see Dallas standing there in jeans and a Badgers sweatshirt.

"Hi." He inclined his head, smiling at all of us though his eyes flicked right past me. He focused on Toff. "Thought I'd come check it out."

"Bummer, you missed the best run of the morning," Toff said.

Jaz threw another wrapper at Toff's head. "He's talking about himself," Jaz said. "If you couldn't guess."

"I thought you had other plans this morning," I asked Dallas, squinting against the now-blinding sun.

He shrugged. "Plans change."

Jaz sized him up, opening her mouth to say something I knew would embarrass me, but fortunately the roar of cheers from down the beach made us all turn to watch the girls ride in. Jake rushed to sweep Claire into a hug, spinning her around and kissing her. I turned away. I wanted to move on, and most of the time I knew I had, but actually seeing Jake kiss Claire the way he used to kiss me felt like a physical blow.

My phone buzzed in my pocket, reminding me it was time to meet Drew for coffee. Anxiety fluttered in my stomach. I'd already had a misstep with Iggy, then the weird homework night with Henry. This was my third attempt to put the RC mission into action. I shot a nervous glance at Dallas, who'd shaded his eyes with his hand, watching the next group of surfers paddle out.

"Take a load off, dude," Toff said to Dallas, giving me the perfect excuse to leave. I stood up, losing my balance a little in the sand. I pictured Dallas doing his one-legged crane stand. I bet he never lost his balance.

"You can take my spot," I told Dallas. "I need to go."

He met my eyes for the first time since he'd arrived. "Battle stations ready. Target locked." The intense expression in his eyes made my stomach lurch. I looked away, reaching down to grab my bag. I needed to get out of here. Too many weird emotions swirling around, watching Jake with Claire, Dallas giving off weird vibes, and Toff showing off his body and making Amy blush.

"I'll see you guys later." I ignored Dallas and plastered on a fake smile for everyone else.

Toff winked at me. "You're gonna miss me getting another trophy, Wordworm."

Jaz smacked him on the arm. "You need to learn some humility, dude."

His grin deepened. "Why? What's the point?"

Dallas's responding laughter made me burrow deeper into my hoodie. That laugh of his... Sighing heavily, I turned away and trudged up the beach, the sound of cheers and crashing waves fading behind me.

Drew was already at the coffee shop when I arrived. He sat at the same corner table Dallas had chosen, frowning at a laptop screen. He wore a British driving cap and a plaid scarf. Maybe he was taking the director look a step too far, sitting there surrounded by the Bean's usual tie-dyed hippie crowd.

He glanced up as I approached, giving me a tight smile. "Hello, Vivian."

"Hi. Thanks for meeting me. I know you're busy." I sat across from him, wishing my churning stomach would settle.

He shrugged. "Always time to discover new talent."

This was the tricky part, pretending interest in the talent show when I didn't have any talents. Recommending books was hardly a crowd-pleaser.

"How's the line-up for the show so far?" I took a sip of tea, stalling.

"Decent." He flicked a glance toward his screen. "Though we don't have as much variety in the musical acts as I'd like."

An image of Dallas bent over a cello flashed on the

movie screen in my head. "Really?"

Drew shook his head. "Lots of singers. Two piano players." He shrugged and straightened his scarf. "Very pedestrian."

Ew. I hated pretentious language, especially during a normal conversation. I imagined Dallas smirking about target recon and squirmed in my seat.

"So tell me about your act. I was surprised you wanted to meet." He sipped from his own cup of tea, Earl Grey, of course. Maybe he thought he was Shady Cove's James Lipton, running his own *Inside the Actor's Studio* show.

"No offense intended," he continued. "I just couldn't recall you participating in drama or music. Or speech competitions." He frowned slightly.

I felt like I was talking to the guidance counselor, not someone I could potentially date. Definitely not someone to go to the Surfer Ball with. Great; ten minutes in and I wanted to bail. Dallas would gloat like crazy. I squeezed my eyes shut. It didn't matter what McNerdy thought. I forced myself to smile at Drew.

Drew raised his eyebrows, watching me curiously. "I don't suppose you have an unusual musical talent? Something not involving Katy Perry imitations?"

That made me laugh and gave me an idea.

"You know the cello guys? The ones who toured with Elton John?" I asked.

Drew tilted his head. "Yes, of course, 2Cellos. The perfect blend of classical and popular music. Commercially appealing." He eyed me speculatively. "I don't suppose you have a way to contact them?"

"No, of course not." I sipped my tea, which definitely wasn't calming my nerves. "But I know someone like them. Well, I mean he plays the cello."

"Is he any good?"

"Uh…" He'd been playing for ten years. He had to be good. Besides, everything about Dallas screamed perfectionist. If he'd tackled the cello the way he did developing our software and researching book categories, he had to be good. Maybe not hot Croatian good but definitely talent-show good. "Yes."

Drew nodded. "So why isn't he talking to me? He's not an arrogant prima donna, is he?"

"What? No. He's…um…shy. He's new in town." I crossed my fingers under the table to cover my white lie. Dallas definitely wasn't shy, but he wasn't a prima donna, either.

"Ah. Vespa Guy." Drew nodded as though he knew all about Dallas.

"Yes, Vespa Guy. Also known as Dallas Lang."

"Well, if he's interested, I'd love to have him audition." He narrowed his eyes. "No promises, though. I don't do favors."

I grimaced, feeling a tiny lick of anger flare in my chest. "I'm not asking you for a favor."

"Aren't you?" Drew reached for a stack of papers and straightened them.

Wow. This was so not going the way I'd planned. I heard Dallas's voice in my mind. *"Was there any sort of recon done for this mission? Or are the targets totally random?"* I heard Jaz, too. *"Drew? Really? He's not your type. At all."* I did a quick check-in with my hormones, which were comatose.

My phone pinged from my bag. Grateful for the interruption, I retrieved it, my hormones fluttering to life when I saw a text from Dallas. *"How's it going? Jaz says he has 0 zing."*

Jaz. She'd told him about the zing meter?

I hesitated, then typed, *"This is a covert mission. Please cease all cellular communications."*

"Do you have any other talent show prospects for me?" Drew drummed his fingers impatiently on the table. "Because if not, I have places to be."

"No other prospects," I told Drew, trying to refocus on the conversation.

He closed his laptop. "Well, thanks for the referral. Tell Dallas I'll be in touch."

I swallowed. How would Dallas react when I told him I'd volunteered him? Maybe I'd just forget to mention it altogether. I could track down Drew in a few days and tell him Dallas had changed his mind. "Sure, I'll tell him," I lied.

Drew gathered his papers and I noticed his leather laptop bag had monogrammed initials. How had I missed all the warning signs?

My phone pinged with another text. *"Msg rec'd. Recommend abort mission. Return to base for refueling."*

I sent him a row of question marks.

"Pizza. Toff and Claire won. C U @ Slice? Everyone's going."

Everyone was going to Slice of Heaven? A twinge of jealousy snaked through me as I pictured Dallas laughing with all the surfer girls. Amy was right. Surfing was sexy. And Dallas had just watched Claire and the other girls rock their stuff.

Maybe it was just as well. If he didn't find his own RC target, I was going to have to find someone for him. And I definitely didn't want to do that.

"Have fun," I texted, my fingers flying quickly before I could chicken out. *"Don't worry about my mission. Worry about your own, soldier."*

I took another sip of tea, which tasted bitter and cold. After Drew left I waited, but Dallas never replied.

"Virtue is a relative term."
—Spock

CHAPTER SIXTEEN

SUNDAY, SEPTEMBER 7

Since it was Sunday, Mom was gone, restoring her serenity with Natasha and the meditation posse. We'd had a good laugh when I had to chase her down the deck steps before she left wearing her jammies. I knew that meant her current book project was going well.

I was grateful for a day to myself in the store. I hadn't heard back from Dallas last night, which bothered me way more than it should. I hoped to make a lot of progress on the inventory without him. The sooner it was finished, the sooner he'd be out of my hair. And my heart.

The bell on the door jingled and Mrs. Sloane entered, leaning on her cane.

"Hi, doll," she said, fluffing her hair. "Romance deficiency. Need my fix."

I smiled, happy to see her. "What are you in the mood for?" Based on all the data entry I'd done last week, I knew our stock better than ever.

"Hmm." She made her way toward the romance shelves slowly, leaning heavily on her cane. I hurried around the counter to give her an arm to lean on. She winked at me.

"That book Amy had us read for book club was excellent. Maybe another gothic?"

I was about halfway through Amy's book. It was old-school but I had to admit the brooding hero had a certain appeal. Dallas had suggested Castle Crazies as the category name for gothics. I'd rejected it. Instead we'd compromised on Castle Cravings. I pushed away the image of us laughing together, arguing over the name.

"This one's awesome." I pulled a book from the shelf. "Just the right blend of scary and swoony."

Mrs. Sloane flipped it over to read the back blurb. "Mm hm," she mumbled to herself. "I'll take it." She gave me a mischievous smile. "I heard about a new werewolf shape-shifter series. It's supposed to be hotter than the one we read for our book club." She fumbled in the pocket of her sweater and pulled out a slip of paper. I read the author's name and smiled. "Definitely hot," I whispered conspiratorially.

"I think I'll stay for awhile. That coffee smells delicious."

We always kept a pot of coffee brewed for customers who liked to sit and peruse books.

"Sure," I said. "You sit down; I'll bring it to you." A few minutes later I sat with her at one of the small tables.

"How's the Shady Cove Retirement Center? Anything exciting happening?"

She snorted. "I knew living with old people would be boring, but that place..." She shook her head. "A few of us like to get out and about. But most of the folks can't go out or don't want to." She took a sip of coffee. "There's a new lady who reads as much as I do. Her name's Bertie. I met her grandson. Nice young man, except he never took off his sunglasses."

Retirement homes scared me. I was terrified of getting old, but maybe I'd end up like Mrs. Sloane, feisty and full of spunk. And reading lots of sexy books.

"I have a list of books to bring back for my friends," Mrs. Sloane said. "The ones who can't get out." She reached into her sweater pocket again, pulling out a piece of paper that had been folded into a tiny square.

I took it, carefully unfolding the paper. The handwriting was spidery and shaky. "Um, I'm not sure I can read this." I felt bad, imagining myself desperate for books and unable to get to a bookstore or library.

Mrs. Sloane took the paper and held it out in front of her, narrowing her eyes. "Bertie has the worst penmanship I've ever seen." She sighed. "I know she likes romances, but I'm not sure which type."

"Um, does she know how to use a computer? Maybe she could order books online."

She laughed. "Sweetie, I know it's easy for your generation, but only a few of us at the center know how to use the internet. And not everyone can afford to buy books."

I fiddled with the zipper on my hoodie. There had to be some way to help people get access to books. The library was small, and only open a few days a week because of budget cuts. Even if the library was open 24/7, it didn't matter to the shut-ins.

As I sipped my coffee, I thought of Dallas's software, of the giant database of books we'd have once the inventory was complete. Maybe the seniors didn't know how to use computers, but Dallas had showed me some of the reports we'd be able to print.

Excited, I leaned across the table. "I have an idea," I said. "What if I brought the books to you and everyone else at the center?"

Mrs. Sloane's eyes lit up. "Do you think you could?"

"I'm pretty sure I can. I should be able to print out a list of all the books we have in stock. Everyone at the center could go through it and mark what books they want. Then I could deliver them." I got even more excited as I thought about it. I could bring my laptop and record transactions and keep track of the trades. We could donate a lot of the older books to the center so they wouldn't have to pay for them. And I could make recommendations based on prior reads.

Mrs. Sloane clapped her hands together. "Oh, Vivian, what a marvelous idea! I can't tell you how happy this will make people."

Matching readers to books was my super power, not to mention, it didn't involve boys or hormones or my RC mission at all. It would just be me and books and readers. Heaven.

"I'll ask Mom to call the director of the center so they know it's legit."

Mrs. Sloane smiled at me. "Don't underestimate yourself, doll. I don't think you need anyone to vouch for you."

'd just locked up the store when Mom called from her cell. "Paul and Toff are coming for dinner."

"Again?" This shared family dinner thing was new. Paul and Mom went out every weekend, but I wondered what this forced family time meant for Mom and Paul. Were they getting more serious? Or just pretending we were the Brady Bunch, only with two kids instead of six?

"Vivvy." Mom's voice sounded disappointed.

"It's fine," I reassured her. "What are we cooking?"

"We're not. You've worked all afternoon, and I'm too tired. Paul and Toff are supplying dinner."

"I hope it's edible."

Mom laughed. "They're getting lasagna from Spinelli's."

"Sounds great," I lied. I didn't want to be social tonight, but I couldn't bail. Mom would be hurt if I did. Plus, Toff would just bust into my room and drag me downstairs to eat. He had boundary issues sometimes.

As soon as we finished dinner, I'd make up some excuse and escape to my room. I needed to post a review of the latest sci-fi romance I'd read, starring a smoking hot spaceship captain. The sci-fi was secondary to the romance, so there was a lot of blog noise about the book not being "real" sci-fi. I'd gotten into an online debate with another review blogger about space operas, *Star Trek, Firefly,* and a whole bunch of other stuff only book nerds and sci-fi nerds cared about.

Drew texted me just as Paul's old VW van pulled into our driveway. I ignored the text, watching from the window as Paul and Toff emerged from the van with foil containers of food and a bottle of wine. From a distance they looked more like brothers than father and son.

My phone pinged with that annoying look-at-me reminder so I opened Drew's message. *"Did you talk to Vespa guy about auditioning yet?"*

Why was he so impatient? *"No."*

"One of my acts dropped out. Ask him if he can try out this week."

I chewed my bottom lip. Maybe I should tell Dallas about it. Maybe he liked being on stage.

"Wordworm! Where are you, brainiac?" Toff's voice floated up the stairs. I closed my eyes in frustration. My life would be so much easier if I could live on a planet of women.

Toff knocked on my door. "You decent in there or is it my lucky day?"

Gross. "Don't you have kitchen stuff to do? I'm sure the parents need your help."

"The parents are busy sucking face, which is why I escaped to your room." He rattled the doorknob. "Let me in. I need to talk to you."

Uh oh. He sounded serious, the laughter gone from his

voice. A tingle of warning crawled up my spine as I crossed the room to unlock the door.

"Hey." He frowned down at me, which made the tingle increase. "Okay if I come in?"

I stepped back, gesturing him inside. "Did someone get eaten by a shark?" A girl could hope, I thought, picturing Jake being pulled under water, arms flailing.

Toff smiled faintly, then plopped into my desk chair. He picked up a paper clip and started twisting it into weird shapes, not looking at me.

Nervous, I perched on the edge of my bed. "What's up, Flipper? You're freaking me out."

He glanced at me, his eyes troubled, then he refocused on the paper clip mangling. "I, uh, heard a rumor." He looked up at me, still not smiling. "Did you…were you and Jake…" His voice faded and he took a breath, dropping his gaze to his paperclip. "Did you two, like, hook up over the summer?"

No. No. No. What had Jake told Toff? Who else had he told? I pictured Dallas and my stomach twisted. I couldn't look at Toff. I tugged at a loose thread on my comforter, swallowing over the lump that appeared in my throat

My chair squeaked as Toff shifted. "So it's true."

"I can't believe Jake told you." I raised my eyes to find him watching me intently. His sky blue eyes were cloudy, his lips a thin line.

He shrugged. "It doesn't matter."

Anger shot through me. "Yeah, it does, Toff. I don't want anyone to know about…what happened."

Toff glared at me. "Why not? Everyone knew how you felt about Jake."

My pulse pounded in my ears. "They did?"

Toff rolled his eyes. "The way you always watched him… hard to miss, Viv." He glared at his paper clip, twisting it. "I just didn't think you were...you know." He broke the paper clip in half.

"Didn't think I was what?" I snapped.

He shrugged, not looking at me. "I never thought you'd sleep with someone like him."

Air whooshed out of me like he'd punched me. A tornado of chaotic emotions swirled through me—embarrassment that he thought I'd done something I hadn't, combined with anxiety about what lies Jake was telling, and to whom.

No, I hadn't slept with Jake, but what if I had? Would that make me a bad person? And what about Jake? I doubted Toff would say the same thing to him. He'd probably high-five him.

"Get out," I whispered, pointing at my door. I was *not* having this conversation with him. I was mortified...and pissed off...and needed him to leave.

"Viv, wait. I'm sorry. I didn't mean—"

"You said exactly what you meant, Toff. Now get out."

He stood up, looking contrite. "Just go." I pointed at the door again, trembling with anger and embarrassment.

He sighed in exasperation, but he left, closing the door quietly behind him.

I finally let the tears flow, wrapping my arms tightly around my torso. Was I going to end up with a reputation just for kissing? The irony practically killed me. And why was it just girls who were called sluts? No one ragged on Toff for hooking up with all the surfer girls. The double standard had always bothered me and to feel like one of my friends was judging me on that same standard infuriated me.

No way was I going downstairs for dinner.

Flopping back on my bed, I pictured the beautiful planet from the *Star Trek* episode where Spock fell in love. Paradise, where everyone was happy all the time. I'd give anything to be able to beam myself there and never come home again.

• • •

Toff and I didn't speak to each other during dinner. Mom had insisted I join them, even when I pleaded an upset stomach. Mom and Paul watched us like we were lab specimens, occasionally sharing worried parental looks, punctuated with frowns and hyperactive eyebrows.

I ate half-heartedly, not even tasting the marinara sauce. I stood up with my nearly full plate. "I'll clean up," I said, turning away from the table.

"But we're not finished yet," Mom protested.

"I just remembered I left dessert in the van," Paul said. "Toff, can you and Viv go get it?"

Like a pouty kid I faced Paul, glowering. "Do we both need to go?"

"Vivvy." Mom revved up her warning voice.

"There's a box of books in there, too, for the store," Paul said. "I got it from one of my tenants who moved out yesterday." Paul owned a duplex close to the beach and rented out one side to a rotating crew of surfers who came to learn from him or just be beach bums for awhile.

Toff's chair legs screeched on the tile floor as he stood up. "I've got it." He set his napkin on his chair and brushed past me.

Mom's face went hyperactive, sending me all sorts of messages. I banged my glass on the table. "Fine," I growled and stomped after Toff.

Outside, Toff leaned against the van looking across the main road toward the sun setting over the ocean. The fading dusty striations of orange and red reminded me of a vintage postcard.

"It's your business, who you hook up with," Toff said as soon as I got within hearing distance.

"You're right, it is. But we didn't...it's not what you

think." I spoke through gritted teeth because if I didn't stay angry I'd start crying. I hated losing control of my feelings like this, especially over someone who hadn't even treated me decently.

Toff turned to look at me. The breeze mussed his sun-streaked surfer hair. His blue eyes fixed on mine, and I knew most girls would love to trade places with me right now. But I didn't feel any zings as we waited for each other to speak. Instead I felt awkward, and angry, and a weird pressure to justify my actions, like my big brother had found me out.

But you didn't do anything wrong, I told myself. *You didn't use Jake. He used you.*

"Do you want to tell me what happened?" His arms crossed over his chest.

I looked away to focus my thoughts.

"What did Jake tell you?" I kept my eyes on the setting sun. Just a few more seconds and it would dip below the horizon, sort of like my heart was about to sink as I told Toff the truth.

He sighed next to me. "It doesn't matter. I want to hear your version."

I leaned against the van, letting the fading warmth from the metal seep into me. Toff had been my friend since kindergarten. He was always there for me, teasing and joking, yeah, but always sweet. I knew I could trust him. Maybe he could counteract whatever rumors asshat Jake was spreading.

"It was a few weeks before school started. Jake came in the store to get books for his grandma."

He nodded, keeping his eyes on the sunset instead of me.

I swallowed. "Anyway, he asked if I...asked me to meet him, down in the cove after curfew." I shrugged. "So I did."

"Of course you did."

"What's that supposed to mean?"

He gave me a rueful smile. "Like I said, you've lusted after him since kindergarten."

I smacked him on the arm. "Kindergartners don't lust."

He raised an eyebrow. "Okay. Puppy love. Crazy crush. Whatever you want to call it. You've had it bad for Jake forever."

I turned away, embarrassed. "Not anymore." I took a breath. "So yeah, I met him. It was…well, you know how I felt about him…"

My voice faded away. I wasn't going to share the gory details but I wanted him to know that whatever Jake was saying wasn't true. "We didn't um…it was mostly just kissing." I felt Toff tense next to me but he didn't say a word. "He, uh, you know…wanted more. But…" I took a deep breath, gulping in sea-scented air for strength, listening to the gulls cry out as they swirled overhead.

"I asked him to meet me for lunch. Smoothies, whatever. More than once. He always had some excuse." I shrugged, fighting back tears. I'd been such an idiot not to see right through him. "Anyway." My voice was ragged. "When I didn't want to…you know…that was it. He dumped me."

Toff stepped away from the van, hands stuffed in his pockets, staring straight ahead, his jaw taut. I shivered as the breeze turned colder now that the sun had set.

"You knew his reputation, Viv." He practically spat out the words.

I whirled toward him. "You're blaming *me*?" White hot anger surged through me. "I should've known you'd defend him. Bros before hos or whatever."

He stepped close, his eyes flashing. "*What*? You think I'm defending *him*?" Toff closed his eyes briefly, running his hands through his tangled hair, frustration emanating from him like smoke from a bonfire. "Damn it, Viv. The guy's a douche. I want to kill him right now." He stared down at me, vibrating with intensity. He bit out his next words. "He's an asshole."

"Yeah," I said. "I figured that much out."

Toff sighed and kicked at the ground. "He always is, but it doesn't stop girls from throwing themselves at him."

"That's total BS, Toff. Why is it cool for Jake to be a total player, but whatever girl he's been with is a slut? You ever hear of a double standard?" I pushed past him, yanked open the van door and reached in to grab the pastry box.

"Viv, wait. You know that's not what I'm saying."

I couldn't deal with him right now. He said he didn't blame me, but it sure felt like he did. It infuriated me, but it also hurt, cutting much deeper than I would've thought. I practically ran back to the house, stumbling up the steps to the deck.

I was done with boys. All of them.

CHAPTER SEVENTEEN

CLARION CALLER - SEPTEMBER 15ᵗʰ
Meet Our New Senior, Dallas Lang
By Vivian Galdi

You've probably noticed the new guy driving the Vespa to school. Senior Dallas Lang (aka Vespa Guy) moved to Shady Cove from Milwaukee, Wisconsin last spring. His dad teaches in the Engineering school at UC, so that must mean Dallas is a brainiac, but we guessed that because of the cute nerd glasses. A rabid Packers fan, Dallas might show up in a cheesehead hat some day. You've probably noticed lots of red University of Wisconsin Badgers clothing in his wardrobe.

Random factoids: Dallas has played the cello for ten years and is a whiz at computer coding. When asked if he might become a professional cellist some day, going on tour like the 2Cello sensations, Dallas refused to answer, making this reporter wonder what other secret talents our new classmate might be hiding.

Dallas misses his friends from Wisconsin but is looking forward to making new friends. In fact, this reporter has it on

good authority that he loves to dance. Pay attention, ladies,
and some of you gents: The Surfer Ball is just around the
corner.

Dallas slammed the newspaper on the lunch table, startling Amy, Jaz, and me.

After my argument with Toff, the last thing I needed was another boy getting in my face. Even a smexy nerd-hot boy who looked even cuter than usual in a faded yellow polo shirt and plaid shorts. "You get mugged by Ralph Lauren?" I snarked. A tiny part of me knew I shouldn't lash out at Dallas, but the all-boys-are-worthless part of me was louder.

Jaz snorted with laughter, but I kept my eyes on Dallas, whose flashing green eyes bore into mine.

"I thought you said nobody reads the newspaper." He crossed his arms over his chest.

"Nobody does." I shrugged, trying to act nonchalant even though it felt as if a swarm of butterflies were swirling from my stomach to my throat. I reached up to brush a stray curl behind my ear and shot a glance at the surfer table. Toff had been watching me like a hawk all freaking day. His gaze shifted from me to Dallas.

"Well, somebody must read it. Three girls asked me to the Surfer Ball this morning." He ran a hand through his spiky hair. A jolt of jealousy surged through me.

"Sounds like Viv did you a favor," Jaz piped up. "Making you instantly popular and getting you a date to the most awesome event of the year."

Dallas rolled his eyes. "I'm not interested in popularity."

"Hey cheesehead!" A voice boomed across the courtyard, and we all turned toward it. It was newspaper Nathan, sports columnist extraordinaire. He grinned at Dallas. "Packers suck, dude! You gotta be a 'Niners fan if you live here."

"'Niners suck!" One of Nathan's friends yelled. "Raiders rule."

"Chargers!" someone else yelled.

Ig chose that moment to cruise by our table. "Save me a dance, Dallas?" He winked, but kept moving as Jaz snorted with laughter.

Dallas turned back to me, frustration etching his face. "See what I mean?"

I bit the inside of my lip. I hadn't expected this. I honestly didn't think many people read the paper, even the online version.

"Sorry," I said, but my heart wasn't in it. I was still too distracted by my own drama. Jake had given me the evil eye in homeroom this morning, and dreadhead Claire had stared at me in the bathroom as if she wanted to say something, but when I'd returned her stare, she'd scurried away.

Besides, who complained about getting asked to a dance by three different people?

Dallas watched me while I stirred my yogurt. What did he want from me? An apology for writing a funny profile that got him noticed?

"I thought it was a good article," Amy said quietly. "Funny. But with some interesting facts about you." She sipped from her juice bottle. "Plus, Viv said you're cute."

"I said his *glasses* are cute," I corrected, kicking Amy under the table. I snuck a glance at him. Yep. Still cute, even when he was angry.

"So, who's the lucky girl taking you to the dance, Dallas?" Jaz asked, elbowing me hard. "Or are you breaking a school record and going with all three girls?"

Dallas sighed and shoved his hands in his pockets. He glared at Jaz, then his eyes locked on mine. "I'm not going with any of them. Vivian, I—"

"Vespa guy!" Drew scuttled up to our table like a beetle,

dressed completely in black, including his fedora. "Just the man I'm looking for. Can you audition today after school?"

Drew squinted and did that stupid face-framing thing with his hands, zooming in on Dallas's face pretending to be a movie director. "Not quite as hot as the Croatians, but you'll definitely attract some interest."

Dallas stared at him, confusion replacing his frustration with me. "What are you talking about?"

Drew glanced at me. "You didn't tell him about the audition? I thought you said he wanted to do the show?"

Could this day get any worse?

"What show?" Dallas asked.

"The Shady Cove Talent Show," Drew said. "Annual tradition of surprisingly decent acts. Directed by *moi*." Drew frowned at me, then refocused on Dallas. "Vivian tells me you're an amazeballs cellist."

Jaz choked on her drink. "Straight guys don't say amazeballs, Drew."

Drew shot her an impatient glance. "I do." He put his hands on his hips and narrowed his eyes at Dallas. "So are you amazeballs? And can you try out today?"

Dallas tilted his head to the sky and closed his eyes. Everything about his posture screamed maximum frustration, and it was all my fault. I never should've told Drew about the cello thing. I grabbed my yogurt and scooted to the end of the bench. "I've gotta go," I mumbled, turning away to avoid eye contact with Drew or Dallas. I took off, practically running.

"Vivian, wait!" a voice called after me but I ignored it, making a beeline for the nearest doors.

Once inside, I hurried to the library. I headed for the farthest table hidden behind a spinning rack of manga. I sank onto the floor and buried my head in my arms. Faces swirled in my mind: Jake, Toff, Dallas, and Drew. All these boys driving me crazy, some in bad ways, and one in a disconcertingly good way, but I'd just totally pissed him off.

I stretched out my legs and tried to focus on my yoga breathing. I visualized my bookshelf at home because it was my favorite calming image. My heart rate had finally begun to slow down when my phone pinged. Three times.

From Toff: *"U ok?"*

From Jaz: *"Where u at, girl?"*

From Dallas: *"Can't make it to work tomorrow."*

I stared at my phone then typed my replies.

To Toff: *"I'm fine."*

To Jaz: *"Witness protection. C U after school."*

To Dallas: *"Whatever."*

I felt like a defective Midas. Instead of turning everything I touched into gold, I turned everything to crap.

"Dang, girl. You sure know how to stir up trouble." Jaz grinned as she fastened her bike helmet.

"Me? You're the biggest trouble stirrer I know."

She fluttered her eyelashes innocently. "I have no idea what you're talking about. Anyway, we're talking about you."

"I don't want to talk about me." I couldn't wait to leave school and get home.

She looked surprised. "You don't want a replay of what happened between Drew and Dallas after you ran away like a scared little baby?"

I glanced anxiously toward Dallas's Vespa. He'd be here any minute. "Let's go. You can tell me while we ride."

Jaz resumed her story once we reached the bike path. "Okay, so after you bolted, Dallas was like, 'What talent show? What are you talking about?' And Drew's all, 'Viv told me you're awesome on cello and you want to be in the show.'

"And Dallas was like, 'When did she tell you that?' And Drew's all, 'She asked me out. I think she likes me but used your audition as an excuse to meet me for coffee. But she's not my type.' You should've seen Dallas's face! He was shocked. Or maybe pissed. It's hard to tell with him."

"Wait," I interrupted, my heart beating one hundred miles per hour. "Drew made it sound like I was into him? Oh my God." Why had I ever put him on my RC list?

Jaz laughed as we pedaled uphill. "That guy's ego is bigger than his whole body."

I shuddered. Now Dallas thought I liked Drew. Great. "I never should've started this stupid replacement crush mission. It's a disaster."

"You know what I'm going to say."

I strained as the hill's incline increased, breathing harder. "Go ahead." The words came out between gasps for air.

"I. Told. You. So."

"Feel better?"

Jaz shot me a grin as we crested the top of the hill. "Yeah. So anyway, after Drew said you weren't his type, Dallas got super pissed off. He told Drew he wasn't interested in auditioning for his stupid show. And Drew said, 'So perhaps Vivian exaggerated your abilities.' And Dallas looked ready to punch Drew, but then Toff came over—"

"Toff? What the heck?"

Jaz shot me a look. "I know, right? So anyway, Toff's all, 'Is there a problem?' And Drew gets all puffed up, which was funny because next to Toff and Dallas he's totally scrawny. And Drew's like, 'The biggest problem just ran away.' And Toff's like 'Shut up about Viv, Drew,' and Dallas was all, 'Yeah, I think the real problem here is you.' And Amy and I were like oh my God, they're both going to beat up Drew."

Jaz took a deep breath. "But they didn't. Drew took off and Toff and Dallas were fist-bumping and all, 'That guy's an ass.' And then they started talking about surfing lessons or whatever." Jaz took another breath. "You've gotta stop this RC madness, dude."

I screeched to a stop and stared at Jaz.

A guy on a mountain bike swore as he swerved to pass us. Jaz dismounted and walked to the scenic overlook. I followed her, the butterfly swarm in my stomach making me want to puke.

"Don't give me that 'Whatever do you mean, dear Jasmine?' innocent face. You know what I mean. Take Toff off your list because Amy likes him and you don't. Take everyone off that damn list except the McNerd."

Her eyes blazed. She wasn't kidding around. "Amy likes Toff?" So I'd been right about that.

Jaz rolled her eyes. "Earth to Vivvy. Don't you ever notice how shy she gets whenever he's around?"

"Yeah." I nodded, thinking of how she almost fainted when Toff unzipped his wet suit. "Why didn't she tell me?"

Jaz shrugged. "She thought since you wanted to put him on your RC list, she wouldn't get in the way of potential true love." She sighed, shaking her head. "For someone who's supposed to be a romance expert, you're totally screwing up, Viv. Big time."

A heavy sigh escaped me and floated on the wind toward the ocean. I wished I could follow it. I felt like a terrible friend for being so clueless. I'd have to make it up to Amy somehow.

"TSTL," I whispered.

"TS what?" Jaz asked, frowning.

"Too Stupid to Live. The worst kind of heroine." *Like me.* "God, it's so much easier to read about this type of drama than actually live it."

"Maybe. But wouldn't you rather fall in love for real than just read about it?"

I started to lean against the stone wall, but it was covered with seagull poop, the perfect metaphor for my day. "I'm not falling in love. Never again."

"You were never in love with Jake. That was lust, pure and simple. I bet you two never even talked for more than five minutes."

Jaz's ridiculous platform boots appeared in my field of vision as I stared at the ground.

"Anyway," she said, "you're not stupid. You're my best friend and I love you, but you have to get a grip." I looked up to see her smiling, but then she crossed her arms over her vintage Journey concert T-shirt. "As for Dallas, he is *so* pissed off with you."

"I know," I mumbled.

"But it's because he likes you. A lot."

I sighed next to her. "I don't know. After the newspaper article and the talent show thing, I'm pretty sure Dallas hates me."

Jaz laughed softly. "Try telling him you're sorry and see what happens."

"What do you mean?" I turned from the waves to face her.

"I'm picturing a moonlit night. You apologize for making him the laughingstock of the school—"

"He's not a laughingstock."

"Debatable. Anyway, he thinks he is and that's what matters. So you apologize. He glares at you for about five seconds, then sweeps you into his arms and gives you the hottest kiss of your life. A million times hotter than Jake."

My whole body burned with anticipation as Jaz described the kiss. The totally imaginary kiss that was never going to happen.

She was right, but I couldn't admit it. I grabbed my bike. "I need to get home. My shift starts in ten minutes and Mom gets panicky when I'm late, especially when she's in the middle of writing a new book."

I didn't see the ocean or the beach as we rode. All I saw were the hurt faces of my friends. And I was the cause of the pain, even though I never meant to be.

Love sucked.

"Come on, Spock. Let's go mind the store."
— Captain Kirk

CHAPTER EIGHTEEN

TUESDAY, SEPTEMBER 16

"I'm so pleased you came up with this idea, Vivian."

I sat across from Ms. Garcia, the director of the senior center, as we discussed the details of my mobile book service. We'd agreed on one afternoon every other week, working around my schedule at the bookstore.

"Let's take a tour," she said, pushing her chair away from her desk.

We walked down a hallway that smelled like antiseptic cleaner mixed with burned food. Ick. I squared my shoulders. The least I could do was come here a couple times a month with books. Books could take people away from reality, and I bet a lot of people here needed that type of escape.

As we rounded a corner, I crashed into a tall body walking quickly. He jumped back, adjusting the mirrored sunglasses on his nose and tugging down his baseball cap.

"Sorry," he muttered, head down.

"Hector!" Ms. Garcia exclaimed. "How nice to see you again. Bertie's lucky to have such a devoted grandson."

I studied him. He looked familiar.

He cleared his throat and dropped his head even lower,

speaking in almost a whisper. "Just checking in to see how she's doing."

"Well, you let me know if she needs anything." Ms. Garcia gave me a little push toward Hector. "This is Vivian Galdi. Her mom owns the local bookstore and Vivian has volunteered to run a mobile book service for the residents. Your grandmother will be able to order books she wants from Vivian's inventory."

Hector raised his head slightly. I assumed he was looking at me from behind his mirrored shades. "Excellent," he said, and the second I heard him speak I knew who he was.

My mouth dropped open, then I clamped it shut. I would not freak out like Jaz; I'd play it cool even though I was standing within sniffing distance of rock star Fisk Vilhelm, code name Hector, apparently.

Ms. Garcia's cell phone rang from her pocket. "Excuse me." She stepped away. "I've got to take this."

Hector/Fisk leaned in close. "Please don't blow my cover. I'm begging you."

I nodded. "I won't. I promise."

He took a deep breath. "It's cool of you to bring them books. My gran likes romances." His neck reddened slightly, and I guessed he was rolling his eyes behind his shades. "She goes through them like crack." He cleared his throat. "I mean, um, candy, or whatever."

I laughed. "It's okay. I sort of consider myself a pusher, of books I mean. Especially romance."

He removed his sunglasses, and I looked into his rock star eyes. Yowza. He almost put Dallas to shame. Almost.

"No kidding? That's awesome. Can I count on you to keep her supplied?" He reached into his pocket, pulled out his wallet, and handed me a hundred dollar bill. "Will this cover her for a while?" He grinned at me. I liked the way his eyes crinkled when he smiled. He seemed normal. Not like a world famous rock star.

I nodded mutely.

"Awesome. But please don't tell anyone you saw me here. I come here a lot to check on my gran. She's so important to me. I'd hate to have to stop visiting her because the paparazzi were camped out here waiting for me."

I nodded vigorously. Thank God it was me he'd run into, not Jaz. It would kill me not to tell her about this, but I couldn't.

"I promise," I said. "That must suck having them follow you everywhere."

He put his sunglasses back on. "Mega sucks," he agreed. "But they don't know I'm in town, so I'd like to keep it that way as long as possible."

"I swear I won't tell." I gave him the split-fingered Spock gesture; it was the only one I could think of.

He grinned. "You're a Trekkie?"

My cheeks heated. Had I seriously just geeked out in front of one of the coolest guys on the planet? Wait til I told Dallas…except I couldn't tell him. I sighed heavily.

"You okay? You look like you just lost your best friend."

"Yeah." I sighed.

He tilted his head. "Uh oh. Even worse than a best friend, isn't it? I'm guessing he was more than a friend?"

"What are you, psychic?" I couldn't believe I was talking to Fisk Vilhelm so easily.

He laughed. "You know how many love-struck girls I see on tour? You've got that same sad look in your eyes." He lowered his shades to look me in the eyes. "I'll tell you a secret. Whatever you did, he'll probably forgive you."

I stared at him, speechless.

He grinned. "I've gotta go. Vivian, right? Your mom owns the bookstore? Maybe I'll try to sneak in there some day." He wiggled his eyebrows. "Incognito."

I nodded, still at a loss for words.

He shoved his sunglasses back up to cover his eyes. "Take care of my gran. I'll make sure to leave plenty of crack money here with Ms. Garcia."

"Okay," I finally managed to speak. "I'll take care of her." I smiled. "And I never saw you here."

He returned my Vulcan salute, then he was gone.

Even though Dallas had texted me that he wasn't coming to work, he still showed up, startling me when he materialized at the counter.

"I thought you weren't coming today," I muttered, yanking out my ear buds.

"Temporary rage quit," he said. "I'm over it." He drummed his fingers on the counter and leaned against it, staring down at me.

"Rage quit?" I forced myself to meet his eyes.

"Gamer term. McNerd lingo." He didn't give me a full smile, but I thought I saw his lips twitch. "You want anything from the Bean?"

Surprised, I stuttered out a reply. "Uh…coffee? Me? No. Too much. Caffeine. I've had plenty today, I mean." I closed my eyes briefly. *Talk much, Viv?*

"Okay. Back in a few."

I held my breath until the jingle of the door's bells signaled his exit. I exhaled slowly. I thought of what Fisk said. *"Whatever you did, he'll probably forgive you."* I needed to apologize. Not for the article because that was funny, and he knew it was coming. But the whole thing with Drew and the talent show…I should definitely apologize for that.

Spock's face loomed in my mind. *"If you must apologize,*

Vivian, why agonize over it? Simply do it and move ahead with your mission."

Mission? I was having plenty of doubts about *that*, especially after Jaz's lecture. But Spock was right. Since Drew and Henry were busts, and Toff and Iggy were off the list, I'd better find some new targets so I could make a decision and stop the madness.

Hiddles wandered in, mewing loudly. I glared at him. "He'll be back soon. Cool your jets, cat." Hiddles hissed, then disappeared down the horror/thriller aisle. How appropriate.

I resumed my data entry. We'd planned another late night of inventory and data entry this week. Another night of just the two of us. My hormones were already in party mode, trying on dresses and shoes, storming around inside me like a deranged herd of sorority girls.

An older couple who'd shared a couch while sorting through potential purchases approached the counter. The woman set a stack of books on the counter just as Dallas returned with a giant green smoothie. I tried to ignore his all-consuming presence as he settled himself in the chair next to me.

"We're finally ready," the woman said. Her husband stood next to her engrossed in a spy thriller.

"I'm glad you found something you liked." I stood up to tally the books. "Are you visiting Shady Cove?"

She nodded. "We're doing a coast tour, so we're just here overnight. I read about this store in a travel magazine." She glanced around, then leaned forward to whisper. "Is it true Macy Gardner owns this store?"

I could almost feel Dallas holding in his laughter next to me. I tried to look surprised by her question.

"No." I glanced at the woman. "That's a common rumor, but it's not true."

"Oh." Her smile faded.

"Told you." Her husband glanced up from his book. "Can't believe everything you read. Probably some rumor started by the owner to drum up business."

I tensed, feeling defensive.

"Actually, this store *is* owned by an author," Dallas said. We all turned to stare at him. He narrowed his eyes at the husband. "She's very well known, but we have to sign a secrecy oath to work here. To protect her privacy." He shot me a look full of such innocence and mischievousness combined that I practically melted.

"Um, yeah, he's right." I turned back to the wife. "I'm not…we're not…allowed to say, or we'd lose our jobs. But I can tell you she's a much better writer than Macy Gardner."

The woman's eyes lit up. "Oh, I wish you could give me a hint."

The husband rolled his eyes. "What a scam."

"Mysteries," Dallas said, standing up and moving close to me, so close my knees almost buckled. He reached across the counter to take the cash the woman held. "Will that be all for you today?" He counted out her change and stuck bookmarks inside her books like I always did.

"Thank you, dear." The woman smiled at Dallas in a grandmotherly way as her husband turned and headed for the door.

"Thanks for shopping with us," I said to their retreating backs, recovering some of my composure.

"What a jerk," Dallas said as the door closed behind them.

I nodded. "No wonder she stocked up on romances."

Dallas crossed his arms over his chest, pinning me with the deadly green eyes. "You're implying people who read romances are unhappy with their own love lives?"

My entire body blushed under his penetrating stare. "No…I didn't mean…I just…" I took a breath. "People read for all sorts of reasons." I sank into my chair. "Anyway. Thanks for standing up for my mom." I forced a wobbly smile. "Even though you still don't know her pen name."

"You're welcome. And not yet, but I'm still working on it." Hiddles appeared out of nowhere as soon as Dallas sat down, jumping onto his lap. I glared at my disloyal cat, who watched me through slitted eyes.

I put my ear buds back in to listen to the hot cello duo, lying to myself that my music choice had nothing to do with Dallas. Dallas glanced at me, then dug out ear buds from his backpack and plugged them into his phone. I wondered what he was listening to but felt too shy to ask.

The bell on the front door jingled and we both glanced up to see Mrs. Sloane enter carrying her tote bag full of books. She waved at me and winked at Dallas. I removed my ear buds and hurried around the counter to meet her. After she settled into her usual chair, I poured her a cup of coffee and sat down across from her.

"Thanks, sweetie." She sipped from her mug. "I had to come in person to tell you. Everyone at the center is so excited about your book service. Ms. Garcia told everyone about it after you left."

"Wow." I leaned back against the chair, feeling a tingle of excitement. "That's great news." I paused. It probably would be best to wait to do my first visit until we'd finished the inventory. If I was going to be lugging books back and forth, I wanted to be able to track things online, not on the index cards.

I glanced at Dallas, who still had his ear buds in. His brow furrowed slightly as he stared at his screen. God, he was adorable.

"Stop it, Vivian. As I've told you before, Vulcans do not swoon."

Stupid Spock.

Mrs. Sloane gave me a knowing smile. "Have you two gone out yet?" She tilted her head toward Dallas. "On a date?"

Horrified, I whipped my head toward Dallas. Thank God his ear buds were still in, but for a second I thought I saw his lips quirk. I turned back to Mrs. Sloane. "No! No, of course not. He's just...we're just...um, he's you know, working here, that's all. There's nothing going on." I couldn't believe I was having this conversation with a silver-haired little old lady. Then I considered the number of romances she consumed and realized I shouldn't be at all surprised.

"Well, the sooner you can start the bookmobile business, the better," Mrs. Sloane said.

"Bookmobile?"

She smiled. "That's what we used to call the mobile libraries. They were giant RVs stuffed full of books. They'd park in front of our school when I was a kid. We'd pack into the bookmobile like sardines, so excited to get new books."

"Cool." I'd never heard of that.

"Have you finished Amy's book for this week's meeting?" Mrs. Sloane took a sip of coffee.

I nodded. "I liked it, even though it was kind of old school."

Mrs. Sloane's eyes twinkled behind her glasses. "There's something about a brooding hero who takes charge. I think we're biologically programmed to respond. Especially when they rescue us from the evil villain."

I laughed and darted a glance at Dallas. His lips were definitely quirking. Was he eavesdropping? His ear buds were still in, but I didn't hear the tap-tap of his keyboard.

"We need to finish the inventory," I said. "But once that's done, I'll be there." I shot another glance at Dallas and caught him staring at me. He was totally eavesdropping. Nosy McNerd. My eyes met his. Nosy, *hot* McNerd.

Swallowing, I turned back to Mrs. Sloane. "I'm guessing just another week or so. It depends on Dallas's schedule since he's helping." I waited, expecting him to speak up about his schedule, but he didn't. Instead the sound of the keyboard clicking resumed. I snuck a glance and saw him frowning at his screen.

I remembered what he'd said about battles and strategies. I had a feeling I was outmatched.

"I've been thinking," I said loudly. "Maybe we should talk about our favorite hero types at the next book club meeting. I'm going to set up a shelf of highlighted books based on hero types."

Mrs. Sloane's eyes lit up. "What a marvelous idea!" She reached up to pat her hair. "But I'm not sure if I can pick just one type."

I nodded, cocking my ears for the sound of Dallas's keyboard, which was silent again. I smirked with satisfaction. Spock's deep voice interrupted my thoughts. *"Vivian, it appears you're becoming distracted from your mission. I sense an awkward attempt at flirtation. Perhaps you should reconsider this conversation."*

I didn't want to listen to Spock right now; I wanted to trap Dallas. But why? Why was playing this game with him so intriguing? *Like I didn't know.*

"Well, we know one of your favorites," I said, ignoring Spock's imaginary glare. "The brooding hero."

Mrs. Sloane nodded. "An oldie but a goodie."

We giggled together. Dallas resumed typing, but sporadically.

"What about you?" Mrs. Sloane asked. "I remember how much you loved that book with the hero who had supernatural fighting abilities."

I sighed, remembering that hero. "My super ninja," I said. He was definitely one of my favorites. I didn't dare look at Dallas because he'd stopped typing again.

"I'm sure you can't pick just one hero type, either," Mrs. Sloane said.

"Definitely not." I stretched my arms above my head, thinking. "I guess I like complicated heroes. You know, not just one archetype."

She nodded. "Moody and brooding but also sensitive."

"Right," I agreed. "Super awesome ninja powers and an artist all rolled into one. Plus an awesome dancer."

Mrs. Sloane laughed. "You know those people don't exist in real life, my dear. That's why we read novels."

"Maybe not. But a girl can hope."

A loud feline protest sounded, followed by a thump as Hiddles landed on the floor. Mrs. Sloane and I turned toward Dallas, who'd stood up. He stared at his phone, then glanced at us. "I'll be back. I need to make a call." Then he turned and disappeared through the door to the kitchen.

Curiosity consumed me as I wondered who he was calling. Spock's voice interrupted my reverie. "*His affairs are not your concern, Vivian. You're veering dangerously off course from your mission.*"

Mrs. Sloane glanced out the windows to the parking lot where the senior center's driver waited patiently, flipping through a magazine. "I should hurry up and pick out a book. We need to stop at the market before we go back to the center."

I nodded and hoisted myself out of the chair. "Pick your hero poison." I gestured toward the romances.

"How about a pirate? It's been ages since I read one of those."

"Swashbuckling historical or modern-day corporate raider?"

"Hmm." She tapped her chin with her finger. "Let's try one of each."

"You got it." I disappeared down the aisle, trying not to obsess over who Dallas was talking with.

Maybe it was just his mom. But he wouldn't disappear for that conversation; I'd already overheard several of those when-will-you-be-home and can-you-stop-at-the-store chats.

Dallas didn't return until after I'd walked Mrs. Sloane out to the car. He stalked inside, vibrating with an intense energy I'd never seen before.

"What's wrong?" I asked.

He moved behind my chair, leaning down to grab his backpack. "I've got to go. It's kind of an emergency."

"Is everything okay?"

He scowled. "Yeah. But I've gotta do something for a few hours." He straightened, looming over me. "I know you want to finish this inventory. I can come back and work late tonight."

I swallowed as I looked up at him. He didn't seem like an adorable McNerd right now. The energy pulsing out of him was powerful and intense and very un-nerdy.

"You don't have to—" I started to say, but he cut me off, waving a hand impatiently.

"I know I don't have to. But I'm committed to finishing this project. I gave your mom my word." He closed his laptop and shoved it into his backpack. "And you," he said, almost under his breath.

"You sure everything's okay, Dallas?"

He stilled briefly when I said his name. "Yeah. Just something I need to do." He slung his backpack over his shoulder and grabbed his helmet. "Text me later about tonight. I'll be available after seven."

I nodded, discombobulated by this new Dallas I hadn't seen before.

Hiddles jumped onto the empty chair and Dallas reached down to rub his ears. "I'm sorry. I don't usually bail like this."

I shrugged. "You're not bailing. Just pressing the pause button."

"Thanks." His lips curved into a brief smile, then tensed into a thin line again. "Later," he called over his shoulder, and he was gone.

"Wow." I turned to Hiddles, who glared at me. "What was that about?" Hiddles curled into a tight ball of fur on Dallas's chair. I reached out to rub his head. He made a weird noise in his throat, but he didn't hiss.

The door jingled and a group of chattering tourists entered. Hiddles jumped off the chair and disappeared.

I put on my most welcoming smile, grateful for the distraction.

My phone pinged with a text from Dallas at 7:03 p.m. while Mom and I sat at the kitchen table eating dinner. *"Inventory?"*

I wanted to tease him about texting three minutes late, but hesitated. I didn't know where he'd gone this afternoon, and if it was something serious, I shouldn't joke.

"No texting during dinner," Mom said, but she winked when she said it.

"It's Dallas. If I don't reply he'll blow up my phone with more texts." I took a sip of juice. "He's, um, persistent."

She nodded. "I've noticed. He's quite disciplined for a teenage boy. Very unusual." She watched me like a hawk, trying to suss out my feelings for him. Sometimes I hated having a writer for a mom.

"Let me reply, then I promise no more texting." My fingers flew across the screen. *"Need 2 finish hmwk. Maybe 8-10?"*

"We're going to work tonight," I told Mom. "Just for a couple of hours. We're almost done."

She frowned. "It's a school night."

I rolled my eyes. "Mom, I'm not ten years old."

She rolled her eyes right back at me. "No kidding. But you still need your rest."

"We'll stop at ten." I paused. "Ten thirty at the latest. I want to get this done, so I can start the mobile bookstore for the senior center."

Mom's face brightened. "It's such a great idea, Vivvy. The director was so thrilled when I talked to her."

My phone pinged. *"C U @ 8."*

I set my phone aside and dug into my quinoa salad.

"There's another surf comp this Saturday," Mom said. "Do you want to go? I can handle the store."

I pictured last week's scene, with Jake and Claire tongue-fencing. "No thanks. I'd rather work."

Mom frowned. "I thought you liked the comps." Mom tugged at my curls, just like I did when I was unsettled.

"I do, but Saturdays are busy. I don't mind working."

She waited for me to say more, but I didn't. Maybe I could just fake an illness for the rest of this week.

Incurable crushitis.

"Did I ever tell you that you play a very irritating game of chess, Mr. Spock?" —*Captain Kirk*

CHAPTER NINETEEN

When I entered the store at 8:10 p.m., Dallas had already set up at his laptop, a stack of fantasy novels next to him, typing with Hiddles on his lap. I wondered when Mom had given him a key.

"Hey." He glanced up, then refocused on his screen, scowling.

"Somebody's grumpy," I said, sitting next to him.

"You would be to if you had to write a bunch of stupid college application essays *and* babysit for your sister *and* finish this inventory *and*—" He stopped short, shooting me a guilty look.

Wow. Okay then. I gulped as I sat next to him. "You didn't have to come back tonight. I could've—"

"Don't worry about it. I've got it handled."

He wouldn't look at me, his jaw tight and shoulders rigid. But in spite of his attitude, he smelled like soap and whatever else made him smell way too good. Why had he showered? My face flamed, imagining activities that could cause him to sweat.

"Can't you, um, use the same college essay for all your

applications?"

He shot me a withering look. "I can tell you haven't started *yours* yet."

I narrowed my eyes and handed him a Reese's peanut butter cup. "Try one. I hear chocolate soothes the savage beast."

He took the candy and unwrapped it, watching me the whole time, then shoved it into his mouth and turned back to the computer. Still not smiling.

"So we've made it to sci-fi and fantasy," I said. "Now it's my turn to make fun of your categories."

He swallowed his candy and raised an eyebrow. "Stereotyping again, I see."

"Trolls, goblins, and brownies, oh my."

He stopped typing to look at me. "Are you creating weird category names for these books, too?"

I shook my head, embarrassed that he hadn't laughed. "No. Just a sorry attempt at a joke." *And lighten your cranky mood.*

"Ah. Noted." His body relaxed, and I could almost feel the tension easing out of him.

He spun his chair so he faced me, eyes all green and glinty behind his glasses, making me crazy. "It's possible I *do* read some of those books. But I'm not an expert like you are with your genre."

"Hmm." I tapped my chin, faking concern. "We might need to hire another genre expert."

"Or I could just research it. I'm assuming there are specialized blogs." He leaned back, crossing his arms over his chest, lips twitching. "Like the hunkaliciousheroes blog. Now *that's* a wealth of information." He cocked an eyebrow. "Granny shoes?"

Oh. My. God. He'd found my blog. How much had he read already? How many rants and raves about love and kissing and burning chemistry and...oh my God.

I hid my face in my hands, then whispered between my fingers. "How'd you figure it out?"

"You only made one tactical error. Unfortunately for you, I found it."

Frustrated, I dropped my hands and faced him. "Enough with the battle metaphors, Lang. Tell me how you did it."

He grinned, apparently over his earlier grumpiness. "You're the only blogger who listed Murder by the Sea as her favorite bookstore."

I closed my eyes. He was right; I'd put it on my page of faves and raves. I wanted to melt into the floor. He might as well have read my diary.

"You're a great writer, Vivian. You're funny, and you have strong opinions. That's cool."

I turned back to my computer, refusing to speak or look at him.

"So you're not speaking to me now?"

I shook my head. How could I possibly speak when I was this embarrassed?

He sighed next to me. "Fine."

We stayed that way, not speaking, keyboards clicking, until Mom texted me.

"My mom's bringing you dinner. She's worried you didn't have time to eat before you came back here."

He glanced up. "She doesn't need to do that."

I shrugged. "She likes feeding people, even though she's a lousy cook."

His laughter made my stomach tumble over. "Lucky for you she got Chinese food."

"Sweet." He resumed typing as his mouth curved into a smile.

We worked in near silence, the only sounds our keyboards and Hiddles purring on Dallas's lap. I wondered if I could block him from reading my blog somehow, but I doubted I could outsmart him when it came to hacking.

"My, aren't you two busy," Mom called from the store kitchen. The smell of sesame chicken made my mouth water even though I'd already eaten. "It's quiet as a church in the middle of the night."

"We're focused," I muttered.

Dallas snorted next to me, but I refused to look at him.

"Smells awesome." He stood up, stretching his long, lean body. I snuck a glance as he moved into his weird karate kid stance.

"What?" He sounded annoyed. "You do yoga; why do you think this is weird?"

"I didn't say it was weird." I spun my chair to face him.

"You're thinking it, though. You have a lousy poker face." He grinned at me, hugging his knee tighter to his chest.

"Good thing I don't gamble."

He switched legs, balancing on the other. "Don't you?"

"What's that supposed to mean?"

He shrugged. "Every battle is a gamble. You never know how a mission might turn out. "

"Come and get it, data monkeys!" Mom called over the clatter of plates and silverware.

Dallas laughed, and returned to standing like a normal person. "Let's eat, Sweet Feet."

I gaped at him, horrified he'd just called me by my blog name, but he was gone before I could think of a retort.

"So how do you like Shady Cove, Dallas?" Mom asked as I joined them in the kitchen. "Are you making new friends?"

He'd just taken a bite of rice and chicken, so I answered for him. "He likes the weather except for the fog. Misses some of his old friends." I paused. "Also, he collects trophies for some secret sport. I'm guessing miniature golf." I gave Dallas a syrupy sweet smile.

"Shady Cove is different than I expected," he said after

swallowing, keeping his eyes on me. "But Vivian has offered to help me out. Introduce me to some people I might like to get to know better."

He shot me a wicked grin, then licked his lips, distracting me from making a snarky retort.

Mom beamed at me. "That's lovely, sweetie. It's so important to make newcomers feel welcome." She turned her high beams on Dallas. "I'm so glad Vivvy is helping to ease the transition for you." She paused to sip water. "Vivvy grew up here, so she knows everyone. Who to avoid. Who you should get to know better."

Dallas's eyes sparked with amusement. "That sounds like our mission." He smirked at me. "Right, Galdi?"

I narrowed my eyes at him while Mom opened a fortune cookie, blissfully oblivious. We continued eating, shooting each other death glares. Except his were full of silent laughter while mine were full of false bravado as I wrestled desperately to calm the fireworks exploding inside of me.

Mom headed back to the house after dinner, reminding us not to work too late. As soon as Dallas and I sat down at our computers, he shot me a sideways glance. "So if you're not going to hide behind your ear buds tonight, you can help me out with something."

My stomach tumbled over. "What?"

He spun his chair and Hiddles meowed from his lap, annoyed. "My replacement girlfriend list. You owe me some names. Considering all the grief caused by your article, it's the least you can do."

My mouth dropped open. "You're serious?"

He nodded. "Sure, why not? Besides, we just told your

mom you were going to introduce me to some people. And you know my shallow criteria from the day you interviewed me."

I took a breath. He was totally messing with me.

"Plus," he said, "this crazy replacement mission seems to be working for you. At least according to Drew."

Now he was taunting me. Or was he? Maybe he thought I actually liked Drew. "Uh, I wouldn't say that."

"No? Drew seems to think so."

"Drew's an idiot." I picked up a book and glared at the beautiful fairy on the cover. I bet she didn't have to worry about replacement crushes. She probably had some hot fey boy chasing after her.

Dallas propped his ankle on his thigh, causing Hiddles to jump off his lap. "So Drew's off the list?"

I shrugged. "Yeah."

Dallas drummed his fingers on his thigh. "Who's your next target?"

"That's on a need-to-know basis. And you don't need to know."

Dallas's gaze didn't waver. "Fine. Then let's talk about *my* list."

Rolling my eyes, I tried to look annoyed rather than jealous. "You don't need a list."

He leaned back, clasping his hands behind his neck, showing off his ridiculously toned arms. I made another mental note to Google hot cello players since I still hadn't gotten around to it. Dallas's arms flexed as he watched me, making my throat go dry. "So you figured out my perfect match already?" He gave me a slow, mysterious smile. "I knew you would. Eventually."

We stared at each other for a long, tension-charged moment. When I spoke, my voice was raspy. "You don't need a list because you already have three names."

He frowned. "No I don't."

I tugged at the skirt I'd worn over patterned leggings today. Jaz told me it was sexy cute. I caught Dallas glancing at the place where my hand had just been. My pulse sped up, wondering if he thought I looked sexy cute.

"*Red alert. Red alert. Focus, Vivian. Focus.*" It wasn't Spock's voice I heard this time, but the warning voice from the original *Enterprise*. How many imaginary voices could live in my mind at once?

"Your list is the three girls who asked you to the Surfer Ball." I forced a smug smile, but I wasn't feeling it.

He blinked at me. "You're kidding."

"Nope." It was my turn to lean back in my chair. "Tell me their names."

He dropped his eyes, and a slight blush crept up his neck. My hormones protested wildly, demanding that I launch myself from my chair onto his lap. I reached for my water bottle again.

"Um, okay." He rubbed the back of his neck, still not looking at me. "One was Jamie something. Tall. Blond."

Also gorgeous, I filled in mentally. Figures. I reached for a piece of paper and wrote Jamie Quinn.

"Next," I prompted, forcing myself to sound bored.

He watched me closely, like he knew I was acting a role. I bit my lip, and his eyes shot to my mouth.

"Next," I said again.

He frowned. "Kylie."

I nodded, scrawling her name on my list. Also gorgeous. Who would have guessed all these girls had a thing for McNerds? I snuck another glance at him. Well, he didn't exactly fit the stereotype.

"And?" I said. "Last one?"

"Um, Tara, I think?"

Great. Of course the gorgeous Tara had asked him

out. Even Iggy had tried to test his gayness with her. Just imagining she and Dallas naked together made me clench my pencil so hard it cracked.

"You don't need my help, Dallas."

He tugged at his jeans. "But I don't know these girls, and you do. You can at least tell me about them."

This was frakking killing me. I could *not* do this.

Just kiss him, my hormones whispered like sirens leading me to certain death. *Just one little kiss. Then you'll know for sure if his feelings match yours.*

My hormones were psychotic. As if I'd just randomly lean across the space between us and—

Dallas's phone rang, making us both jump.

"I'll see what I can find," Dallas said to the caller. "But no promises." He disconnected. "My sister," he said, smiling sheepishly. "She wants to know if you have any more books in the Crystal Unicorn series."

"I'll check." I was grateful for an excuse to get away from him since my imagination was stuck in a repeat loop, fantasizing about kissing him.

Vivian to Spock! May-day! May-day!

I lingered in the kids' section, trying to slow my heart rate. How many guys could show up at a new school and have three uber hot girls throw themselves at him? Not many. I wished I was Becca's age, preoccupied with unicorns instead of crazy fantasies that turned me into a stuttering idiot.

I glanced at the clock: 9:35. He'd be leaving soon, then I could escape to my bedroom fortress. I couldn't wait to bury myself in a book and shut out thoughts of Dallas and stupid Drew. And Jake the Snake.

"Here." I set two Crystal Unicorn books on the desk. "No charge."

Dallas glanced at me. "Why not?"

"Consider it a peace offering, for the talent show thing." I shrugged, not meeting his gaze. "Sorry about that." I glanced up, relieved to see he looked intrigued rather than mad.

"Hmm," he said. "If I were into Crystal Unicorns, this might be a fair trade." His eyes were full of laughter, making my insides do cartwheels. "But since I am *not* a Crystal Unicorn fan, I think you need to come up with a better peace offering."

Sinking into my chair, I twisted a curl around my fingers. His eyes tracked my hand, then flicked to my face. "Well?" he prompted. "You have any better ideas?"

The ideas I had could never be said aloud. "Not really."

"I do. How about popcorn?"

"Popcorn?" I stared at him, confused. "How can you still be hungry?"

"I'm always hungry. Plus you ate half my dinner." He tilted his head toward the kitchen. "We both know there's a case of popcorn in there."

"So I make popcorn and you forgive me for throwing you under the bus with Drew?"

His easy grin made my breath catch. "Not quite. You have to watch something with me while we eat the popcorn."

I raised my eyebrows. "You're going to force me to watch a McNerd show, aren't you? Let me guess. *The Big Bang Theory?*"

His eyebrows knotted. "Go make the popcorn."

I glanced at the clock. "I told my mom we'd be done at Ten. Ten thirty at the latest."

"If we start now we'll be done by ten thirty." He wasn't giving up. "Come on, Galdi. Live dangerously."

"Fine. But then we're even, Lang."

"Popcorn," he ordered, pointing toward the kitchen.

I texted Mom while listening to the kernels explode inside the microwave like fireworks. *"Be home a little after 10:30."*

Her response flew back. *"Do I need to come over there?"*

Oh my God. *"No!"*

"Don't push it, kiddo. 10:45 or I'll come check on you."

What did she think she'd find? Dallas and me…no, I couldn't go there. I poured the popcorn into a bowl and grabbed two sodas from the fridge. When I emerged from the kitchen I heard the tinny theme song from the original Star Trek series.

"No way." I laughed as I plunked down the popcorn and sodas.

"Way," Dallas said, grabbing a handful of popcorn.

I wished we were in my house, snuggled together on the couch in front of our television. I squeezed my eyes shut, pushing away the image.

"You okay?" Dallas asked.

I opened my eyes and focused on the screen, embarrassed. Spock and some random crew member were dressed in weird orange hazmat uniforms decorated with gold swirls. I loved watching shows from the sixties because the styles were weird yet retro cool. I reached for a handful of popcorn, my hand brushing Dallas's.

"Sorry," we said at the same time, yanking our hands out of the bowl. I wondered if he'd felt the same jolt of connection I had, but I wasn't about to look at his face. Instead, I focused on the crewman I knew would end up dead because he was nameless and wearing a red shirt, which meant certain death in the Star Trek world. Lo and behold, he contracted some alien virus two minutes later.

We both cracked up at a goofy scene where the infected crewman threatened people with a butter knife, but then the guy ended up stabbing himself with it.

"Could you get injured from a butter knife?" I asked.

"Apparently so. Maybe because they're futuristic butter knives with laser edges." Dallas shot me a sideways grin.

I took a drink of soda. "So why'd you pick this particular episode?" I asked.

"Watch and learn, young Padawan."

"You're mixing up your references. *Star Wars…Star Trek*."

He rolled his eyes. "Like *I* don't know that? Just watch."

The episode was vaguely familiar, but since I'd watched them with my dad before he and Mom had split, I couldn't recall them easily.

But then a shirtless Sulu ran down a hallway, yelling and brandishing a fencing foil. Oh no. This was the episode where Nurse Chapel told Spock she loved him, and he freaked out, because he got the virus, too. The virus made people's emotions rise to the surface, sort of like when they were drunk.

I scooted my chair away from Dallas as if that would alleviate my rising anxiety. "So I'm guessing you're making me watch this because of Spock," I said, as an insurance ad filled the screen.

Dallas turned, his chair bumping into mine since we sat so close together. "Yep. I figured if you're following some weird Spock strategy as part of your mission, you should see that he doesn't always follow his Vulcan code. Sometimes his humanity wins out."

"But he only loses control because of that stupid virus. I'm not in danger of getting some alien virus that will make me all drunk and stupid."

Dallas shoved his glasses up his nose. "You honestly think you can stay logical about this? Totally ignore your feelings?"

I swallowed nervously, hardly believing we were having this conversation.

"I think I can try." I breathed. The show resumed and I turned away from him. "I'm sticking to my mission," I said softly, more to myself than him.

"All because you want a date to the stupid Surfer Ball?"

My face burned. "I-I know it sounds stupid to you…but

I'd really like to go with someone nice. Someone fun."

He watched me in that intense way that made it hard to breathe. "I'd never call you stupid." He took a drink from his soda, still watching me. "But I don't see why you're putting all this effort into something you can fix so easily."

We stared at each other, not speaking, until I broke the stalemate. "What do you mean?"

"Just ask your obvious target to the stupid dance and get it over with. I'm sure he'll say yes."

"The obvious target?" Was he saying what I thought he was?

He nodded. "I'm sure *someone* appreciated your fake Spock tattoo. Probably not Drew, though. Or the homework guy."

I turned away, focusing on Dallas's laptop screen where Nurse Chapel told Spock she loved him and he freaked out, telling her he was sorry he couldn't love her back. He escaped to a hallway and cried. Usually I laughed at the over-the-top acting in Star Trek, but for some reason I almost felt like crying, too.

Dallas scooted his chair away from the desk. "More popcorn," he said, grabbing the bowl.

"Let's pause it." I reached for his keyboard, but he put out a hand to stop me, sending sparks shooting up my arm.

"No," he said softly. "I've seen it plenty of times. You keep watching." He disappeared into the kitchen while I watched Spock have a meltdown. That would *not* be me. I'd maintain my Vulcan cool and complete my mission. The last thing I needed was more drama in my life.

I made notes on the list of girls who'd asked Dallas to the dance. When he returned with a fresh bowl of steaming popcorn, I handed him the list.

"What's this?" he asked.

"Your replacement girlfriend list. Start with Kylie." She was the nicest of the three.

My heart broke into a million pieces as I imagined them dancing together.

We both ignored Bones yelling on the screen while Dallas read my notes. He raised his eyes to mine. "You honestly think she's my top target? The best match for a McNerd like me?" He took a bite of popcorn and chewed slowly, then swallowed, his gaze never wavering from mine. "You can't think of anyone else who might be a better match?"

We stared at each other for a long moment, neither of us blinking. It took all my Vulcan cool not to snatch the list out of his hand and tell him his perfect match was sitting right here. But I didn't.

Love was dangerous. Unpredictable. I was better off reading about it. So instead of telling Dallas the truth, I just nodded, reaching for more popcorn, not even flinching as the steam burned my fingers. For the next few minutes, it took everything in me to keep the tears from falling.

"Of my friend I can only say this: of all the souls that I met on my
travels, his was the most… human."
— Captain Kirk

CHAPTER TWENTY

FRIDAY, SEPTEMBER 19TH

Somehow I managed to avoid Dallas the rest of the week, and today was a teacher planning day so we didn't have school. I had a busy day planned, including posting a new book review and interviewing Reg and his friends for the newspaper.

And *not* inviting Dallas to join me for the interviews.

Today's blog post was all about the aliens, specifically Aelyx from the Alienated series and Daemon from the Lux series. I'd bribed Jaz with a couple of free smoothies in exchange for a cool anime style drawing of the hot aliens looking steamy and kissable, and I'd posted a funny kissing quiz. The quiz asked about the best place for a first kiss (car, couch, or back row in a movie theater) and the all important first kiss question: tongue or no tongue?

After I found the perfect animated GIF to post with my blog, I texted Amy, asking her to give it one last look. She replied with a row of hearts and a thumbs-up, so I hit publish and closed my laptop, relieved to check one item off my to-do list.

I stopped into the bookstore to see Mom before I headed to the beach to find Reg and was surprised to see Dallas leaning on the counter talking to Mom.

He glanced up, but his smile was tight, and I wondered if he felt as awkward as I did after our last conversation about the girls on his RC list.

"Hey." I pulled at the strings of my faded *Dibs on Mr. Darcy* hoodie.

He stepped back from the counter clutching an envelope. "Just stopped by for my paycheck," he said. "I've gotta run."

Mom glanced between us, her invisible writer's antennae scanning us for signs of conflict or drama.

"Oh, uh, sure." *So articulate, Viv.* "Well, uh. Have a good day." I shrugged, hating that we'd been reduced to this awkward formality with each other.

He nodded again, then focused on my mom. "Thanks again, Ms. Galdi."

"Of course," she said, her smile way too bright. "We'll see you tomorrow, right?"

Ugh. Tomorrow. Inventory. More alone time with him. I pretended to be fascinated by a stack of self-help books that had to be from the seventies. *Get Your Groove Back: Guide to a Groovy Middle Age* and *Far-out Fitness: Fun Ways to Lose the Fat.*

"Yeah," I heard Dallas say. "See you then."

I waited until I heard the door close before I made eye contact with my mom.

"What's going on with you two?" she asked, eyes narrowed suspiciously.

"Nothing." I flipped through the *Far-Out Fitness* book. Had people actually worn leg warmers in public back then? With those awful exercise leotards? Yuck.

"Vivian Josephine Galdi. Come here."

Uh oh. The middle name meant business. I shuffled to the counter, avoiding direct eye contact.

"Did you and Dallas have a fight? Did you two go out and

break up already without telling me?"

"No!" I met her penetrating stare with my own. "We did *not* go out. We're just...I don't know. Not seeing eye-to-eye on some stuff."

Mom crossed her arms over her crime scene tape T-shirt. "I hope you're being nice to that boy, Vivvy. He's so sweet. And he's new in town. I'd hate to think my own daughter was giving him grief."

I tugged at my hair. "I am *not* giving him grief! There's nothing going on with us. No dating, no fighting. *Nothing*." And that was the problem, wasn't it? Because I wanted something but was unwilling to admit it.

I pushed off the counter. "I've gotta go. I'm heading to the beach to interview Reg and a few of the other guys, if they're willing." And I wasn't inviting Dallas; I didn't need a bodyguard.

Mom's cranky face disappeared, replaced by an approving glow. "I'm so glad you're doing these interviews, sweetie. If anyone can do them justice, it's you."

Wow. How did she do that, go from judgy mom to cheerleader mom so fast? And I thought I was moody. "Thanks Mom. I'll see you for dinner, okay?"

Her smile lit up her face. "Paul and Toff are joining us. Pizza."

I stifled a groan as I turned to leave. Pizza with Flipper, just what I needed.

Not.

Stopping into the Bean, I loaded up on croissants, donuts with sprinkles, and muffins for Reg and his friends. I was grateful Jake wasn't around to make snide remarks about my bulging sack of yumminess, but as I exited the store I almost crashed into Dallas.

"W-what are you...are you stalking me, Dallas?" Flustered, I stepped away, almost stumbling over an oversized flower pot.

Dallas's gaze narrowed. "No. I was going to get a smoothie. I didn't know I wasn't allowed in the Bean at the same time as you."

Ouch. "Sorry," I muttered, shoving my pastry bag into my bike's basket.

"Where are you headed?" Dallas asked.

I hesitated. "To the beach," I said, inwardly wincing at the partial truth.

"Want company?"

His question stunned me. "I-I-uh..." I stared at his faded Nikes.

The shoes pivoted away from me. "Never mind," he muttered.

My hand shot out, grasping his bicep, which flexed under my grip. As Jaz would say, *Da-yum*. "W-wait," I stammered. "I...well...I'm going to do the homeless interviews for the *Clarion*." I shrugged, meeting his wary gaze. "You can tag along if you want."

He cocked an eyebrow. "Tag along? Like a puppy?"

That made me snort-laugh, but he didn't share my amusement. I quashed my nervous laughter. "No, not like a puppy." I held up my empty hands. "I forgot the leash."

"Good thing I respond to voice commands."

"Do you respond to treats?" I teased, "Or are you motivated by slavish devotion to your human?" As soon as the words tumbled out, I wanted to kick myself.

Surprise flickered in his eyes, but he didn't miss a beat. "Let's find out." He closed the gap between us, smirking down at me. "I promise I'm potty trained."

Blushing, I turned to unlock my bike. "You'll have to run to keep up with me."

"Challenge accepted."

I should've known competition would motivate him.

Spending more time with him was a mistake, especially since I'd told him to focus on his own RC list, but my inner Vulcan was off duty. Straddling my bike, I shot him a challenging grin. "Last one to the overlook is a Klingon."

Ten minutes later, I won the race, but only by a hair. Dallas ran fast and was barely out of breath after sprinting next to me.

I handed him a water bottle and he took it, tilting his head back to drain it.

"Okay, Lois Lane." He winked. "Let's do this."

Reg grinned as we approached his bench. "Pastry Princess. What are you doing out here on a school day?"

"No school today." I handed him the bag and started pouring cups of coffee. I'd brought a thermos of coffee from home along with paper cups. "I was hoping maybe I could interview you." I glanced at the other two guys on the bench. "And your friends, if that's okay."

Reg took a bite of a chocolate sprinkle donut and chewed, watching his friends. They took coffee cups but eyed us warily.

"This is my friend Dallas."

Dallas nodded and held up a hand in greeting. "Hi. Nice to meet you."

Reg nodded, still chewing. I shot Dallas a nervous glance and he gave me an encouraging smile, just enough to bolster my confidence.

"It's for the school newspaper," I explained. "To raise awareness about the need for shelter donations."

"I don't want anybody's pity," Reg said. "Not interested in being a sob story."

The other two nodded, still eyeing me suspiciously. I

noticed that one of them didn't look too much older than me underneath his spotty beard. The other man might've been in his early forties. It was hard to tell since living on the streets took such a toll on the body. I could feel Dallas tense up next to me, and I wondered if he was scared. I gave him a reassuring glance, but was surprised to find that he looked more protective than fearful. Not at all like a loyal puppy.

"No, no," I said, hating that I'd already messed up somehow. "It's not like that at all. I want to write about your life. Your history. Your family. Whatever you want to tell me."

The older man snorted. "Ain't seen my family in years."

"Mine kicked me out," said the younger guy. "Tried to go back once, but they'd moved." He shrugged like he didn't care but I saw the flash of pain in his eyes. I couldn't even fathom the pain, the rejection.

"My daughter says I can live with her if I want," Reg said. "But I won't do that to her. I get these…episodes. The VA says I need meds, but I ain't putting more shit into my body."

Glancing at Dallas, I settled into a cross-legged position on the pavement and retrieved my journalism notebook from my backpack. Dallas sat next to me, apparently content to let me run the show. "Is it okay if I take notes? I promise I'll let you read the article before it's published."

The three men eyed each other as I waited, holding my breath. Dallas squeezed my knee, then removed his hand, his supportive gesture startling me.

"I don't read too good," said the younger guy, ducking his head.

"I'll read it to you," I said, glancing at Reg for approval. He took another bite of his donut and chewed slowly. After swallowing, he took a long swig of coffee, then announced, "Viv's all right. I trust her." He nodded toward my notebook. "Go ahead, Princess."

We stayed for a long time, me listening and taking notes,

Dallas quiet at my side. At one point I asked if I could record them on my cell phone, but Dan, the fortyish guy, got twitchy so I didn't.

In the end, Chris, the guy closest to my age, talked the most. It was like he'd been waiting forever for someone to listen to his story and once he started he couldn't stop.

The sun's warmth dissipated as the fog rolled in. An involuntary shiver shot through me and Dallas tugged off his sweatshirt and handed it to me. I glanced at him, taken aback at the protectiveness I saw in his eyes. I tugged the Badgers sweatshirt over my head, inhaling his eau de nerd scent, hoping to burn it into my nasal passages forever.

"Thank you so much." I stood up. "I'm going to write three articles- one for each of you." I hesitated. "If that's okay with you. I'll meet you back here so you can approve them first."

Reg nodded and after a beat, Chris and Dan grunted in agreement.

Dallas stood up and shook their hands, and so did I, taking note of their dry, cracked skin and the dirt caked underneath broken fingernails and in every crevice. I wished I had Jaz's artistic skills to capture the contrasting image of my clean, manicured hands clasping theirs.

Dallas and I ambled up the beach path together. He wheeled my bike and I trailed next to him, my mind spinning with the stories I needed to write, hoping I could do them justice.

"You're good," he finally said.

I paused, searching his eyes for a hidden meaning. "Good at what?"

"Asking the right questions. Knowing when to be quiet."

His compliment warmed me even more than his sweatshirt. "Thanks."

We walked on in companionable silence. I scanned the

beach for glimpses of Fisk but saw nothing to report back to Jaz.

When we reached Mom's store, I tried to return his sweatshirt but he shook his head.

"I know where to find you." He tugged at his hair. "Thanks for letting me tag along."

"You were very well behaved, even off your leash." I tilted my head back, grinning. "Even without treats."

"Slavish devotion, remember?"

My teasing persona fled, leaving behind a stammering idiot. "Uh oh—I..."

"See you tomorrow, Vivian." His grin took my breath away.

And then he was gone, zipping away on his Vespa as I buried my nose in his sweatshirt.

Slavish devotion indeed.

"No! Leave me!"
—Spock

CHAPTER TWENTY-ONE

SATURDAY, SEPTEMBER 20

The Lonely Hearts gathered in the store's kitchen, feasting on sugary and salty snacks. The group was especially loud and rambunctious today, so I tapped on a glass with a knife to get everyone's attention. Staring at the butter knife reminded me of watching the *Star Trek* episode with Dallas.

"Okay, everyone, settle down," I said, pushing away images of Dallas and me huddled in front of his laptop, sharing popcorn and soda. "Before we discuss the book, I want to talk about an idea for the store."

The chatter faded and everyone waited, smiling and expectant. "So most of you know Mom's computerizing things. We're almost done setting up a database."

Mrs. Sloane spoke up. "With the help of that handsome young man."

Amy glanced up from her yarn and needles, waggling her eyebrows suggestively.

"Right." I sighed. "Anyway. While working on the inventory, I came up with the idea of setting up a special display featuring romances by hero category."

"Like the tall, dark, and brooding type," said Mrs. Sloane.

"Yes." I smiled conspiratorially. "We're calling those the Heathcliffs." That had been Dallas's idea. I'd been shocked he knew about *Wuthering Heights*. He'd just rolled his eyes and said he wasn't a cultural Neanderthal.

"What other categories?" asked Megan. She took notes on her laptop like the diligent grad student she was.

I hesitated. "Well, I'll tell you some of my ideas, but I'd like your input, too."

"How about Power Rangers?" asked Amy.

"What?" I stared at her.

"Remember that kids' show? Maybe it would be a good name for those Navy SEAL heroes."

I grinned. "I like it."

Everyone got excited, tossing out funny category names. When I told them about the McNerd category, Megan cheered and did a goofy seated robot dance.

We were all laughing so hard that Mrs. Sloane had to cup her hands around her mouth to project her next comment. "The funniest sex scene I ever read involved a McNerd and a protractor."

We all collapsed into raucous laughter, none of us hearing the back screen door open. When everyone suddenly froze, I knew exactly who'd wandered into the kitchen. I hyper-focused on Amy, whose expression told me Dallas had definitely overheard Mrs. Sloane. Mortified, I refused to turn around to face him.

"Um, sorry," he mumbled behind me. "Didn't mean to interrupt." His footsteps moved quickly across the kitchen and as soon as the door banged shut behind him, everyone collapsed into laughter again.

I took a deep breath, willing myself to focus. "Okay, ladies. Time to talk about the book."

...

As usual, Amy stuck around to help me clean up after the meeting. After I'd dried the last cup to within an inch of its life, she yanked the dishtowel out of my hands.

"You can't avoid him forever."

"Sure I can. All I need is my sleeping bag and I can live in the kitchen for the rest of my life."

Amy laughed. "With his timing, he'd just barge in here while you were changing clothes."

"Oh God. Don't even say it." I shivered.

"Just pretend nothing happened."

I rolled my eyes. "Really? Pretend he didn't hear something totally inappropriate about hot McNerds and protractors?"

Amy giggled. "What book did she mean, anyway? I need to read it."

The kitchen door flew open and Mom rushed in, looking harried. "Vivvy, I need you. A group of Lodge guests just descended on us. They all want romances." She grinned at me. "Poor Dallas. I think he wanted to melt into the floor when they started talking about vampire and werewolf… um…you know."

"Sounds like an emergency," Amy said. "You'd better go save the McNerd."

Mom looked confused. "The what?"

"Never mind," I said, pushing past Mom. "I'll take care of it."

"Call me later," Amy mouthed.

I heard the women all the way across the store. They'd found the romance section, and sounded just as rambunctious as my book club.

After what seemed like forever, amidst much raucous

laughter and commentary, I'd found everyone at least one book. When the boisterous group descended on the counter to pay, debating about which heroes were sexiest, Dallas jumped up.

"Be back in a few," he mumbled, brushing past me and sending shock waves through my body. He kept his eyes averted so I wasn't able to gauge his mood by his eyes like I usually did.

Once the women left, I examined the pile of books next to Dallas's laptop and noticed he was almost done with the fantasy and sci-fi books. So today was it—our last day working together.

I glanced at his screen and read the tab names open on his internet browser. *Insider Gaming Cheats. Cello Masters.* I leaned closer to his screen. *Hunkalicious Heroes.* He was reading my blog again? Heat flooded through me as I recalled my current hot aliens blog and my first kiss quiz.

He had one more tab open. *Fisk Vilhelm Screen Debut.* Huh. That was weird. Then again, maybe not. Apparently Dallas was a bit star struck.

According to Jaz's secret intel, Fisk was still staying at The Lodge in one of the private cabins. I'd kept Fisk's secret though I wished I could tell someone that I'd met him and how cool he was.

When the bell on the door jingled I jerked away from Dallas's laptop, guilt flooding through me. Checking out his internet tabs was almost like him eavesdropping on my conversation with Mrs. Sloane. Or wandering into the middle of a book club discussion.

His soapy clean smell filled my nose as he moved behind my chair along with the smell of smoothies. He placed a cup next to me. I could tell by the color and smell it was chocolate and peanut butter, my favorite.

"Thanks." I smiled at him as he sat down with his green

228 THE REPLACEMENT CRUSH

smoothie. He always went with the healthy choice, just one more annoying example of his impressive self-discipline.

"Sure," he said, avoiding eye contact. He skimmed the jacket of a book and started typing.

Was he mad at me? Or just embarrassed from the McNerd protractor thing? Not to mention the raucous debates from The Lodge guests. Ugh. It was kind of amazing he hadn't run out of the store screaming today. I tried not to think about how much I'd miss him once our project was finished.

I took a long slurp from the smoothie straw, making that loud bubbling noise that drove my mom nuts. I watched him from the corner of my eye and saw his lip quirk up at my noisy drinking. I opened a desk drawer and fished out a five-dollar bill, then slid it across the desk. He stopped typing to stare at the cash.

"What's this for?" he asked.

"My smoothie."

He frowned. "Don't worry about it." He paused. "Besides, it has the antidote."

It was my turn to frown. "What antidote?"

"For the Spock virus. The one that made all his human emotions spill out. If you drink this smoothie, you'll be able to retain your Vulcan cool and complete your mission."

I stopped slurping, detaching my lips from the straw. His eyes darted to my mouth, then he turned away, focusing on his screen again, but I saw a hint of a blush creep up his neck.

Maybe we both needed the antidote.

A pizza box sat on the table between Dallas and me in the store kitchen. It was almost midnight. We'd both been determined to finish the inventory tonight, and we'd done it.

When he told me he needed to wrap it up tonight because he had a lot of other commitments, I pasted a fake smile on my face and told him I understood, even as I wondered if his commitments involved dating Kylie.

We didn't talk much, instead focusing on our food. Dallas drained his soda can and wiped his mouth with a napkin. I half-expected him to belch. Toff would've. But Dallas wasn't Toff.

"So you can start your mobile book service now," Dallas said.

"Yeah, I'm looking forward to it." I didn't tell him that I'd wanted him to help me with it, that I'd imagined us choosing books together, laughing at the selections made by the sweet little old ladies.

Dallas closed the lid of the empty pizza box. I couldn't believe how much food he could eat and stay so fit. Maybe he ran marathons in his spare time.

"Can I ask you something?" He spun the empty soda can between his hands.

I shifted uncomfortably, hitching my leg under my thigh. "Depends. Are you going to make fun of my blog again?"

He smiled down at the table. "No, I wouldn't do that."

"Ha. You already have."

"Okay, so maybe I did a little bit." He fiddled with a package of unopened red pepper flakes. "It's hard not to tease someone who likes reading about hot aliens." He glanced up, flashing his dimple.

"Please, *please* stop reading my blog," I begged, my cheeks burning.

"What's the verdict on the first kiss quiz?" he persisted. "Tongue or no tongue?"

Despite my complete and total humiliation, I entertained a brief fantasy of straddling his lap, ripping his glasses off his face and...tongue. Definitely tongue.

I needed to switch to reading murder mysteries. Gruesome, violent ones with no romance.

"So did you have a real question for me?" I asked, hoping to steer us back to neutral territory.

He tugged at his spiky hair, then pushed his glasses up his nose. Two signs he was nervous. Which meant I should be, too. "Well, this...uh...replacement crush mission. I'm still trying to understand your illogical logic. It doesn't make sense, for someone like you."

My stomach clenched. "What do you mean *someone like me*?"

He cleared his throat. "Someone so smart. Funny." He shrugged, then locked his eyes on mine. "Someone so pr—so, uh, popular."

Had he almost called me pretty? My pulse pounded in my ears.

"You think I'm popular?"

He shrugged. "You know everyone. You have lots of friends. People like you."

I narrowed my eyes suspiciously. "Are you stalking me, Dallas Lang?"

"Hardly."

Ouch. I winced and started fiddling with my own empty soda can.

"I'm not a stalker," he said. "I'm an observer."

I snorted. "Same diff. Just semantics."

He shook his head. "Big difference. Stalkers are obsessed. No objectivity whatsoever."

"Oh, so you're an objective observer now? A scientist of human behavior? And you're giving me a hard time for being a Vulcan?"

His lips quirked. "I'm not a Vulcan. I'm more of a... McNerdist, if you will."

I giggled, flustered by the way his eyes lit up while I

laughed. "All right, Mr. McNerdist. What does your scientific observation tell you?"

He rocked back on the kitchen chair, balancing carefully on two chair legs. Hiddles readjusted himself, anchoring his claws into Dallas's jeans.

"We've already established that you're definitely not a Vulcan," he finally said. "At all. But you're trying to be." He hesitated, his eyes hooded. "Because someone hurt you. Jake, I assume."

Suddenly the room felt too small, and the silence roared too loudly in my ears. It wasn't exactly shocking that he'd figured it out. But now I realized just how much he'd observed.

"So what?" I hoped my sarcasm hid my anxiety.

"So attacking this…boyfriend hunt or whatever like it's a game of Battlefield, trying to sink an enemy and capture a prize you don't even want…it's stupid." He took a breath and returned the chair's weight to all four legs. "Because even missions with good intentions cause collateral damage and people get hurt." He paused again, then plunged ahead. "You don't seem like the kind of person who'd hurt someone intentionally. But I think you will, if you haven't already."

My breath escaped in a startled gasp. I jumped up from my chair and grabbed the pizza box. I had to get away. I was completely freaked out at how he'd somehow seen into my heart. How he saw parts of me I was trying to keep hidden.

But accusing me of hurting people? I hadn't done that. Drew didn't like me and neither did Henry. So far my mission was a failure, but I'd only hurt myself.

"Vivian. Wait."

I didn't stop when he called after me. I rushed down the deck stairs and tossed the pizza box into a trash bin, slamming the slid. Breathing heavily, I moved out of the glow of the porch light on the deck, leaning against a wall shadowed in darkness. The damp night air made me shiver, and I wrapped my arms around my body, wondering what it would feel like to have Dallas wrap his arms around me.

"Vivian." His voice was soft, hesitant, reaching me before his shadow loomed over me.

"What?" I pressed against the wall, wishing I'd disappear through it into Narnia.

"I'm sorry." He stepped closer, and his low voice sent shivers racing up my trembling body. "I didn't mean to upset you."

I shrugged, unable to speak or look into his eyes, half-hoping and half-dreading what I might see there.

"You're cold," he said, stepping closer. Much too close.

"And you said you weren't a stalker." I tried to joke but my voice trembled as much as my body did.

He moved closer, just inches from me. The heat radiated between us like our own private sun.

"Just observing," he said, and before I could take another breath, he pulled me into his arms, pressing me against his body. My hands splayed against his chest and I felt the rapid beating of his heart underneath my palm.

Mayday! Mayday! My hormones jumped ship, crashing into the sea of desire that rushed through me. He tilted my chin up, making my breath catch as my eyes met his.

"You're sure you aren't interested in chemistry? Not even as bonus criteria?" His voice was low and sexy.

"I'm s-sure," I barely stammered out the words before his lips claimed mine.

His kiss was gentle at first, soft and warm. I thought about resisting, pushing him away. I knew he'd never force me. But I wanted this kiss more than I'd ever wanted Jake's. So instead of resisting, I leaned into him, reaching up to wrap my hands around his neck. I didn't try to hide my desire for him; instead I matched his hunger with my own.

My body felt like a firecracker shooting into the sky, exploding into a million electric sparks, as I finally gave in to the feelings I'd tried to hide, allowing my hormones free rein. Dallas pushed me against the wall. I hoped the building was strong enough to support us because it felt as if we'd just exploded a supernova. Our kiss deepened as he moved his hands up the length of my body, into my hair, tugging his fingers through it. My legs no longer felt solid and he seemed to sense it, dropping his hands from my hair to encircle my waist, crushing me against him, teasing my mouth open with his tongue.

Kissing Jake had been hot, but kissing Dallas was a volcanic explosion. I melted into him, letting my inner Kirk beat the crap out of my inner Spock.

I finally let my fingers touch his hair, running my hands through it. It was soft, just like I'd hoped. He groaned into my mouth, pressing himself even tighter against me, pinning me against the wall like a trapped butterfly. I shoved his glasses onto the top of his head, capturing his face between my hands.

Then, as quickly as it started, it was over. Dallas jerked away from me, breathing raggedly. Cold rushed into the space between us, and I reached out my hand, wanting to pull him close again. He stepped back, lowering his glasses onto his nose.

"Wh-what?" I whispered. I felt like he'd slapped me.

"Don't do this unless you mean it," he said, his voice rough, his eyes glittering down at me. "I know this isn't on your list." I could still feel the heat emanating from him.

I leaned against the wall for support. "What list?"

He chuckled softly. "Your criteria list, Vivian." He took a long breath to compose himself. "No chemistry, remember? No zing or whatever the hell you and your friends call it. But *we* definitely have it, so I guess that means I'll never be on your list."

He hadn't sworn around me before. My own breath came in uneven gasps. I'd never been kissed like that. Ever. He crossed his arms, looking down at me. "Or have you changed your mind? Are you ready to give up your stupid mission now?"

Had I changed my mind? My God, if that kiss didn't do it, nothing could.

But wasn't this exactly what I wanted to avoid? Amazingly hot kisses that made me lose control and possibly lose my heart? I wasn't sure if I could handle that again. Not after Jake.

"I...I'm not sure...of anything right now." I could hardly think straight. I needed time to process what had just happened. I liked Dallas so much, but I was still reeling from what Jake had done to me. Could I really afford to let another person have control of my heart? Could I risk it?

He stepped back as if I'd slapped him. "So you're going to pretend this isn't what you want? You're going to keep playing Vulcan and deny your feelings for me?"

"I...I don't know, Dallas. I'm...not sure what I feel... what I can handle."

His laughter was sharp, tinged with a bitterness that made me shudder. "Well, that sucks." He tilted his head back, looking up at the stars, the same stars I thought I was soaring through while we kissed. He closed his eyes and sighed heavily. "I think it's obvious how I feel about you, Viv. But I'm not going to wait around for you to decide how you feel about me. If you want to stick to your stupid mission, just leave me out of it. Not like I was ever one of your targets, anyway."

He turned away, disappearing quickly into the shadows. I closed my eyes, leaning against the wall, unshed tears burning my eyes.

Viv. He'd finally called me Viv.

I heard his Vespa hum to life, then the sound faded as he drove away, out of my life, but not out of my heart.

"Mind your own business, Mister Spock. I'm sick of your half-breed interference-do you hear?"
—Captain Kirk

CHAPTER TWENTY-TWO

It was like Dallas and I didn't know each other anymore. He never caught my eye in the halls at school, or texted me, or stopped by my lunch table to make some random McNerd observation. He and Toff, however, seemed to be bonding. I'd heard from Jaz that Toff was teaching Dallas to surf and he was supposedly a natural at it.

Of course he was. I remembered my joke about life being a corny movie where the new guy comes to town and sweeps all the surfing competitions. If we'd still been friends...or more than friends...I could've teased him about it.

Toff and his dad still showed up for dinner once a week, but things weren't the same between Toff and me. He was full of unspoken questions and I didn't have any answers. My mom asked me if we'd had a fight. I told her no, we were just drifting apart, earning me a lecture about the importance of maintaining friendships, especially those I'd had since forever.

Amy and Jaz stopped telling me that my RC mission was a bad idea. Instead, they nodded like brainless zombies when I tossed out potential target names. Names I didn't even care about. I missed Jaz's feisty arguments and Amy's speeches about true love, but they'd apparently made a secret pact to tolerate me like the crazy cat lady everyone felt sorry for.

So far, the RC mission had tanked. Iggy suggested I give Henry another chance, since he was kind of a McNerd, though not nearly as appealing as Dallas. Even though I didn't want to, I'd gone to a movie with him; but when he tried to kiss me, I turned away. I was pretty sure no one would ever come close to kissing me the way Dallas had. My hormones had been so bored they hadn't even woken up when Henry made his move.

But that wasn't the worst part. When we'd left the theater, we'd seen Dallas and Kylie in the lobby, holding hands and laughing. Unlike me, he hadn't looked as if he was there under duress. My heart felt as if it splintered into a million tiny pieces while I watched them together. I was hurt and surprised that someone who'd put so much passion into our kiss and had said what he had about his feelings for me, had apparently moved on so quickly.

Dallas glanced my way as I trailed Henry across the lobby. He'd stopped laughing, his eyes latching onto mine. He'd untangled his hand from Kylie's and for several deranged seconds, I thought he might cross the lobby to swoop me into his arms. But instead he'd just turned away, his face reminding me of the night he'd stormed out of the store on his mysterious errand, full of intensity and frustration.

The only activities keeping me sane were boring homework, my review blog, and the senior center book delivery service. Maybe it was pathetic that the highlight of my week was wheeling an overflowing cart of books into the stale-smelling lobby of the senior center, but at least when I was there I forgot about my stupid boy problems.

...

It was a quiet afternoon at Murder by the Sea when the door swung open and I glanced up to see the Unabomber slinking into the store, hiding under a grey hoodie pulled low over his forehead and oversized dark sunglasses. He glanced around the store, then spotted me. As he moved quickly toward me, I realized who it was.

"Hey," he whispered. "Gran's out of crack. Can you hook me up?"

I stifled a giggle. "Go through that door." I pointed to the "Employees Only" door to the kitchen. "I'll be right there." I hesitated. "There's soda in the fridge, if you want. Cookies on the counter."

He shot me a quick grin before striding quickly toward the kitchen. I glanced around the store. No one had noticed him or looked ready to buy anything, so I put our small bell on the counter and the worn sign that said, "Ring for service," then followed Fisk into the kitchen.

He sat at the table drinking a soda and eating from the package of cookies. He'd pushed the hoodie off his face and removed his sunglasses. Dang. No wonder Hollywood wanted him on the big screen.

I was dying to snap a photo of him for Jaz, but I knew I couldn't. Maybe someday I'd tell her about this. Then again, maybe not, since she'd kill me for keeping it a secret.

"How's it going, Vivian? Keeping the senior center supplied with granny porn?" He grinned at me.

"It's not porn!" I took a cookie from the package as I sat down across from him. "And I guess I'm not doing a good job with the supply if you're here."

He took a drink from his soda. "Honestly, I just wanted to check out your store. Get away from The Lodge for a while."

I nodded, thinking how hard it would be to stay trapped

undercover. "That must be weird, having to hide out all the time."

He shrugged. "It is, but I'm the one who signed up for this fame gig." He grinned at me again. "I miss doing stuff like this, though. Just hanging out like a normal person."

"Right. Hanging out with a boring high school girl; I'm sure you totally miss that."

He laughed. "You're not boring. What you're doing for the senior center is cool." He spoke around a bite of cookie. "So is it true your mom's a famous writer?"

"Sort of famous. And yeah, it's true. But I can't tell you her name. Secrecy oath." I smirked. "You understand."

He nodded, still chewing. "Oh yeah." He glanced around the kitchen. "This is nice, though. Kind of reminds me of home."

"Where's home, anyway?" Jaz would know, but I didn't share her freakishly encyclopedic knowledge of celebrity bios.

"Minnesota. The frozen tundra. My gran raised me, that's why she's with me now. I'm all she's got."

That was shockingly sweet. And the frozen tundra thing, that was exactly what Dallas had said about Wisconsin. I studied Fisk's friendly, beautiful face. I sort of wished Dallas was here; it would be funny to see if he got star struck around Fisk.

"What are you thinking about?" Fisk asked. "You drifted away there for a minute."

I refocused on Fisk and shrugged. "Just, um…nothing."

His eyes narrowed. "It's a guy, isn't it?"

I laughed nervously, feeling myself blush. "There you go with the psychic thing again."

He grinned as he fished another cookie out of the package. "Rock star. Psychic. Same thing." He took another bite. He ate almost as much as Dallas. Fisk pointed a finger at me. "Ah-ha. More blushing. You're totally thinking about a guy, and I know it's not me."

That cracked me up. "How do you know I'm not totally flustered to be hanging out with a famous rock star?"

He shot me a cocky grin. "I can tell these things. I spend half my life surrounded by teenage girls who think they're in love with me. And that's definitely not you." He winked. "So tell me about him."

My grin faded and I fiddled with the strings on my hoodie. "Not much to tell." I shrugged, then met his eyes. "It's like a bad song lyric, you know? Girl meets boy. Girl falls for boy; boy falls for girl. But stupid girl rejects boy because she's an idiot. Now boy acts like he doesn't know girl. And girl is very sad."

He'd leaned back in his chair while I spoke, studying me thoughtfully. "You're breaking my heart, Vivian. Seriously. Why don't you just tell him how you feel?"

I shook my head, horrified to realize a few tears had leaked into my eyes while I'd told him the sarcastic version of my very real pain. "I can't. He's moved on to someone else." I raised my eyes to his. "And this is why I spend most of my time with book boyfriends instead of real boys. I stink at human relationships."

He stopped chewing. "That sucks. You deserve better. Maybe he's not worth it if he gave up so easily."

"No," I said softly. "He didn't give up. I did. I pushed him away, told him to move on." We sat in silence, then I tried to smile. "I wish I was like you, Fisk. I'd write an awesome song about it."

He nodded. "Yeah. It's pretty hard to resist a love song apology."

"Unless it's a bad song, like Adam Sandler in *The Wedding Singer.*"

Fisk laughed. "Still worked for him, though. He got the girl."

"It was the Billy Idol effect."

We laughed together but were interrupted by the bell ringing from out front. "Be right back," I said, jumping to my feet. I hurried to the door, opened it, then almost slammed it shut when I saw who was standing at the counter. *Vivian to Spock: Mayday!* I leaned against the door, my stomach doing back flips.

Fisk cocked an eyebrow. "Problem?"

I bit my lip. "It's him. The guy from my song. I mean, from my life."

Fisk grabbed another cookie. "So go out there." He grinned at me. "I can be your Billy Idol back-up. Go out and tell him how you feel."

My heart thudded in my chest. "No. No way." I eased the door open a tiny crack... Dallas stood there, hands in his pockets, looking around the store and frowning. Becca stood next to him holding a couple of books. Dallas reached out and tapped the bell again. I couldn't help but smile. It must be killing him that no one was out there to wait on customers.

I took a deep breath. "Okay, I'm going out there. But just to wait on him. He's with his little sister, anyway."

Fisk shrugged. "Okay. You're probably right. You need to build up to your big apology. You can't just wing it."

I didn't bother to tell him I'd never have the guts to apologize to Dallas, to tell him how I felt. Even my hormones were chickening out, telling me to hide out here with Fisk. But I had to do my job.

Pushing through the door, I pulled at my hair, wondering if I looked like a total train wreck. Not that it mattered. Dallas tensed when he saw me approach, but Becca grinned. "Hi," I said, not making eye contact as I walked behind the counter. "Sorry to keep you waiting."

He cleared his throat. "That's okay." He took the books from Becca and set them on the counter. I rang up the sale without speaking or looking at him, keeping my eyes on the cash register.

"Eleven dollars and thirteen cents, please," I mumbled, still refusing to make eye contact. He slid a twenty dollar bill across the counter, and I took it, careful to avoid touching his hand. I counted out the change and finally looked at him.

He watched me with his usual McNerdy intensity but didn't say a word. He turned his hand over, palm up, waiting for the change. I dropped it in his hand.

"Do you want a bag?" I croaked, cursing my rusty voice.

He shook his head, shoving the change in his pocket. Becca grabbed the books off the counter and grinned at me. "Thanks!"

"You're welcome. Hope you like them." I smiled at her, grateful to focus on someone other than Dallas. He reached down to take her hand and they turned to leave, but Dallas hesitated, turning back to me.

"I read your articles on the homeless guys. They were... insightful. Thoughtful." He hesitated. "You did them justice."

Taken aback, I simply nodded and mumbled a thank you. His gaze stayed on me a beat longer, then he and Becca left.

I rushed back to the kitchen, almost crashing into Fisk when I flung the door open. He jumped back, barely avoiding me.

"Sorry," I muttered, swiping a tear away. I needed to be alone, not have a breakdown in front of a rock star I barely knew. "Were you spying on me?"

He shrugged, but a guilty flush crept up his neck. "I was curious." He grinned at me. "Artistic curiosity, in case I write that song." His grin faded. "So that was him? The guy with the glasses?"

I nodded. Fisk probably thought Dallas was a dork. "He's a great guy," I said, unable to keep the defensiveness from my voice. "He's super smart. And sweet. And just so..."

My voice faded away. This was ridiculous, me talking to Fisk like he was Dear Abby.

He rubbed a hand over his chin, watching me almost as intently as Dallas did. "I'm sure he is. He'd have to be to fall for a girl like you." I couldn't quite read his expression. I could tell he wasn't laughing at me, but he looked as if he was hiding something. Probably trying not to laugh at my teenage drama. Then his face bloomed with his rock star grin. "I know it's stupid to take advice from a weird rock star eating your cookies, but I have to say it again, Vivian. Talk to the guy."

I gave him a half-hearted smile. "You're not at all what I expected, Fisk. For a rock star, I mean. You're almost normal."

He laughed. "Almost. But not quite." He pulled his hoodie over his head and put on his sunglasses. "I've gotta get back to my gilded cage. But thanks for the cookies and the conversation. It was just what I needed."

"Wait. I need to get books for your gran."

He shook his head. "That was just an excuse for me to leave prison. She should be fine until your next visit."

"Okay." I nodded. I couldn't believe we'd talked about me the whole time. I'd had a rock star all to myself and hadn't asked him anything. Jaz would kill me if she were here. "So is it true you're rehearsing for a movie at The Lodge? Getting all buffed? Is The Rock up there, too, training you?"

He grinned, his teeth blindingly white underneath his dark shades. "Top secret, Vivian. You know how it is."

I returned his grin. "Got it. You were never here."

He made a goofy clicking noise with his tongue and pointed his finger at me. Suddenly I saw him as he might have been as a teenager, super cute but a little dorky, before he was discovered and famous.

"We always have cookies," I said. "And soda."

"Thanks, Vivian. I'll keep that in mind."

And then he was gone, slipping out the back door like a shadow, leaving me alone to think about Dallas, and my own Vulcan stupidity.

"I have been, and shall always be, your friend."
—Spock

CHAPTER TWENTY-THREE

The first weekend in October was foggy and chilly. Mom offered to let me attend the surf competition on Saturday, but I said no. Jaz texted me a few photos, both of which were like a punch to the heart. One was of Toff doing his bicep-curling pose after winning the longboard competition. I missed cheering him on and razzing him about his lack of humility.

The other was a photo of Dallas standing by himself, staring at the ocean. "*I bet he's thinking about you,*" Jaz texted. "*You should text him. Call him. Plan a sneak kissing attack.*"

Jaz. She wasn't giving up. I smiled sadly and deleted the photo.

Mom disappeared as usual on Sunday, and I opened the store at noon. Not many people were up and around yet, so I put up the "Be right back" sign and hurried to the Bean for a triple-shot mocha. As I hurried back to the bookstore, I nearly collided with Claire.

"Sorry." I jumped back as if she'd bit me.

Her eyes were red-rimmed, her face pale. "My bad," she said. Then she blinked her eyes in recognition. "Vivian, thank

God. I was looking for you. Are you…do you have a minute?"

That was the last thing I expected her to say, but she looked so miserable I couldn't say no. "Sure," I said. "But I need to get back to work." I nodded toward the bookstore. "You can talk to me in there. We probably won't have any customers for at least half an hour."

"Okay," she whispered. "I'll get a drink and come over."

As I sipped on my drink and booted up the store's computer, I wondered why Claire wanted to talk to me, of all people. When Claire entered the store, she looked around nervously, as if worried we weren't alone.

"Hi," I said. "Come on in."

She chewed on her lip, looking like a scared animal, ready to bolt.

"Do you want to sit in the back?" I pointed toward the kitchen. "No one will bother us. If I hear the front door, I can help the customers while you can stay back there."

Nodding, she nearly sagged with relief. We walked to the kitchen in silence, then took chairs across from each other at the table. Claire sipped from her to-go cup, staring down at the table.

"Are you okay?" I asked, starting to freak out a little bit.

She shook her head, still staring at the table.

"Do you want me to, um, call someone? To come get you?"

She raised her eyes, looking frantic. "No," she said. "Don't do that."

We sat in silence again, until she finally let out a long, shaky sigh. "Can you…will you…" She took another breath. "Will you tell me what happened between you and Jake?"

Adrenaline shot through me, pinning me to the back of my chair. A million questions swirled through my mind. "Why do you want to know?"

She dropped her eyes and a tear slid down her cheek. Oh

no. Was she jealous? I could at least reassure her about that. "Not much happened with us. You should ask him. He told me himself we were never really *a thing*."

Her face jerked up. "Seriously?"

"Yeah." I nodded. "We just…um…kissed mostly." I took a deep breath, wondering what he'd said to her. "It was no big deal." She didn't need to know that it was a big deal, to me.

Her face seemed to cloud over. "But he said you guys…" Her voice trailed away and her cheeks turned pink. I was suddenly in my bedroom again, watching Toff break a paper clip in frustration when he'd assumed the same thing Claire apparently did.

"Jake said what?" I snapped. If he was telling more people we'd actually done the deed, I'd break my vow never to speak to him so I could kill him.

She took a long drink from her cup and tugged at her dreadlocks. "He said…that you…" A tingle of warning shot up my spine. "He said you, um, didn't want to…you know. At first. But that you changed your mind." She barely met my eyes. "He said if um…someone like you…could, you know, that I shouldn't keep saying no."

A powerful surge of anger tore through me and I gripped the edge of the table. My pulse pounded in my ears. "No," I finally managed through gritted teeth. "That's a lie. A total lie." I took a steadying breath. "He wanted me to sleep with him, yeah, but I told him no. He basically dumped me when I wouldn't."

Her eyes widened in shock. "Really?"

I nodded. "The first day of school…I totally thought it was me he'd be kissing at lunch. Not you." I shrugged, forcing a smile. "That was the day he officially cut me loose."

Her mouth formed a small *O* shape. "Seriously? Oh my God. I had no idea. I'm so sorry."

I brushed a tangle of curls behind my ear. "Look, it doesn't matter. I mean, him dumping me doesn't matter. Him saying that we had sex—that totally matters. I can't believe it. I'm going to kill him."

She shook her head. "He's not telling everyone. Just me, I think. He was trying to…um…persuade me, I guess."

Anger surged through me again. "So he basically said if a weirdo bookworm like me was willing, you should be, too?"

She dropped her gaze to the table, nodding. "I don't think you're weird, though." She glanced up. "This place is cool. And I like your blog. And your *Hit or Miss* column in the school paper."

It was my turn to look shocked. "You read my blog?"

She smiled hesitantly. "Yeah. I love to read." She frowned slightly. "Why doesn't anyone think surfers are smart?"

"I don't think that," I said, but part of me wondered if I did. The truth was I hardly knew Claire. Even though our school was fairly small, she was a sophomore and spent all her time with Jake and his posse. For all I knew, she was on the honor roll.

"How'd you hear about it? My blog, I mean?"

She shrugged. "Amy told me. I like your reviews. You're honest, but you're never mean even if you don't like the book."

"Wow," I said softly. "Thanks."

We sat in silence, both of us twisting our hair and staring everywhere but at each other. Then I had a horrifying thought. "Did Jake try to…did he force you…" I couldn't say the words, terrified of her answer.

She shook her head and a few more tears slid down her cheeks. "No. But I broke up with him last night because he said he was sick of waiting…" She couldn't finish speaking, but she didn't need to.

"Asshole."

Claire nodded. "He is. But I still sort of like him." She sniffled. "That's the worst part. Even though I know he's a jerk. I can't just turn off my feelings."

Boy, did I ever know about that. "Yeah." I sighed. "I went through that, too."

She leaned across the table, looking hopeful. "So what did you do? To get over him?"

I thought of my RC mission. Of the bad dates. Of Dallas and our kiss, and how I'd pushed away the one guy I wanted to keep close.

I leaned back in my chair and sighed. "Nothing that would help you. I think you just need to tough it out." As I watched her, my jealousy and resentment faded away. She was a girl just like me, falling in love, then getting her heart broken. "Keep reminding yourself of what a jerk he is. Remember he lied to you to get what he wanted."

She nodded but didn't say anything.

"I think you'll know when you're ready for sex. And if you feel like you're being forced, he's definitely the wrong guy." Dallas would never force a girl; I knew that deep in my heart. "Your first time should be special with someone you trust and love. Not wasted on somebody like Jake."

"Maybe," she finally spoke, giving me a sad smile. "But he's an awesome kisser."

I sighed. "Yeah. He is." I thought of Dallas again and my stomach fluttered as my body remembered our white-hot kiss. "But I've had better."

"You have?" She perked up. "Who?"

"It doesn't matter." I took a deep breath. "So you honestly like my blog?"

She grinned, a real one this time. "Go-go boots all the way, baby." She reached out a hand to fist-bump me and I returned the gesture.

"So," I said. "You should come here next Saturday. One

p.m. Lonely Hearts Book Club." I scooted my chair away from the table. "Come on. I'll loan you a copy of the book we'll be arguing about."

I never would've dreamed I'd bond with Claire, but she stayed in the store for another hour talking about books and eating M&Ms from the book club snack stash. We didn't agree on everything, but she had thoughtful opinions. I told her she'd be a great addition to our club.

When she left with a bag of books, she was smiling. I hoped she'd stay strong in her resolve to ignore Jake and his stupid lies.

I didn't know what to do about him spreading rumors. Claire didn't think he'd told anyone else, but he'd told Toff the same lie. I stared at my phone for a long time before working up the nerve to text Toff, but I finally did.

"U around? I need 2 C U."

He replied immediately. *"U ok?"*

Guilt over how I'd been ignoring him since our argument about Jake washed over me. Even though most of our relationship was based on teasing and joking, I knew he cared about me.

"Yeah. But I need to c u."

"Name it. I'm there."

I glanced at the clock. It was almost time to close the shop. Mom had texted me she'd be home late and to eat without her.

"6:00 at the cove." Hopefully we'd be the only ones there. The last thing I needed was to encounter somebody doing the nasty with Toff and me as an accidental audience.

"C U then."

•••

Empty beer bottles and dead cigarettes dotted the sand in the cove, along with kelp strands and broken seashells. I unfolded my ratty beach blanket and sank onto it, hugging my knees to my chest and staring out to the ocean. The sun had just set and it was cold, but I didn't care. Stars winked above me. I closed my eyes listening to the rhythmic pounding of the surf.

"Hey." Toff flopped next to me.

I opened my eyes, grateful to see his easy grin. "Hey, yourself." I smiled, but it felt hollow.

He pushed a strand of hair behind his ear. "What's up, Wordworm? It must be bad if you're asking me for help."

Instead of making me laugh, his comment made tears well in my eyes, surprising me. I turned away, but not before he saw the tears. He wrapped an arm around my shoulders, pulling me close.

"Viv, what is it? Now you're freaking me out." He pulled me even closer, and I was grateful it felt like a brotherly hug, nothing more.

"I need to know something." I took a breath, then plunged ahead. "Remember when we talked about Jake? And you asked if I...if we..." My voice trailed away as his grip loosened.

"Yeah," he said, his voice wary. "What about it?"

"I want to know who else he told."

He sighed heavily, dropping his arm from my shoulders. The cool breeze raised goose bumps where his arm had been.

"Does it matter?"

I turned to face him, anger flaring in my chest. "Of course it matters. It was a lie, Toff. And you're not the only one who's heard about it."

He frowned. "What's going on, Viv? Is Jake hassling you?"

I turned back toward the ocean. "Not directly. But he's… using me, sort of. Telling people that he and I… even though we didn't."

Toff's body tensed next to me. "I'll kick his ass. Just say the word."

I leaned my chin on my knees. "I'd like that. But I want to do it. I'm thinking maybe a crossbow. Or poison."

Toff laughed softly. "Don't forget castration." Even though the darkening sky hid his face in the shadows, I could tell his jokes hid discomfort. "Jake says that about every girl he dates."

"Seriously?" My heart pounded in my chest.

Toff nodded, looking out to the ocean rather than at me. "According to him, he's slept with every girl who's just said hi to him in the hall." He glanced at me. "We all know he's mostly full of it, but I also know he's not a complete liar…" He shrugged.

He picked up a seashell and chucked it toward the water. "I've been thinking about what you said. That double-standard thing. You're right; it's not fair." He picked up another shell and hurled it across the sand. "But that's not what I meant, that night we argued. I wasn't calling you a slut. I'd never say that about you."

I drew circles in the sand with the toe of my shoe as I worked out what I wanted to say. "It's weird how you and I have always been friends…way before our parents mortified us by dating."

The sound of his laughter warmed me, and made the knot in my stomach loosen.

"Yeah," he said. "I guess I've just always felt like I should look out for you or whatever. Like when kids used to call you Chunky Monkey when we were younger. I saw you crying one day under the slide and I felt bad for you."

"Oh wow. So you're a pity friend? Great."

He fake-punched me on the shoulder. "I guess you grew on me, sort of like algae."

"You sure know how to make a girl feel special, Flipper. Next thing I know, you'll ask me on a pity date."

He laughed. "Yeah, right. Somehow I don't see that working out. You'd drag me to a boring foreign romance movie. With subtitles."

"And you'd take me to that greasy burrito place I hate."

"I'd fall asleep in the movie."

"We'd get kicked out because you snore so loud." I shoulder-bumped him.

"And because of the burping since I ate all those greasy burritos."

"You. Are. Disgusting." I fake-punched him three times, once with each word.

He leaned back on his elbows and grinned up at me. "You always said you wanted a brother."

Tugging my knees into my chest, I returned his grin. "Yeah, it's like this creepy Brady Bunch thing our parents are doing to us, huh?"

He snorted. "You're definitely not hot enough to be Marcia. Sorry, Jan." He crossed his eyes at me. "Anyway, we were friends before they started dating."

"True," I said. "I'm glad we're agreed on the pity date. We'd kill each other." I hesitated, then plunged ahead. "What about Amy? Ever think of asking her out?"

He glanced at me, brow furrowed. "The redhead?"

I nodded, hoping maybe he'd show a flicker of interest.

"Huh. I never, uh, looked at her…like that."

"I thought you looked at everyone *like that*."

He pretended to look offended. "Dude, that hurts. I'm not a *total* man-whore."

"Uh-huh."

"Amy, huh?" He sat up and chucked another seashell toward

the waves. "I'm sort of on a hiatus from chicks right now."

"Fancy word, bro."

He shot me a dark look. "Watch it, Wordworm. You're not the only one who can read."

"Ooh, fighting words."

He grinned. "Anyway. I'm taking a break from girls."

I decided to stop joking. "You okay? Somebody break your heart?"

He shook his head. "Nah. Just...you know. Gotta focus on grades and stuff to stay on the team."

"Uh oh. Need any help?"

"Not from you, Wordworm." He winked. "I prefer hot tutors."

I threw my hands up in frustration. "You just said you were taking a break from girls!"

His grin was sly. "I meant a break from relationships. That's different."

I shook my head in disgust. "P.I.G.," I spelled out.

"Nope. Just a guy who appreciates a nice view."

"Oh my God, Toff! Never mind what I said about Amy. She's too sweet for you."

He was quiet for a moment, then shrugged. "Probably so." He glanced at me. "Anyway, I'm relieved to hear I'm off your stupid list. What the hell were you thinking, putting me on there?"

Son of a...Jaz would be lucky to make it to Christmas.

His low laugh rumbled over the sound of the waves. "You had to know she'd tell me. That chick has a big mouth."

I dropped my head to my knees. "She might as well have rented a billboard," I mumbled into my jeans.

"She's worried about you. And she knows we're friends."

I raised my head and met his gaze, which was warm and sympathetic.

"Anyway," he said, "it's a good thing we cleared this up

because if you *had* been stupid enough to ask me out, Vespa Guy would've kicked my ass."

"What?" My voice was barely a whisper.

Toff narrowed his eyes. "Viv, as much as I like you, sometimes you're kind of a dumbass." His face softened into an easy grin. "You seriously don't know how Dallas feels about you?"

I shook my head, wondering if the raw hope leaping around inside of me was visible on my face.

Toff rolled his eyes. "Man, this big brother gig sucks. But I can't watch you mope around like an abandoned puppy." He sighed and shifted to face me. "Seriously, Viv. What is up with you and Dallas? He's dating some chick he doesn't even like, and you're going on these…mission dates or whatever the hell you call them. Why are you two being so stubborn?"

"What do you mean, he doesn't like Kylie?"

"Well, I mean…he sort of likes her. But not the way he likes you. Any guy who wastes time reading your sucky blog has like, serious feelings or whatever."

I gaped at him. "Dallas told you about my blog?"

Toff nodded. "See what I mean? He's lucky I like him, or I would've totally busted his chops about it in front of the other guys."

I didn't know what to do with this information. I hoped it was true, but I also felt horribly guilty about Kylie. I'd practically forced Dallas to ask her out. I didn't want her to be part of my collateral damage, too.

"I had my chance with Dallas and I blew it. Honestly, he's better off with someone who appreciates how awesome he is."

Toff rolled his eyes. "You're totally overselling the guy."

I opened my mouth to protest but Toff spoke first. "Kidding. He's cool. And at least I know he isn't a jackass like Jake." His eyes glittered with anger under the moonlight. "You sure you don't want me to kick that guy's ass? Cuz I will."

"Nah," I said, standing up to brush sand off my legs. I smiled down at him, thinking of all the times he'd had my back over the years. "I'm glad we talked, Flipper. Believe it or not, I kind of missed you."

He stood up and grabbed the blanket, shaking the sand off. "Of course you did. I'm missable. Lovable. Kissable. All the 'ables.'"

I laughed as we folded the blanket into a messy square. "And so, so humble."

He grinned and yanked my hair, then tucked the blanket under his arm.

We walked back to our bikes, laughing and teasing each other, our easy friendship settling around me like a comfy old hoodie. I truly had missed him.

Almost as much as I missed Dallas.

"Curious how often you humans manage to obtain that which you do not want." —Spock

CHAPTER TWENTY-FOUR

MONDAY, OCTOBER 6

Henry waited for me at my locker, his face pinched yet determined. I slowed as I approached, anxiety blooming in my stomach. "Hi, Henry."

He nodded, moving slightly so that I could open my locker. I spun the lock, grateful for something to do because I had a premonition things were about to get weird.

"Vivian. How are you today? You're looking well."

He sounded like he'd rehearsed his lines, which made me even more anxious. "I'm groovalicious, Henry. How are you?"

He didn't smile at my stupid joke. "Very well, thank you." He shoved at his glasses, reminding me of Dallas, but not. He cleared his throat. "Do you have t-time for a question?" His voice wobbled and my heart fissured because I feared I knew exactly where this was going.

"Um, sure. I have newspaper at three thirty but I have a few minutes." *Please, please don't let him ask me out again.*

His Adam's apple bobbed up and down, then he spoke, his voice still unsteady. "I'm here to ask you to accompany me to the Surfer Ball." His entire face flushed beet red. "I know it's traditional for girls to ask guys, but I-I um..." His voice faded, like he'd forgotten his lines.

I was appalled by the raw hope in his eyes. Hope I was about to crush. Maybe I should just say yes, just go to make him happy. But after my discussion with Toff, I'd vowed to be true to myself, and others, even if it meant I couldn't have the guy I wanted. I didn't want to hurt anyone else, and saying yes when I meant no would only hurt Henry in the long run. I took a deep breath.

"Thank you for asking me, Henry. That's sweet. But I…I can't go with you. I'm sorry."

He dropped his gaze to the floor. "You have another date."

It would be easy to lie, but I wouldn't. No more pretending. "No. I'm not going to the dance. I just…don't want to go."

He raised his eyes. The hope was gone, and now he looked hurt. "That day you asked me for pre-calc help. You didn't need my help."

I bit my lip, feeling myself blush with guilt. "Well, I…"

"Don't bother, Vivian. I know it's true." He shifted his books. "I thought maybe you asked me to meet you because…" His cheeks flamed. "Never mind."

Oh my God. What had I done? I heard Dallas's voice: *"You know about collateral damage, right? Somebody always gets hurt."*

Henry turned away, but not before I saw the expression on his face. He looked like I must have when I saw Dallas holding Kylie's hand.

"Henry. I'm sorry. I really am." My words echoed down the hallway but he kept walking, head down, his gait hurried.

Tears pooled in the corners of my eyes. God, I was an idiot. Why had I ever thought anyone could be logical about love? Or that I could just pick guys off a list like I was grocery shopping? My stomach twisted in knots as I watched

Henry disappear into the crowd.

If true love ever did find me, I'd send it packing because I didn't deserve it.

After a long, boring newspaper meeting, I closed my locker, grateful the drama-filled school day was over. I closed my eyes, breathing deeply but when I opened them, Nathan stood there, staring down at me, looking as nervous as Henry had earlier this afternoon.

Oh no. What had Iggy done? I couldn't handle any more boy drama today.

"Hey, Vivian." He flashed me a tight smile. "Do you have a sec?"

Not again. Swallowing nervously, I nodded but moved toward the doors. "I need to go, but you can walk with me."

"Sure," Nathan said, falling into step with me. "So, um, this is kind of awkward…" His voice was low. "It's…uh…about Iggy."

Oh my God. He must know about my list, thanks to blabbermouth Iggy. Could this day get any worse?

I stopped and turned to face him. "Please don't." I sounded desperate. "Iggy wasn't supposed to tell anyone."

He frowned, his eyes clouding with confusion. "So…Iggy knows already?"

It was my turn to look confused.

"I think we're talking about two separate things." He took a breath. "But what I wanted to ask is…you and Iggy are friends, right?"

I nodded, anxiety chewing up my insides.

He stood very still, but I could sense his apprehension. "Do you think…" He stopped and took a breath. "Is he…um, seeing anyone right now?"

It took so long for his words to compute in my addled brain that Nathan turned away, but not before saw I how devastated he looked.

"No, no!" I finally sputtered, as the pieces finally fell into place. "He's not. Seeing anyone."

Nathan turned back to me, eyes lighting with hope. "Really?"

I nodded, grinning with relief. I couldn't wait to tell Iggy our gaydar sucked. "I think he'd definitely be interested."

Nathan smiled shyly. "You think so?"

"Oh yeah. He's very…aware…of you."

Nathan cleared his throat and glanced away, embarrassed. "Okay. Cool." He glanced at me. "So what were you talking about? What did you think I was going to ask you?"

Laughter bubbled out of me and he frowned. "What's so funny?"

"Nothing. Nothing at all. Do you want Iggy's number?" I dug in my pocket for my cell but Nathan shook his head, waving his phone at me.

"Already got it, for newspaper stuff."

"Cool." I tilted my head toward his phone. "What are you waiting for?"

He grinned. "Thanks, Viv."

"*GUESS WHO TEXTED ME FOR A DATE??!!!*" Ig's text message might as well have been a holler from the rooftops. I grinned at my phone as I unlocked my bike. Nathan worked fast; good for him.

"*I know,*" I replied. "*So much for our gaydar.*"

"*Right??? First time it's failed me!*" Followed by smiley faces, hearts, and rainbow emoticons.

At least someone's love life was looking up. I was happy for Ig and Nathan, even as sadness over my own stupidity pressed in on me like the ocean fog, filling me with damp sadness and bleak regret.

I rode my bike home slowly, hoping to unknot my tangled emotions. My mission was a complete bust. None of my targets were right: not Drew, definitely not Toff, and then poor Henry who thought he was right for me…but I'd broken his heart because he wasn't the right target.

When I saw Reg kicking back on the bench, his head tipped back soaking in the last rays of sunshine before the sun dipped behind the horizon, I coasted to a stop.

He opened one eye to look at me when I sat next to him. "Pastry Princess. How's tricks?"

I gave him a half-hearted smile. "Trickier than usual." I stretched out my legs. "Have you ever been in love, Reg?"

He turned to face me, opening both eyes. "Hell, yeah. Best time of my life." He wheezed as he shifted on the bench. "Also the worst." He shrugged and shot me his familiar yellow-toothed grin. "Somebody break your heart?"

"Yeah. Me." I shook my head. "I'm an idiot."

He sighed next to me and rearranged his body to face the setting sun again. He closed his eyes. "We're all idiots when it comes to love."

"So…" I tugged at my hair. "No words of wisdom for me?"

He laughed. "Now, what could you learn from an old coot like me?" He wheezed again. "I'll tell you this. The biggest mistake I ever made was walking away from the only woman who loved me in spite of my crazy-ass self."

For the thousandth time, I saw Dallas turning away that night he'd kissed me under the stars.

"Yeah." I sighed. "I get that."

"Anyway," he said. "You got years ahead of you. You got time to figure it out."

It didn't feel like that to me. I felt like a time-bomb was ticking, but I didn't know how to turn it off.

"You like to read, Reg?"

He shot me another one-eyed glance. "Used to. Horror, mostly. The gory ones."

I laughed. "I'll bring you a couple of books tomorrow." I don't know why I hadn't thought about doing so before now, but it felt like a tiny step on my path to redemption. I needed to atone somehow, for hurting Henry. And using Drew, however briefly. I squeezed my eyes shut.

No wonder Dallas continued to ignore me. If I were him, I'd run the other way, too. I was a freaking train wreck.

"See you, Reg." I stood up and grabbed my bike.

"Lookin' forward to it," he called after me.

I rode slowly along the path, watching the joggers on the beach, kids playing in the sand, couples holding hands. If only I could grab a tiny bit of that peacefulness and implant it in my aching heart, so swollen with regret.

Dallas was right about collateral damage. I just never expected that I'd be the victim.

"Insufficient facts always invite danger."
—Spock

CHAPTER TWENTY-FIVE

made my announcement quietly at lunch.

"You're sure?" Jaz asked.

I nodded, then opened my RC notebook and ripped out the list, shredding it into tiny pieces. Jaz and Amy high-fived each other, grinning.

"Finally," Jaz said, heaving a relieved sigh. She gathered up the torn pieces of paper. "I'm going to burn these as an offering to Cupid. Maybe he'll take pity on you."

I snorted.

Amy beamed at me. "I'm so proud of you," she said. "Now you can focus on true love again."

"Maybe some day," I mumbled.

The truth was I loved Dallas, and I wasn't going to quash those feelings by going out on any more stupid fake dates with anyone else. I couldn't be with Dallas—not now—but at least I'd be honest with myself. I glanced across the courtyard looking for him like I always did, but I didn't see him.

Claire approached our lunch table, twisting her hands nervously. She shot me an anxious half-smile. "Okay if I sit here?"

Even the art Goths paused their arguing to hear my answer.

"Sure." I gave her my friendliest smile. I scooted down my bench, making room for her. I knew Jaz and Amy would give me the third degree later, but they welcomed Claire, looping her into a discussion about Fisk Vilhelm, asking Claire if she'd heard he was hiding out at The Lodge.

I knew how hard it must be for her, not wanting to be around Jake. I darted a glance across the courtyard and saw him glaring daggers at us. Screw him; he'd earned this by the way he treated her. I returned his glare, refusing to drop my eyes from his. Loud laughter distracted me, and my eyes shifted to Toff. He caught my eye and grinned. I returned his smile, grateful we were friends again.

"So Claire's coming to book club next week," I said, turning back to my friends.

Amy looked surprised but recovered quickly. "Yeah? That's cool." Amy turned to Claire. "Are you reading our next book? Even if you can't finish it before we meet, you should still come to the meeting."

Claire tossed her long dreads over her shoulder. "I'll have it finished by then." She gave me a sad smile. "Not like I'm doing much else, except homework and surf practice."

Jaz took a long drink from her water bottle and slammed it on the table. "He's a total douche. When is someone going to kick his ass?"

The art Goths paused to stare at Jaz.

"Who's a douche?" asked one of the Goth girls.

"Jake Fon—" Jaz began but I put up a hand to silence her. "What?" Jaz snapped. "You're not going to defend him, are you?"

"Jaz, don't," I begged. I didn't want a scene and I knew Claire didn't, either.

"So Jake dumped you or something?" The girl asked

Claire. "I don't know if he's a douche or not, but he's hot enough I might overlook it."

Claire grabbed the remains of her lunch and stood up. "I'll see you later," she mumbled.

"Claire, wait." I stood while shooting a death glare at Jaz. Claire had joined us because she needed a safe place; she wasn't ready to go all vigilante on Jake's ass.

Claire scurried across the courtyard and I rushed after her.

"Claire!" It was hard to run in the new wedge heels Jaz had convinced me to buy. As I rounded a corner, I wobbled, fell off my heels, and crashed into a tall, solid body. Strong hands grabbed me, saving me from falling on my butt. A familiar scent and a touch I'd felt once before sent my hormones into full charge-the-Alamo mode. I felt my face flush as I raised my eyes. "Thanks."

Dallas's green eyes locked onto mine. It felt as if we were frozen wax figures in a museum, locked into a forever pose. I hadn't been this close to him in weeks, but everything in me responded as if our kiss had just happened. I blinked, breaking our stare, and he dropped his hands from my shoulders. I was vaguely aware that Kylie stood next to him. I took a wobbly step backward, cursing Jaz for talking me into these stupid shoes.

"You okay?"

I'd missed that sexy nerd voice.

Kylie gave me a sympathetic smile.

"Yeah," I took another step backward. "Just trying to catch up to someone."

Dallas frowned, then glanced over his shoulder "Claire? She ran by us a minute ago."

"Yeah." Of course he'd noticed Claire. The observant McNerd missed nothing.

I shrugged an embarrassed smile at them, then took off toward the parking lot, walking fast instead of running, but

Claire had disappeared.

Frustrated, I headed back toward the courtyard, but out of nowhere, hands gripped my shoulders and spun me around.

Jake.

I told myself not to panic and made myself stand taller. "What do you want?"

He tossed his hair out of his eyes. "I want you and your freaky little posse to stop talking shit about me."

My mouth dropped open. "Are you serious? You're the one who's talking about me! Telling people that we...we..."

His lips curled in a sneer. "That we what, Viv? Did what I know you wanted to do, if you hadn't chickened out?"

Panic and anger shot through me, making me shake. "I didn't...I never..."

"Oh, I know *you never*," he snarled. "That part was obvious."

My hand had a mind of its own, reaching up to slap him, but his reflexes were fast. He caught my hand, gripping it so tightly I winced. "Don't even think about it, Viv." He twisted my wrist and I almost whimpered.

"Let go of me." My voice shook as I looked around desperately for help, but the chimes had rung and everyone had gone back to class.

He didn't let go. "You stop whining to your bodyguard Toff about me. And tell Jaz to shut up, too."

What had Toff done? He must've said something to Jake. Stupid Flipper playing big brother. And Jaz—her big mouth was going to wreak havoc for all of us.

I made myself look him in the eye. "You stop spreading rumors about me, and maybe my friends and I will stop telling people what an asshat you are."

This time he twisted my wrist so hard that tears sprang to my eyes. I wondered if I should yell for help. But no one would hear us out in the parking lot. He'd timed it perfectly because he was sneaky. Slithery. A total snake.

I considered kneeing him in the groin but worried he might retaliate and hurt me. Shivers racked my body as my panic increased. "Please," I begged, hating the whine in my voice. "Just let go, Jake. I'll drop it if you will."

I hated myself for caving in to his bullying, but my fear ratcheted up with every shaky breath.

His grip loosened slightly. He leaned in, and I smelled sweat. "You swear?"

I nodded and jerked my arm out of his loosened grip.

"Good." He stepped close, eyes dark and threatening. "Call off your dogs, Viv, or you'll be sorry."

My legs shook so badly I feared I'd collapse.

He turned and stormed away, and I finally did collapse, sinking onto a nearby bench.

What had just happened? And what could I do about it? If I told anyone, he might really come after me or my friends. I despised him even more now, but maybe for my own safety I needed to lay low.

Toff stopped me as I was leaving my locker with Jaz and Amy. "You okay, Flipper? I saw you bolt off after Claire."

"Are you spying on me, creeper?" I hoped a joke would distract him. I didn't need him going after Jake again and making things worse.

"Nah. I was just bored with all the rock star babbling." He grinned at us, and I noticed his gaze lingered on Amy. Her cheeks instantly flushed, highlighting her freckles.

"I hear you know how to bust into The Lodge," Jaz said. "You wanna take me sometime?"

I shook my head frantically at Toff and Amy giggled.

"No way, freak show," Toff said. "You'd totally get us arrested."

Jaz squealed in frustration. "Why does everyone think I'm a stalker?"

"Because you *are!*" Amy and I exclaimed in unison.

Toff pushed off the wall of lockers, grinning. "Gotta split, psychos." He flipped us a salute as he sauntered away.

"Soo cute," Amy whispered, then she bit her lip, obviously mortified she'd said that out loud.

Jaz and I grinned.

"He's cute," I agreed, "but his ego's enormous."

Amy nodded, watching him leave, laughing with his friends. "Yeah. But so is his heart."

"Oh, Amy." I sighed. "You've got it bad."

"I know." Her voice was so quiet we had to lean in to hear her. "But I can't help it." She glanced at me. "*You* know how it is, even though you're still pretending you don't like Dallas."

"Yeah," Jaz agreed, shoulder-bumping me as we turned to leave. "Queen of repressed desire, that's you."

I stopped to glare at her. "You know, sometimes I want to…to…"

"Strangle me?" she offered helpfully.

"That. And other stuff."

"Stop it, you two," Amy admonished us. "I'm not done talking about Toff."

We stared at her, shocked, then burst into laughter.

"Talk away, sister," Jaz said. "At least you aren't squashing your feelings like some people."

We argued amiably all the way to the bike racks and Jaz even let Amy get in a few more dreamy sighs and starry-eyed observations about Toff. Cocooned between my friends I let myself relax, telling myself Jake had just been spouting off, that he wouldn't really do anything.

I had to believe it.

...

Mom sat at the computer, glaring, when I arrived at the store for my shift.

"Hi." I snapped open a can of soda and plopped into the chair next to her. Dallas's chair.

If I closed my eyes, I could still feel his hands on my shoulders when he'd stopped me from falling and see his intense eyes on me, full of unspoken questions. Or maybe I'd imagined that part.

Mom muttered under her breath, still glaring at the computer.

"You're free to go kill people," I said. "The second shift has arrived."

"Hm?" Mom didn't seem to hear me. She whacked the monitor, swearing.

"Whoa," I said. "That doesn't work, Mom."

"I know. That's why I called him."

Goose bumps rose on my arms. "Called who?"

Mom turned the chair, finally focusing on me. "Dallas, of course. I think I broke something. I can't get the reports to run."

"Let me try." The last thing I wanted was Dallas turning up here to play rescue hero.

Mom stood up. "Go for it, but I've tried everything."

I moved into Mom's vacated chair and stared at the screen where Dallas's custom error message blinked on the monitor: *"Dammit, Jim, I'm a doctor, not a coder. Try again and make sure to follow all the steps."*

Hilarious, Dallas. I closed the error message and followed all the steps from his cheat sheet, which I'd memorized. The stupid error message popped up again.

"See?" Mom said, hovering over me. "I think it might

be my fault. I added some new books today but I was sort of distracted, and I'm not sure I did it right."

I groaned in frustration. "Mom, you're supposed to leave that stuff for me."

She looked guilty. "I know. I was trying to distract myself. I'm struggling with a plot issue and sometimes it helps if I focus on something else."

I sighed heavily. Mom's phone pinged with a text. I held my breath as I waited for her to tell me what I already knew.

"Dallas says he can come by later. He asked if someone's available after the store closes tonight."

I felt her eyes on me. Frickety frak.

"Can you meet him here, hon? I'm on a crazy deadline, and it's probably better if it's you, anyway. You two worked together on the software and you speak his language."

I whirled around to face her. "No, I don't."

"You know what I mean. Please, Vivvy. We need to fix this. I don't know what happened between you and Dallas but—"

"Nothing happened," I snapped.

Silence pressed down on us until I finally caved. It wasn't like I had a choice. I sighed extra long and loud so she'd know how unhappy I was. "Fine. Tell him I'll be here."

"Thanks, sweetie." Her fingers tapped on her ancient phone. "Maybe this will give you two a chance to—"

"Mom, don't. Just don't." I felt her mind-reading stare, but I put up an imaginary force field to keep her out.

She gathered her papers and tea cup. "I could order a pizza for you guys."

Ugh. Not that again. The last time we'd shared a pizza it had ended in that world-rocking kiss. And him telling me goodbye, permanently.

"He can eat popcorn," I said grumpily.

"Vivvy. What's wrong with you? You two got along so well."

I ignored her and shut down the computer, hoping a restart would fix the problem so Dallas wouldn't have to come, after all.

She left the store, calling over her shoulder, "Let me know if Dallas is hungry, and I'll order food."

"Whatever," I muttered under my breath.

Once the computer restarted I tried to run Mom's reports but got the stupid error message again.

Hiddles wandered over, weaving between my legs. "You feeling okay, cat? I'm not him, you know." He glanced up at me and meowed, then jumped into Dallas's chair. "Yeah, today's your lucky day. You can grab some lap time when he gets here."

As soon as I said the words, I imagined myself sitting on Dallas's lap, re-enacting one of my favorite kissing scenes from my ninja hero book. I needed to get a grip. Hiddles rolled over on the chair, lying on his back and exposing his fat stomach. I reached down to pet him but he batted at me, claws out as usual.

The door swung open, letting in a swarm of tourists. I put on my best fake smile and sent a prayer request for strength to whoever watched over pathetic weirdoes like me.

'd just flipped the OPEN sign to CLOSED when Dallas's Vespa pulled up in front of the store. I wondered if I could escape or if he'd already spotted me. Where would I hide, anyway, under the desk with the cat?

He approached the door, running his fingers through his crazy spiky hair, helmet dangling from his hand. My hormones stormed like an out of control riot, flooding my body with adrenaline and giddy anticipation.

"Shut it, girls," I whispered as I unlocked the door.

"Hi." He didn't look happy as he brushed past me, smelling of soap and awesomeness. His hair was damp and I realized he'd just taken a shower. I wondered why and decided not to think about it, especially when Kylie's face popped to mind.

He stashed his helmet under the desk and dropped his backpack in the corner. I smiled as he reached down to pet Hiddles, then I reminded myself that nothing was like it used to be.

Determined to ignore him, I turned away, wandering over to my "Pick Your Hero" display and straightened the books. I avoided the McNerd book, since the guy's glasses reminded me of Dallas.

Dallas cleared his throat. "Um, Vivian? Can you please come here?"

Had I really thought I could avoid him all night? Taking a deep breath and hoping not to fall off my wobbly shoes, I approached the desk but didn't sit down. He raised his head, locking eyes with me.

He blinked behind his glasses and reached up to tug his hair. "Um, can you please sit down and show me what you did?"

Still standing, I said, "My mom tried to run some reports and got your error message. I tried and got the same error."

He nodded and unzipped his hoodie. His T-shirt had a picture of Spock saying "I find your lack of logic disturbing."

"Nice shirt," I said, narrowing my eyes. Was he mocking me with his wardrobe choice?

A muscle in his jaw twitched. "Thanks." He cleared his throat. "Do you know if she added any new data today?"

I nodded. "She did. She said she probably messed up. She was distracted." I shrugged and forced a smile. "Distracted by poisons."

His lips quirked. "Ah, of course." He glanced at the

screen and sighed. "This might take a while."

I glanced at the clock. Almost 7:30. I remembered Mom's offer, and so did my stomach. "Did you, um…are you hungry?"

He looked up, and I watched his Adam's apple move as he swallowed. "Maybe some popcorn?"

Grateful, I escaped to the kitchen and nuked two bags. I grabbed sodas, remembering all the other times I'd done this for us. *"Calm yourself, Vivian,"* Spock said. *"This doesn't mean anything. It's not like you and Dallas were a thing."*

Now Spock was talking like Jake? Had I completely lost my mind?

I sat next to Dallas, careful not to reach for popcorn at the same time he did.

He frowned and rubbed his chin as he stared at lines of code, absently reaching into the bowl for popcorn. I pulled my history textbook out of my backpack and started reading.

"Do you have a lot of homework tonight?" He snapped open his soda can.

I shook my head, not looking at him. "Not much."

"Can you scoot your chair over here? I need to show you something."

I shot him a glance from the corner of my eye, then scooted my chair over a tiny bit. He sighed next to me. Through my hyper-aware peripheral vision, I saw him tug at his hair. I knew he was frustrated. But with me or the software? Maybe both.

"So when you add new books, you have to be sure to hit the submit button or it won't save to the database."

"I know that, Dallas." I winced at the defensiveness in my voice.

He raised an eyebrow. "Okay, so maybe you need to remind your mom?"

I nodded.

"Also, if you don't enter anything in the author field, the book doesn't show up on the report. That's a bug, unfortunately. But I can fix it so you'll at least see the titles on the report. Then you'll know to add the author names later."

I nodded again. I didn't want to say anything that sounded whiney or defensive. I scooted my chair away and pretended to study.

We sat in silence for awhile, Dallas's fingers flying over the keys, pausing occasionally to grab a handful of popcorn. I wondered what it would be like to kiss him now since he'd taste like butter.

Suddenly I remembered his *Star Trek* bible. The book was a giant brick, but I'd been carrying it around with me for reasons I chose not to analyze. I retrieved it from my messenger bag and set it on the desk.

"You don't want it anymore?" He flipped it open, paging through it like he'd discovered a long-lost friend.

"No."

He glanced up, frowning slightly. "I thought you liked it."

I swallowed. "I do. I mean, I did. It's great…it's just…" I shrugged. "I'm sort of done with *Star Trek*."

His eyebrows shot up. "How is that possible? That's like saying you're done with chocolate and peanut butter." His glance strayed to the candy dish which overflowed with Reese's peanut butter cups.

I bit back a smile. I couldn't do this with him. Not when he was with Kylie and I was with…no one.

"Cold turkey," I said. "It's the best way to stop bad habits." *Or obsessions you can't control.*

He reached for his soda and took a long drink. Then he crossed his arms over his stupid shirt and narrowed his eyes. "Speaking of bad habits, how's everything going with your replacement mission? Any luck?"

Why was he doing this? Nervous energy flooded my body. I thought of the shredded RC list and the guilt I still felt about Henry. I took a shaky breath. "It's over."

Dallas's eyes widened behind his glasses. "So…mission accomplished? Target acquired?"

I almost smiled at his battle lingo. God, I'd missed this. Missed him. "No." I kept my eyes on his. "Mission fail."

He took another handful of popcorn and chewed slowly, watching me. I forced myself to maintain eye contact until he finally spoke. "I always thought you picked the wrong target."

I felt a blush flood my cheeks with warmth. Of course I'd picked the wrong target, but I couldn't admit it. As far as I knew, Dallas was still with Kylie. I wasn't going to be a home wrecker. Or crush wrecker. Whatever. I'd done enough damage already.

"So, no Surfer Ball date?" He brushed his hands together, sending white crumbs flying. He frowned, looking around for a vacuum probably. I bit back a smile watching his neat-freakiness in action.

"Nope," I said. "Unless you count the hunkalicious hero I need to read about and review."

The corner of his mouth curved into a sexy smile. "What type? Castle Craving? Power Rangers?"

No way was I confessing to reading about a McNerd hero. "I have a stack of ARCs I need to pick from. I haven't decided yet."

He ran a hand through his hair, and I remembered how it had felt when I ran my own hands through his hair the night we kissed. Heat bloomed everywhere in my body.

"You should go anyway," he said. "Go with your friends. You don't need a date. It's not the fifties."

He was right, of course, but I couldn't tell him the main reason I'd decided not to go was I didn't want to see him and

Kylie wrapped around each other all night. That would kill me.

Instead, Claire would spend the night at my house watching movies, since Jaz and Amy were going to the dance. They kept trying to convince us to join them, but Claire felt like I did, not wanting to see Jake entwined with anyone else.

"I'm sure I'll get a full report on my phone," I said. "Pictures of all the perfect couples. Whatever." I reached toward the popcorn bowl and he pushed it toward me. I took a big handful, grateful for something to keep me from babbling.

"Maybe if you…" he began, then stopped. He turned away, his jaw tight.

"Just don't worry about me, okay?" I snapped, suddenly overwhelmed by the emotions tidal-waving through me. I couldn't have this conversation with him. It hurt too much. "Your replacement mission obviously worked out better than mine," I said through a clenched jaw. "I'm sure you and the perfect Kylie will have a perfect Surfer Ball experience."

He faced me, his eyes narrowed. "Whoa. Why are you mad at me? I'm not the one who decided to act like a Spock robot and not date people I was attracted to."

I wanted to throw my popcorn at him. "Why do you care anyway, Dallas? It's not like we…" I let my voice trail away, hearing Jake's voice in my mind. *"It's not like we were a thing."*

He leaned back in his chair like I'd slapped him, then spoke through gritted teeth. "Look, I know that night we… that you and I…" His voice trailed away. "Things weren't the same between us after that."

"No kidding. One minute you kissed me like…like you meant it, but then you stormed off. Then next thing I know you're dating Kylie." I was appalled at the raw emotion in my voice. I hoped he'd only hear the anger, not the desperate regret underneath.

His eyes darkened and his jaw clenched. "You're giving *me* grief? You, who had a whole list of replacement boyfriends you wanted to take out for a test run? Who said you didn't care about chemistry or connection? Who basically told me to get lost after we kissed?" His face reminded me of the Hulk before he blew up into the green monster. "I thought..." His green eyes flashed like a storm burned inside of him.

"You thought what, Dallas?"

He turned away, his whole body tightened with anger. "I thought after we..." His shoulders heaved with a heavy sigh. "Maybe it meant more to me than it did to you." He met my gaze again, but the angry storm in his eyes had been replaced by wariness, telegraphing a question I didn't want to answer.

I couldn't do this with him. I jumped up and hurried to the kitchen, closing the door behind me. This sucked, to infinity and beyond. I swiped at the tears on my cheeks. Screw it. I was going home. Mom could deal with Dallas.

A knock sounded softly on the door. I pretended not to hear it as I stepped onto the back porch; but before I could escape, Dallas's voice stopped me.

"Vivian. Please don't go."

I didn't turn around, standing frozen on the dark porch, praying he'd apologize but also wanting to run for the house. His footsteps echoed on the kitchen tile, then he stood directly behind me. I smelled his clean scent and heard his deep sigh.

"I'm sorry." His voice was low, and strained. "Please turn around. Look at me."

I shook my head, staring toward our house where a lone lamp shone out of Mom's attic office. Everything looked blurry through my tears.

His hands settled on my shoulders and I flinched. Why was he touching me? His voice was almost a whisper. "I don't know...I just...God, you make me crazy, Vivian. The last thing I want is to hurt you."

My skin burned under his touch. I stepped out of his grip and spun around.

"You're wrong, Dallas. When I kissed you, it did mean something to me." *So much I can't even tell you.* I took a shaky breath "I don't know if—if maybe you heard something about Jake and me, and that's why you think…" I couldn't say any more about those lies. "You know what? Forget it. I'm going home. Just text my mom when you're done."

"Viv, wait—"

But I didn't wait; I left quickly, not daring to look back.

t was almost eleven when I heard the whine of Dallas's Vespa fade away into the night. Mom had gone to the store after I'd stormed into the house. I'd refused to tell her what we'd fought about, but she'd returned a short time later and knocked on my bedroom door.

"Dallas is as close-lipped as you are. But he's staying until he fixes the software. He said he'd finish tonight."

"Whatever," I mumbled into my pillow. Of course he'd finish tonight; he didn't want to spend any more time with psycho Vivian. I flopped over onto my back. "Isn't he special?"

She sighed so loudly it seemed to float under my door and right into my heart. "Vivvy, I don't know what is going on with you two. My guess is a lovers' quarrel." She paused. "A very intense one. I hope you two can work it out."

Lovers' quarrel? No wonder she wrote mysteries instead of romances.

"We hate each other," I called through the door. "So I guess it's a haters' quarrel." I paused. "Whatever you do, don't break the computer again. I'll quit if he has to come back and fix anything else."

She laughed softly on the other side of the door, and I threw my pillow across the room. Then I picked up my cell and scrolled through the messages Dallas had sent while I'd pouted in my room. Three apologies. Four pleas to return to the store. Five stupid emoticons: sad faces, goofy faces, even a stupid Spock face.

It killed me that he might have heard I'd slept with Jake, and now assumed that kissing him hadn't meant anything to me, when the opposite was true. The unfairness of it overwhelmed me.

I pulled up Jake's number and typed a new text message quickly, before memories of his threats stopped me. *"You said you'd back off. Stop telling lies about me. You'd better not tell any lies about Claire, either. I'm sorry I ever let you touch me."*

I stared at the unsent text. I wasn't going to let him keep causing trouble for me. No matter what Dallas or anyone else believed, what mattered was the truth.

Maybe I was just a nerdy bookstore girl, but didn't I matter as much as anyone else? Didn't Claire? Didn't we deserve to be treated decently if someone dumped us? Or even if we broke up with them?

I was tired of worrying about Jake and his lies, but I was even more tired of scurrying around like a scared rabbit, hiding from him on campus, too afraid to tell my friends about his threats. I took a deep breath and hit send.

Then I scrolled through Dallas's apology texts one last time before deleting them, wishing I could delete my feelings for him, too.

"If there are self-made purgatories, then we all have to live in them." —*Spock*

CHAPTER TWENTY-SIX

WEDNESDAY, OCTOBER 8

I told Jaz about my fight with Dallas, then she told Amy, so by the time we gathered for lunch I knew they'd be taking my metaphorical temperature.

"Are you okay?" Amy asked. "Do you want some tea? I always keep chamomile in my locker, in case of emergencies."

"You and Natasha." I sighed, leaning my hand on my chin. "I don't want to talk about Dallas."

"What happened?" Claire asked, fiddling with a dreadlock. I was glad she'd rejoined our lunch table after yesterday's scene.

"Big-time drama," Jaz stage-whispered.

Claire raised her eyebrows at me. "You guys used to date, right?"

I opened my mouth to protest, but Toff slid onto the bench next to Amy, making her blush and disrupting my train of thought.

"'Sup, my lovely harem? What's the big gossip today?" Toff grinned at us and tore open a bag of potato chips.

"Dallas and Viv had a huge fight," Jaz said.

"Dude, seriously?" I glared at Jaz. She had no filter.

She shrugged and tilted her head toward Toff. "He's one

of the girls now, right?" She grinned at him. "You know how Dallas and Viv are. Pretending they can't stand each other when they really want to tear each other's clothes off."

"So it's gonna be one of those lunches, huh?" he asked. "A bunch of he said/she said drama. So what happened? You steal his calculator or something?"

"Hilarious, Toff." I tossed a raisin at him and he almost caught it in his mouth. "No. This was a real fight." I sighed and my gaze drifted across the courtyard.

Dallas sat at a table with Kylie and her friends, but he was staring directly at me. I met his gaze and held it. Toff threw a potato chip at me. "Dude. You're like a dog in heat."

My face flushed. "You're gross, Toff."

"But accurate," he said.

Jaz and Amy giggled while I glared at them. I turned to Claire. "We never dated. We just worked together."

She frowned. "Oh. But it always seemed like…" Her voice trailed away and she shrugged.

Jaz rolled her eyes. "They totally want to. But they're the most stubborn people on the planet."

"Truth," Toff said as he opened another bag of chips. He was like a human garbage disposal. "So is anyone going to tell me what happened? Or do I have to find a translator who speaks girl?"

"Dallas had to fix something on the store computer last night," Amy said. I watched her maintain eye contact with Toff. I knew it was hard for her, but she did it. "Then he and Viv got into a fight about kissing and—"

Toff glanced at me and raised an eyebrow, then turned back to Amy. "Go on."

"Well, they argued because right after he kissed her, he started dating Kylie."

"Seriously?" He looked surprised. Maybe Dallas hadn't told him about our kiss. Unlike Jake, Dallas wasn't spreading any rumors about me. Toff glanced over his shoulder toward Dallas. "So I have to beat his ass, too? I thought I just needed to hurt Jake."

I closed my eyes in frustration. "It's not like that. I told you..." my voice cracked. I gave him a pleading look. "Remember how I told you I blew my chance with him?"

I felt Jaz, Amy, and Claire staring at me. I hadn't told them about my beach chat with Toff.

Toff sighed and stuffed more chips in his mouth, chewing slowly. I shook my head, sending him silent messages not to do or say anything to Dallas.

"What's going on?" Jaz asked. "Are you guys like reading each other's minds or something?"

Toff's lips narrowed, the stubborn tilt to his jaw making me wonder if he was going to seek out Dallas as soon as lunch was over. But then his expression softened and he encompassed everyone with his easy grin. "Wow. And you think guys are hard to understand? You bitches are psycho."

We all laughed but Amy swatted him on the arm. "Don't call us that."

"Bitches or psycho?" He leered at her and she blushed. He turned back to me. "So you fought about all this last night? Just decided to harass the poor guy while he was fixing your computer?"

I shot a glance in Dallas's direction, but he wasn't at the table.

"Just forget it," I said, giving Toff my strongest warning glare. "It doesn't matter. I'm never dating anyone ever again. And I'm definitely never kissing anyone ever again."

Everyone stared at me, then broke into peals of laughter.

"What?" I protested. "You think I'm kidding? Trust me, from now on these lips are totally celibate."

Everyone laughed, but I knew it was true because if I couldn't kiss Dallas, I wasn't kissing anyone.

"Insults are effective only where emotion is present."
—Spock

CHAPTER TWENTY-SEVEN

Jaz and I raced down the hallway, running late after spending longer than usual at the lookout site. Today I agreed with her; it was definitely Fisk jogging along the beach. I'd even signed her log, wishing I could tell her why I recognized him so easily.

I skidded to a stop at my locker, focused on the combination lock, until I noticed Jaz frozen like a statue.

"What?" I frowned at her, then followed her gaze to the top of my locker.

SLUT gleamed down in angry black ink. I stopped breathing, reaching out to the wall of lockers for support.

"Son of a bitch," Jaz whispered.

I gaped at the word, wondering who did it.

"Jake," growled Jaz. "I'm going to kill him."

"Oh." My breath whooshed out of me. Of course it was Jake. "But we can't prove it."

Jaz rolled her eyes. "Who else would do it? Motive and opportunity, just ask your mom."

One of the security guards stalked toward us, his expression grim.

Jaz pointed to my locker when he stopped next to us. "Did you see this?"

He nodded, scowling. "That's the second one today."

"The other one is Claire's locker, right?" asked Jaz.

The grooves in his scowl deepened. "Sounds like you know who did this."

"Not for sure," I said, shooting a warning glare at Jaz, remembering the pain as he twisted my wrist.

"To the principal's office, ladies. Now."

Before Dr. Blake released us, she assured us she'd look into Jake's possible involvement. She also said the custodial staff would try to remove the slur but might not be able to right away.

"You can cover it up with something in the meantime. We have some posters lying around the office if you want. Just don't try to retaliate with Mr. Fontaine's locker. That's not how students at our academy respond."

"You don't have to worry about that." I wasn't going to get in trouble doing payback on his locker. Who knew what he might do?

She nodded. "I'm sorry, Vivian. You can be sure he'll have a serious consequence."

She hesitated. "Would you be interested in restorative justice mediation with him? If he admits he did it?"

Much as I liked my hippie school, sometimes I wished they'd punish offenders like normal schools. Maybe put him in a stockade.

"Probably not. Just, um, send him to the brig or whatever."

Dr. Blake frowned as she wrote on her legal pad. "Noted."

• • •

handed my tardy slip to Ms. Kilgore, consciously avoiding eye contact with everyone. I felt Jake's eyes on me, and Toff's. Had he seen my locker? And what about Dallas? I slid into my seat, heart racing, willing myself not to cry. I couldn't let Jake see how he'd impacted me. When I thought of how he'd touched me, kissed me...how could someone do *that* and then turn on me, threaten me?

As soon as Ms. Kilgore released us, I flew out the door, ignoring Toff as he called after me. I spent the rest of the morning head down, ignoring the whispered comments and giggles aimed my way.

I ignored texts from Amy and Toff, Amy offering chamomile tea and Toff offering to kick some ass. When it was time for lunch, I thought about skipping so I wouldn't have to retrieve my lunch from my locker, but I told myself I needed to be brave.

At my locker, I was shocked to discover the graffiti had been graffiti'd. Instead of SLUT, it now said:

SLUvT

T R

A E

R K

I stepped back, trying to decipher it. Star Trek Luv? Who would...I spun around, looking for Dallas, but he wasn't there. He'd been here, though. I could feel it. For the first time all morning, I smiled.

The rest of the afternoon I stewed about my locker, chewing my nails down to the quick. I wanted to confront Jake, but I was afraid to. He'd turned into such a jackass. If I was honest with myself, I'd admit that he'd always been a jerk; but my stupid hormones had made me overlook that important fact.

I lingered in the hall as everyone swarmed around me, jostling and laughing on their way to the final class of the day. As I started for the library, I spotted Jake leaning against a wall of lockers, watching me with a smirk. His smug expression fueled a fire I didn't even know I had. I stormed down the hallway, shouldering my way through the crowd, headed right for him. His eyes widened as I approached, but he didn't move.

"You need to back off." My voice shook and I knew he heard the tremor because his smirk deepened. Anger stampeded through my veins like wild horses, spinning me into a rage strong enough to overcome my fear. I thought of Claire in tears in the store. Of how humiliated I'd felt when he'd dumped me, saying we were never *a thing*.

"I mean it, Jake. You can't treat people like...like trash you can just throw away when you get tired of them." I glared at him, standing my ground even though I was shaking. I reminded myself I was doing this for Claire, too, and for every other girl he'd lied about because I knew we weren't the only ones.

His eyes narrowed. "I warned you, but you couldn't just let it drop, could you? Just because you were jealous of Claire, you had to get even and tell her some bullshit to make her hate me."

Shocked, it took me a moment to come up with a comeback. "I told her the truth, Jake. Are you crazy? You really think every girl wants you, don't you?" Laughing bitterly, I shook my head. "Newsflash, Jake: You're an ass. And you can't keep using people and lying about it."

This time he was the one to laugh. "Who's going to stop me? You and your little gang of loser friends?"

I was dimly aware that several people had slowed, eavesdropping on our argument. In my peripheral vision, I saw a tall blond figure approaching. Fast.

I took a breath. "I want you to stop lying. About me. About Claire."

He took a step closer, clamping a hand around my wrist. "Maybe Vespa guy would've stuck around if you *did* put out, Galdi—"

The blond figure appeared next to us, breathing heavily and looming over Jake.

"You don't want to do this, Fontaine," Toff growled.

"Fight!" Voices chanted around us, then a classroom door swung open and Mr. Yang bore down on us.

"Gentlemen. Is there a problem?"

Jake released my wrist.

Toff and Jake glared at each other. If looks could kill, they'd both be slit to ribbons.

"No problem," Toff bit the words out.

"Right," Jake snapped. "No problem."

Mr. Yang crossed his arms over his chest until Jake gave up and turned away. I watched him go, my heart beating erratically. Mr. Yang turned back to Toff.

"Everything under control, Mr. Nichols?"

Toff nodded. I could feel the raw energy pulsing out of him. I glanced down the hall just in time to see Jake turn around and raise both hands, flipping us off in stereo.

Toff took a step forward, then stopped when I pulled on his arm.

"You two need to get to class," Mr. Yang said. He pulled a pad of paper out of his pocket and scribbled tardy passes for us.

"Thanks," I said, taking both passes. Toff glared down the hallway after Jake's retreating figure.

"Get to class. Now." Mr. Yang frowned.

"Let's go." I pushed Toff forward, hurrying to match his long, angry stride.

"What the hell were you doing, Viv? You need to stay away from him."

"You saw what he did to my locker." I was practically jogging now, trying to keep up.

He stopped short, and I knocked into him. His normally clear blue eyes were dark and stormy, reminding me of a thundercloud. "Yeah, I saw it, and I plan to do something about it." He glared at me, like somehow this was my fault.

"You can't fight him. You'll get suspended. Kicked off the surf team."

He rolled his eyes. "I'm not an idiot, Viv. There are other ways to deal with him." He ran a hand through his messy hair. "Just stay away from him, all right?" He took a breath, and suddenly the storm in his eyes was replaced by pleading. "Please?"

We stared at each other for a long moment. I remembered our night on the beach together, how he'd said he first felt sorry for me when I was teased as a little girl. Frustration wound through me, tightening my insides like a coil. I hated that he felt obligated to protect me.

"I needed to stand up for myself," I said.

He huffed an exasperated sigh. "Yeah, I wish all girls would stand up to him. But he's dangerous. You know what they say about poking snakes, right? Just keep away from him, Viv. You told him off, now let it go."

"But if nobody calls him out, he wins! He gets to keep being an ass, and using people, and...and—" My voice caught. My rage had cooled down and was threatening to dissolve into tears.

Slowly, Toff reached out a hand, but I batted it away. His jaw tightened, and I saw the hurt in his eyes. I wanted to tell him I was sorry, but instead I stood frozen in my self-righteousness, frustrated that he wanted me to just ignore Jake.

Spock wouldn't ignore Jake; he'd do the Vulcan nerve pinch and paralyze him.

"I don't need a bodyguard, Toff." I matched his intense gaze with my own. I worried he'd do something stupid to Jake and end up suspended or worse.

His eyebrows shot up. "I'm your friend, Viv. I care about you. You're practically my freaking sister. I'm not going to just let him—" He stopped, shoving his sleeves up his muscled forearms. His breathing was ragged. "Never mind. Do whatever the hell you want." He spun away from me and stormed down the hall, slamming his fist against a locker before rounding the corner and disappearing from view.

As the sound of his fist banging on metal echoed in the hall, I staggered back as if he'd slapped me.

Why couldn't I ever get it right? Why did I keep hurting the people I cared about the most?

CHAPTER TWENTY-EIGHT

HUNKALICIOUSHEROES.COM
Romance Reviews for Ravenous Readers

Book Review: END OF DAYS, Genre: horror
Rating: ***Bare Feet
Reviewed by: Sweet Feet

Author Richard McAlister is a master of the scary-as-hell, nightmares-for-weeks stuff. I don't usually read horror, but next week is Halloween, and I needed a break from the lovey-dovey stuff. Why? Don't ask.

Anyway, this book scared the holy heck out of me. I ended up sleeping in my mom's room on her floor. No lie. So if that's your thing, snatch it up. I'm not even going to tell you what happens in this book because then I'd have to relive it and have more nightmares.

Highly recommended for people trying to kick the romance thing (in real life, I mean. Never the books.)

***This one's out of my usual genre. Bare feet = run like mad.

"Where there's no emotion, there's no motive for violence."
—Spock

CHAPTER TWENTY-NINE

Time slowed to a crawl, the days as gloomy as my mood as the date of the Surfer Ball crept up on me. Dallas hadn't tried to talk to me or hadn't sent any more apology texts after that night in the bookstore. Toff didn't eat lunch at our table anymore, and I knew it was because of me. Jake left me alone, so I was hopeful his anger had finally abated since he'd defaced my locker.

I hadn't read a romance in weeks, but now that the night of the Surfer Ball had finally arrived, I needed to find something to distract me.

After I locked up the shop, I perused a new stack of donations, lingering over an Austen sequel about Mary Bennett. Heck, if awkward Mary Bennett could find love… My phone pinged with a text from Claire.

"Hey! We beat San Antigua! Now u have 2 come 2 the ball. At least to the party. I changed my mind & am going to the dance."

San Antigua High was the reigning surf team champions. They'd won state for several years in a row. For our small school to beat them in some of the league final events was huge. I pictured Toff doing his bicep curl pose and smiled. As if he'd read my mind, his text pinged my phone, with a photo of him celebrating. *"Party on the beach after the dance, Wordworm. U better show."* We'd hardly spoken since the incident with Jake, so his text felt like an olive branch I couldn't ignore.

Texts from Jaz and Amy arrived in quick succession with the same basic message, telling me to at least come to the party even if I wasn't going to the dance. I sank into one of the store's overstuffed chairs, weighing my options.

It would be a huge party. Lots of celebrating. Lots of hooking up, especially for the surfer gods triumphant in their victory. I wondered if there was any way I could get Toff to notice Amy. Really notice her. I rubbed my forehead. I'd done a horrible job of matchmaking for myself; why did I think I could do it for my friends?

I should go. I hadn't done anything fun in forever. But what if Dallas was there with Kylie? And Jake would probably be there. I sighed, curling into the chair. I couldn't avoid everyone forever.

I sent a group message. "OK. Not the dance, but the beach party. But I need a ride." Mom had left earlier this afternoon with Paul, telling me she wasn't sure if they'd be back tonight or tomorrow morning. I wasn't going to ride my bike miles down the coastal highway in the dark.

Three offers of rides pinged back at me. I smiled at my phone. Maybe my love life was a train wreck, but I had awesome friends.

Before Amy and Jaz picked me up for the party, they peppered me with texts and Snapchat photos from the

Surfer Ball. The girls from the surf team looked amazing in their rainbow of mermaid dresses, shimmering in the laser lights at the dance.

Jaz Face-Timed me when it was time for the Poseidon award. I wasn't at all surprised to see Toff crowned King of the Sea amidst a roar of cheers. He strutted across the stage waving his trident scepter, rocking a three-pointed golden crown, a smug grin plastered on his face. I knew Amy must've been swooning.

Amy and Jaz still wore their ball dresses when they picked me up. I wore jeans and a bulky sweatshirt since I wasn't trying to impress anyone. They chattered nonstop all the way to the beach, but I noticed they were careful not to mention Dallas, and I didn't ask about him.

The party was wild. Two huge bonfires lit up the beach and music blared from competing speaker systems. I could smell the beer and weed when I stepped out of Amy's car.

"Wow," I said. "Looks like a rager."

"I wonder how long 'til the cops show?" Jaz said as she picked her way across the beach, her dress shoes clutched in her hands.

"That's why we're so far out of town," Amy said. "So they don't show. At least not for awhile."

"How do you know that?" I asked.

She slanted me a smile. "Toff told me."

Jaz and I stared at each other, each wondering the same thing.

"Don't do that," Amy said. "Nothing's going on between us."

"Oh, really?" Jaz said. "I noticed you two dancing a few times tonight."

Even in the dark, I could see Amy blushing. "That was nothing. He danced with everybody. That's just how he is."

Before I could ask more probing questions, Claire ran up

and hugged me. "You came! I'm so happy to see you."

"Congratulations." I returned her hug. "I heard you smoked the short board division."

She grinned proudly. "It was sick. I still can't believe I won."

A loud roar caught our attention, and we all turned toward the source. The guys on the surf team had formed a human pyramid, dressed in their tux jackets and board shorts, with Toff on the top, waving his scepter.

We laughed and cheered, especially when the pyramid collapsed, sending all of them sprawling. Toff spotted us and jogged over, grabbing me in a sideways hug. "Wordworm. I'm shocked and honored you made an appearance."

"I'm here for Claire, not you," I teased.

He grinned down at me. "Liar." He reached out to tug on my curls. We looked at each other for a long moment, then his mouth curved into his easy grin, and I knew he'd forgiven me for our argument about Jake.

"Is, um, Jake here tonight?" I asked, apprehension coiling through me.

Toff shook his head. "Haven't seen him. Probably because I warned him not to show."

Relieved, I returned his grin. "Excellent. Take us to the food, Flipper."

We trailed along, laughing and joking as we made our way through the huge crowd. Jaz handed me a plastic beer cup. "Live a little, Viv. Don't worry, I'll be the DD tonight."

I took a sip. I didn't drink much, but maybe she was right—I should try and have fun tonight.

I turned to look up the beach and my gaze landed on Dallas, who stood by himself, looking right at me. Even though it was windy and cold on the beach, I was suddenly flooded with heat. His eyes locked on mine, and I felt as if the *Enterprise*'s tractor beam had latched onto me, pulling me in.

He wore a tux, but his bow tie hung loose and his pants were rolled up. He was barefoot, holding his dress shoes in one hand. Everything in me wanted to run toward him, but I knew that was the crazy hormones talking. He was here with Kylie. I broke eye contact and turned back to my friends.

I danced with my friends, pretending to have fun, but my heart wasn't in it. My eyes kept searching for Dallas. Occasionally I'd spot his silhouette, but then I'd turn away, not wanting him to catch me staring. After awhile I decided to walk up the beach by myself to clear my head and try to shake off my sadness. I had to let go of my McNerd obsession. Whatever could've happened between us was in the past. He'd moved on. So should I.

The sounds of the party faded as I strolled along the beach, letting the cold waves lap over my feet. I loved the beach at night with the canopy of stars overhead. Nights like this I pretended I was a visitor from another planet, that I'd just beamed down from my spaceship like a Star Trek explorer, the only form of sentient life. At least if that were true I wouldn't have to worry about my love life.

"Hey!" a voice called after me and I pivoted. I couldn't make out the figure in the darkness but as he jogged closer I was shocked to recognize Jake.

My pulse thudded in my ears as he caught up to me. Apparently he'd ignored Toff's warning and decided to crash the party. When I saw the anger slashing across his face, my internal warning system activated. Panicked, I looked around, but we were the only ones on this deserted section of the beach.

"What's up?" I asked, forcing lightness into my voice. Could I defuse this somehow? Convince him to leave me alone?

He stood so close he could have kissed me. Or hit me. He glared down at me and my eyes darted around again, searching for witnesses, but there weren't any.

"Who the hell do you think you are, Viv?" His voice echoed in the night air, and he stepped even closer.

I took a step back. "What are you talking about?"

His eyes narrowed, but before I could react, he grabbed my sweatshirt, pulling me in close. "You're the reason Claire dumped me. You and your frigid bitch bullshit. Then you ratted me out because of your locker. Now everyone's pissed at me because Toff made it sound like I practically raped you or something." His hands twisted in the fabric of my shirt, and my heart hammered in my chest.

"Let go of me, Jake." I wanted to scream, but fear tamped down my volume and the words came out as barely a whisper.

"Why should I?" He pulled me in. In his drunken belligerence, he tried to kiss me, but ended up slamming his forehead into mine. My head spun, and when my vision cleared I could see the anger in his eyes. "You bitch. You're just a scared little whore, but I know what you want."

I tried to shove him away but he'd wrapped a leg behind me and I was trapped. Terror tore through me as I struggled against him. I turned my face away from him, but he yanked it back, hurting my neck and scratching my face. Far in the distance, I heard shouting. I thought I saw shadowy figures running toward us in the darkness, but they were far away.

"No!" I found my voice at last, yelling as loud as I could and pushing my hands against his chest, but he was much stronger than me. Adrenaline flooded through me as tears welled in my eyes. I tried to remember what I'd learned in the self-defense class Mom had forced me to take. I tried to lift my knee to aim for his groin, but he held me tight, his sour, beer-soaked breath in my face, his dark eyes full of venom. His fingers pressed into my arms, and I knew I'd have bruises in the morning.

"I'm gonna make you like it. Make you beg for it." He sneered. "Your bodyguard Toff isn't around to save you."

"No!" I was sobbing now, using all my strength to try to

pull away. Then suddenly I was wrenched out of his grip, strong arms wrapping around my shoulders and hugging me against a tall, firm body, while another body flew through the air, tackling Jake with a grunt, and pinning him to the sand.

Shaking and sobbing I turned to see whose arms held me. Toff's worried face loomed over me. "Holy crap. Are you all right, Viv?"

I nodded, unable to form words. We both turned back toward the sounds of swearing and fighting. Jake staggered up from the sand. He and Dallas faced each other like wild animals, circling each other warily. Somewhere along the way, Dallas had lost his tuxedo jacket and his tie. And his shoes.

"You want her?" Jake sneered. "She's all yours, geek. She won't put out, though. Not unless you make her." Jake's words hit me like a punch, making me stagger against Toff, whose arms tightened around me.

"I might need to get in on the ass-kicking," Toff whispered in my ear. "If that's okay with you."

I nodded mutely, my eyes transfixed by Dallas. Rage and power rolled off him in waves I could practically feel.

"Shut the fuck up," Dallas growled. His eyes never left Jake's face.

"Make me," Jake snarled.

Dallas was lightning fast. One minute they faced each other, the next, Dallas spun like a top. His leg shot into the air and his foot connected with Jake's head. Jake collapsed onto the sand, Dallas leaning over him, Jake's shirt twisted in his grip.

"You sure about that?" Dallas asked, his voice low and threatening. "Cuz I'd love to make you shut the hell up. Permanently."

"Oh, yeah." Toff laughed next to me. "I knew he was good but I didn't know how good."

"What?" I glanced at him, confused.

Toff shot me a weird look. "Google him, dork."

A strange spidey sense tingled the top of my head. Google Dallas?

Toff squeezed my shoulders reassuringly, then rushed toward Dallas and Jake. Toff leaned over Jake's prone figure and yelled in his face. "You're a fucking snake, Fontaine, and I'm going to make sure everyone knows it. You try that shit with any other girl and I will personally rip off your dick and shove it up your ass."

"Don't forget his balls," Dallas growled, tightening his grip and making Jake wince in pain.

"Them too." Toff glanced at Dallas and they shared a victorious, testosterone-laden grin that sent shivers up my spine.

"Let me go," Jake whined, his voice plaintive.

Dallas leaned closer to Jake, turning so that his ear was next to Jake's mouth. "Speak up. I can't hear you."

Toff's laughter ricocheted off the waves and I hugged myself tight. I felt as if I was having an out-of-body experience watching all this unfold. What would have happened if they hadn't showed up?

My eyes connected with Dallas's as he stood up, letting Toff take over the asshole-wrangling. We stared at each other, and I swore I could feel electrical currents bouncing in the air between us.

"You okay?" he asked, his eyes fixating on me so intensely I took a step back.

I nodded, then stumbled in the sand, overwhelmed with the desire to crumple as I was overcome by tears, realizing how close I'd come to a horrible assault.

Dallas was next to me in just a few quick strides. He glanced over his shoulder at Toff. "You got him?"

Toff had pulled Jake to his feet and held him like a cop with a perp. "Yeah." He nodded brusquely. "You take care of Viv. I'll throw away the trash."

"Fuck you," Jake said, but his heart wasn't in it. Toff yanked him hard, dragging him away from us like a wild dog.

"Wait," I said, so softly my voice disappeared into the wind. "Toff, wait!" He heard me this time and stopped. I took a shaky breath and walked toward them, Dallas hovering next to me.

Jake glared at me, blood running from his nose, his tuxedo shirt torn and ripped. I trembled, but I had to do this. "This is the third time you've tried to hurt me." I heard Dallas inhale sharply and remembered he didn't know about the incidents in the parking lot or the hallway. I took a breath and tried to catch Dallas's gaze, but he was staring directly at Jake now. "If you ever touch me again, I will call the cops. I'm…I'm not scared of you, Jake. You lied about me. If anyone's a slut, it's you."

"Screw you, Vivian." He barely got the words out before Toff had him immobilized.

"That's no way to talk to a lady," Toff growled at him.

Jake snorted. "She's not a lady. She's a—"

I felt Dallas vibrating next to me, but before I could stop him, he launched himself at Jake again, wrapping his hand around Jake's throat.

"Dallas, wait," I pleaded. This was so unlike him; I'd never even seen Dallas kill a spider.

I was afraid he'd hurt Jake again, more than he already had. Much as I loathed Jake, I didn't want Dallas to end up in jail, and I was afraid he might.

Dallas turned to me, the raw emotion in his eyes stunning me.

"L-let him go, Dallas. Please." We stared at each other for a long moment until he tore his gaze from mine and exchanged a look with Toff. He unclenched his hand from Jake's throat, but I noticed Toff tighten his grip around Jake's chest.

Dallas took a step closer toward him, and I saw sheer terror in Jake's eyes. "So I lied about us. So what?" He turned his face toward me. "You would've let me f—"

He never finished his sentence because Dallas's fist slammed into Jake's stomach and he crumpled, even though Toff still held him.

"Dude," Toff said to Dallas. "I'm taking him away before you do any more damage." Then he yanked Jake's hair. "You're even dumber than you look, asshole. You do realize he could probably kill you if he wanted to, right?"

Dallas ran a hand through his hair as he watched them go, breathing heavily. He was shaking, too, but I knew it wasn't from fear. I wasn't sure I could handle the intensity rolling off of him. He was like an amped up superhero who needed to fly to the moon and back to calm himself down.

I realized he'd lost his glasses during the fight. I turned away, scanning the beach for the black frames. I knelt in the sand, feeling around for his glasses, my eyes filling with tears. I wanted to go home, to hide under my covers and release all the emotions warring within me.

Dallas knelt next to me, the smell of sweat, adrenaline, and his soap filling my nose and making my head spin. I kept digging, pushing away broken seashells and strands of kelp.

"What are you doing?" he asked, his voice surprisingly gentle for someone who'd almost snapped a guy's neck.

"Looking for your glasses."

He laughed softly. "They're in my jacket. Back by the bonfire."

My hands stilled in the wet sand. I sat back on my heels and finally looked at him. A long, shaky breath eased out of me as I met his eyes.

"Why'd you take them off?" I whispered.

He shrugged. "Thought I might be doing some wild dancing." His smile didn't reach his eyes.

"Did you? Do a lot of dancing?"

He kept his eyes on mine. "No."

My heart raced. The adrenaline pumping through me tonight was making me queasy. I dropped my gaze from his face, taking in his torn and bloody shirt. "I don't think you're going to get your deposit back on your tux rental."

"It was worth it."

I looked up into his eyes, wishing I could lose myself in them forever. I squeezed my eyes shut, reminding myself he'd come here with Kylie, not me.

"Is it…okay if I touch you?" he asked softly as he stood up. I opened my eyes to see his hands reaching out, waiting to pull me to a standing position.

I nodded, letting him tug me upright. Electricity shot through me, and I stumbled back, the impact of what had almost happened hitting me full force.

He held onto me, his grip firm. "It's all right, Vivian," he whispered. "He's gone. He's not coming back." He lifted one of his hands, lightly brushing the scratch on my cheek. His eyes darkened when I flinched. I hadn't realized how rough Jake had been. He had truly wanted to hurt me.

I nodded, but I couldn't speak. Trembling, I let myself fall into him. As his arms enfolded me, I wondered if this was what it felt like to be hugged by an avenging angel. He sighed into my hair as I melted into his warmth. His hands stroked my back as I cried softly, dampening his shirt with my tears.

"I'm s-s-orry," I whispered, though I knew I had nothing to apologize for.

"Shh," he said, his lips in my hair. His arms tightened around me. "God, Viv. If we hadn't come after you…" His voice trailed away as he pulled me even closer.

"Why did you?" I asked, pulling away just enough to look up into his glorious eyes.

His eyes roamed over my face. "I saw you walk off by

yourself. Then I saw Jake run after you. He came out of nowhere. I think maybe he was hiding out. Waiting." His face tightened into an angry grimace. "I grabbed Toff and we came after you."

"Why?"

He sighed, pain etching his face. "The graffiti on your locker. The stuff Toff told me about…What an ass he is. I knew whatever he was up to wasn't good, and I sure as hell wasn't going to stand around and do nothing."

I nodded, then dropped my gaze. His hand cupped my chin and tilted my face up.

We stared into each other's eyes, the moonlight shining down on us, the waves crashing behind us. I wanted to linger forever in the comfort of his arms. I wanted him to kiss me, but I was afraid to hope for that. And truthfully, I wasn't ready for anyone to touch me like that. Not yet. Right now, I just needed to get home, far away from Jake and the craziness of this night.

And I needed to Google Dallas. I couldn't wait to do that.

"I'm taking you home," he said, reading my mind.

"Okay." I hesitated. "What about Kylie? How will she get home?"

He shifted slightly, keeping his arm tight around my shoulders. "She didn't come with me."

I turned my face to look up at him. "She didn't?"

He shook his head. "She asked me, but I said no. I came by myself." He sighed. "I think I caused my own collateral damage. But I couldn't keep—" He broke off, his gaze dropping to my mouth, then he turned away toward the bonfires. "You should let your friends know you're leaving with me."

"Yeah," I said, fumbling for my phone. What had he meant by causing collateral damage?

He reached for my phone. "Want me to do it?"

I nodded, overwhelmed again by his sweetness. Then

I panicked at what he might see if he pulled up my text histories. I imagined Dallas reading the messages Jaz sent about him, and my cheeks burned red. Thank goodness it was dark out. I clutched my phone to my chest. "I'll do it."

A hint of a smile tugged at his lips.

We paused while I fired off a quick message to Jaz, Amy, and Claire.

He pulled his phone out of his pocket. "I'll tell Toff to give your friends a ride if they need one, after he deals with Jake."

I frowned. "I thought Toff was drinking."

Dallas glanced up at me. "Nope." A grin flashed across his face. "Like that guy needs any extra chemicals."

I laughed softly, flushing under Dallas's warm smile.

He sent his text, then pulled me in close. We walked in silence across the beach, then climbed the crumbling steps. Cars lined the road as far as I could see. Far in the distance, I heard sirens. The party would be breaking up soon. I shot off another line of texts to my friends, warning them to head out sooner rather than later. The sound of sirens made me wonder what Toff would do with Jake.

"I'm down this way." Dallas pointed and I let him lead me. I couldn't wait to get home and crawl underneath my covers. I might even have to dig my old stuffed bear out of the closet to sleep with tonight. A sudden vision of curling up next to Dallas in my bed overwhelmed my senses and I stumbled.

"You sure you're okay? To ride on the back of the Vespa?" Concern etched his face.

So I was finally going to live out one of my swoony fantasies. "Yeah. I'll be fine."

We reached his Vespa and he handed me the Union Jack helmet. "What about you?" I asked.

He shot me a crooked grin. "My skull's thicker than yours."

"I'm not sure anyone's is." Dallas seemed surprised that I

was able to crack a joke at a time like this, but I felt safe with him.

"Your glasses," I said, suddenly wondering how he'd drive without them. He pressed a button on his scooter and popped open the Vespa's seat, revealing a storage compartment. He pulled out a leather jacket and reached into the pocket for a pair of glasses that looked exactly like his usual pair.

"Always prepared." He grinned as he put them on. He held out the jacket. "You should wear this."

"No." I pointed to his torn and bloody shirt. "You need it more than me. I'll be fine."

I tugged the helmet on while he zipped up his jacket. He reached over to buckle the strap under my chin, adjusting the strap to fit me. His warm fingers against my throat made me shiver.

"Ready?" He cocked an eyebrow and I nodded, biting my lip.

He settled himself on the seat, and I climbed on behind him. He started the engine and we pulled away, winding slowly up the coast, just as I'd fantasized so many times.

I reveled in the feel of his muscles, wondering if he felt the same way about me pressing against him. I closed my eyes, pushing away images of Jake. Son of a... I wanted to kill him. Maybe Dallas would do it for me since he was apparently a bad-ass ninja, just like in my favorite book. I closed my eyes, leaning into his back. We swerved slightly and my grip tightened around him.

"Sorry," he called over his shoulder, his voice swallowed by the wind. I dropped my hands to his thighs, and felt every muscle in him tense at my touch. I wished we could ride forever, just the two us, following the road wherever it took us.

Much too soon, we pulled into my driveway, slowing next to Mom's car. So she'd come home after all. Great.

Dallas lowered his feet to the ground and killed the

engine. We sat there, neither of us moving, then I decided I'd better disentangle myself before I made a fool of myself clinging to him like a desperate cello groupie.

He dismounted, and I unbuckled my helmet and handed it to him. He looked toward our house, tugging at his hair. The glow of the TV made the living room look blue. Movie night. I hoped Mom and Paul weren't making out on the couch like a couple of teenagers.

"I'll walk you up," Dallas said.

The cold night air and vivid memories of Jake's attack made me long to be connected to him again. I wanted his arms around me, but he stood motionless, waiting, and watching me.

Sadness and regret, so much regret, washed over me. I turned to walk across the gravel driveway. He matched my pace, his body just inches from mine. The backs of our hands brushed against each other as we mounted the steps, and I sucked in a breath. Did he feel the electricity crackling between us or was it just me?

We reached the top of the stairs and turned toward each other. My body tingled with anticipation. He ran a hand through his hair, then shoved both hands in his pockets.

"Are you going to tell your mom? About Jake?" His voice was low and intense.

"I don't know. Maybe." I knew I had to, but I couldn't even think about it right now.

He nodded. "Toff and I are witnesses. You know we'll be there for you, right? If you want to, um, do something official, or whatever."

The thought of calling the cops made my knees buckle. I grabbed the deck chair closest to me. Dallas's face tightened with anger. "Son of a... I'm going to fucking kill him." He grunted. "Sorry. I meant to say frakking kill him."

I laughed softly. "I don't know if I'm more shocked by your ninja skills or your f-bombs." I forced a wan smile.

"Anyway, I want to frakking kill him, too."

A smile tugged at his lips. "You going to hit him with a stack of books?"

I loved that he knew it was the perfect moment to make a joke. I stared at my feet. "No. But I think I might hire a ninja to do it for me." I raised my eyes. "You know any kick-ass karate guys?"

His eyes narrowed but his lips quirked slightly. "Nope."

"I can Google it in five seconds, you know."

His smile deepened. "You're going to Google hit men? I bet your mom already has." He shrugged, still smiling. "Research."

I reached out to swat him playfully on the shoulder, then dropped my hand, afraid to touch him because what if he didn't want me to?

His eyes tracked my hand as it dropped to my side, then he raised his eyes to mine. His jaw tightened before he spoke. "Vivian, I—"

"Vivvy! I didn't know you were home." Mom's voice shattered the chemistry between us as she stepped onto the deck.

"Hi, Ms. Galdi." Dallas looked relieved. What had he been about to tell me?

"Dallas!" Mom oozed giddiness, darting me a smug look. "What a nice surprise. Do you want to come inside?"

I was grateful Dallas wore the leather jacket. Mom would've freaked at the bloody shirt.

Paul appeared behind Mom in the doorway. "You kids are home early. I thought tonight would be a late one with all the celebrating."

Dallas and I shared a pained glance.

"I wasn't feeling well," I said quickly. "Dallas brought me home."

Mom frowned, reaching out to touch my forehead like I was five years old.

"I should go," Dallas said, taking a step back from all of us.

Mom tilted her head. "You sure? We have brownies, fresh from the bakery."

Paul grinned. "I splurged. White flour instead of wheat."

Dallas ducked his head. "Thanks, but I need to go." He glanced at me. "Remember what I said, okay?"

I nodded, swallowing over the lump in my throat. I needed to get to my room, stat, so I could fall apart.

"Bye." He nodded at Mom and Paul, his glance sweeping over me quickly, then he turned and jogged down the steps, disappearing into the darkness.

"Vivian, what's going on?" Mom asked.

I pushed past her, tears streaming down my face, and ran to the safety of my room where I locked the door and cried myself to sleep.

"Has it occurred to you that there is a certain inefficiency in constantly questioning me on things you've already made up your mind about?" —*Spock*

CHAPTER THIRTY

Sunday morning dawned as gray as my mood. I'd dreamed of Dallas and Jake: swirling images of desire and repulsion. I woke sweat-soaked and nauseated, telling myself to breathe. Telling myself I was safe.

I grabbed my phone, suddenly remembering I'd fallen asleep without Googling Dallas. Text messages from Jaz, Amy, and Toff filled my screen, but I ignored them. Instead I opened my phone's internet browser and typed in Dallas Lang, Wisconsin.

My screen filled quickly. *"Dallas Lang, Wisconsin State Teen Martial Arts Champion. Dallas Lang: Regional Champion. Dallas Lang: Can He Win Nationals?"*

Holy. Crapoli.

I sat up, staggered to my desk, and powered up my laptop. I needed a big screen for this kind of data. As I waited for my system to come to life, I picked up The Lovers tarot card the weird psychic lady had forced on me. I'd meant to throw it away but that seemed like bad karma. Today it felt like the card burned my hands, even though I knew it was just my imagination.

I Googled Dallas Lang again, only this time I clicked on images for results. The photos made my mouth go dry.

In the first photo he held a trophy above his head, laughing. Shirtless. My eyes honed in on the tattoo curling around the top of his shoulder. I couldn't tell what it was, maybe a dragon? Whatever it was, it made me reach for a glass of water. He looked like a freaking action movie star. Plus, he wasn't wearing glasses, just like last night. I remembered when I'd interviewed him over coffee and stupidly asked him if he ever wore contacts.

He'd shot me that sexy smile and said, "Sometimes."

My eyes scanned the article. "Dallas Lang, reigning state teen champion of Taekwondo, triumphed again, beating highly ranked Bradley Closs in a sparring match that should have been on pay per view. After the match, Lang and Closs posed for photos, surrounded by a surprisingly raucous group of female fans."

I snorted and kept reading.

"When asked how he continued to dominate state and regional matches, Lang, ever the gracious winner, praised his sensei and his dojo." I reached for my phone and typed a text.

"Solved: the case of the mysterious trophies." I glanced at the time: 9:03. Was he awake? So what; he'd see it eventually. I hit send and returned to my Googling, lingering over the images.

My phone pinged at 9:42 a.m.

"You going to write another article?"

I smiled as I typed my reply. *Do you want me to?"*

"No."

"Why so modest?"

"Why so curious?"

"It's my DNA. Mystery author mom. Remember?"

"I remember."

My breath came in shallow beats.

His next text came after a few minutes of radio silence.

"How are you?"

I knew what he meant. He wanted to know how I was mentally, physically, and every other way after last night.

How was I? When I didn't think about Jake and instead salivated over photos and articles about Dallas, I was fine. More than fine. But when I thought of Jake grasping me in his angry vise grip, I felt a panic attack swarm over me like a hive of angry bees.

"You there, Vivian?"

"I'm okay."

"Can I call you?"

Spock started to protest, but I ignored him. *"Sure."*

Seconds later my phone rang. "Hey." His sleepy voice sent my hormones into red alert mode.

"So." I swallowed. "Apparently you *are* a ninja bad-ass. For real."

"Apparently." His reply was soft and sexy.

"You weren't going to tell me?"

He sighed into the phone. "I would've. Eventually. If we'd…um…spent more time together."

I closed my eyes, willing my racketing pulse rate to slow. "So is your body like a lethal weapon? Did you have to register with the sheriff's office when you moved here?"

He laughed, sending shivers to all the wrong places. "I'm registered with the FBI. Covers all the states." He sounded more awake now.

"How convenient." I wondered if he slept in his underwear. My entire body burned as I tried to ignore the tattooed, bare-chested images flashing through my mind.

"So," he said. "Seriously. You doing okay?"

I sighed into the phone. "I guess."

"Did you tell your mom yet?"

"No."

He didn't say anything. We breathed together and I

wondered if he was picturing me in my bed the way I was picturing him.

"You're working today, right? Since Sunday's the day your mom takes off?"

Warmth licked through me. "Stalking me again?"

"Observing. Big difference, like I told you before."

I leaned into my pillow, wishing he was next to me.

"So are you?" he asked. "Working today?"

"Yeah." I hesitated. "What are you doing today?"

Silence for a few seconds, then a sigh. I pictured him tugging at his hair. "I have some stuff to do. Homework. Some other stuff. "

"Ninja stuff?"

He laughed softly. "Maybe."

We breathed together again. I formed the words in my mind, selecting and discarding carefully before I finally spoke. "Thank you, Dallas. For—for saving me. For being a real-life hero. And for bringing me home last night." I took a deep breath, hesitated, then let more words spill out. "You made me feel safe, Dallas."

I thought I heard his breath hitch but I wasn't sure.

"I'm glad we were there," he said. "Really glad."

Neither of us said anything, then I tried to make a joke. "Your moves are way more impressive than a Vulcan nerve pinch."

He laughed softly. "So you're on Team Kirk now?"

I swallowed. Every nerve in my body tingled with an energy I couldn't control if my life depended on it. "That's a big leap. From Vulcan to crazy train."

"Kirk's not crazy. Just passionate." He paused. "Anyway. For what it's worth, I think you should tell your mom. You don't have anything to be ashamed of, Vivian."

My breath came short and fast. "I-I feel as if...I don't know. As if I should've somehow been able to take care of myself better."

He swore under his breath. "That's stupid. It's simple physics, Viv. You couldn't have fought him off."

I sighed into the phone. "Maybe if I had your ninja moves, I would've had a better chance."

This time he sighed. "Maybe. But he had a major advantage over you. That's why I hate guys like that." He was quiet for a moment. "That's why I started in martial arts when I was a kid. After getting beat up one too many times, I wanted to learn how to fight back."

"Achievement unlocked," I whispered, and he chuckled into the phone.

"Seriously, you shouldn't feel as if you…failed or whatever. Sometimes other people have to step in, especially when it's not a fair fight. Or a full-on attack, like last night."

I started trembling, remembering how scared I'd been.

"Viv? You still with me?"

I rubbed at my eyes, at the scared and angry tears. Maybe I should've told Mom. I didn't want to be in the store by myself today.

"You should call Toff. Jaz. Amy. All your friends. Have them hang out with you at the store today."

But he was the one I wanted next to me.

"I wish I could come by," he said, reading my mind, "but I need to be somewhere at ten thirty." He hesitated. "Call Toff, okay? He's got your back. You know that, right?"

"Yeah," I murmured. "I know."

"Promise me you'll call your friends, okay? And tell your mom?" He hesitated. "I'll see you at school, Vivian."

Vivian, not Viv. Call my friends. Like he wasn't one of them. I exhaled, releasing a long breath. "See you," I whispered, then I disconnected before he could hear the tears in my voice.

Jake's angry face filled my mind, but I pushed it away.

I wouldn't let him intrude. No matter what happened with Dallas and me, today and every day from now on was going to be a Jake-free zone.

No assholes allowed.

spent the afternoon working in the store, grateful to be busy. In between customers, I texted Jaz, Amy, and Claire, who were losing their collective minds about what had happened last night. They all wanted to come see me in person, but I delayed them, despite Dallas's advice, telling them the store was too busy. I was afraid I might melt down with my friends and I didn't want that to happen in public.

Toff texted me late in the afternoon. I guessed he'd slept in, after partying half the night. *"How's the Wordworm?"*

"Groovy," I texted.

He sent back a row of cross-eyed, tongue-rolling smiley faces. *"Hippie."*

"Yeah. So what?"

"Seriously. How's my favorite dork?"

"Good." I hesitated then typed again. *"I Googled Dallas."*

"Kick ass, huh? R U even more in luv with him now, dork?"

And what if I was? Did it matter? *Call your friends,* Dallas had said, leaving himself out of that equation. He was remarkable, and he'd saved me, but he would've done the same for anyone.

"Drop it, Flipper."

I set down my phone while I assisted a couple of kids looking for *Diary of a Wimpy Kid* books. By the time I looked at my phone again, Toff had blown it up with more messages.

"So for real, Viv. You ok?"

"Jake will never bother you again. Ever."

"Viv?"

"WTH? U lip-locked with ninja boy?"

I blushed when I read that one. If only.

"I'm here. Just busy @ work. Thank you Toff. 4 last night. 4 everything."

"U know I'd do anything 4 u." Then he sent the tongue-out smiley face. *"Almost anything."*

He was my brother, whether I wanted one or not. *"What did u do with Jake?"*

"Tied him to an anchor. Dropped him overboard."

"Seriously. What did you do?"

"Made sure he got home safe. Tucked him in with his teddy bear."

He wasn't going to tell me. Maybe it was just as well.

"He won't bother u again. Or anyone else. Bruce Lee and I took care of it."

My breathing slowed. I wondered what Toff and Dallas had done after Dallas dropped me off last night. Jake was still alive or I'd have heard otherwise. He was lucky. I smiled to myself; I was starting to think like my mom, plotting Jake's imaginary death.

A dad and his little boy approached the counter with a stack of *Thomas the Train* books. After they left, I texted Toff again.

"Is it okay if you and your dad don't come over for dinner tonight? I kind of need a break."

"Whatever you need, Wordworm."

I sent him a row of dolphin emoticons. *"Thanks Flipper."*

•••

Mom nibbled on a piece of pizza while we curled up on the couch, half-watching an old episode of *Veronica Mars*.

"So," she said around a mouthful of cheese and veggies. "About last night…"

"Isn't that an old movie? Black and white, right?"

She narrowed her eyes. "Nice try, Vivvy." She chewed and swallowed. "Tell me the truth. Are you okay? And what's going on with you and Dallas?"

I'd worried about this conversation all day, turning it over in mind. How much to tell her, if anything? I knew Dallas and Toff had scared the hell out of Jake. He wasn't going to mess with me, or any other girl in Shady Cove.

But was that enough, or should I report him? If so, for what? He'd grabbed me, yeah. Threatened me. But was that reportable? I closed my eyes. If Toff and Dallas hadn't shown up… I didn't know what to do.

"I promise I'll tell you, Mom. I just need some time. But as for Dallas…I guess we're not fighting anymore."

She grinned. "No more lovers' quarrel?"

I shook my head, blushing. We were hardly lovers. What were we now? Friends again? Or just a guy who'd rescued a girl?

She sighed happily, totally misinterpreting my blush. "I'm so glad." She reached for another slice of pizza. "Whenever you want to talk, sweetie. About anything."

I nodded. "I know," I whispered. "I will. Just not yet."

We sat in comfortable silence, watching TV and eating pizza. I wondered what Dallas had been doing all day. I'd hoped for another call, or at least a text, but I hadn't heard from him.

Before I could lose my nerve, I picked up my phone and typed a quick text message. *"Harvey Climpet."*

A few minutes he later he sent his reply: *"???"*

"Google it, ninja."

It took him less than a minute to figure it out.

"Your mom writes under a man's name?? Well-played,

Spock. Hu'tegh."

My butterflies did a little jig when they saw the nickname.

"Hu'tegh?"

"Google it."

So I did. Hu'tegh was Klingon for 'damn.' What a McNerd. I typed quickly. *"So this is how Wisconsinites get around the no swearing rule?"*

"Yep." A hesitation, then another text. *"U doing ok?"*

Mom cleared her throat. "No texting during dinner, Vivvy."

I raised my eyes. "Are you serious? We're watching TV."

She nodded toward the pizza box on the coffee table. "And eating dinner."

Shaking my head, I sent Dallas one last text. *"G2G. But yeah. I'm good."* Everything in me wanted to add an X and an O to the end of my text, but no way would I do that until I could figure out how he really felt about me.

It was time for me to put on my big girl panties and tell Dallas how I felt. How I'd always felt.

And if I was finally going to tell him, I had to make it good.

"Are you out of your Vulcan mind?!"
— *Dr. "Bones" McCoy*

CHAPTER THIRTY-ONE

WEDNESDAY, NOVEMBER 5

"Hello, Vivian. Today's not your usual book delivery day. Can I help you with something?" Ms. Garcia's warm smile welcomed me as I stood in her office doorway.

"I wondered if I could speak with Mrs. Sinatra. Just a quick, um interim, book drop-off." Fisk had told me his gran's code name that only he used.

Ms. Garcia raised her eyebrows. "How did you—" She caught herself and tried to look official. Fisk/Hector must have told her who he really was and sworn her to secrecy, too. "We don't have anyone here by that name."

I grinned and held up a bag full of paperbacks. "She reads fast. Her grandson asked that I keep her supplied." I still hadn't met Fisk's gran since she wasn't very mobile. Mrs. Sloane brought her list when I set up shop in the community room and then delivered the books to her.

Ms. Garcia's face relaxed. "Isn't *Hector* a sweetie? All right, come with me." I followed her down the narrow hallway, waving and saying "hi" to my regular customers until Ms. Garcia knocked on a closed door.

"Come in," said a wobbly voice. Ms. Garcia opened the

door and ushered me inside.

This room was nicer than the others: better furniture with lots of plants and flowers on all the surfaces. And a framed poster of Fisk winning the *America Sings* competition several years ago before his career took off.

"Well, hello, sweetheart," Mrs. Sinatra aka Fisk's gran said. "To what do I owe the pleasure?"

I held up the bag. "More books." I waited until Ms. Garcia closed the door, then spoke quickly. "My name is Vivian. Bookstore girl?" I smiled hopefully. "I've met your grandson and I need to get a message to him. But I don't have his number since he's, like, famous." I took a breath. "Can you call him for me, please? I hate to intrude, but it's important."

She frowned. "Is everything okay?"

"Not really." I decided to confide in her. "I'm trying to fix something I messed up. And I think Fisk can help me."

She nodded. "All right, hon. I'll tell him. He knows where to find you?"

I nodded. "Thank you." I patted her hand. "I'm glad I got to meet you. Your grandson's a great guy and he cares about you a lot."

"He's the bee's knees," she said, and I grinned, thinking of Iggy and how much he'd love my plan. But I couldn't tell him or anyone else.

I slid off the bed, grateful for her help but also nervous.

If Fisk came through, this was going to be the scariest, dorkiest thing I'd ever done in my life.

For a rock star Fisk was shockingly prompt. He'd sent a message through his gran, via Ms. Garcia, that he'd come by the store tonight after closing. I'd just shut the door when I saw the Unabomber emerge from the shadows. I grinned at him and unlocked the door.

"Hi," I said. "I didn't expect you to respond so fast."

He glanced around the darkened store, then tugged off his hood and sunglasses. "I figured it was urgent." He stared down at me, looking genuinely concerned. "What is it, Vivian?"

Suddenly I felt like a complete idiot. I'd just paged a freaking rock star to help me fix my dorky teenage love life. Who did I think I was?

"Vivian," Fisk prompted. "What's going on?"

"Um, let's talk over cookies." He laughed but followed me to the kitchen.

Once we'd settled at the table with snacks, he pointed at me. "Quit stalling. What's up?"

I took a deep breath. I'd come this far; I couldn't give up now. "I need you to be my Billy Idol."

He frowned and stopped chewing. "What?"

"Like in *The Wedding Singer*," I rushed on, before I could chicken out. "On the airplane? When Adam Sandler sings to Drew Barrymore. And Billy Idol's there."

He blinked at me, waiting.

"But I can't sing. I'm even worse than Adam Sandler." I pointed at him. "But you can, obviously." I took a deep breath. "I want you to sing to Dallas. Oh, and I want you to do it for our town's talent show as a special guest star. It's for a good cause…we raise lots of money for the food bank and homeless shelter and…it might help me win back the guy I'm in love with," I finished, breathless.

Fisk stared at me for a long moment, chewing and swallowing his cookie. He chugged from the soda can, then leaned back in his chair. "Let me see if I understand. You want me to serenade this guy you rejected? His name's Dallas?" His eyes crinkled like he'd just told me the punch line to a joke.

I nodded, biting my lip. I was out of my Vulcan mind. No way would he do it.

"But," he continued, "instead of sneaking to his house and serenading outside his window, you want me to perform at the town talent show. Full of a bunch of sorry acts, I bet. Magic tricks, middle schoolers break-dancing, that kind of stuff. Right?"

I shifted in my chair, surprised at how defensive I felt of our town's show, but before I could say anything Fisk gave me his camera-loving grin. "I'm in, Vivian. Just tell me when."

No way. No freaking way. I struggled to find my voice. "Really?" I squeaked. "You mean it?"

"Sure, why not? I haven't performed in months. I could use the practice." He winked at me. "And I'm a sucker for Romeo and Juliet stuff."

I finally relaxed enough to laugh. "It's not as if we come from warring families."

He shrugged. "Still, you know what I mean." He ran a hand through his rock star hair. "Have you thought about what song you want?"

I'd thought about it a lot. I'd researched lyrics and bands, and I'd also considered Fisk's voice, which was amazing and unique. I'd re-watched the *America Sings* episode when he won, and one of the judges had compared him to Freddie Mercury. That's when I knew what song it had to be.

"You love Queen, right?" I asked.

He eyes lit up. "Lay it on me, Viv."

I grinned. "*Somebody to Love.*"

He returned my grin. "Awesome. I'll kill that song."

"I know."

Then he frowned, making me panic. "What about a band? Back-up singers?"

"Uh," I stuttered. "Um, I…well, I was going to put you in touch with Drew, the director of the show. Maybe he can figure that out." Would our school band work? Maybe with the school choir?

"Can he keep my appearance a secret? I can't have this turn into a circus, Vivian, much as I want to help you. I'll need to disappear right after the show so no one suspects I'm staying in town."

Was Drew trustworthy? I had a feeling he'd keep this secret because it would be such a coup to get Fisk to perform. Knowing Drew he'd advertise the secret guest star all over town and get the buzz going. Then he'd get all the credit when Fisk showed up.

I realized this was a way for me to make up to Drew for the stupid list stuff and for lying about Dallas wanting to be in the show. And I didn't care who got the credit for Fisk performing.

All I wanted was for Dallas to listen to the song and confess that he still loved me, just like Drew Barrymore did with Adam Sandler on the airplane after he sang her that awful song. *If* he still loved me.

No pressure, Viv, I told myself. *You're just going to announce your feelings in front of the whole freaking town. No pressure at all.*

"Let's do it," Fisk said. "I'll come back here tomorrow night at nine o'clock after you close. Bring the talent show director but nobody else, okay?"

I nodded, swallowing nervously. "I don't know how to thank you, Fisk."

He tipped the last of the soda into his mouth, then smirked at me. "Let's wait and see how Romeo reacts to the song before you thank me."

My shoulders sagged. "Maybe this is a dumb idea. In fact, I *know* it's a du—"

"No way," Fisk interrupted. "You're not backing out on me, Viv. I've even got a Freddie Mercury costume already." He grinned at me. "Should I wear a fake mustache to complete the look?"

"No." I laughed. "You can't deprive the rabid Vilhelm fans of your gorgeous face."

He winked. "True. Can't disappoint my fans." Then he looked serious again. "One thing, Viv. Last time you said this Dallas guy had, uh, moved on from you to someone else."

I stared at my shoes before peeking up at him. "Yeah, he did for awhile. But now he's not with anyone."

Fisk nodded. "Good." He narrowed his eyes at me. "What else can you tell me about this guy? How well do you know him?"

That surprised me. "Well, we worked together. He's like a genius coder. He programmed software for the store." I hesitated. "We have a lot in common." Way more than I'd been willing to admit. "He always makes me laugh. And he's one of the sweetest guys I know."

"Cool." Fisk nodded. "Anything else?"

I thought about telling him how Dallas had saved me. About his room full of trophies for his Bruce Lee bad-ass-ness. But Fisk didn't need to know those details. "Why so curious?"

His lips quirked. "If I'm playing Cupid, I want to make sure you two are a good match."

My face flamed with heat as I remembered the insanely hot kiss. "We're, um, very compatible."

Fisk's grin turned mischievous. "I can see that by your purple face. That's all I needed to know."

Drew almost lost his composure when the Unabomber took off his sunglasses, but he reined it in at the last second, clearing his throat and tossing his scarf. "Fisk Vilhlem. I'd heard a rumor you might be staying at The Lodge."

Fisk nodded, after shooting me a wink. "Yep. I want to

help out my friend Viv, and I hear you're the guy who can make it happen."

Drew stood up straighter. "Of course."

Fisk glanced at me. "Vivian, do you mind if Drew and I talk in private?"

I blinked in surprise. "Why?"

Fisk crossed his arms. "You need to trust me." He glanced at Drew. "Also, you'd be bored listening to all the technical details I need to work out with my director."

Drew looked triumphant. I wanted to smack him, but I let him gloat. I owed him that much.

"Okay." I shrugged, feeling slightly hurt, but I reminded myself that Fisk was doing me an incredible favor. "I'll be out front, shelving books or whatever."

Drew gave me an imperious nod and I rolled my eyes. Fisk winked as I turned to leave the kitchen.

Fisk was right; I had to trust him. So instead of trying to eavesdrop, I sorted books and thought about Dallas, and imagined all the different ways he might react to my song. Worst case scenario, he'd reject me. But since he was Dallas, he'd do it privately so I wouldn't be publicly humiliated. I could handle that. I could keep it together until I could collapse in the privacy of my own room.

Best case scenario...well, that was easy to imagine, and it sent my hormones into delirium. So I focused on that, enjoying the fantasy while I alphabetized horror novels, hoping my own story wouldn't have a grisly ending.

"A little suffering's good for the soul."
—Dr. "Bones" McCoy

CHAPTER THIRTY-TWO

Monday, November 17

I t was the last week before Thanksgiving break. Everyone was in screw-off mode at school. Main Street glittered with holiday lights and decorations. Mom and I put up our store Christmas tree decorated with miniature book ornaments we'd collected over the years.

At school, Dallas wasn't ignoring me, but he wasn't hanging out with me, either. I'd expected more after all that had happened, but he kept a formal, careful distance. He smiled at me in the halls and said hi every day, but that was it. The graffiti had been cleaned off my locker, leaving no trace of him.

During lunch, he hung out with Toff, who'd returned to the surfer's table. They kept an eye on our table when Jake slunk through the courtyard, but they didn't join us. Jake had been banished from the surfers' table; no one knew where he was spending lunch. Rumor had it he was eating in his car.

Jaz and I stood at the bike rack after school. Dallas nodded to us before taking off on his Vespa, but he didn't stop to talk.

"He's not completely ignoring you, so that's a good sign," Jaz said.

"He's not going to ignore someone he rescued." I sighed. "He's a nice guy."

"So you think it's just courtesy kindness? Him talking to you every day?"

I stared at her. "Funny, Jaz." I hesitated. "I don't know. I mean, that's all he does. Says hi, then leaves. It's like he's checking me off his to-do list."

"Tell your mom to break the computer again. Then he'll have to come to the store." She grinned as we rode our bikes toward the beach path.

I snorted. "I don't think so." I shrugged. "Maybe it's been my imagination all this time." I thought of the intensity between us on the beach after the fight. The way he'd looked at me; the way he'd held me. Was it all my crazy imagination?

Well, I'd find out the truth soon enough. The talent show was Saturday. According to the cryptic updates Drew whispered to me in the hallway, Fisk's performance was going to rock the house. The band and choir practiced at school, not knowing who the guest star was. Then Drew brought recordings of those sessions to The Lodge for Fisk to practice with. I had to admit, it was pretty smart of Drew.

Drew had asked me to help with the advertising. It was the least I could do since he was doing me a favor, not to mention I wanted to generate a big crowd so the shelter would benefit.

I'd bribed Jaz with smoothies to create the flyer. She came up with an amazing sketch of a glowing Shady Cove Main Street, complete with a looming "Special Guest Star" sign that looked just like the famous Hollywood sign in the L.A. hills. I'd posted flyers in all the stores and restaurants, the town visitor's center, the rec center, and all over our school. All kinds of rumors were flying about the guest star, speculating about everyone from Mick Jagger to Justin

Beiber, depending on the age of the person guessing.

Now all I had to do was stand on stage in front of everyone I knew and dedicate the song to the boy I loved.

"Vivian, are you certain this is wh—" Spock's sternest face loomed in my mind.

"Shut it, Spock," I said out loud, ignoring Jaz's surprised expression.

I was done listening to the Vulcan.

"There's only one kind of woman. You either believe in yourself or you don't." —*Captain Kirk*

CHAPTER THIRTY-THREE

I spent Friday night tossing and turning, stressing about the talent show. To distract myself I read old reviews on my blog where I rambled about love and heroes and perfect book boyfriends. I pulled books off my shelves and reread some of my favorite passages. Some made me tingle, some made me cry. I curled up under my blankets, then threw them off, jangling with nervous energy.

I'd hurt too many people, pretending I was the star of the show and others were just minor characters without real feelings. I thought of Henry's hurt face when I'd turned him down for the Surfer Ball, and Amy, willing to sacrifice her feelings for Toff if I wanted to date him. And Toff, one of my best friends, willing to be my knight in shining armor even when I told him not to be.

Pulling my blanket under my chin and closing my eyes, I finally let myself think of Dallas. I'd hurt him, too, maybe more than anyone. All I wanted was a second chance, but maybe I didn't deserve it. I was like a one-girl tornado, leaving a pile of rubble in my wake. Maybe I didn't deserve to be slut-shamed on my locker, but I wasn't an innocent victim, either. I sat up and grabbed my laptop.

Dear Hunkalicious Followers:

Thank you all for being such loyal fans and followers of my blog. Whenever I read a new book, I can't wait to share it with you. But it's time for me to take a break. I've learned a few things about myself lately, one of which is I've been so busy trying to be the star of my own story, I've hurt a lot of people. It's embarrassing to admit it, but I'm telling you because I know you understand. You've read enough stories where the main character is an idiot and you spend half the book screaming at her to stop the crazy.

Well, that's been me lately. I led some people on, which was totally thoughtless of me. I was so busy thinking about my feelings I didn't stop to think about theirs. I kind of wish they read this blog so they'd know I am sorry, but I'll just have to tell them in person.

Some of my friends do read this blog and to them I can only say: You were right. I'm a total idiot. I'm not a Vulcan. I'm just a girl...a stupid, silly girl who tried to be someone she isn't. I promise I won't do it again.

Finally, there's one person who used to read this blog but probably doesn't anymore. I owe him the biggest apology of all because he offered me his heart and I rejected it, even though I wanted it more than anything. He's the smartest, funniest, sweetest McNerd I've ever met. I wish I'd told him how I felt...how I still feel, but for now I'm just going to pretend he's reading this and that he'll forgive me some day.

I don't know when I'll resume my reviews. Maybe after

the holidays. Maybe not. But meanwhile don't forget about all the other blogs listed on my sidebar—they're all awesome and funny. Even though we don't always agree, they'll give it to you straight.

Until next time...

I closed my computer feeling as if a huge weight floated away. I still needed to apologize to Henry, but at least this was a start. Lying on my bed, I closed my eyes. I had one more thing to do.

I needed to talk to Mom about Jake. I kept reliving my fear and panic from the night he'd chased me down, and the nightmares hadn't stopped. I couldn't let anyone else go through that. I had to report him. Toff and Dallas were witnesses and I knew they'd back me up. Plus, Mom was friends with the sheriff because she was always bugging him with research questions. I was nervous, but I knew it was the right thing to do.

After the talent show, after whatever happened with Dallas, I'd tell Mom. And I knew that even if Dallas rejected my love song apology, he'd still back up my story.

Hiddles wandered into my bedroom and jumped on my bed.

"Whoa, little guy. You lost?" He ignored my sarcasm and curled up next to me, burrowing into my chest, purring loudly. Tentatively, I reached out to pet him. He didn't flinch or jump off the bed. Instead, he nudged my hand with his head. We lay there together as if we'd always been best buddies, until I finally drifted to sleep.

"Please, Captain. Not in front of the Klingons."
—Spock

CHAPTER THIRTY-FOUR

Drew texted me right after I'd closed up the shop. *"Got your dedication ready?"*

My pulse pounded in my ears. I'd had it ready for days. *"Yes."*

"Meet me backstage before the grand finale."

"Ok."

This was it. I had an hour to get ready, which felt like not enough time and way too much time all at once. I flipped over the "closed" sign and reached down to pet Hiddles, who was rubbing against my leg. Maybe he knew I needed a little encouragement.

You can do this, Viv. Just pretend you're in one of your books.

The question was, what type of book? Would I finally get my happy ending or was this going to be an ugly-cry ending?

• • •

met Jaz and Amy in the theater lobby, already crowded with excited people. The secret guest star combined with the start of the holiday season had everyone in a bubbly, happy mood.

Jaz narrowed her eyes at me. "What the hell are you wearing?"

I pulled Mom's trench coat tighter around me. "Never mind."

She stepped closer. "What's under that creeper coat, Viv? You're not going to streak across the stage, are you?"

My face burned. I wasn't naked, but I might as well be. I was already regretting my outfit, but it was too late now. "No," I snapped. "No more questions. Let's go find seats."

None of my friends knew about my secret plan. No one but Drew and Fisk, an unlikely duo if ever there was one.

We found Toff waiting for us with some of his surfer posse. "Hey, gorgeous chicas. I got us front row seats."

My anxiety made me irritable. "Why so stoked, Flipper?"

He smirked at me. "Wordworm. It's vacation. We made it to the league championships. Time to kick it." He fist-bumped me, grinning, then he leaned over and whispered in my ear, "I got your text. The ninja's coming. But he has to sit with his family."

I nodded, unable to speak. I'd called in a favor, asking Toff to make sure Dallas would be there.

"Are you going to maul him after the show or what?" He leered at me, but I couldn't joke with him. Instead I shrugged, feeling as if I was going to puke. He frowned. "You need to chill, Viv. Just kick back and enjoy the show."

Right. As if.

We made our way through the crowded lobby. I spotted Henry standing by himself, frowning up at a framed poster of *Gone with the Wind*.

"Give me a minute," I said to Jaz and Amy. They followed my gaze to Henry, then shot me matching frowns as Toff and his friends headed through the doors. "Go on. I'll find you guys."

Henry kept his eyes on the poster even when I stood right next to him.

"According to my mother, this is one of the bestselling books of all time," he said.

"I'm not sure about that, but I know it was a big deal."

"Does your mom sell millions of books?" He finally turned toward me, his face pinched and anxious. Was that because of me? Ugh.

"No." I shrugged. "But she does okay." I took a breath. "Listen, Henry, I owe you an apology. It's way overdue. I'm so sorry. For…you know…leading you on."

He touched the sides of his glasses, readjusting them over his ears.

"You're a nice guy," I said, meaning every word. "You deserve someone who appreciates that. Not just…someone being stupid. Like me."

He nodded, his lips drawn thin and tight. "Correct. But I did learn something from the experience."

"Oh? What's that?" The house lights flashed and my phone vibrated in my coat pocket.

"Don't trust smart girls who ask for homework help."

My stomach clenched. "I'm so sorry, Henry. I never meant to—"

"I know." He shrugged and his ears turned red. "Anyway…you um, might want to work on your…dating strategy in the future."

I bit back a smile. "Room for improvement?"

He nodded. "Definitely."

The theater lights flashed again. "I agree. Look, we should go." I hesitated. "There might be room in our row, if you need a seat."

His face finally bloomed into a full smile. "No need. I'm meeting someone and she's saving me a seat."

"Yeah? That's great."

We walked into the theater together and Jaz waved wildly from the front row.

"Have a great night, Henry."

"You, too. And don't give up, Vivian. Statistically, you're bound to find a good match."

I laughed as I ran down the aisle. *Let's hope so, Henry.*

Toff pointed to a seat next to him. "Rock star seating." A velvet rope reserved our entire row, which was full of surfers and my friends. Nathan and Iggy sat next to each other, heads close together and laughing. Iggy glanced at me and winked. Claire waved from where she sat with some of her surfer friends.

"How'd you manage this?" I asked Toff.

"Not everyone is immune to my charms. Just you."

I laughed, and he reached out to tug my hair. "Just kick back and enjoy the show, Viv."

Impossible, but at least I could try, until I had to sneak backstage and seal my doom.

Or my redemption. It could go either way.

The lights flicked on and off one last time and everyone cheered, then settled down. The first act was a group of tiny ballerinas, including Dallas's little sister, Becca. They were adorable, especially when they spun the wrong way and crashed into each other, giggling. The audience cheered loudly. That was part of the deal: lots of cheering no matter how bad the act was. It was part of our town's happy hippie ethic.

Each act was a little better than the previous one. I had to admit Drew did a decent job of upping the expectations with each performance. By the time we got to the grand finale, everyone was buzzing with anticipation.

This was it. I stood up, my legs shaking. "I've got to go," I whispered, squeezing past Jaz and Amy.

"What?" Jaz didn't bother to whisper. "You can't go now! It's the grand finale."

I pinned her with my fiercest glare. "I know. And you'd better cheer for me. Really loud."

Her eyes widened as she gaped at me. "Viv? What are you doing?"

I ran down the aisle, unbuttoning my coat as I rushed back stage, digging into my pocket for the props.

Drew grabbed me as soon as he saw me.

"You're late," he hissed.

"I'm s-sorry." I dropped my coat on the floor and he stared at me, eyes wide.

"Wow," he said. "Unexpected. But, uh, wow."

Fisk appeared next to me. "You're a knock-out, Viv." He glanced at my face and grinned. "In a freaky way. Are you ready?"

I looked out to the darkened stage. The school band had set up their instruments and the choir members climbed onto the stacked risers, jostling each other and giggling. It was hard to make out faces in the dark.

"No," I said, "but I'm going to do it anyway."

Fisk fist-bumped me. "Excellent."

I finally focused on him, taking in his tight white pants and yellow military jacket covered in brass buttons. "You *do* look like Freddie Mercury. From the Wembley Stadium concert videos."

He grinned. "Only hotter. With better teeth."

"Places everyone!" Drew hissed loudly, and suddenly all was quiet. He turned toward me. "You're on, Vivian."

Fisk squeezed my shoulder. "You've got this."

Giving him a grateful smile, I walked onto the stage.

I faced the packed auditorium. I heard quiet rustling behind the closed velvet curtains and Drew hissing at everyone to be quiet. I clutched the cordless mic he'd given me.

Everyone stared at me expectantly. I heard tittering laughter and saw a few people pointing at my outfit.

That's what happens when you wear a red Star Trek mini-dress uniform, black tights, and shiny leather boots. And Vulcan pointy ears.

"Hi," I said, my voice shaking. "I'm Vivian Galdi. I'm glad you all came to the annual talent show." I took a deep breath, searching the crowd for my friends, grateful they were in the front row. Toff grinned up at me, waving his hand in a shaka brah surfer gesture.

Jaz looked as if she wanted to kill me and hug me at the same time. I knew my mom and Paul were out there somewhere, and that Mrs. Sloane was cheering me on with her friends from the senior center, ensconced in the handicapped row in their wheelchairs. And Dallas, sitting with his parents, was probably wondering what the heck I was doing. I couldn't see him, but I knew he was there.

"The grand finale is going to blow your mind. I can say that because I picked the song." I took a deep breath again. *Pretend you're on a movie set.* The crowd started murmuring, so I spoke louder, right into the mic. "You might be wondering why I'm dressed like this." A few hoots and catcalls made me smile. "It's because I'm trying to apologize to someone. For being a stupid Vulcan, when I'm really just a human."

"Go humans!" Toff yelled. I saw Jaz reach out and smack him on the chest.

Over the audience's laughter, I heard a clatter from behind the curtains as if someone had dropped something. "So." I took another breath and read from the note card in my shaking hand. "The song you're about to hear is a classic, beloved by those who heard it originally in the seventies. If you haven't heard it before, I know it will become one of your favorites."

I paused and looked out at the crowd, desperately scanning for Dallas. "Freddie Mercury was a genius, and Queen was arguably one of the greatest rock bands of all time." Hoots and cheers came from all corners of the theater. Goose bumps rose along my arms. This was happening. Really happening.

"This song is dedicated to everyone who's made mistakes, especially about love. In particular, it's dedicated to someone who I've spent the past couple of months making a lot of mistakes with." My voice was quivering, but I had to push through. "I was on a mission, kind of like *Star Trek*." I gestured to my outfit, unable to focus on anyone now.

I hoped to God Dallas wasn't in the bathroom or in the lobby loading up on popcorn. That'd be just my luck. I took one more breath and pushed on. "But my mission was a fail. An epic one. Because I picked the wrong target. More than once. So this song is for him, and for everyone who's looking for…Somebody to Love."

As soon as I said the song title, the audience erupted into cheers. I felt the curtains whoosh open behind me and I stepped back. Drew appeared at my side, taking the mic from me and steering me off stage so I could watch from the side. Beads of sweat dripped into my eyes. I took shaky breaths. I'd done it. I focused on the stage, at the band members and the choir.

And at the lone folding chair in the middle of the stage, lit by a spotlight, where Dallas sat dressed in black jeans and a tight black T-shirt, cello propped between his legs, staring at me as if I was an alien.

Which, technically I sort of was, with the pointy ears and all.

Oh my God. What was he doing on stage? How? Why? I searched frantically for Drew, but he was gone.

We stared at each other, unmoving. I noticed he wasn't wearing his glasses, as his gaze took me in from head to toe. His eyes widened but that was as much as I could tell from where I stood.

"Go, Vulcans!" Toff yelled, making everyone laugh. Dallas's lips quirked up as he stared at me, but before I could return his smile, the choir's perfect a capella harmony rang out, singing the first line of the song, and the music jolted Dallas into action. He bent over his cello, the soaring music he made taking my breath away.

As the band performed along with the choir, I stood transfixed, watching Dallas's fingers fly over the frets, and the bow dance across the strings. He was every bit as mesmerizing as the Croatian guys.

Then a familiar, powerful voice rang out, taking over the solo while the choir continued singing the chorus. The entire audience gasped, then erupted in screams as Fisk Vilhem pranced out from stage left, microphone in hand, his soaring voice channeling all the passion and emotion of Freddie Mercury.

The audience jumped to their feet, screaming and cheering. Fisk owned the stage, pounding out the vocals like the rock star he was. My eyes darted back and forth between him and Dallas, bent over his cello. They played off each other, grinning and gesturing, whipping the crowd into a frenzy.

Fisk hollered at the crowd, "Everybody!" He held the mic out and everyone chanted along with him. "Find me somebody to love!" Before I realized what had happened, he'd crossed the stage and dragged me out of the wings, steering me to center stage, right next to Dallas, pointing to us as he sang.

I stood there like an idiot in my *Star Trek* uniform, laughing nervously in front of the cheering crowd while Fisk sang like a wicked angel. I glanced at Dallas, whose head was bent over his instrument as his arms moved and his muscles flexed, willing him to at least look at me. As if he read my mind, he raised his head and winked. At least, that's what the hormones saw, but they were whipped into a frenzy. They might be hallucinating.

Fisk extended his arms toward Dallas, encouraging more raucous cheering and applause, and everyone cheered as his cello solo soared high into the rafters. I remembered Drew asking, "Is he any good?"

Yeah. Really frakking good.

Everyone stayed on their feet, swaying and clapping along to the final chorus, and I found myself singing along, not caring whether or not I could keep a tune. The music pounded through me, erasing some of my anxiety. No matter how Dallas reacted, I'd just done something brave, and honest, and it felt amazing.

The last line of the song soared out of Fisk's mouth, his voice making every hair on my body stand up: "Can anybody find me...somebody to love?"

The choir took over, echoing the words in a rhythmic chant. Fisk leaned over Dallas, grinning as Dallas worked the cello like a master. Dallas glanced up and returned his grin, and in that moment I realized that they knew each other. Like, really knew each other.

What the heck?

As the song ended, the theater erupted into chaos. The curtains closed and pandemonium broke out onstage, too, as the band members and choir rushed to surround Fisk, begging for autographs and bubbling with hysteria since they'd just performed with a real rock star.

Several security guards appeared from nowhere to surround Fisk and to pull him offstage. He blew me a kiss as he hustled by. "Good luck, Viv." He shot Dallas a cryptic glance over his shoulder, then he was gone.

I finally turned to face Dallas, who stood on the stage apart from everyone else, watching me with his arms crossed over his chest. His cello rested in a stand next to him. I pictured Adam Sandler walking down the airplane aisle singing to Drew Barrymore, not caring what anyone else thought. I had to be brave like that.

I already looked like a dork. I might as well finish this.

Slowly, very slowly, I approached him, tuning out the laughter and cacophony behind us. He watched me with his usual McNerdy intensity, even more visible without the glasses. I saw his eyes travel up and down my body, taking in the full ridiculousness of my outfit. A muscle twitched in his jaw as I stopped right in front of him. I wondered if he was trying not to laugh.

I took a deep breath. "Once upon a time, you told me your criteria. For your replacement girlfriend." I cleared my throat and stood up taller in my boots, which were killing my feet. "I believe I meet those requirements."

His eyes widened, then he ran a hand over his mouth. Was he hiding a smile? I couldn't be sure. "You think so?"

I nodded. I was insane. Completely out of my Vulcan mind and my human heart. But I wasn't going to stop until I'd told him everything. Just like Spock when he got zapped by those alien spores. Just like in my favorite books, this was my grand gesture, and I was going to do it right.

I inhaled, then let the words tumble out in a rush. "I was an idiot, Dallas. You were always my mission target. But I was…afraid. I didn't want to get my heart broken again."

He watched me, his eyes never moving from mine. How did he stay so still like that? I wasn't even sure if he was breathing.

"But you know what? I don't care anymore if you break my heart. Because the thing is, I…I really like you Dallas. A lot. You're an amazing guy. You're sweet, and smart, and funny…and brave…and I just…just needed you to know that." I waited, but he said nothing as he stood there like a McNerd statue, so I let my hormones take over my vocal cords again. "I wish I could rewind the past couple of months and go back to that night you kissed me. But I can't. All I can do is tell you I'm sorry I ever let you walk away."

He finally moved, tilting his head slightly. "Maybe we should discuss this logically, Spock."

My mouth dropped open. "What?"

He was definitely smirking. He took a step closer, and I could smell his minty, soapy Dallas smell. I would *not* swoon.

"First," he said, "about my criteria." He took another step toward me, reaching up to twirl a strand of my hair around his finger. My heart sped up, then stuttered to a stall like a plane tanking into a free fall. "Number one: pretty. We both know I'm shallow." He shrugged. "Can't help it." His eyes roved over my face, stopping on one of my pointy ears. "You meet that one."

"In spite of the ears?" I joked, proud of myself for not collapsing into a puddle of nerd-worshipping mush.

His gaze moved from my ear to my face. "Because of them, not in spite of them. Number two, smart."

"But a special kind of smart," I interrupted. "Not the kind who beats people up with her smartness."

"Right," he agreed. The hand not entwined in my hair reached out to wrap around my waist and pull me in close. "Smart as in apologizes on her blog to everyone she's hurt."

So he'd read my blog? All I could do was stare into his eyes, which remained fixed on mine. I wondered how long I could go without breathing before I passed out. I desperately wanted to feel his lips on mine before I lost consciousness.

"Number three." He ducked his head and grazed my lips with his. "Has her own opinions." His lips spread into a slow grin. "Likes to argue." His lips drifted up to my nose, making me giggle. "Check."

"Get a room!" Toff's voice bellowed onto the stage, followed by laughter and cheers. Dallas and I turned to face our friends, who huddled in a tight knot at the bottom of the stage, grinning up at us.

"Dude," Dallas warned, "you know I can kick your ass."

"Please do." Jaz smirked. "I'll pay you extra if you mute him for life."

"Viv finally gets her man, just like me!" Iggy hollered, then he high-fived Nathan and planted a kiss on his lips, inspiring more cheering.

Claire shot me a thumbs-up from the aisle where she hung out with her surfer friends. Amy moved close to the stage and motioned me over. I stepped away from Dallas and leaned down so I could hear her over the rowdy crowd, some of whom were still singing or chanting for Fisk, hoping for an encore.

"It's just like in our favorite books," she said, beaming up at me.

"What is?"

She winked. "Your mission failed for a reason, Viv. True love can't be strategized. It just...happens." Her gaze darted nervously to Toff, then she turned away, blushing.

Dallas appeared next to me, tugging me away from the edge of the stage. "Thanks for your support, guys, but Viv and I need to...talk. Alone."

Everyone catcalled as Dallas pulled me off center stage into a dark corner where old stage sets blocked us from view.

We were alone in near darkness and he held me so close I felt his chest rise and fall against mine.

"Before we got interrupted," he said, his voice low and rumbly, "I was thinking about kissing you."

My heart thudded against my ribs. "Maybe you should stop thinking and just do it."

He laughed softly, then his lips grazed mine so softly I could hardly stand it. I wanted pressure. Lots of it. So I pulled him against me so tightly that all I felt was lean, hard muscle and hot, hot skin, even through his clothes.

But before I could kiss him, his lips devoured mine, kissing me so passionately I completely forgot where I was. I kissed him back, reaching up to run my fingers through his hair. I felt him groan deep in his chest, and suddenly we were moving, me walking backward, him pushing me against the wall.

He raised his head and even in the dim glow from the exit sign I could see his eyes were dark with desire. "You even meet bonus criteria." He paused. "Which almost makes up for the temporary insanity of you pretending I didn't meet your criteria."

He pulled me in closer and I flashed on Amy's favorite gothic. There was a scene where the heroine almost fainted when the hero swept her into his arms for a kiss. I thought it was stupid when I read it, but now I wasn't so sure.

"Bonus criteria?" I whispered. "Like what?"

"Convincing rock stars to do your dirty work," Dallas murmured, running a hand through my hair and making me shiver. "Supplying dirty books to sweet little old ladies. Keeping homeless guys supplied with donuts." He took a small step back but didn't let go of me. "And the best one of all." His eyes traveled up and down, eyeing me hungrily. "Looking unbelievably hot in a *Star Trek* uniform." His lips quirked. "You have to wear that every day now, you realize that, right?"

I shoved him playfully in the chest. "Shut up. This dress is not one of your criteria. Not even bonus."

He cocked an eyebrow and pulled me in close again. "You honestly don't think that dress is going to be on a McNerd's list? Maybe you're not the hot nerd expert you think you are."

"Who said I was a—a hot nerd expert?" I sputtered.

He grinned, resting his forehead against mine. "You set up an entire sub-genre in the store about guys like me."

I smiled against his lips. "You're kind of full of yourself right now, McNerdy." It was a total turn-on but I wasn't going to tell him that. Besides, with the way I was looking at him, I don't think it could've been more obvious.

"Of course I am. The hottest *Star Trek* babe in town just told the whole world she wants me. I just performed with a freaking rock star. I'm totally the hottest nerd around."

"Yeah," I said, nipping at his lower lip. "You are." Then I kissed him with all the pent-up frustration of the past two months, hopefully reminding him of criteria number four: feisty.

I felt like I might float away on giant bubbles of giddiness as Dallas kissed my neck, then worked his way up to my ear, making heat streak through me. He laughed softly. "I have to try this," he whispered, then he nibbled on the pointy fake ear.

"Hey!" I tried to shove him away but he just laughed and kept nibbling. "Those weren't cheap, buddy," I protested, even though they were.

"I'll buy you a new pair." His voice was rough and sexy against my neck, making me sag against him.

"So I have a few questions," I managed to say in between gasps as he moved his kisses to the other Vulcan ear.

"I have a few answers." He tucked a strand of hair behind my ear. "Go."

"After the fight with Jake…you hardly talked to me. I mean, I knew you were worried about me, but you were so distant." I hesitated. "Not like, um, you are right now."

His arms tightened around my waist. "I was giving you space. I thought you might need it, after Jake." He sighed. "And I felt guilty about Kylie. I only dated her because you rejected me. It wasn't fair to her or you. I got my feelings hurt and I didn't care who I hurt in return."

I looked down, overwhelmed by guilt. "I'm sorry."

"My mistake, not yours." He lifted my chin, forcing me

to meet his gaze. "I apologized to her. She wasn't happy, but I couldn't keep pretending." He shrugged. "I was going to ask you out over winter break." He kissed me softly. "You beat me to it."

After more kissing, I pulled away again. "One more question. Why are you here?"

He stared at me like I was nuts. "Um, because you just told the entire town you're madly in love with me. And admitted your stupid mission was an epic fail."

I shoved against his chest, laughing. "You think I'm madly in love with you, Dallas Lang?" I smirked, and he feigned offense. "Okay, so maybe I am. What I mean is, why did you perform? With Fisk?"

He leaned against the wall, pulling me into him. "Fisk asked me. He said he'd agreed to help out at the talent show, but he wanted a special accompanist." He shrugged, grinning. "He and I practiced together at The Lodge because he said he wanted it to be a surprise. I had no idea you were behind the whole thing."

I frowned, trying to figure it all out. "But how do you know him? I mean, it's not like he Googled Shady Cove cellist and…" My voice trailed away as the pieces clicked into place. Dallas darting out of the store when his cell pinged with messages. Dallas's Midwestern ninja competition dominance. The funny look Fisk gave me when he saw Dallas in the store. The questions he'd asked about how well I knew Dallas.

"You're Fisk's secret ninja trainer, aren't you?" I whispered, as his lips brushed mine again, almost distracting me from my Lois Lane questions. "For the movie he's filming?"

"Not exactly," he whispered, his lips against mine. "We're about the same size, so his sensei asked me to spar with him. They wanted to keep it low key. No paparazzi. Or stalkers like your buddy Jaz."

"That's why you always had to run out of the store. Ninja training."

He kissed me again, then pulled away to look into my eyes. "Now you tell me how you know him. How you talked him into this."

"Um, it's kind of a long story. But I knew I had to tell you how I felt. And I wanted to make it…big. Because I screwed up big. Fisk and I are kind of buddies. He came to the shop a few times to get out of The Lodge…and I supply his grandma with book crack." I laughed as his brow furrowed in confusion. Before he could cut in, I continued. "You know me. I read too many books with insanely happy endings. Go big or go home, right?"

"Are you saying I'm your HEA? Or at least your HFN?" His smile was teasing, but I knew he wanted a real answer.

"Mission accomplished, Captain Kirk. Target acquired."

Much later, after so much kissing I thought my lips might fall off, we left the theater together holding hands. "I almost forgot." I stopped to dig through my messenger bag, then pulled out the clumsily wrapped present.

"You got me a present?" He looked surprised and happy.

"Last ditch bribery attempt. In case the song didn't work or the, um, kissing."

He raised an eyebrow, giving me a heated look. "You didn't need to worry about the kissing."

I blushed under his hot gaze. "Open it."

He shot me a crooked grin, then tore open the paper in one fast move.

"Geez." I laughed. "You're worse than a little kid."

"I love presents." He grinned again as he held the ball of

fur. "You got me a Tribble?"

I nodded, biting my lip nervously. "Dorkiest present ever?"

He laughed. "Yeah. But it's from you, so it's also the best present ever." He tossed the wrapping paper into a nearby recycling bin, then pulled me close as we strolled down the beach path lit by twinkling Christmas lights wrapped around the lamp posts.

"Psst."

We turned to each other. "Did you hear that?" I asked. Dallas nodded.

"Psst. Over here."

I squinted in the darkness. The Unabomber sat on the homeless guys' bench, hidden in the shadows.

"Fisk! What are you doing here?"

"Shh," he whispered, but when he stood up to meet us, he was grinning. "I don't even want to ask what took you two so long to leave the theater."

I knew we were both blushing, but Dallas spoke first. "Shut it, Hollywood."

Fisk took off his sunglasses and laughed, then slugged Dallas in the shoulder. "Was that the best song ever or what? We've already got like a zillion hits on YouTube."

"No way," I said.

"Sure." Fisk waved his phone at us. "Everybody had their phones. Plus somebody filmed it as part of the fundraiser DVD." He grinned at me. "You're captured forever on the internet as the nerdy girl with the Spock ears."

"Great." I groaned.

"Anyway," Fisk said. "I wanted to make sure you two kids finally admitted how madly in love you are."

"Dude," Dallas said. "Don't forget I can still kick your ass."

"Not for much longer," Fisk said. "I'm getting pretty good."

Dallas grinned at him. "Yeah."

"You totally played us," I said, knowing my smile was even goofier than Dallas's. "You're like a real-life Cupid."

Fisk shrugged again, but he looked ridiculously pleased with himself. "I haven't had that much fun in a long time." He glanced back and forth between us and waggled his eyebrows suggestively. "So?"

"So you don't have to worry," I said. "We, um, got everything cleared up."

Fisk's eyebrows shot up. "Is that what the kids are calling it these days? *Clearing things up*?"

"Watch it, Hollywood," Dallas growled. "You know I'm not impressed by your shtick."

Fisk grinned at him. "That's why I love you, man." He glanced at me. "You, too, Viv. You two are awesome. You belong together."

"Is this when you break into song again?" I teased. "Because I wouldn't mind an encore."

"Name it," Fisk said, glancing around. "Nobody here but us."

"No thanks," Dallas said. "I'll see you later. Prepare to have your butt kicked at our next training."

They fist-bumped each other and did the dude hug, then Dallas took my hand and we started walking. We hadn't gotten far when I heard Fisk's unmistakable voice floating behind us on the breeze, singing an old Paul McCartney and Wings song about silly love songs.

"I haven't had enough of silly love songs," I said to Dallas. "Have you?"

"Not as long as they're dedicated to me," he said, stopping to pull me into him. "By you."

I reached up to remove my Vulcan ears, but he stopped me. "Not til I get a picture first. Vivian the Vulcan admits she was wrong and that she wanted the McNerd all along."

"Um, according to Fisk I've already done that on YouTube for the whole world to see."

"Yeah, but this is for us. Just us." He pulled out his phone and took a selfie of us, me making a judgy Spock face and him making a crazy Kirk face.

"We're pretty hot," I said, laughing. "For a couple of nerds."

"Oh yeah," Dallas said. "Total dork royalty."

"The McNerd king and his Bookworm queen." I locked my hands behind his neck, standing on tiptoes to nibble on his earlobe.

He stumbled backward, pulling me with him. "God, Viv. You're killing me."

"We wasted a lot of time," I breathed into his ear and attempted a Scottish brogue. "Time to kick it into warp speed, Captain. I can't hold on much longer."

He laughed into my hair, his hands tight around my waist. "Whatever you say, Spock." His lips claimed mine again and my body felt like a star soaring through an electric galaxy, sparking and crackling with an internal fire that would never go out.

We clung to each other like two lost space explorers who'd finally found each other after navigating a dangerous galaxy full of black holes and asteroids.

Sighing happily, I let the hormones take control.

It was the least I could do, since they'd been right all along.

ACKNOWLEDGMENTS

As always, I have many people to thank for helping me transform this story from a glimmer of an idea to an actual book:

My family and friends, whose support never wavers and whose love never falters.

My amazing critique partners: The Wild Writers and Lynn Rush.

My agent Nicole Resciniti, for loving this story and talking me off the ledge more than once.

My editor Liz Pelletier, who always pushes me to take my stories to the next level and tolerates my weird text messages.

Stacy Abrams, for bringing insightful editing and fresh eyes to this story.

Beta reader Allie Bass, who generously shared her surfer expertise.

Finally—to the book blogging community, this book is for you. I'm in awe of your passionate love of books and the time and dedication you give to reading and reviewing. Thank you for your ongoing support of authors and for all of your reviews: the go-go boots, the granny shoes, and everything in between.

READ ON FOR A SNEAK PEEK OF
HOW (NOT) TO FALL IN LOVE
BY LISA BROWN ROBERTS

CHAPTER ONE
SEPTEMBER 1

"Hey Darcy! You'd better get outside. There's a tow truck hooking up your car."

I stared at Ryan, with whom I'd been in lust since seventh grade, trying to make sense of his words. It took a moment to realize he was not, in fact, admitting he'd been madly in love with me for the past five years, but was instead jabbering about my car.

"Tow truck? My car?" It was like he spoke Klingon and I didn't have a universal translator.

"Yeah." His blue eyes flashed with excitement. "You should hurry. They can really screw up your transmission." He tossed his messily perfect bangs out of his eyes. "I guess they're serious about us not parking in the handicapped spots. But dude, that's harsh."

Handicapped spots? I never parked in those. My brain finally kicked into gear and I slammed my locker shut.

"Thanks." I took off down the hall, out the main doors, then cut across the manicured soccer field toward the parking lot. As I ran, my stomach roller-coastered. Did I really park illegally? Dad would kill me if he had to pay to get my car out of an impound lot.

My Audi was already loaded onto the tow truck by the time I got there. A swelling crowd of my classmates milled around, pointing and exclaiming. The one using great dramatic expression and lots of gesturing was Sal, my best friend and queen of the theater club, AKA "DQ" for Drama Queen. Sal was always on the verge of being in full costume, like today in her weird grandma prairie dress and suede-fringed boots with fake spurs. She looked like a demented cowgirl, especially with her short, spiky black hair and goth makeup.

"I demand to see a warrant! You can't just come onto private property and take someone's car. My father is a lawyer and—"

"Can it, kid," said the tow truck driver. He hopped off the back of the truck where he'd been adjusting the cobweb of chains trapping my car. He paused before climbing into the truck, then his voice boomed loud enough to reach the whole crowd. "When the bills ain't paid, the car goes away."

I froze. Bills not paid? That was impossible. My dad was Tyler Covington, the face of Tri!Umphant! Harvest Motivational Industries. He had his own TV show. Just on PBS, but still. Money couldn't possibly be an issue.

No one had noticed me yet. Maybe I could duck behind the other cars and hide until the tow truck left. Unlike my dad and Sal, who both thrived on an audience, I was queen of the mice, always skittering around corners and on the watch for potential traps.

Sal spotted me. "Darcy!" Everyone turned to stare. So much for avoiding the spotlight. "Darcy, come tell this man this is your car. Show him your driver's license or something!" Sal was freaking out like it was her car being towed.

The tow truck man leaned out of his window. "Like I said, if you don't pay your bills, you don't keep your car." The truck roared to life, slowing as it passed me. The driver tossed an envelope out the window. As it fluttered to the ground, Sal ran to grab it.

"When you come get your car out of the impound lot," the driver called, "bring cash. We don't take bad checks." He laughed and cranked the steering wheel hard, making my Audi wobble like a toy as he exited the parking lot.

The hive of students buzzed with excitement as Sal rushed over to hug me. Her thick black eyeliner magnified the panic in her worried brown eyes. "Oh my God, Darcy. I can't believe this. What an ass. This can't be right. He can't just take the car from—"

I held out a hand for the envelope. "Let me see it."

She handed it over and I tore it open.

Notice of Intent to Sell

This notice informs owner TYLER COVINGTON that vehicle 2013 Audi VIN 214081094809148 has been repossessed due to nonpayment after notice to cure was sent via certified mail. This vehicle will be sold in thirty days at auction. All proceeds will be used to pay off the loan. To redeem this vehicle, bring full payment in form of cashier's check to High Plains Deals impound lot, 1301 Mountain Avenue, Denver, Colorado.

A few kids wandered closer to us, oozing curiosity. Sal glared at them. "Back off. Give her some privacy, dorks!"

Something was wrong. Horribly wrong. This couldn't be happening. But it had, in front of the entire school. The parking lot was full, with everyone leaving for the day. I imagined Ryan's face when he heard my car had been towed because it wasn't paid for, and I felt sick.

Ugh.

Things like this didn't happen at Woodbridge Academy. WA was the most elite private school in Denver. Ninety percent of the kids came from wealthy families. The other ten percent were scholarship students.

"I can't go back in there," I whispered, tilting my head toward school where my books waited in my locker. My hands shook as I crumpled the repossession notice and tried to unzip my messenger bag. Sal took the paper and refolded it neatly. She unzipped my bag and tucked the letter inside, then put her arm around me.

"We're getting out of here. Now." We hurried to her car, a yellow Beetle with daisy hubcaps and DRAMAQN on the license place.

She tore out of the parking lot, slowing only to flip off a couple of football players who yelled at her to slow down. The Beetle squealed around corners, hopping the curb more than once.

"God, Sal, chill out. This isn't a NASCAR race." I was going to hurl if she kept driving like a spaz.

She glared at me and then refocused her stare over the dashboard. "We have to get you home. Your parents need to call the tow truck company and get your car back before that asshole ruins it towing it around like a load of trash."

My stomach clenched. Did mistakes like this really happen? Did banks screw up that badly?

Sal shifted gears angrily. The way she drove her car it'd be lucky to last another year.

"Sal." I hesitated. "What if it's true? What if we do owe a bunch of money on my car? And somehow didn't pay the bills?"

She glanced away from the road to gape at me. "Are you nuts? Your family is freaking loaded, Darcy. This has to be a mistake." She chewed her bottom lip. "You can probably sue, you know. For damages to your car, pain and suffering, all that jazz. I'll ask my dad about it."

I rolled my eyes. Sometimes her never-ending drama wore me out.

"Forget it," I said. "I'm sure my dad will fix this."

"Exactly," she agreed, blowing through the stop sign at the end of my block. Her car lurched to a stop in our driveway.

"Thanks for the ride," I said, "but maybe I'll sue *you* for whiplash."

She didn't laugh. "Just get inside and get this handled. I've got to get back to school for auditions."

"Sorry." I felt a twinge of guilt. She didn't need to drive me home; I could've called my mom.

"Don't apologize. That's what best friends are for, right?" She grinned at me then peeled out of the driveway. I wondered how many speeding tickets her lawyer dad made go away.

I opened the wrought iron gate on the side of the house, looking for my dog, Toby, but he wasn't waiting for me like usual. I hurried past the swimming pool, already covered in anticipation of winter, and through the French doors into the kitchen. I had to find my dad to get him to call and get my car back.

Something was off. I didn't smell dinner cooking, which was weird since Mom, who could have her own Food Network show, always had exotic ingredients simmering on the stove.

Toby came running from the dining room, wriggling with happiness, and I dropped to my knees for a dog hug.

"Hey, boy. What's going on?" I looked into his devoted Labrador eyes as I rubbed his chocolate brown fur. "We'll run in a little bit. I need to find Dad first." I opened the pantry to grab him a Scooby snack. He caught it easily when I tossed it in the air.

"Mom?" I called, as I left the kitchen. I was starting to get worried. "Dad?"

No answer.

I wandered into the dining room. We only used it for dinners with Dad's premier clients and family holiday extravaganzas. The rest of the time it lurked empty yet imposing. The sleek, spiky silver chandelier made me think of knife blades poised above us while we ate, but Mom bought it during a European shopping spree, so we were stuck with it.

"Mom?" I yelled louder this time. Toby barked for emphasis.

I heard muffled voices from the library. It sounded like Mom and Dad talking, not Mom and one of her perky tennis buddies having their post-game Perriers. That was a relief. I couldn't deal with perky after the drama in the parking lot.

I flung open the door. "You guys won't believe this. Some jerk took my..." I trailed off when I saw it wasn't Dad with Mom, but J.J., Dad's business partner.

"Darcy." J.J. turned toward me, flashing his movie star smile. It was almost as blinding as my dad's trademark grin.

"Sorry to interrupt," I said, backing toward the door. "I thought Dad was in here." I glanced at Mom, who sat in a leather wing chair, her fingers twisting her gold serpentine necklace. Why did she look like she was fighting back tears? I glanced at J.J., whose smile had vanished.

Something inside my stomach twisted and I reached down to pet Toby, wanting to keep him close. "Everything okay?"

J.J. and Mom exchanged one of those condescending we-have-to-tell-her-something-but-let's-not-tell-her-too-much looks.

"What is it?" My stomach knot twisted tighter. "Is Dad okay?" Visions of fiery plane crashes played on the TV screen of my mind.

"Sure, sure. He's fine," J.J. blustered, not looking at Mom. "But he's, ah, had a change of plans. He won't be home tonight."

"But he's got the game tonight. He can't miss that." Dad was the official team motivator for the Denver Broncos and never missed a game. I stared at Mom, who was staring at J.J. She still hadn't looked at me. I heard echoes of the cackling tow truck driver's laugh and a nibble of fear tickled the base of my neck.

"Mom? What's going on?" Now they both stared at the ground. Toby leaned against my leg and let out a soft whine.

"I need to talk to Dad," I said. "Because this crazy thing happened at school today with my car."

J.J.'s head jerked up. "What happened?" His voice was sharp, surprising me.

"Were you in an accident?" Worry creased Mom's face.

"No." I rubbed Toby's head. He leaned into my hand, making me feel safe like he always did. "Worse. This jerk tow truck driver took my car from the school parking lot, in front of everyone." I cringed, reliving the humiliation.

J.J. and Mom stared at each other, their expressions making goose bumps rise on my arms.

"But I thought her car was paid for," Mom whispered, her eyes fixated on J.J.

J.J. glanced at me. "Darcy, your mom and I need to talk. Alone."

I swallowed. Normally I'd leave without question, but something was seriously wrong. "No."

Mom raised her eyebrows. "Darcy. Please."

The knot in my stomach had morphed into a balloon now, swelling with anxiety and worry. "No," I repeated. I never argued with adults, but I was freaking out and needed to know what was going on. "Dad's not home for a Broncos game, which he never misses. Some jackass stole my car right in front of me. What's going on?"

"Don't say jackass," Mom said softly, but her heart wasn't in it.

J.J. loosened his tie and walked to the window, staring out at the trees bending in the breeze. I waited. I'd win this battle, no contest. I spent most of my life waiting and watching other people. Most of the time I was like a shadow no one noticed.

"Your father," Mom started, then stopped to swallow

and compose herself. Her cloudy gray eyes met mine. "Your dad is taking a little vacation." She fiddled with her watch. "He's been working too hard. He needs a break."

My heart sped up. A break? Was that code for something else? A break from us? From Mom? I looked at her red-rimmed eyes. God, I hoped this didn't mean divorce. I glanced at J.J., who still stared out the window.

"So is he going up to the cabin for a few days?" I asked. "Or staying in L.A.?"

"Honestly, I'm not sure what he's doing." Mom turned to look at me. "He called J.J. from the airport to say he'd be back next week sometime."

"He called from L.A.?" I looked at J.J., willing him to turn around and tell me what he knew.

Mom spoke again when J.J. remained silent. "No, he called from our airport. As soon as he got off his plane, he got in his car and hit the road."

"He what?" That didn't make any sense. What was Dad doing? My heart raced even faster. He was a freak about keeping his word, never being late, never missing appointments. Missing tonight's game was completely unlike him.

"You have to tell her," J.J. said, his voice low. "It's already started, with her car."

The fear I'd been tamping down tore through me now as he turned toward us, his expression hard and unreadable.

"What's started?" I hated how weak and tinny my voice sounded. Why couldn't I sound strong and passionate like Sal or my dad?

"We… There might be…" My mom tried to speak but couldn't finish, tears choking her voice.

"Harvest is going broke, Darcy," J.J. bit out the words. "Which means your family is, too. So don't plan on getting your car back anytime soon."

I stumbled backward as if he'd slapped me. His words echoed in the room as Mom collapsed into sobs.

"I...but I..." I struggled for words, fear and confusion shutting down coherent thought. "But," I tried again, my voice rising in panic. "My dad... Where's my dad?"

J.J.'s mouth thinned into a bitter smile. "That's the million dollar question, isn't it?"

No one spoke, all of us staring at each other in frozen silence. I couldn't believe what J.J. said. My dad wouldn't just go AWOL. Every minute of his life was scheduled and planned. And broke? What did that even mean?

"I need to go," J.J. said. "Since Ty's not here for the football game, somebody needs to greet his clients in the stadium box." He wiped a sheen of perspiration from his forehead.

"You'll let me know?" Mom whispered. "If you hear from him again? And tell him to call me. Please."

J.J. frowned at Mom. "He hasn't called you?"

Tears spilled down her cheeks as she shook her head.

He heaved a deep sigh then lumbered across the room. He closed the door behind him without saying good-bye.

For some reason, I thought of this old movie with a badass guy who does slow-mo acrobatics to avoid flying bullets. He has to choose whether to take a red pill and wake up to reality, or take a blue pill and stay in a fake world. That was me right now. Did I want to take the blue pill and live in denial of whatever was happening with my dad? Or did I want to take the red pill and have the truth crash down on me?

I was such a wuss. I'd pick the blue pill every time.

GRAB THE ENTANGLED TEEN RELEASES READERS ARE TALKING ABOUT!

THE SOUND OF US
BY JULIE HAMMERLE

When Kiki gets into a prestigious boot camp for aspiring opera students, she's determined to leave behind her nerdy, social-media-and-TV-obsessed persona. Except camp has rigid conduct rules—which means her surprising jam session with a super-cute and equally geeky drummer can't happen again, even though he thinks her nerd side is awesome. If Kiki wants to win a coveted scholarship to study music in college, she can't focus on friends or being cool, and she definitely can't fall in love.

ROMANCING THE NERD
BY LEAH RAE MILLER

Until recently, Dan Garrett was just another live-action role-playing (LARP) geek on the lowest rung of the social ladder. Cue a massive growth spurt and an uncanny skill at basketball and voila...Mr. Popular. The biggest drawback? It cost Dan the secret girl-of-his-dorky dreams. But when Dan humiliates her at school, Zelda Potts decides it's time for a little revenge—dork style. Nevermind that she used to have a crush on him. It's time to roll the dice...and hope like freakin' hell she doesn't lose her heart in the process.

LOVE ME NEVER
BY SARA WOLF

Seventeen-year-old Isis Blake has just moved to the glamorous town of Buttcrack-of-Nowhere, Ohio. And she's hoping like hell that no one learns that a) she used to be fat; and b) she used to have a heart. Naturally, she opts for social suicide instead...by punching the cold and untouchably handsome "Ice Prince" — a.k.a. Jack Hunter — right in the face. Now the school hallways are an epic a battleground as Isis and the Ice Prince engage in a vicious game of social warfare. But sometimes to know your enemy is to love him...

OLIVIA DECODED
BY VIVI BARNES

When Olivia receives an expensive bracelet on Valentine's Day, she suspects her ex, the bad-boy hacker Jack, is behind it. But when the gifts begin getting creepy, she enlists his help to discover who the stalker is. Jack is busy helping Nancy run the Briarcreek home, trying to stay on the up-and-up even though the temptation to hack for money is always there. When Nancy tells him someone is hacking into their house accounts, Jack is shocked to discover the hacking is traceable to his computer — and it was used to purchase an expensive bracelet. Jack and Liv must work together — and fight the simmering attraction still between them — to figure out who is stalking her and setting him up as a thief and put a stop to it for good.

LOLA CARLYE'S 12-STEP ROMANCE
BY DANIELLE YOUNGE-ULLMAN

While she knows a summer in rehab is a terrible idea (especially when her biggest addiction is decaf cappuccino), Lola Carlyle finds herself tempted by the promise of saving her lifelong crush and having him fall in love with her. Unfortunately, Sunrise Rehabilitation Center isn't quite what she expected. Her best friend has gone AWOL, she's actually expected to get treatment, and boys are completely off-limits... except for Lola's infuriating (and irritatingly hot) mentor, Adam. Like it or not, Lola will be rehabilitated, and maybe fall in love...if she can open her heart long enough to let it happen.

CHASING TRUTH
BY JULIE CROSS

Three months after the scandal that rocked the nation—the suicide of Simon, the teenage son of a California senator and Eleanor's date to homecoming—Eleanor Ames is left wondering if leaving her con-artist family for the private school life was worth it. Just when things are beginning to return to normal at school, Miles Beckett shows up, and he won't stop asking questions about Simon's death. The thing is...Ellie has questions too. Can she uncover what happened to Simon without falling in too deep with Miles?